**One could never be quite certain
that a demon wasn't still around.**

They walked on out of the demon realm. There were
no more odd events. Evidently the demon had gotten
bored with them. That was a relief.

The fungus along the marked route turned brownish.
The air became chill. Gloha closed her wings closely
around her body, insulating it with the feathers. Cynthia suffered less, because she had more furry mass,
but she did take a jacket out of her backpack and put
it on over her shirt to protect her maidenly human
torso. Evidently she had never adopted the centaur
mode of undress after gaining some experience with
the form, and had retained some of her clothing in case
of need. Trent, already completely garbed, seemed to
have no problem.

They turned a corner, entered a moderately large
chamber—and came face-to-snoot with a dragon. The
creature had antennae instead of eyes, which made
sense down here, but in other respects seemed formidable enough. It had dragonly form and mass, metallic
overlapping dark gray-green scales, atoutly taloned
feet, one and a half squintillion teeth, and an attitude.
It moved forward, inhaling, growling.

"Wait!" Trent cried, advancing to meet it. "We have
a pass for this path."

Too late.

Tor Books by Piers Anthony

Alien Plot
Anthonology
But What of Earth?
Demons Don't Dream
Geis of the Gargoyle
Ghost
Hasan
Isle of Woman
Letters to Jenny
Prostho Plus
Race Against Time
Shade of the Tree
Shame of Man
Steppe
Triple Detente

With Robert E. Margroff:

Dragon's Gold
Serpent's Silver
Chimaera's Copper
Mouvar's Magic
Orc's Opal
The E.S.P. Worm
The Ring

With Frances Hall:

Pretender

Edited with Richard Gilliam:

Tales from the Great Turtle

HARPY THYME

PIERS ANTHONY

TOR
fantasy®

A TOM DOHERTY ASSOCIATES BOOK
NEW YORK

This is a work of fiction. All the characters and events portrayed in this book are fictitious or used fictitiously, and any resemblance to real people or events is purely coincidental.

HARPY THYME

Cover art by Darrell Sweet

A Tor Book
Published by Tom Doherty Associates, Inc.
175 Fifth Avenue
New York, N.Y. 10010

Tor® is a registered trademark of Tom Doherty Associates, Inc.

ISBN: 0-812-53484-0
Library of Congress Catalog Number: 93-37000

First edition: January 1994
First mass market edition: February 1995

Printed in the United States of America

0 9 8 7 6 5 4 3 2 1

Contents

$\overline{1}$
GLOHA

Gloha flapped her feather wings until she was high above the harpy hutch. The Land of Xanth spread obligingly out below her, so that she could see all the way to its medium-far corners. There was Lake Ogre-Chobee, with its ogre tribe on the shore and its toothy reptilian swimmers. There was the great Gap Chasm with its horrendous six-legged Gap Dragon. There was all the monster-infested jungle between them. She loved all of it.

But she couldn't pause to appreciate the sights. She had important business. She had to go see the Good Magician so she could ask him a Question. With luck and a year's Service, she might have his Answer. Then maybe she would have her heaving little heart's desire.

She leveled off and flew swiftly toward the Good Magician's castle. She knew exactly where it was, but had never thought she would one day have to go there. That was because she had just somehow assumed that her life would work out well on its own, after the frustrations of childhood worked their way out of her system the moment she turned eighteen and became party to the Adult Conspiracy. Unfortunately, when she actually became party, she realized that she needed a male of her kind—and she knew of none. She was the only person of her new species in Xanth. That had become a problem.

So now she was off to the Good Magician Humfrey, and after doing her year of Service for his Answer, she would be able to settle down with the man of her dreams and live happily forever and ever after and torment their children unmercifully by not letting them know the secret of stork summoning. She was nineteen years old now, and would be twenty then, which would still leave her a faint bit of her youth for her true love to appreciate before they both became adult dullards the following year. She was not so vain as to assume that she would be different from all the other adults who had ever existed. It was too bad that life had to consist of the two problems of childhood and adulthood, with only that brief window of romance wedged in between, but that was the way it was. She knew; she had observed. She was mostly humanoid, and that was the way humanoids were.

She reached the region of the castle, and paused in her flight. There was a mean-looking vapor hovering over it. That looked uncomfortably like Cumulo Fracto Nimbus, the worst of clouds. But what would he be doing here? He wouldn't dare harass the Good Magician.

Reassured by that thought, she resumed flight. But the closer she got, the larger the cloud loomed, and the uglier it looked. Soon she realized that this wasn't merely the magic of perspective, that changed things according to their distance; that cloud was looming uglier on purpose. It *was* Fracto!

She flew lower, to pass under the mean-spirited blob. But Fracto extended his vapors downward to intercept her. She tried to go around, but he sent boiling fog out to the sides to cut her off. His big amorphous mouth formed a gassy O. HO HO HO! it gusted.

This was a real nuisance. Gloha had never liked Fracto, and this encounter was making her emotion ripen into active detestation. Of all times for the blowhard to be in her way! He must know where she was headed, so was getting his flatulent jollies from interfering with her. Somehow he always seemed to know when something important was happening, like a picnic, and he always came to spoil it.

How was she going to get through to the Good Magician's castle? She realized now that the evil cloud would stay here as long as she did, just so he could ruin her mission. She hovered in the air, and waved her fine little fist at the big ugly cloud. "Oh, you make me so angry, I could utter a bad word!" she exclaimed.

HO HO HO! A twisty gust reached out to blow her skirt up over her head so that way too much of her lithe little legs was exposed.

"Now stop that!" she cried, quickly pushing the skirt down. She realized belatedly that she should have worn slacks on this trip. But she had wanted to look dainty and feminine, because she would probably meet one of the Good Magician's five and a half wives. After she got through the challenges that would bar entry to the castle, of course. The Good Magician always had three challenges, to discourage those who weren't really serious about their quests for information. He didn't like to be bothered frivolously.

Then something clicked in her pretty little head. The challenges! This must be the first one! The disreputable cloud must owe the Good Magician a debt, and so was doing him a Service. It wasn't coincidence at all. She had to figure out how to get past Fracto.

That put an entirely different complexion on it. Her own comely little complexion relaxed. All she had to do was figure out how to get past this messy old cloud, and she would be a third of the way through. There was always a way; she just had to find it.

Could she insult Fracto, and make him blow himself out? That was the way Grundy Golem would do it. But Grundy had a mouth that was the envy of harpies; he could spew out insults faster than they could. Gloha was half harpy, because her father was Hardy Harpy, so she should be able to spew out a stinking stream of invective. But somehow she had never cared to acquire that ability. Her mother was Glory Goblin, who was beautiful and good, and Gloha just preferred to emulate her. If her brother Harglo were here, *he* could have let out an oath that burned a hole in the cloud. But this was a challenge she had to handle by herself.

So steaming Fracto was out. Avoiding him seemed to be out too, because he was hovering right over the castle she had to reach, by no accident. What was left? Outsmarting him? She just knew she was smarter than a creature whose brain was swirling vapor, but how could she prove it? This seemed to be a situation in which intellect didn't count for much. All he had to do was sit there and wet on her if she tried to get through.

Well, maybe she would just have to get wet. It wasn't as if she were made of spun sugar, whatever impression she preferred to give others.

Gloha set her firm little face in an earnest little expression and flew directly toward where she hoped the castle was, on a level course.

Fracto puffed up like a mottled wart. He opened his sodden maw and breathed out a sickly gust of wind. It surrounded her, coating her true little tresses with smog and her winsome little wings with dirty ice. Foul air clogged her nice little nose and fuzzed her open little eyes. Suddenly she was flying blind, and losing altitude. She was in danger of crashing!

Gloha sneezed. The force of it shot her spinning back out of the foul air, and she was able to blink her eyes clear. She still had some altitude, and was able to pull out of her tail-spin.

She brought out her handsome little hankie and wiped her face. Fracto's ugly puss was laughing and spitting out broken bits of wind and cloud that drifted in stenchy colors. It seemed that she couldn't just try harder; the awful cloud had too much ill wind.

Well, if she couldn't fly there, she would walk there. She was a goblin girl with harpy wings, and though she had spent most of her time with winged monsters, she was at home on the ground too. Fracto couldn't stop her from using her fast little feet.

She glided down to the ground before the evil cloud could work up another foul gust to blow her away. She had hoped to find an enchanted path going there, but saw none. So her lovely little lady slippers touched down in an isolated glade, and she began to walk. There was an ordinary path that would serve; she had noted its direction as she descended, and was sure it would take her there. She would simply have to watch out for hostile monsters and other ilk, because they would be able to harass her on an unenchanted path.

Fracto was furious. He huffed and he puffed and he blew up such a storm that in two and a half moments snow was pelting down. In the remaining half moment it was piling up so thickly that all trace of the path was gone.

Oops. How was she to find her way now? She knew she would get lost in the trackless snow. She couldn't even make her own tracks, because the snow was covering them up just about as fast as she made them. In addition, it was cold; her tight little tootsies were freezing.

She would have to take shelter until the storm blew over. Maybe she could find a blanket bush and hide under the blankets, and the snow would cover her so that Fracto wouldn't know where she was, and would drift away. At least she would be warm while she waited.

But she saw no blanket bushes, and no pillow bushes.

This glade was singularly bereft of useful plants. There was only a big snowball at the edge of the glade. She certainly didn't need that!

But as her teeth began to chatter in an unladylike manner, her mind squeezed out an odd thought. What was a giant snowball doing here? The snow had just started, and it was covering the ground with a level layer. It couldn't form itself into a snowball. Was there an invisible giant doing it? But there was no depression where the snow would have been taken from, and there was no smell of giant. "That snowball—that's no ball," she muttered, making temporary tracks toward it.

Then she realized that she had made a pun. "That snowball" had become "That's no ball," spoken the same way. And that gave her the cue.

She marched up to the ball and touched it. Her hands passed through its seeming surface. She stepped forward, and found herself within the entrance to a tunnel. It looked like a snowball from outside, but it was warm and dry inside. This was the way past Fracto's storm. All she had had to do was figure out the secret, and she was on her way. Her mild little mind had prevailed over the cloud's fury, and she had mastered (or maybe mistressed) the first challenge.

But there would be two more, and they wouldn't be any easier than the first. She had gotten through as much by luck as by wit, and might have used up her supply of both. Should she give up her quest?

But then she would never find her Perfect Mate and True Love, and would have to endure unhappily forever and ever alone, which was a fate worse than marriage. She wasn't ready to face that dreary prospect. After all, she had so much to offer the right man, she hoped. She glanced down at her fancy little figure, just to be sure.

So she proceeded resolutely down the passage. She would at least make an efficient little effort, and if she failed, then she would go somewhere and cry.

The passage opened out into a good-sized lighted cave.

Along the sides were darkened alcoves, and at the far end was a monster. Uh-oh—she suspected that the next challenge was upon her. Instead of a cantankerous cloud, she would have to get by an aggressive animal.

But there had to be a way to do it without getting eaten. She merely had to figure out that way again. Somehow. Maybe if she proceeded very carefully it would happen.

So she took a tour of the chamber, looking in the alcoves. This turned out to be a slightly baffling tour.

The first alcove held a fat bird with a beautiful fan-shaped tail. Gloha cudgeled her balky little brain and managed to remember news of a bird like this, perhaps confined to Mundania: it was a turkey. She looked at it, and it looked at her, and that was it. The bird wasn't confined, but didn't seem inclined to depart its alcove. It was just there.

"You certainly are a beautiful bird," Gloha said politely. The turkey gobbled appreciatively.

She moved on to the next alcove. There was a rather unprepossessing young human man. Because he was human, he was about twice as tall as she was; goblins were twice as tall as elves and half as tall as humans. She wasn't sure how either other species could stand being so pitifully small or so dangerously large, but it wouldn't be polite to call attention to such failings, so she didn't. "I say, can you talk?" she asked the youth, who seemed to be no older than she was, though it was hard to tell with humans.

"Sure," the youth replied.

"What is your name? Mine is Gloha."

"Sam."

He did not seem to be much for conversation. "What are you doing here, Sam, if I may ask?"

"I'm part of your challenge."

That was certainly direct! "And what is your role in this challenge?"

"I'm a flunky."

"A flunky? I don't think I know that position."

He didn't respond. She realized that he merely answered

questions, and as briefly as possible. Naturally the challenge creatures didn't volunteer much information.

"What does a flunky do?" she asked. Then she was afraid he would just say that he flunked. But Sam did give a meaningful response, fortunately.

"He does stupid errands for other folk."

"What errand will you do for me?"

"None."

So much for that. That time she might almost have preferred a less straight answer. She moved on.

The next alcove held a tub of dirty water. That didn't seem to be of much interest, so she went to the following one.

That alcove held a large four-footed animal, like a unicorn without a horn, with long ears. "Hello, creature," she said.

"Hee-haw!" it brayed back.

That gave her the cue. It was a Mundane donkey.

The next alcove held a sort of springlike metal thing sitting on a step. There were several steps, but it wasn't using them. But when she came to stand before it, it leaned over and its top end toppled to land on the next step below. The rest of it followed smoothly, making a turn from the upper pile of itself to the lower pile, until all of it was down. Immediately it bent again, and started sinuously transferring itself to the next step. When it reached the bottom of the little stairway, it stopped. That was all.

The next alcove held a vaguely humanoid creature with a most versatile tail. It jumped from bar to bar, swinging with its hands, feet, or tail. It moved very cleverly, never missing a bar, never falling. It chittered at her from its furry face. She pondered, and realized that this was another odd creature: a monkey.

So it went: each alcove held a creature or thing. They were all part of her challenge. But how did they relate? She could see nothing similar about them; this was like a little zoo with assorted displays.

At the far end was the monster. It stood taller than she was, on all fours, with a huge powerful foresection and a rather small hind section. It was in no alcove; it was in the exit from the chamber. She realized that she had to get by it, but the moment she approached it, it rose up and snarled with such ferocity that she had to step quickly back. It wasn't confined or chained, but it didn't pursue her.

She realized that this was the one she would have to deal with. So she stiffened her knocking little knees and came to stand just beyond the monster's snarl range. "If I may inquire," she said in her most timidly civil little voice, "what are you?"

The monster eyed her appraisingly. He licked his formidable chops. "Hi. I am the Yena," she said.

Gloha blinked. She had thought the monster was male. She looked again, trying not to blush because of the impolite nature of the act, and saw that it was indeed male. She must have misheard. "The Yena?"

"That's what I said, goblin girl," she replied.

Gloha looked yet again. The monster was female. How could she have thought otherwise? "Thank you," she said faintly.

"You're welcome, you tasty little tart," he said.

Gloha found herself getting confused and embarrassed. Once she had passed the magical age of eighteen she had sought information about the secrets hidden by the dread Adult Conspiracy, and had been somewhat disappointed when she learned their nature; she had almost wished she hadn't bothered. But she had gotten it straight, she thought. Now she wasn't sure. How could she be sure, when the creature's unmentionable region kept changing? When it might not be exactly the way a male goblin's region would be, not that she had ever seen such a region anyway? Of course the creature's voice was changing too, being now gruff and then dulcet. What a confusing (not to mention embarrassing) situation!

"You—you must be part of my challenge," she said after

a moment. "I—I'm supposed to get past you, so I can go on to the next."

"And if you fail to find the key, I will get to crunch up your bonnie little bones," the Yena agreed.

Gloha had been afraid of that. But now, irrelevantly, she realized that there was something odd about the creature's mane. It was severely knotted. In fact it seemed to be twisted with balls of metal.

She pondered, and decided that it was better to inquire than to ignore. "Your mane—" she started after a pale little pause. "Would you tell me why it has metal in it?"

The Yena smiled, showing his distressingly big sharp teeth. "Ah, you are admiring my locks," she said.

"Um, yes. They are—unusual."

"Indeed," he agreed. "I'd give anything to be able to comb them out. But each one is locked in place."

Gloha picked up on a subtlety. There was something the Yena wanted. "Anything?" she asked hesitantly.

He considered. "Well, anything, within my power, of course. I'm not exactly a wealthy monster."

"Even—even letting a minor little morsel get through without being eaten?"

She peered closely at Gloha. "You're catching on, morsel," he agreed. "But of course you would have to deliver."

Gloha realized that she had found only half the key to this riddle. She had to find a way to comb out the Yena's locks. But what could that be? They were solidly metal, and surely would not respond to her cute little comb.

Yet somewhere in this chamber must be the answer. Because that was the way it was, with challenged. Everyone knew that. What everyone didn't know was how to get safely through a particular challenge. That tended to discourage querents from bothering the Good Magician—which was of course the point. Humfrey didn't like to be bothered by folk who weren't serious. His time seemed to be impossibly precious, so he prevented it from being wasted.

She gazed around the chamber. What would comb out a metal lock? Surely not a donkey or a turkey. The flunky? She didn't see how; the metal would still be too hard to abolish. The same went for the monkey, and how that murky water could help was beyond her. Water made iron rust, which would be worse than ever, because it would make the locks impossible to work.

Something began to percolate through her meticulous little mind. These things here—there *was* something similar about them. They were all keys! Donkey, monkey—even the mur-key water. And a key should do for a lock, to unlock it. One of these keys must unlock Yena's locks.

But which one? And how would it work? She couldn't bring the donkey to comb Yena's locks; it just wouldn't work. There was something she still hadn't figured out. She didn't want to make a mistake, because that would get her eaten, which she probably wouldn't enjoy.

She went back to look at Yena. Now she saw that each lock of the monster's mane was different. Some were big padlocks, others were little keyhole locks, some were several types together—combination locks—and one was weird. "What lock is that?" she inquired, pointing.

Yena craned her head about to look. "That is the Lock Ness," he said. "It is a monster."

Indeed it was. It was a huge tangle of serpentine cables of metal knotted into a lock that seemed impossible ever to unlock.

"I suppose that if you could unlock that one, the others would be easy," Gloha said.

"Surely so. But if anyone tried to unlock it and failed, making it even worse, I would be most annoyed. I'd probably have to pulverize that person."

Gloha had suspected as much. She returned to the alcove exhibits. One of these had to be the key to that awful lock—if she could only figure it out. If she guessed wrong, she was doomed.

She looked at the don-key. She just didn't see how its

hooves could do anything as intricate as unlocking a lock.
The same went for the tur-key's claws. The flun-key was a
man, who might have the necessary dexterity, but he had no
tools to work on that horrendous Lock Ness. In fact none of
these creatures and things seemed like likely prospects.

Maybe she had not yet fathomed the proper pun. Which
of these keys was punnishly designed to open such a lock?
Not the don, tur, flun, mon, mur, or—what was that slinky
spring that marched down the steps called? The question
brought the answer: it was a slin-key. That was no good either.

Then another theatrical little thought percolated through
her petite little perception. Slinky—that was the way the
Yena would like to have his/her locks. All combed out and
slinky smooth. And the slin-key was metal, showing that
metal could be prettily flowing. So maybe it could lend its
attributes to the metal lock mess—uh, ness—and make it
similarly smooth.

She wasn't at all sure that her reasoning was right, but
since everything else seemed wrong, she gathered up her
cornered little courage and made her move. She reached
into the alcove and picked up the slin-key. It flexed irides-
cently in her hands but did not protest. She carried it to the
Yena. "I think maybe this slin-key will smooth out your
Lock Ness," she said with an adorable little ad-lib.

The Yena swelled up hugely. "Oh you do, do you?" he
inquired ominously. "Are you sure?" she added.

"I—I'm not s-sure," she confessed in a dainty little dither.
"But it s-seems the best chance."

"Remember, I'll chomp you if it doesn't work."

"Y-yes, I realize that," she said, shaking. "But I must try
it."

"Well then, what's keeping you?"

"N-n-nothing," she said with a successful little stutter.
She lifted the slin-key and put it to the Lock Ness.

The tangled cables twisted like snakes. They slithered
around and through each other, forming a pattern like that of

the slin-key. Then they flowed down and became slinky smooth, exactly as she had hoped. After that, all the other locks smoothed out similarly, making the fearsome Yena look positively handsome or beautiful, as the case might be. The entire hide glistened like polished water, showing her real little reflection.

Gloha almost went into a sweet little swoon.

"Well, you did it," the Yena said, standing aside. "You may pass on to the next challenge."

Gloha stiffened her nice little knees and prepared to walk on. "I'm just glad I got the right key."

"Oh, there was no danger of getting the wrong one."

"No danger? You mean you were only bluffing about chomping me?"

"No, I wasn't bluffing about that. But any of the keys would have worked."

She was aghast. "Any? But then where's the challenge?"

"It was a challenge of courage, just as the first was a challenge of nature. You rose to it, so you pass."

"Courage? But I was terrified!"

"That's the nature of courage: to do what you have to do, without yielding to fear. Every sensible person feels fear on occasion, but only cowards let it govern them."

"I never realized!"

"Well, it wouldn't have been as good a challenge if you had," the Yena said sensibly.

"I wonder what the third challenge will test," Gloha said musingly.

"Understanding, of course." The Yena curled up and went into a snooze, his tail twitching contentedly across her fur.

Gloha walked down the passage. She hardly cared to admit it, but her understanding had already been strained to the limit of her broadened little brain. She wasn't at all sure she could evoke any more understanding than she had already. But what was there to do but go on?

The passage was getting warmer. In fact it was getting hot. Gloha would have removed her bright little blouse, but that would have been unseemly. Certainly she couldn't take off her snug little skirt. So she spread her wings a bit and waved them slightly, making a delicate little draft to cool herself. This was certainly a change from Fracto's blizzard outside!

The heat increased. The floor got so hot that her sunny little sandals started smoking. She had to practically dance to stop her feet from getting burned inside them. Even so, she was soon surrounded by smoke.

Then she spied a water fountain by the side of the hall. She skipped to it and touched its magic button. A fortunate little fountain of chill water spouted, and she put her longing little lips to it and drank deeply. That cooled her, and the smoke dissipated. What a relief!

She proceeded on down the hall, no longer bothered by the heat. Now she didn't have to jump and flap her wings to cool her feet, but she was so glad to be safely by that region that she jumped anyway, dancing along. This hall was large enough so that she could stay in the air longer than a regular jump, by flapping her wings. She couldn't actually fly here, but at least it made walking fun. This was more like a frolic. All too soon she knew it would get serious, so she enjoyed herself while she had the chance.

The passage widened into another chamber. In the center was a small plant. She couldn't make out its details, but appreciated its presence. Plants always improved places, especially if they had nice flowers.

She walked toward the plant. But something funny occurred. She seemed to be slowing, though she was walking at the same pace as before. She just was making slower progress.

Realizing that this could be a problem, she hurried. But though she ran, she still moved more slowly. She saw now that her lazy little limbs were not going at the rate she thought; she was running, but they were molasses slow. She jumped, and she rose slowly into the air, then slowly fell.

Something was definitely amiss! She felt fine, but she wasn't getting anywhere. What could account for this?

What else but the challenge? It was upon her, and she had to figure it out. The Yena had said it would be a challenge of understanding. So she would have to understand.

She had a bright little bit of feminine intuition. She lifted her purse and let it go. It fell slowly toward the floor. So slowly it would take several times as long as it should to get there. She reached for it, but her hand moved almost as slowly as it did, making it hard to catch. Meanwhile she herself was still in the air from her slow jump.

She paused. She settled slowly to the floor and looked at the plant. Now she recognized it: thyme. The herb that affected time. That was why she was slowing: she was in its field of effect. She would have to figure out how to get around it.

That was indeed a challenge. She really did not know much about thyme, except that the closer a person got to it, the more powerful was its effect. So if its effect was to slow her down, she needed to get away from it, because by the time she reached it she would be moving at no speed at all.

But now she saw that there was no way out of the chamber except the passage on the far side—beyond the plant. She would not be able to reach that passage without going closer to the plant than she was now. That would take, literally, almost forever.

There was certainly plenty to understand! How could she pass a plant she couldn't pass in her lifetime?

Well, the first thing she had to do was back off, so as to be able to operate at normal velocity. She was afraid she was even thinking slowly at the moment. In fact, it might be a longer moment than it seemed.

She backed away. Slowly her feet moved, and her body nudged backward like a small river barge. But as it moved, it gained speed, and soon she was back to normal.

She stopped at the edge of the chamber. She knew it was pointless to go back up the passage she had come down, because that didn't lead to the Good Magician's castle. She had to go forward—past the plant. Somehow.

There had to be a way. That faith had gotten her through the first two challenges. There must be something here that she just had to understand. As before.

She looked around. Now she spied seven glass cups on the floor at the edge of the chamber. Each was on its own built-in pedestal, or maybe it was just a two-way container, the same either way up, so that it looked like an hourglass. They seemed to contain assorted seeds. Each was labeled. One said SEC, and the next said MIN, and the next HR. Farther along one said DY, and another WK. Then MNTH, and finally YR. What could they be?

She started to reach into the first cup, to take up some of the seeds and see what kind they were. But she hesitated, because she didn't yet understand the nature of either cups or seeds, and if understanding would enable her to get safely through, a lack of understanding might wash her out in a hurry. She should figure out the meanings of the labels before she took any action.

Another thought percolated through her meandering little mind. A thyme plant—hourglass cups—these must be the seeds of thyme! Of time. Some of them might enable her to pass the mother plant. If she just figured out the right ones, and how to use them.

Now the labels started making sense. SEC—that would stand for Second, the briefest measure of time. MIN would be Minute. And so on, through Hour, Day, Week, Month, and Year. The SEC seeds were tiny, while the others were respectively larger, until the Year seed was so big that just one of it filled the cup.

What would happen if she lifted out that huge Year seed? Since the thyme plant itself slowed her down, that would probably speed her up, and a year would pass in maybe an instant. That wouldn't do her much good. But if she took a Second, that would hardly be worth it, because even an ordinary second passed pretty quickly. Which kind of seed could she use, and how could she use it?

She decided that if she took some seeds and walked toward the thyme plant, they should cancel out the slow effect, and enable her to maintain her speed. So she could get through on something like a normal schedule. If the seeds worked the way she was guessing they did.

She returned to the SEC glass and picked up one seed. The chamber blinked, and the seed was gone. What had happened?

She thought about it, and decided that the blink had been time jumping forward one second. She was now one second ahead of herself, as it were.

She tried her purse-dropping trick again. But this time as she let it go, she scooped several secs from the cup.

There was a triple blink, and suddenly the purse was on the floor, much faster than it should have been. Now she was sure: to touch a seed of thyme was to feel its effect, which was opposite to that of the thyme plant.

But how could she use any of these seeds? She needed to get them to the slow vicinity of the plant before touching them. She couldn't keep dashing back to the cup for more.

"Silly me!" she exclaimed as a dim bulb flashed just over her honeyed little head. She picked up the SEC cup itself. Seconds were all she cared to use; they were more manageable, and she could use them in handfuls if she had to.

She carried the seconds glass as far as she could before the slowdown was bothersome. Then she picked out one sec. This time there was no blink; instead she speeded up for an instant. The seed had canceled out a moment of the thyme's slowdown. It was working!

She moved ahead, dipping out more secs. Her progress was somewhat jerky, being either fast or slow, but that was to be expected. She had to use two seeds at a time as she got near the plant, and then three. When she was closest to it, she had a small handful of secs at a time. She didn't want to use them all up before she completed her journey across the chamber! But once she was beyond it she was able to get by with fewer secs, and finally she made it to the far hall, and she still had some secs left. That was a relief.

She set down the cup and started down the hall. She had made it through the third challenge!

But as she turned a corner, she came up to a broad desk set to block it. A woman sat behind the desk, writing on a pad of paper.

Gloha stopped, surprised. "Who are you?" she inquired.

"I am the SB," the woman replied, pointing to a name-plate that said SB. "I'm here to handle the Sin Tax."

"Syntax? you must be a writer."

"Sin Tax," the woman repeated. "S-I-N-T-A-X. You must pay. I am the Sin Bursar. It's my business to see that you pay."

"But I haven't sinned!" Gloha protested innocently.

"You were smoking, drinking, gamboling, and having secs," SB said evenly. "Those are all taxable."

"Smoking? But my shoes were burning up! And it was just one drink of water I took to cool off. And then I was so happy to be cool again that I did dance a little, but I never thought—" She paused. "What was that last?"

"You had most of the seconds available. You used them up. Now you have to pay the tax."

Gloha realized that she was stuck for it. Ignorance was no excuse, whether a person stuck her finger in a beehive or used the contents of a seed cup. "How do I pay the tax?"

SB toted up the total on her pad. "That's four counts. You will have to perform four tasks. You will have to wash her, dry her, sock her, and box her."

"Washer, dryer, soccer, and boxer?" Gloha repeated, baffled. "I don't—" But she stopped herself before saying "understand." After all, she had to understand, in order to get through this challenge, which she now realized wasn't yet done. "Could you explain that a bit more?"

SB touched a button on her desk. A panel in the wall opened. Beyond it Gloha saw a strange yet rather nice creature. It had the head and front legs of a horse, and the hind section of a winged dragon. So it was a winged monster, and therefore a creature Gloha could relate to, as she was a winged monster herself.

"There is the Glyph. Clean her up and pack her for shipment," SB said, and returned to her writing.

Gloha entered the Glyph's pen. Now she saw that the poor creature was quite dirty. Her wing feathers were soiled, her fur was grimy, her scales did not glisten, and her hooves were caked with mud. The poor creature needed attention. Gloha would have been glad to help her even if it wasn't to pay the Sin Tax.

There was a trough and bucket beside the stall, and brushes too. Gloha dipped the bucket full of water, and approached the Glyph. The creature shied nervously away from her. "Hey, take it easy, Glyph!" Gloha said soothingly. "You don't have to be afraid of me. See, I'm a winged monster too." She spread her wings and pumped them a couple of times.

The Glyph settled down. Gloha washed her, getting the fur and scales and hooves clean so that they glistened and shone as they should. Then she brushed off the wings so that the feathers turned light and bright. She fetched towels and dried her. But she wasn't sure how to sock her. She wasn't about to hit this nice creature.

Then she saw a plant with odd dangly foliage. It looked like a blanket bush, only smaller. She brought it to the Glyph, and the plant immediately reached around the Glyph's feet and legs. Tendrils stretched material, in a moment and a half both legs had socks. The socks sank in, and seemed just like nice black fur decorating the legs from the knees down.

Now it was time to box her. Gloha saw wood panels to the side of the stall. She could use these to make a big enough box around the animal. She went to fetch the first panel. But as she put her hands on it, she paused. Something was nagging her.

She turned. The Glyph was looking at her. Their gazes met. She had reassured the animal, and now the Glyph trusted her. But Gloha didn't trust the situation.

She left the panel and returned to the hall. "Why does she need to be boxed?" she demanded.

SB looked up from her writing pad. "It's on the bill of lading. One boxed Glyph."

"That's not good enough. Why does she have to be boxed, when she's tame? Why can't she just be led to where she's going? It's cruel to put an animal in a box."

SB checked her pad. "She's going to be a sculpted figure on a fancy building. She has to be crated for shipping."

"I don't understand," Gloha said, using the word she had tried to avoid. But she was upset. It was too late to take it back anyway.

"Why don't you?"

"This Glyph is a fine sensitive animal. She's been badly treated before; she should never have been left so dirty. Boxing her will be more bad treatment. I will never understand why that should be."

"What never?" SB asked.

"No, never!"

"What never?" SB repeated.

Gloha hesitated. She knew she was throwing away her chance to pass the third challenge and get in to see the Good Magician. But she liked the Glyph, and couldn't bear to see the creature mistreated. Who wanted to be stuck on a building, anyway? "No, never," she said in a tone that was neither cut nor little.

"Then you must share her fate," SB said. "Go mount her."

"You mean ride her? I'm sure she's a fine steed. But what's the point, if she's not going anywhere?"

"Wherever she is going or not going, you will go or not go too. That's the rule. I'm here to enforce the rule."

A realistic little realization came to Gloha. "You're doing your Service for the Good Magician!"

"Of course. That's the rule."

"What was your Question, if I may ask?"

"I asked him how I could be a writer. He said I should work on my syntax. Only it turned out to be the Sin Tax. I'm confined to this desk for this boring job. But I must say it concentrates the imagination beautifully. I have written several chapters of my novel between taxes."

"So you're getting to be a writer after all," Gloha said. "While you're doing your Service."

"Yes. I think I'll have a chapter about a crossbreed winged goblin girl and her friendship for a crossbreed winged animal. Do you think my readers will like that?"

"I hope so. It seems interesting to me."

"Now go ride the Glyph." It was evident that SB's affability did not extend to neglecting her duty.

Gloha didn't argue. She was satisfied to share the Glyph's fate, if she couldn't improve the animal's lot. She went to the stall and climbed on the Glyph's back, between the wings. "I'm sorry I couldn't save you," she said, patting the neck under the now-beautiful mane. "But I just couldn't box you, no matter what."

The ceiling disappeared. Open sky appeared. The Glyph spread her giant wings and launched into the air. She was through the hole in the roof and into the sky almost before Gloha knew it.

"But—but you're free!" Gloha said, amazed.

The Glyph neighed happily. Gloha could have let go and flown herself, but preferred to stay with her new friend. Where were they going?

A castle came into sight below. The Glyph angled down toward it. There was a nice solid flat roof with a pile of hay on it. The Glyph landed on this.

"But where are we?" Gloha asked, not yet over her amazement.

"The Good Magician's castle, of course," a voice answered.

Gloha saw a pretty young woman standing by a stair

leading up to the roof. "But I shouldn't be here," she protested. "I messed up on the third challenge."

"Oh, I don't think so," the woman said, coming forward. "I am Wira, the Good Magician's daughter-in-law. I came here to lead you to him."

"I'm Gloha," Gloha said, disgruntled. "I—I told the SB woman I didn't understand, and it was a challenge of understanding, so she said I would share the Glyph's fate, and—" She broke off, realizing that something else was odd.

Wira was petting the Glyph. The Glyph was nuzzling her face. It was evident that the two knew each other. Wira brought out a sugar cube and the Glyph ate it. Then Wira petted the animal again and stepped away. "Come on in," she said to Gloha.

"The challenge of understanding—it wasn't about riddles or directions," Gloha said. "It was about decency."

The girl smiled. "Of course."

Gloha joined her, and they walked to the stairs. The Glyph began eating the hay, contentedly.

2
SECOND SON

The interior of the castle was pleasant and surprisingly light, considering the thickness of its walls. Probably magic accounted for that; after all, Humfrey was the Magician of Information, so he would know how to have a nice residence.

Wira led her to the kitchen, where a woman was seated at a table, facing away from them. "Mother, put on your veil, if you haven't already," Wira said.

"That's all right, dear; I heard you coming," the woman said. She turned, and her face was covered by a full, thick veil. Tiny serpents framed the region of her face; they seemed to be in lieu of hair. The effect was fairly attractive; they were pretty little snakes.

"This is the Gorgon," Wira said to Gloha. Then, to the other: "This is Gloha, who just passed the challenges. She has come to see Father."

Gloha was amazed anew. She knew of the Gorgon, of course, but hadn't expected to meet her. The woman's mere glance could turn a person to stone; that was why she was veiled. She was Magician Humfrey's fifth but perhaps not quite final wife; it was a complicated situation.

But what was also confusing Gloha was an oddness about Wira. Suddenly she remembered: Wira was blind! She had moved around the castle with such assurance that Gloha hadn't been reminded. So Wira, alone of people, had no fear of the Gorgon's gaze, because it was mostly the sight of the Gorgon's face that petrified others. It was for Gloha's safety that Wira had reminded the Gorgon about the veil.

"So nice to meet you, dear," the Gorgon said politely. "The Good Magician is ready to see you now." She returned to her business, which seemed to be the slow petrifying of a wedge of cheese: Gorgonzola, of course. Gloha had heard that it was one of her specialties, because she merely had to stare at it long enough.

Now it occurred to Gloha that the cheese must be able to see, at least a little, in order to be affected by the Gorgon's stare. One never could tell what things could do. She knew that when King Dor was around, inanimate things were highly responsive. If a girl stepped over a stone, the stone might make a remark about her legs, and possibly even blab the color of her panties, to her great embarrassment. So maybe it did make sense that cheese could see.

Wira led the way to another winding stairway. It was so gloomy dark that Gloha hesitated for fear of misstepping.

"Oh, I'm sorry," Wira said contritely. "I forgot that you are sighted." She moved a hand, and the walls glowed, showing the stairs.

"Thank you," Gloha said. "I normally don't use stairs anyway; the harpy hive doesn't have them."

"Oh, it must be fun to fly," Wira said. "Of course I would never have been able to do it, even when I was young."

"When you were young?" The woman was twice Gloha's height, because she was full human, but she looked no older than Gloha herself.

"When I was a child, I mean. I'm technically forty-one,

but I've been awake for only nineteen years, so the Good Magician used youth elixir to youthen me back to my subjective age. So I think of myself as nineteen, and I am, physically, but my youth was a long time ago."

"You slept for twenty-two years?" One amazement was piling on another.

"Yes. My family couldn't afford to keep me, because I wasn't very useful, so they had me put to sleep when I was sixteen. Then I met Hugo in the dream realm, and he was sixteen too, and we knew each other for ten years asleep. Then we all woke together, when Magician Humfrey returned here, and got our ages set and started living normally for the past three years. The Good Magician likes to keep his age at about a hundred, though he's really a hundred and sixty, the same as his half wife MareAnn."

"She's physically a hundred, too?"

Wira laughed. "Oh, no, she prefers to be somewhat younger. She says that now that she's lost her innocence, she might as well be of an age to get some fun from life. It seems that old women aren't as appealing as old men, and of course they can't afford to get worn or dirty. She won't say how old she is now."

"Life certainly seems complicated here," Gloha said, not sure she would be able to keep all these ages straight, even if some weren't known.

"Oh, no; life is pleasantly simple here," Wira demurred. "It's only the background that is complicated. Just forget it and you'll have no trouble."

That seemed like good advice.

They reached a small chamber buried somewhere in the deep interior of the castle. It was filled to overflowing with books, scrolls, and stoppered little bottles. In the midst of it was an ancient gnomelike little man hardly larger than Gloha herself.

"Good Magician, here is Gloha," Wira said. "To ask her Question."

The gnome pulled his gaze from his tome with such difficulty that Gloha almost thought she heard a tearing sound. "Go see my second son," he said grumpily. His gaze plopped back to the tome.

"But I haven't even asked my Question!" Gloha protested.

Wira nudged her. "It's better not to try to argue with him. He doesn't pay attention."

"But I came all this way, and went through all those challenges, and I want to get what I came for."

"Please, don't annoy him." Wira guided her away with such concern that Gloha had to go with her. "He's already grumpy enough."

But when they were safely away from the Magician, Gloha voiced her protest more firmly. "I don't think it's fair to make me go through all the challenges to get here and not even let me ask my Question. What's the matter with him?"

"The Good Magician always has good reason for whatever he does. We just don't always understand it. When Mela Merwoman, Okra Ogress, and Ida Human came two years ago with their Questions, he listened to them and refused to answer them. Mela was so annoyed she threatened to show him her panty and freak him out. But later they learned that their Answers would have been a lot less satisfying if he had given them then, because there were other things they had to do first."

"I don't understand."

"Well, for example, Mela wanted to know how to find a good husband. He told her to ask Nada Naga. That didn't make any sense to her, but when she asked Nada, Nada sent her to her brother Naldo, who was then Xanth's most eligible bachelor prince, and he married Mela. Because he saw her freak-out panties, which he wouldn't have seen if there hadn't been complications on the way."

"So she might have lost him, if the Good Magician had told her to go after him," Gloha said. "I see the point. And maybe my case is similar, because I'm looking for a good husband too. But my problem is worse, because I fear there is no male harpy-goblin crossbreed for me. Certainly the

Magician's second son isn't one!" She paused, suffering another unpleasant thought. "In fact, he only has one son, doesn't he? Hugo, whom you married?"

Wira was surprised. "Oh! I hadn't thought of that. I'm sure he hasn't had any more children since Hugo. One of the wives would have mentioned it." Then she brightened. "But he does have five and a half wives, and maybe some of them had children before he went to Hell. So Hugo may not be the first son."

"Suppose he's the second?"

"Then you can ask him. I can quickly find him for you."

"You can?"

"Like this." Wira paused, then whispered, "Hugo, dear."

There was a scrambling on the stairway. A disheveled young human man appeared. "You called, dear?"

"Isn't love wonderful?" Wira asked Gloha. "I'm so glad I met him." Then, to Hugo: "Father told Gloha to see his second son. Is that you?"

"I don't think so," Hugo said uncertainly. "Father had several children before me, I think. So I must be the third or fourth, but I'm not sure."

"Do you know where I can find a good husband?" Gloha asked. "Preferably a flying goblin about my age."

Hugo shook his head. "I don't think there are any other flying goblins. The goblins and harpies were at war for a thousand years or so before your parents got together, so I don't think any of them, you-know." He had to stop, because he was starting to blush.

"He's so sweet," Wira murmured. "Sometimes I wonder whether he ever really joined the Adult Conspiracy." She winked, to indicate that she wasn't quite serious. Then, again to him: "Do you have any idea who would know about all Humfrey's sons?"

"Maybe Lacuna. She recorded his whole history."

"Yes, that's a good idea," Wira agreed, and Hugo smiled with pleasure at the compliment. Gloha had to agree: love *was* wonderful. If only she could find it for herself.

Meanwhile they went downstairs to see if the Gorgon knew. "I should think that would be the business of his prior wives," she remarked. "They will all show up here, in due course." She considered briefly, and a wisp of smoke rose from the spot on the cheese where her masked gaze rested too long. "I believe Dara had a son, however."

"Who?" Hugo asked.

"Dara Demoness. His first wife."

"Oh, you mean Dana Demoness," Wira said.

"No, I mean Dara. Do you think I don't know her name, after meeting her in Hell?"

"But Humfrey calls her Dana."

"Humfrey never did pay much attention to details. She never bothered to correct him, for fear he'd be grumpy. Names aren't as important to demons as they are to us."

"I don't think I can wait five months to check with all the other wives," Gloha said. "I'm getting constantly older, and my young little youth is fleeting."

The Gorgon laughed. "Believe me, dear, your youth will last long enough if you keep your fine little figure."

"Do you really think so?" Gloha asked, beginning to hope.

"Assuredly. You can keep your youth for several years merely by hiding your blasé little birthdays from men. All smart women know this."

"And hide your intelligence, too," Wira added.

"I never knew about such things," Gloha said, impressed.

"Which is part of your charm, dear."

"Maybe you should go home," Wira suggested, "and I'll ask the wives as they appear. Then I'll send you a message when we learn who his second son was."

"Thank you," Gloha said gratefully. She realized that this was her best and only chance to pursue her quest.

The Gorgon served them a snack of funny punwheel cookies and candy-striped milk, to fortify Gloha for her flight home. The Gorgon seemed slightly uncomfortable; her ringlet snakes were panting. The castle was warm, and it looked hot under the thick veil.

"If I may ask—" Gloha inquired with a halting little hesitation.

"By all means, dear," the Gorgon said, wiping her brow. "We aren't as fussy about questions as the Good Magician is."

"Why don't you get some vanishing cream from the Good Magician to make your face invisible—"

"I did that once, but it was awkward going about faceless, so I still had to wear a veil."

"And then mask it with the illusion of your face?" Gloha finished. "So that you would look just like you, snakelets and all, but wouldn't stone anyone."

The Gorgon paused, her veil flexing into an attitude of astonishment. "Why, I believe that would do it, when I'm Xanthside," she said. "Then I could have the spells nullified when I returned to my job as a horror actress in the dream realm. Thank you, dear; I shall see Humfrey about it immediately." She got up and headed for the stairway.

"He's grumpy today," Wira called warningly.

"He wouldn't *dare* grump at me," the Gorgon replied. "Not until after he provides those spells."

Wira giggled, and Gloha joined her. If there was one person who wasn't intimidated by the Good Magician, it was the Gorgon, and not merely because she was his wife.

They finished the cookies and milk. Then Wira opened a window, and Gloha bid her adieu, spread her wings, and took off. "Do visit again sometime," Wira called after her. "There won't be any challenges if you don't come with a Question."

"Maybe I will," Gloha called back. It had been nice visiting with a young woman her own age.

Then she mounted up, up into the sky, flying for home. It was good to be airborne again!

But in a moment she suffered a change of mind. That was one of the privileges of being feminine. She had been for a while at the happy hive; it was time to visit her goblin relatives, which included her mother Glory Goblin. So she changed course and headed for the Gap Chasm where the Gap Goblins lived.

Soon she was there. That was just as well, because the day was getting tired and the sun seemed hardly able to keep itself in the sky; any moment it would singe the trees to the west and dunk itself in the ocean and go out, leaving Xanth in darkness. She glided over the gloomy deep chasm and down to the village perched at its brink. The goblins didn't worry about falling into the chasm; if one did, well, there were plenty more goblins who didn't. In a moment she was hugging her mother, who was still one of the prettiest of goblin women despite being an ancient thirty-seven years old.

Then Gloha explained about how she had gone to see the Good Magician Humfrey, and failed to get a good Answer to her Question. "But the Good Magician always knows what he's doing," Glory said. "I remember when your Aunt Goldy met the ogre who was doing his Service for his Answer. That was a funny thing—the ogre was so stupid that he had forgotten the Question by the time he reached the castle, but he did the Service anyway. His Service was to protect the half nymph Tandy, and by the time he was done with that, he married her and was happy, and that was his Answer. And along the way Goldy got her magic wand and found a husband of her own, all because of her association with the ogre."

"And she was the mother of Cousin Godiva Goblin," Gloha agreed, having heard the story before. "And grandmother of Gwenny Goblin, who's only three years younger than me, and has already had adventures galore and become the first lady goblin chief, and I'm not even married yet!" she finished in a wail.

"Well, you're special, dear," her mother reminded her.

"The only one of my kind! How can I ever find a suitable man?"

"Maybe Humfrey's second son will know."

"And maybe he won't! And maybe it will take five more months to find out who the second son is. And I'll be pushing t-twenty!" For now she was suffering a delicate little doubt about the efficacy of extending youth by hiding birthdays. Suppose it didn't work? She'd be sadly stuck.

Glory saw how serious the matter was. "Maybe your Aunt Goldy will have a notion. Why don't you go ask her?"

"Thanks. I will." Gloha spread her wings.

"I didn't mean right this instant! Don't you want to stay and see your Grandfather Gorbage?"

"Not if I can avoid it."

Glory nodded understandingly. Goblin men just weren't the most pleasant folk. However, she had a more persuasive point. "Are you sure you want to fly in the night? When the other winged monsters might not recognize you?"

Gloha folded her wings. "Maybe I *will* visit with you tonight," she decided. "It's the family way."

"How nice of you, dear." Mothers had a special talent for getting their way.

But in the morning, before her grandfather could show up, Gloha gobbled her breakfast and bid her mother a modestly tearful parting. There were forms to be followed, after all.

Gloha took off and flew north toward Goblin Mountain where her Aunt Goldy lived. It was nice to have an excuse to visit there, now that her cousin-once-removed Gwenny was chiefess. If only the other goblin tribes could be governed by women too! Then the whole of goblindom would be so much nicer. But anything like that was a long way away, if ever.

The sun had dried itself off and recovered enough strength to climb the eastern sky. Gloha had never been quite certain how it managed to find its way to the east after drowning in the water to the west, but assumed that there was some kind of magic to handle it, because the sun's course was fairly reliable. The clouds, which had gotten somewhat damp and drippy in the night, were drying off and turning white and fluffy again. There was no sign of Fracto, fortunately.

She passed the region of the flies, and the dragons, and the elves, until she spied Goblin Mountain. Or was it? She hadn't been there in months, and what she saw below was distinctly odd. "Odds goblins," she murmured. Instead of a structure resembling an enormous anthill with the pox, she saw a prettily tiered network of gardens with flowers. That *couldn't* be it.

Then she remembered: the male goblins no longer governed Goblin Mountain. A female was in charge. So flower gardens made sense.

Reassured, she dropped down toward it. As she got close, she saw more detail. The flowers grew in patches of color, and the color spelled P-E-A-C-E. That was Gwenny's work, all right.

She landed by a prettily manicured front gate. There was a goblin guard, neatly uniformed. He snapped to attention as she approached. "A courteous greeting, Lady Gloha," he said politely. "Whom do you wish to see?"

Gloha was taken aback. What was the matter with this goblin? He should have greeted her with an insult or a threat, or at least a sexist innuendo. That was the way male goblins were. It was expected. She didn't trust this.

Then the goblin flashed a surreptitious scowl. "Don't look so surprised, wingback. This isn't *my* idea. At least I got half a look up under your sexy little skirt as you came down."

Gloha smiled as she smoothed down her skirt. So this was just a veneer over normalcy. Goblin nature had not been repealed. "I want to see Goldy."

"Very good." He turned to his talk-tube. "Gloha to see Goldy, presently." Then he turned to Gloha. "Get your galoshes going, goody-gams."

Gloha nodded, appreciating the goblin-style compliment. She walked on into the tunnel. Soon she found Aunt Goldy's apartment. She knocked on the portal.

It opened. There stood the gobliness, even ancienter than Glory because she was ten years older. But she looked better than she had, probably because she now had more status than before. All females did. "Why, how nice to see you, dear," she said, giving Gloha a hug. "Do come in."

The apartment was nicely finished, with flowers and pleasant pictures all around. Gloha sat gracefully on a cushion, resting her gams, uh, limbs, and especially her wings. "I went to see the Good Magician about a husband, and he told me to see his second son. But I don't know who that is. Mother thought you might know."

Aunt Goldy pondered. "I remember when I traveled with the ogre—his girl Tandy—there was something about her. I never did quite figure it out. But maybe the ogre did. Maybe you should go ask him."

"Ask the ogre? You know ogres and goblins don't get along well."

"This one's different. He's half human. He's a decent creature, and not nearly as ugly or stupid as he should be. He figured out how to work the magic wand, after all, then gave it to me so I could win a goblin chief. He has a way with these things. Talk to him, and maybe he'll help you find that second son."

Gloha shook her bemused little brain. "This is pretty farfetched. Are you sure you aren't getting senile?"

"Not at all sure, dear," Goldy said cheerfully. "Maybe you should ask someone else." But she did seem oddly sure of herself. She surely knew or suspected something, but wasn't about to say exactly what it was lest she seem truly foolish.

At least Gloha could check with the ogre. Then maybe she could find Lacuna and ask her. Someone, somewhere, was bound to know. "What's the name of this ogre?"

"Smash. He's Esk's father, I believe."

"Oh, Esk! I know of him. Esk Ogre. He married Bria Brassie, and they have three children."

"They do? I knew only of one."

"The stork brought them two more, I think. Twins."

"How curious. There seems to have been a rash of twins recently. Maybe the storks are up to something."

"Maybe it's a conspiracy," Gloha said, smiling. "An Adult Conspiracy."

"That must be it," her aunt agreed.

Before she left, Gloha went to see her cousin-once-removed Gwenny, who at sixteen was more like a straight cousin. She was the chiefess of Goblin Mountain, but perhaps would have half a moment to spare.

Gwenny was at a meeting, negotiating a treaty with the naga folk, but her Companion Che Centaur came out to see Gloha. He was a winged monster too, and they were friends. They hugged each other. He was only eight years old, but already he was substantially larger than Gloha, because he was of a larger species. He was also more intelligent, because that was the nature of centaurs.

"I'll tell Gwenny you were here," he said. "I know she would want to see you, but this treaty is so important that she just can't break away. The goblins and naga have long been enemies, and now they will be friends, or at least allies. The details are critical. Prince Naldo Naga is attending, though he'd rather be playing water games with his buxom wife Mela Merwoman, so you can appreciate how important it is."

"Yes, of course." There it was again: married folk having fun. Mela had a daughter two years older than Gloha, yet Mela had no trouble finding her man. "But it's nice to see you, too."

"I understand you are looking for the Good Magician's second son."

"Yes. But I don't know who he is. Do you know?"

"No, but I'm sure the Muse of History would know."

"I don't want to struggle with Mount Parnassus to see her! Aunt Goldy thinks Smash Ogre may know something."

Che cocked his head. "That is possible. At worst, he won't know anything, and then you can ask the Muse."

Gloha thanked him and went her way. Each person had a different idea whom she should ask. Maybe one of those people really would know. Yet once she found the second son, she would still be at the mere beginning of her quest, because the Good Magician hadn't said that his second son had the Answer. Who knew what convolutions remained? She really wasn't very pleased with Humfrey's offhand dismissal of her Question. Who cared about all the other folk whose Good Magician Answers had turned out, in retrospect, to be good? She didn't even have his Answer, just a stupid referral.

She emerged from the mountain and took off before the goblin guard could make any more smart-faced remarks. But she couldn't stop him from getting another peek under her skirt before she got out of range. She really did have to change her outfit, the moment she got home. But first she would see the ogre, because his home in the jungle was closer than the harpy hutch.

She flew south, crossing the Gap Chasm again. She saw a dark cloud, and quickly flew lower before it could see her, in case it should be Fracto. Then she spied the ogre's twisted-ironwood-tree house and descended.

A really ancient woman of fifty or so met her at the door. This was Tandy, the ogre's wife.

"No, Smash is out searching for stones from which to squeeze juice for stone soup," Tandy reported. "He's half ogre, you know, and every so often he likes to exercise his ogre nature. You may have noticed how all small dragons have vacated the area for now. But perhaps I can help you with your concern."

"I'm looking for the Good Magician's second son. Do you know who that is?"

"No, but I know someone who might be able to point him out. That's my father Crombie. That's his talent: to point to anything."

Gloha considered. "That might do it. But isn't your father pretty old, considering how aged you are?"

Tandy smiled in a way that reminded Gloha oddly of Aunt Goldy, who was of that general generation. "Exceedingly old. I think he recently had his ninety-first birthday. But he was once a major character in Xanth; and old characters never die, they just fade away. We just have to talk to him before he fades too far."

"That makes sense," Gloha agreed. "Do you know where he is now?"

"Oh, yes. He lives down in the underworld with my mother Jewel the Nymph."

"She must be horribly old too."

"Yes and no. Nymphs are ageless, really, remaining young and sexy forever or until they turn mortal. Jewel turned mortal when she married Crombie and sent off to the stork for me. So if we figure she was an apparent age of twenty then, she would be an apparent age of seventy now. That's probably manageable."

"I suppose so," Gloha agreed doubtfully. "But I'm not sure I could find my way through the underworld."

"Unfortunately I'm only half nymph; I look my age. But I'm still spry enough to show you the way to my father's home."

"Oh, wonderful!" Gloha exclaimed with guileless little glee, clapping her happy little hands.

"First we have to get to Lake Ogre-Chobee," Tandy said, scribbling a note. "The entrance to the underworld is there. Fortunately that's not too far from here. I can't fly, of course, so it will be slow, but we'll get there."

Gloha hoped it wouldn't be *too* slow. She did want to get there before the five months it would take to check with Humfrey's other wives was done. But of course she didn't say that, because it might upset Tandy and make her even slower.

Tandy pinned the note to a chair. Gloha saw that it said "SMASH—visiting folks—back soon. TANDY." Then Tandy went out to her kitchen garden, where she dug out a plant.

"Oh—to eat along the way?" Gloha asked.

"No, this is a light bulb, to make my poor old body light. In my youth I rode a night mare, but I am beyond that now." Tandy tucked the bulb into a pocket, and indeed, she did seem to step lighter now.

"I don't suppose you also grow heavy bulbs," Gloha said.

"Oh, yes, I do. But Smash uses them, when he's feeling light-headed; they bring more gravity to his thoughts."

They set off through the jungle. Gloha was concerned about encountering land monsters here who might try to eat them, but then saw that Tandy's shirt said OGRE'S WIFE across the back. That probably protected her from most creatures. Who among them would care to risk the wrath of an ogre?

The light bulb did seem to make Tandy faster on her feet; she was quite spritely. She fairly bounded along, while Gloha flew low. They followed a path marked by saplings twisted into pretzel knots and boulders cracked open by powerful blows. An ogre path, obviously.

Then they heard something. It was a weird sort of squishy noise smelling of fresh mud. It seemed to be moving on a course that would intercept their path somewhere ahead. "What is that?" Gloha asked nervously.

"I'm sure I don't know," Tandy replied. "Let's go see."

Gloha had an opposite notion, but did not want to be negative, so she agreed. They hurried forward toward the place the noise would soon be. In a moment Gloha was flying ahead, outdistancing Tandy.

It turned out to be a mud slide. Rich brown mud was coursing through the forest. The only problem was that there was no slope from which it was sliding. It was moving along the level ground, or even uphill.

The mud slewed to a stop. "Ho!" someone called from beyond.

Gloha flew up to see who it was. There to her special amazement was an old, old man sitting on a huge dinner plate set on the mud. Behind him was a prettily decorated cabin with little white curtains in the windows.

Gloha hovered before the man, perplexed. He looked vaguely familiar. "Hello," she said with a timid little tremor. "Did you call?"

"Why, hello, winsome little winged goblin girl; you must be Gloha," he said. "Yes, I called; I thought you might be able to help us. I'm King Emeritus Trent." Then, perhaps assuming that she wouldn't recognize the name: "Ivy's grandfather."

"Oh!" Gloha said with a squeamish little squeak. "I thought you had faded away."

"Not quite," Trent said. "We four grandparents are going to visit Esk's grandparents for a fade-out party. But we seem to have lost our way."

"You four? Where are the others?"

Trent turned his face back. "Hey, Sorceress, lift the veil," he called. "We have a visitor: Gloha Goblin-Harpy."

Immediately the cabin vanished. There sat three other old folk on plates: two women and a man.

"Uh, hello," Gloha said again with a certain awed little awkwardness.

"My wife the Sorceress Iris," Trent said. One of the old women became a beautiful young woman with a shining silver crown and button-bursting bodice. Except that it was laced, not buttoned, so she was a lace-lashing lady.

"So nice to meet you, Gloha," the sorceress said dulcetly, with a grand nod of her head.

"My friend Bink, Ivy's other grandfather," Trent said. The other old man became a handsome medium-young man in halfway casual clothing. He nodded.

"And last and least, his wife Chameleon, in her stupid phase," Trent concluded.

The other woman did not change. Gloha saw now that she was old but amazingly lovely; she needed no magical enhancement, despite being in ordinary garb. For now Gloha remembered from her history lessons that the Sorceress Iris' talent was illusion; she could make anyone or anything look any way she wanted. But Chameleon didn't seem to need illusion. Gloha hadn't believed that anyone that old could look that good.

"We hope you can help us, Gloha," Chameleon said. "We seem to have lost our way."

That was so obvious that it needed no restatement. Then Gloha remembered the thing about Chameleon: she changed with the moon, becoming beautiful and stupid, then ugly and smart. So she couldn't be counted on to speak intelligently.

Something Trent had said registered. "You're going to see Esk's grandparents? Why, so are we! I'm with Tandy, who knows the way."

"What a fortunate coincidence," Queen Iris said. She sent a curiously significant side glance at Bink. "You and Tandy must join us and show us the route."

"Oh, I'm sure we'll be glad to," Gloha agreed. "Let me go tell Tandy!" She darted away before belatedly realizing that this might be impolite. After all, if she remembered her history lessons correctly, all of them had been kings of Xanth at one time or another. But it was too late to correct her lamentable little lapse, so she just flew on.

In a moment she found Tandy, who had continued walking. "There are four—they want to—same place we're going—it's a coincidence," she said breathlessly or perhaps witlessly.

Tandy questioned her on the several pieces of her statement, and managed to fathom the general little gist. "That *is* a coincidence," she agreed. "For such a party to get lost right where we were going—there must be magic involved."

"Oh, yes, the Sorceress Iris is spreading illusion all around," Gloha agreed.

They reached the mud slide. The cabin was back on top of it, hiding the three, but King Trent remained in his handsome younger form. "And to what do we owe the honor of your presence here in the wilderness?" he inquired of Tandy.

"Gloha is looking for the Good Magician's second son, and I thought my father Crombie might point out the direction," Tandy replied.

"Oh, Humfrey is involved in this," Trent said, as if that had great significance. "Well, if you will show us the route, we shall give you a ride on Swiftmud here." He indicated the bank of mud on which his plate sat.

"I *would* rather ride than walk," Tandy agreed. "And perhaps Gloha would rather ride than fly. We shall be happy to make the deal."

So Trent set out two more plates, and Tandy managed to scramble up to one without getting too muddy, while Gloha flew to the other. Then the cabin expanded to enclose them all including Trent, and they were in what looked like a luxurious palace chamber.

"But don't stray from your plate," Chameleon cautioned with a smile.

Gloha extended a cautious finger to the cushioned floor beside her, and felt mud. Everything was illusion except the mud and the plate. But it was pleasant in this seeming cabin. "If I may ask—" she started.

"We are not quite as young as we once were," Trent said. "So now we prefer to travel in comfort. I transformed a mud grub into Swiftmud, and Iris provided plates from her kitchen. This seems to be an adequate mode of travel. Except that Swiftmud is not particularly bright, and strayed from the assigned route when we weren't watching, and now we aren't entirely sure where we are. But we suspected that there would be a fortunate coincidence, and now it has occurred. Show us the way, Tandy, and we shall slide there forthwith."

Tandy looked around. "I think I'll need to be outside for that."

Abruptly the cabin wall contracted, and Trent and Tandy were outside, while Gloha remained inside. In a moment Swiftmud started to move again, sliding smoothly and probably swiftly along. Yes—Gloha saw trees whizzing by outside the curtained porthole. They were on their way.

"Have some anthony and tell us your story," Iris suggested, extending a smaller plate on which several brushes and combs were piled.

"Anthony?" Gloha asked blankly.

"Ant-honey," Iris said more carefully. "Honey from ants. Sometimes in my age I slur out the hyphen. Some like it better than bee-honey or sea-honey."

"Thank you." Gloha took a honey comb from the plate and took a naughty little nibble. It was very good.

The others took honey brushes and chewed on them. Then Gloha explained about her quest to find a good winged goblin man for a husband, and the frustration of her visit to the Good Magician's castle.

"Yes, Humfrey is like that, now more than ever," Iris said, licking spilled honey off her fingers. "Age hasn't sweetened him."

"But he always has reason," Bink said. "I remember when he said he couldn't fathom my talent."

"What *is* your talent?" Gloha asked. "I mean, I know you're a Magician, because my centaur history book said so, but I don't think it said what your talent is."

"Well, that's an odd thing," Bink replied. "I think I have a notion of its nature, but every time I try to tell someone about it, somehow I don't."

"I don't understand," Gloha said.

Iris and Chameleon smiled and looked away.

Bink sighed. "I suppose I could make a demonstration." He took a breath. "My talent is—"

The Swiftmud lurched to a halt, almost pitching them from their plates onto the icky surface of itself.

"Whose fault is that?" Trent's voice called from outside the cabin.

"Oh, it must be mine!" Gloha cried with a chaotic little chagrin.

"Nonsense," Trent said. "This is bigger than all of us."

The cabin vanished, so they could all see what was outside. Swiftmud perched at the edge of a huge cleft in the ground. Trent had halted it just in time to prevent them from plunging into the chasm and getting horribly muddied.

"It must be an extension of the Gap Chasm," Tandy said. "But I don't remember any such fault in this region."

"Probably the original forget spell hasn't yet worn off all the tributaries," Trent said. "But I must admit it came as a surprise. I'm not sure how we'll get past it."

"If we could identify it, we might know more about it," Tandy said. "All the offshoots of the Gap Chasm have names."

"Right," Trent agreed. "So we must answer my question: whose fault is this?"

Gloha realized that he hadn't been accusing her before. Still, she felt somehow guilty. She struggled with her minor little memory of geography and managed to evoke a name. "Could it be San Andrea's Fault?" she asked. "The one that cracks on into Mundania?"

"Yes, it must be San Andrea's fault," Iris agreed. "I never thought much of San Andrea anyway."

"The question is," Iris said tartly, "how are we going to proceed? This fault appears to extend right across our route. If we detour, after losing time by getting lost, we shall be late for our engagement. We don't want the others to fade out without us."

"I can fly across," Gloha said. "But I'm too small to carry anyone else. I might haul a rope across, though, if that would help."

"I don't think we have time to make a rope bridge that would hold Swiftmud's weight," Bink said. "I wish we had thought to get no-fault insurance. Then we wouldn't have encountered any fault."

"We never think of what we're going to need ahead of time," Chameleon said. "Otherwise you and I would never have adventured in the Gap Chasm the first time, Bink."

Bink smiled. "You were almost as lovely then as you are now, dear."

She returned the smile. "And lovelier than I will be next week."

"Save those reminiscences for the fade-out party," Iris snapped. "I'll make us all beautiful then. How do we get there in time?"

"We can proceed, but it may not be entirely comfortable," Trent said. "Swiftmud is a fairly versatile creature; he can slide along any surface without losing his grip. But we might prefer to walk."

"At our age?" Iris asked. "You forget you're ninety-six

years old, and I'm not a great deal younger. If we try to walk any distance, we shall both fade out sooner than planned."

"Then we had better ride," Trent agreed. "But we shall need to use some of your magic glue."

"Glue?"

"For our bottoms."

"What are you thinking of!"

"So we won't fall off our plates when Swiftmud slides down the face of the fault."

Iris considered. Then she dug into her purse and brought out a tube of glue she had evidently harvested from a glue plant.

They took turns applying it to their plates, having to stand on an extra plate Iris provided from somewhere while doing it. Then they sat down again, and their legs and posteriors fastened firmly to each plate. Gloha was nervous about it, and decided not to use the glue. "Maybe I can help find the way through the fault."

"That seems sensible," Chameleon agreed. Gloha felt a thankful little flash of gratitude; not only was the woman lovely, she was nice. Gloha had been afraid that someone would find fault with her suggestion about the fault. After all, it was the nature of faults to be found.

Trent gave a command, and Swiftmud started forward. He slid to the edge of the fault, and over it, making a square angle turn down. One by one the plates made that awesome turn. The others remained on their plates, but Gloha couldn't; she had to fly free.

She looped around and hovered near Swiftmud as he slid at an even pace straight down the wall of the fault. The five passengers remained firmly glued to their plates, but they did not look inordinately comfortable. Gloha suspected that under the illusion their hair and perhaps other parts of their bodies were sagging somewhat. Then the cabin reappeared, hiding them. That made Gloha feel better, at least.

She flew down to investigate the depths of the fault. It narrowed steadily, until it disappeared in a dark crevice too small for Swiftmud to enter. But it was also too wide for the creature to cross, she thought, unless it was capable of making a U-turn across nothing. What now?

She flew to one side, and then to the other. She found a section with a U-shaped connection of stone. That should do. In fact it looked ideal.

She flew back to Swiftmud. "Follow me," she said.

Swiftmud obligingly followed her to the side. She landed on the U-stone. "Cross here," she said.

Swiftmud did. Then it proceeded up the other wall. In due course it returned to the surface, and got level again.

The cabin vanished. "Very good," Iris said. "Now we must go full speed ahead, to make up for lost time."

"As soon as we get unstuck from our plates," Chameleon said, trying to fidget without being able to move her shapely posterior.

"Of course." Iris produced a tube of unglue, and they became unglued.

Gloha settled back to her plate as Swiftmud accelerated. Now the scenery fairly whizzed by. Gloha's hair flowed back in the wind, and so did Chameleon's. The others seemed unaffected, perhaps because their appearances were now illusory, confirming her prior suspicion. Gloha was glad of that, because in their natural states they did look stomach-irkingly aged. She had not realized that it was possible for a person to be older than fifty or so, but understood that some folk just didn't have much choice in the matter.

Soon they reached the great wide broad expanse of Lake Ogre-Chobee. "We had better pause for refreshment," Iris said, "before getting into the labyrinth of the underworld."

So Trent guided Swiftmud around the edge of the lake, looking for a campsite with pie trees and pillow bushes. Instead they found a village whose houses were all black. Sure enough, a sign said BLACK VILLAGE.

"I don't remember a village here," Trent said.

"It must have formed within the decade since our last

visit here," Iris said. "I can clothe us with the illusion of invisibility if you wish."

"Don't bother. Just make us young and anonymous for now. I'm sure the natives are friendly." Indeed, there was a sign a bit farther along saying FRIENDLY NATIVES.

All six of them became young, except for Gloha, who didn't change. She was impressed by Iris' powers of illusion.

Swiftmud proceeded slowly down the center street. Soon a man came out. He looked ordinary, except that he was black. "What can I do for you tourists?" he inquired in friendly fashion. He wore a nameplate saying "SHERLOCK: Safe—Courteous—Reliable."

"We were just looking for refreshment," Trent said. "We're on our way to the underworld."

"You have come to the right place," Sherlock said. "We settled here last year and are promoting tourism. We have all manner of refreshments and entertainments, including regular presentations at the Curse Friend Playhouse. Or you can simply sun yourselves on the Ogre-Chobee beach and feed the tame ogres and chobees."

"Tame ogres?" Iris asked dubiously.

"It happens," Tandy reminded her.

"Oh, yes," Sherlock agreed. "We have Okra the Ogre Tamer, who can make an ogre named Smithereen perform ogre feats of strength for just a smile. Nobody believes it until they see it. And the chobees will allow themselves to be petted, for just a few marsh mallows and maybe a toe or two." He smiled. "A bit of safe, courteous, reliable humor there."

"Just fetch us some fresh pies to take along," Iris said.

Sherlock turned his head. "Pie assortment, to go," he called. Then, to Trent: "And what do you have in trade?"

"Do you need any illusion?" Iris inquired.

"We prefer to have no illusions," Sherlock said. "We like things here as they are."

"Do you need to have any person or creature transformed to something else?" Trent asked.

Sherlock considered. "Actually there is someone we'd like to transform. But it's his nature that needs transforming, not his appearance."

"What is his nature?"

"He's always trying to organize things into a state so he can run it. We have no need of this, but he just won't stop. His name's Nator. We even call the way he acts natorial. It's really bothersome."

Trent pondered. "I seem to remember a type of creature that enjoys that sort of organization. There are a number of them, but none of them want to be the leader. So they are usually in a state of confusion or a state of frustration."

"Nator would love to solve their problems," Sherlock said. "But are they human?"

"Not really. Does it matter?"

Sherlock considered again. "Perhaps not." He turned his head again. "Hey, Nator! Would you like to be a goober?"

Another man came out. "What's a goober?"

"Creatures who exist in a state with no leader, because no one wants to do it."

"I'd certainly like to shape them up!" Nator said.

Trent gestured. Nator became a creature vaguely resembling a cross between a peanut and a pink jellybean with multiple legs and long antennae. The antennae quivered. Then the goober ran away.

"Wait!" Sherlock called. "We don't know whether you like it yet."

But then they saw a green jellybean emerge from the jungle to meet the pink one, and a purple one arriving from another direction.

"They are very quick to locate each other," Trent said. "I'm sure Nator will be all right. They are highly social creatures."

"And they won't mind his being natorial?"

"They should love it. He'll be goober natorial."

A young black woman arrived with an armful of fresh pies. "I hope these are all right," she said. "They are black berry, which is our favorite, and green berry, purple berry, gray berry, and blue berry. And one goose berry. Be careful of that one; it's very fresh."

"Those are fine," Trent said. "Fair exchange. Thank you."

They took the pies. Gloha got the goose berry. It honked as she took a bite, but she avoided its other effect by flying up. Geese were flying creatures, and their food tended to make others try to fly, except those who were already doing so. So the pie's freshness didn't bother her; she knew how to handle it.

They bid parting to Sherlock and the young woman, and Swiftmud resumed sliding. A number of the black folk had come out during the dialogue and exchange, and were looking curiously at the mud. Gloha didn't blame them; it was a most curious creature.

"We shall have to tell Dor about this new village," Trent remarked. "It does seem like a nice place to visit."

"This region has been cleaned up," Bink remarked. "It used to be primitive country, but now it is parklike."

"That must be the work of the Black Villagers," Chameleon said. "Now I remember: I did hear something about a Black Wave that arrived from Mundania, but I never heard where they settled. Now we know."

As they ate their pies, Swiftmud slid out across the surface of the lake, having no more trouble with it than with the vertical walls of the fault. Soon they were surrounded by flat water. Gloha was impressed, because she had never seen so much water in one place. Not when she was actually on it.

This was an interesting journey. But was it getting her any closer to the achievement of her desire? She still had no idea how to find the man of whatever dreams she might want to have, assuming he existed. If only the Good Magician had Answered her Question, instead of dismissing her without even listening. Instead of sending her on this wild goose pie chase for his second son, who might not exist either.

3
RECONCILIATIONS

They had hardly finished their pies before they reached the dome-city of the Curse Friends. Sherlock, curiously, had called them "Curse Friends"; maybe he had misspoken. Actually the city didn't show on the surface; there was only a whirlpool there. A big one.

Swiftmud floated right toward it. "We aren't going into *that*, are we?" Gloha asked with a feeble little fright.

"Oh, that's right, you haven't been here before," Tandy said. "This is the way to the underworld. One of the ways, anyway, but goblins lurk along the others. Don't be concerned."

Gloha tried her best to be unconcerned as Swiftmud got caught by the vortex and floated around it in a diminishing spiral. The central hole loomed up hugely. Then they tilted into it and whirled around and around, going down.

After that it was a blur. Gloha squeezed her expressive little eyes tight-shut closed.

There was a bump and splash, and the awful spinning stopped. Gloha's eyes peeked open just a tiny slit.

They were in a dark cavern, floating on a somber lake. Gloha pried loose her jammed little jaw. "What happened?" she asked doubtfully.

"We landed at the bottom of the vortex," Tandy answered. "From here it's mostly smooth sailing to my mother's apartment."

That was a relief. If Gloha had had any idea what this trip would be like, she would have hesitated to make it. But no one else seemed concerned, so she crammed her startled little stomach back into place and pretended to be satisfied.

After a somewhat timeless time, because there was no sun here to mark it, just a faint glow in the water and on the stone walls, they came to a landing. An unusual woman came out from a doorway. She wore a gown set with so many bright gems that it made the whole region three and a half times as bright. "Oh, you're here!" she exclaimed. "But who is this?"

"Mother, this is Gloha, who has come to see Crombie," Tandy said. "Gloha, this is Jewel the Nymph."

Indeed she looked like a nymph, being of exquisitely crafted figure. Except for one thing: she was old. Gloha had never heard of an old nymph.

"Jewel was timeless until she loved and married Crombie," Bink reminded her. There was a certain diffidence about the way he related to the nymph that Gloha would have found perplexing if she had thought of it, but at the moment she was meeting too many people to have time for extra thoughts. About the only one who was really clear in her mind was Magician Trent, because she remembered him best from her history lessons. "Then she began aging from her apparent age of twenty, just as mortals do. We still call her Jewel the Nymph, but she's really no longer a nymph, and she will join our fade-out party."

Oh. That did not seem horribly clear, but Gloha was in no mental shape to be confused, so she just smiled and ac-

cepted things as they seemed to be. Though she was halfway sure that things weren't exactly as they seemed to be.
What was there about Bink's attitude toward Jewel that
bothered her? Jewel was Tandy's mother; that was enough.

"You are barely in time," Jewel said. "Crombie has almost faded."

"We were delayed while traveling," Iris said somewhat
sourly. Gloha felt guilty again, remembering that the last delay had happened when Bink tried to tell her about his talent. The fault had shown up right then, without warning. Of
course that couldn't have been *her* fault, yet somehow it
seemed so.

"Gloha must talk to my father before he fades any further," Tandy said. "She is still young; most of her life is
ahead of her."

"How nice," Jewel said. She led the way to a bedroom
chamber.

There, amidst piled blankets and cushions, was a horribly
wizened ancient old man. Gloha wasn't sure just what fading out entailed, but if this was it, she didn't much like it.
Crombie seemed to be on the far side of sleep, lying on his
back, his eyes staring up at the ceiling without focusing.
She remembered how Wira's eyes had never quite focused
on things; his were somewhat like that.

But she had to talk to him, and hope he could help her.
"Sir Mister Crombie, the Good Magician Humfrey told me
to talk to his second son, but I don't know where he is or
even who he is, and my Aunt Goldy thought maybe Smash
Ogre would know, but he was out and Tandy thought maybe
you would know or at least be able to point the direction."
Then she took a breath.

The decrepit figure stirred, weakly. The withered old
mouth opened. "Can't," he breathed.

Gloha didn't know what to say. This had become her almost only hope, and now it was dashed. So she burst into
tears.

The figure stirred again. "Ask—else," it breathed.

A thought found its way through her misery. Ask something else? If he could point out anything—or almost anything—why not ask him where her ideal man was? If he could point the way to that one, she wouldn't need to talk to Humfrey's second son anyway.

"Where is my ideal man?" she asked.

One arm moved. It fell off the bed, but it was pointing a definite direction. Gloha made careful note; she had a kind of answer!

But she needed more. "Is there anything that can help me in my search?" she asked.

The arm moved again. This time it pointed at King Emeritus Trent.

"Magician Trent can help me?" Gloha asked, startled. "But he's—" She caught herself before uttering the trite little truth that he was far too anciently old to be able to do anything much more than make it through his share of the fade-out party, and might have trouble even with that. "He's otherwise committed," she concluded.

Trent himself seemed startled. "He must be pointing to something beyond me," he said.

"Such as the wall," Iris said with half a smile. "I'm sure that will be a great help to her."

"Something beyond the wall," Trent said with the other half of the smile. "Just as was the case when he pointed toward her ideal man."

"Perhaps he got the questions reversed, and meant that *you* are her ideal man," Iris said with a quarter of a new smile.

Trent laughed. "How nice it would be to think so! But I think she is looking for one about seventy-six years younger. Here, I'll get out of the way, and Crombie can point again." He eased himself down and to the side, sitting on a cushion near Crombie's head.

Gloha was relieved to get the chance to clear up the confusion. "Mister Crombie, sir, could you point again to whoever or whatever might be able to help me in my quest for my ideal man?"

The withered arm shuddered and moved again. The gnarled forefinger pointed up beyond the decrepit head. Directly at Trent again.

Gloha was both chagrined and intrigued. It did seem that Crombie's talent was working, because the man wasn't even looking and couldn't have known exactly where Trent had moved. But how could ancient aged old King Emeritus Trent help her? There had to be some confusion.

She had asked directions four times: for Humfrey's second son, for her ideal man, and for something to help her, twice. Crombie had been unable to point for the first, but had seemed pretty sure about the other two. The confusion was more likely to be in the first than in the last. Odd that he had failed there. Did it mean the second son was dead? Then why had Humfrey told her to ask him? Was she supposed to find his ghost? That didn't seem quite reasonable; ghosts seldom answered questions.

Then Gloha suffered another astonishing little intuition. But she would have to verify it, because there was something confusing about it. "I—could I talk to Crombie alone?" she asked timorously.

"Why not?" Jewel said. "We can organize for our party."

The others left the chamber. Gloha emboldened herself enough to take Crombie's weathered and almost crumbling hand. Some of her young little vitality seemed to cross over and mend his old gross senility. "We are alone, Mister Crombie," she said. "I promise not to repeat what you tell me, if you want it that way. Will you tell me why you couldn't tell me where Humfrey's second son is?"

The wrinkled ash-gray head rolled from side to side. The worn lips quivered. "No," he shuddered.

"I have a suspicion," Gloha continued relentlessly. "I think the Good Magician had a reason to send me to his second son, and I think you do know where he is."

"No," Crombie creaked again.

"I think that maybe, just possibly, perhaps *you* are that second son. That I found my way to you despite not knowing."

He rolled his head some more, but didn't say no again.

"What I don't understand is why you don't want it known. Maybe if you told me, I would understand."

He was still reluctant, but in the face of her accurate little assessment he managed to recover enough to tell her the story. He was the son of Humfrey and the Mundane woman Sofia, whom Humfrey had married because she was the finest living sock sorter. Humfrey had had a son with his first wife, the Demoness Dara, and a daughter with his third wife, Rose of Roogna. But Humfrey had been more interested in his work than in his family, and more interested in training Magician-level children like Trent and Iris than in his own child. So Crombie had been pretty well ignored and alienated.

"Oh, I'm so sorry to hear that!" Gloha said with more than a slight little surge of sympathy. "No wonder you weren't happy. But still I don't understand why you don't want to be known as his son."

So Crombie told her about his experience with the Demoness Metria: how he had met her when looking for a better mother, and how she had helped him fight off the spooks of the night bedroom, and stayed with him until he turned thirteen and became aware of the female of the species. Then she dissolved into smoke and drifted away. He realized that she had stayed with him only in order to get into Humfrey's castle and spy out his secrets. He had looked for a girlfriend, and thought he found one, but when he wanted to see her panties she had puffed into smoke and he realized that the demoness was having more fun with him. He knew it was Metria, because she had a thing with words: she seldom could remember precisely the right one, and had to hunt through her vocabulary for it. That made her unique among demons, and always gave her away. But more impor-

tant, she was female, and her mischief was always of a female nature. So he had sworn off women forever.

"I can see why," Gloha said. "She shouldn't have teased
you like that. Everyone knows that all any man wants of a
young woman is to see her panties. That's how Mela Merwoman nabbed Prince Naldo Naga, and she wasn't even
very young. That's how I'll nab my ideal man, if I ever find
him. But why did that make you not want to be known as
Humfrey's son?"

So he told her how he had grown up and left home and
gone out on his own, becoming a soldier. He had been supremely embittered by the disinterest of his father, and of
course his mother was a woman, so there was nothing there
for him. Later he had discovered a nice nymph, and she was
all right, because nymphs weren't women, they were innocent creatures. So he had married her, and been satisfied,
though she had loved someone else.

Gloha got a giddy little glimmer of something that surely
was none of her business. "Whom else did she love?"

"Bink. He drank love elixir without realizing it, and saw
her, and loved her though he was already married. In time
she came to love him back, but by then his love had been
nulled by the Time of No Magic. So she was left hurting.
But I liked her, and I brought her a love potion, and then
she loved me too. Of course it still took a while for her
other love for him to fade, if it ever did, because it was natural."

That explained Bink's odd attitude toward Jewel. He had
once loved her, and she had once loved him. That was the
sad memory of what might have been between them. How
romantic!

"Didn't it bother you that her love for him was natural,
while her love for you was magic?"

"No, I knew the situation. All I asked of her was that she
be a good wife to me, and that she was."

So Crombie had made his own life, and that was all right.
Fortunately his daughter Tandy was half nymph, so he could

stand her. But he never saw reason to let his connection to the Good Magician be known. Humfrey had never given any indication of caring, after all.

Gloha got an intriguing little insight of another intuition. "But suppose Humfrey did show he cared about you?" she asked. "I mean, everyone knows that he'd rather grump than breathe, and would never admit to any human passion, but just suppose he let slip a hint that he remembered you and wanted to know how you were doing? Would that make it all right for you to be known as his second son?"

Crombie thought about it, and seemed to be trying to fight off the notion, but its allure was too much for his frail old resistance, and he finally had to admit that that might make it barely all right. But he knew that Humfrey would never let slip anything like that, so it didn't matter. Now he would fade out in peace with his friends, and all would be forgotten.

"But you said Trent and Iris were the ones who took your father's attention from you," Gloha said. "Why should you be friends with them?"

"They didn't know how it was," Crombie said, his voice growing stronger. "They think there was some other reason, such as the demoness. So they let it be, and haven't told anyone. And indeed, I worked for them for years, when Trent was king, and he was a good employer. No fault in him. So now I don't want to embarrass them by having it known."

"And your daughter Tandy doesn't know?"

"She doesn't know. Neither does Jewel. So let's leave it that way. After the fade-out party it won't matter."

"Well, that party may have to be postponed."

The decrepit figure developed some semblance of animation. "Postponed! I can't make it beyond the day!"

"But you pointed to Trent as the one to help me find my ideal man. So he'll have to help me look. So he won't be able to join your party now. Wouldn't you rather wait until he can?"

"You are making typically female mischief!" he exclaimed, his insecurely fastened bones rattling with the effort.

"Well, that's my nature," she said with a golden little grin. "I think Humfrey misses you, and wants to be recognized as your father, but can't do it if you don't agree. He can't even admit that he wants it, for fear of your rejection. So he sent me to see you, hoping I'd jog something loose. I'll bet that if you gave even one nod of agreement, he'd be here to make amends."

"Never!" Crombie said with what might well pass for emphasis.

"What, never?"

"Of course never! The Good Magician is incapable of admitting to making any mistake ever in his long life."

Gloha had a tiny little tinge of doubt. So she suppressed it before it could grow. "Well, we can test it. Nod your head." Gloha hoped she was right. It would make halfway sense of half the confusion she had been experiencing.

"I don't have the strength."

"Maybe I can help you sit up." She leaned over him.

"All right! I'll nod! Then will you leave me alone?"

"Of course," she said with sweet little sweetness.

She put her hands on his bony old shoulders and hauled, and he managed to lurch into sit-up position. Then he nodded his head once, and fell back exhausted.

There was a silence. Nothing happened. Gloha realized that she had misfigured it. "Well, I guess you're right," she said. "I'll go away and let you be."

"Thanks," he breathed. He seemed almost disappointed.

She got up and went out of the doorway. Good Magician Humfrey met her there. "Are you through?" he inquired grumpily.

"Yes, I must be," she agreed sadly. She went on by him, letting him go in alone.

Then she paused. Her mouth dropped into an open little O. The others laughed.

"You did it," Trent said, looking even younger than before. The Sorceress of Illusion was overdoing it a bit, making him seem to be in his twenties. He now wore a bright shirt and trousers, with shiny boots and even a bold sword in its sheath. He looked utterly dashing. "I was hoping you would. I think I owe you a favor."

"Oh, you don't have to—"

"Humfrey brought some Fountain of Youth elixir. He'll give some of it to Crombie so he can survive the postponement of the fade-away party, and he gave some to me. So now I am in shape to help you on your quest."

Gloha looked at him again. "You mean—?"

"This isn't illusion any more. This is my physical age. Of course I'll take some more elixir, with reverse wood, to neutralize the effect after this is done. Then we ancients of Xanth can fade out in style."

"Oh!" Gloha said, feeling maidenly faint.

"However," Iris said sharply, in that tone which suggested that there was a formidable caveat coming to the surface, "the rest of us should not be expected to twiddle our tired thumbs while you two enjoy yourselves gallivanting around the country, slaying dragons and such. What are we going to do—play tag with monsters?"

Trent considered for a good three quarters of a moment. "Maybe you could rest in the Brain Coral's pool."

Chameleon laughed, but Jewel was serious. "Why not?" Jewel asked with nymphly innocence.

Iris answered her. "The Brain Coral likes to collect things in its pool, but it doesn't like to let them go. So unless we want to give up our freedom immediately, it is best to remain well clear of it."

"That's not so," Jewel protested. "I have been there many times on my errands, placing gemstones for mortals to find. Sometimes when I've been tired, the Brain Coral has let me rest in its pool, and then released me much refreshed. It honors any deal it makes."

Trent reconsidered. "Perhaps my humor was ill advised. We may have misjudged the Brain Coral."

"If it actually lets people go," Bink said, "that might be worth considering. The Good Magician knows it as well as anyone does; he could say."

"Did someone speak my name?" the Good Magician asked, appearing in the doorway. Beside him stood Crombie, looking about ten years younger and forty years happier. "My son and I could not help overhearing."

"Your son?" Jewel asked, surprised.

"It's a long story," Crombie said. "What's this about the Brain Coral?"

"Jewel says that the Brain Coral will honor a deal," Bink said. "When I was young I regarded it as an enemy, but that was some time ago."

"The Brain Coral does what it feels proper," Humfrey said. "When you sought to free the Demon X (A/N)th and thereby bring on the Time of No Magic, it fought you, knowing better than you did. But when you are not bent on mortal folly, it is not your enemy."

"So if we made a deal to rest in its pool until Trent returns for our fade-out party, it would let us go at the right time."

"Assuredly," Humfrey agreed. "But it would ask a price for such a service."

Bink turned to the others. "Then maybe we do have something to do while we wait. I understand that a sleep in the Brain Coral's pool is like an instant; you go in and come out immediately, yet centuries may have passed."

"That will do," Iris agreed.

"But you can take time out from that sleep," Jewel said. "You can be conscious if you want to, and talk with other folk there. There are some really interesting creatures in storage, with fascinating histories."

"Then let's go and inquire," Trent said. "See if we can make a deal."

"You go," Jewel said. "I want to learn this long story about who is whose son."

"Gloha and I will go," Trent said. "It's our mission."

The others exchanged a shrug, not objecting. It did seem that the rapprochement between Magician Humfrey and Crombie had excited their greater interest.

"Now just where is the Brain Coral's pool?" Trent asked.

Crombie pointed a direction. It seemed to be downstream, so they went to Swiftmud, who was muddily snoozing on the dark underworld river.

"Sip the water there," Humfrey said. "That will enable you to communicate with it."

They set off through the caves. Now Gloha was able to admire the glowing colors of the walls and ceiling, and the convolutions of stone under the clear surface of the water. This was really a rather pretty place, in its somber way.

They came to a cavern that seemed to be half filled with water. But when Gloha peered down through the water she saw that it was much deeper than she had thought, so that she could not see the bottom. The sides were shallower, and there on slopes and ledges were all manner of things and creatures. All were still; none were swimming or showing signs of life. It was an eerie display.

"This must be the place," Trent said brightly. Gloha had not yet gotten used to his youth and vigor; she would hardly have recognized him if she hadn't known about the youthening. He was a handsome and self-assured man, not at all doddering. Youth elixir was wonderful stuff.

They dipped their hands and brought sips of the water to their mouths. It tasted faintly of medicine.

What do you want of me, King Trent?

"I am about to start a quest with Gloha Goblin-Harpy, and my friends need a place to park for the duration."

What do you offer in exchange?

Trent smiled. "What do you want?"

What is your quest?

"To find my ideal man," Gloha said. Then she had a halfway bright notion. "I don't suppose you have a nice winged goblin male in storage?"

No. I have a winged centaur filly, however.

Gloha shook her head. "I can't marry her."

But perhaps this is our avenue of exchange. I understand that there is now a winged centaur male.

"Che Centaur—Chex's foal," Gloha said. "The only one of his kind. But he's still very young. Just eight years old."

Cynthia is not too much older. It is time for her to emerge and learn the ways of contemporary Xanth. By the time she does, Che may be grown.

"Cynthia," Trent said. "That name seems familiar."

It should, Magician! You transformed her back in 1021.

"I did? I'm not sure I remember. I transformed so many in those wicked days. Was that about the time I transformed Justin Tree?"

About. She came to me, and has been here seventy-two years in suspension. Xanth has changed somewhat in that period. She will need time to adjust, and it will be better if another winged monster assists her, and if she is protected from harm until she is competent.

"I begin to get your gist," Trent said. "You want us to see to that chore, in exchange for parking our friends here."

"Oh, let's do it!" Gloha cried. "I'm sure she's a nice person."

Trent glanced at her obliquely. "It would be better to verify that before making the commitment."

She realized that it was barely possible that his extra seventy-five years or so of experience counted for something. "I suppose," she agreed cautiously.

Then enter the pool and listen to Cynthia's story.

Trent looked at Gloha, and Gloha looked at Trent. This was safe? But if it wasn't, the Good Magician would come to see what had happened. So they shrugged, almost together, and prepared to enter the pool.

But there was a complication. Their clothing. It wouldn't be good to get it soaked, but it also wouldn't be good for the two of them to be unclothed in each other's presence. The Adult Conspiracy had firm things to say about that, even when no children were involved. Trent was a mature male man, and Gloha a fully formed (if petite) approximately human crossbreed woman. It would not be appropriate for him to see her panties.

Don't be silly. Leave your clothing on. Just jump in.

They exchanged another glance and shrug. Then they held their noses and jumped off either side of Swiftmud.

Gloha was afraid she would choke, but she had no trouble. She didn't seem to be breathing, but felt no discomfort. She just slowly sank down into the depth, which no longer seemed unpleasant. She saw Trent descending nearby.

"This is an interesting experience," he remarked without opening his mouth.

"Very," Gloha agreed without opening hers. In addition, her clothing didn't seem to be wet; it neither clung to her nor floated out from her. It remained about the same as it was in the air.

"I think we must be communicating in thoughts rather than sound," Trent remarked. "But our ears think it is sound."

"That sounds right to me," she agreed with a small little smile.

They landed on a pleasant ledge set with pretty shells. There was a winged centaur filly, with brown hair and mane, white wings, and a blouse and jacket covering her human section of torso. That was unusual in a centaur, for that species was normally completely open about bodily appearance and function.

"Cynthia, I presume," Trent said.

"You remember, Magician Trent!" the filly replied.

"It isn't often I transform such a lovely person."

"You haven't changed at all! But I suppose some time has passed above."

"Some has," he agreed. "This is Gloha Goblin-Harpy, who would like to get to know you.'

Cynthia looked at Gloha for the first time. "Oh! You're a winged monster too!"

"Yes. And the only one of my kind, perhaps. I would like to know your story, if you care to tell it."

"I'm happy to tell it, if you care to listen. Make yourself comfortable."

They found nice boulders and sat on them. They were so light, down here under the pool, that even the rough stone was comfortable.

Cynthia began to talk. Gloha soon not only heard her voiceless voice, but saw her sightless scene, as the ambience of the Brain Coral's pool made the scene come alive.

Cynthia was in most respects a regular run-of-the-mill human maiden (though perhaps prettier than most, she was tempted to believe) whom the stork had delivered to a nice family in the North Village barely sixteen years before. Her magic talent was moderate but convenient: she interacted remarkably well with children. She used this magic to make others happy with her baby-sitting. When the children's parents were away, Cynthia was, as a centaur put it, "In Loco Parentis"; that was his way of saying that she was like a substitute parent. Or as the children put it, "Crazy see-see!" which was their way of saying that she was fun and apparent.

But all was not well in Xanth. The Storm King was not paying proper attention to the weather, so that on some days the local pillow bushes got so dry that their feather stuffing leaked out and floated away, while on other days it rained so heavily that the pillows got all sodden and squishy. Meanwhile there was news that Evil Magician Trent was making mischief, trying to shake up the current monarchy. Though Cynthia didn't care much for the way the Storm King was handling the kingdom, she was almost certain that a hostile takeover wasn't the way to improve things.

Cynthia went to the edge of a placid lake to admire her brown-haired and brown-eyed reflection, as was expected of pretty girls her age. She saw a grapevine growing near the water, so she approached it. Grapevines were gossipy plants, notorious for their news about things that shouldn't concern right-thinking folk, so naturally no one listened to them. But Cynthia happened to be alone, and no one would know, so she yielded to temptation and put her ear to a grape.

"The horrendous Evil Magician is nearing the North Village, terrifying the denizens," it gushed, splattering purple prose on her delicate shell-pink ear. "Who can stop this monstrous incursion before it is Too Late?"

Oh, this was bad news indeed! She was firmly against the Evil Magician invading her peaceful village with his nasty transformations. She would have to try to stop him. Unfortunately she had not the least idea how to do it. All she could think of was to intercept him and try to persuade him to leave this village alone. She was a resourceful maiden with a talent for dealing with children; she would think of something to stop his childish behavior. She hoped.

One day while she was picking rambling roses she saw him approaching. She knew it was him, because she happened to see him change a butterfly into a pink elephant. The elephant seemed none too pleased with the transformation; it trumpeted a brassy melody and galumped off, flapping its ears like wings. That was definitely a sign of magic. So she moved to intercept the man before he could pass her by.

Suddenly she was face-to-face with him. She opened her mouth to utter a paragraph of remonstration as her eyes met his. And stopped, stunned.

Not by his magic. By his attractive face and general good looks. She had assumed he would be ugly, or at least somewhat crude and rough around the edges. Maybe stooped, with a limp and a sneer. Instead he was somewhere in the vicinity of divine, being tall and upright and even-featured.

"A greeting, pretty maid," he said, accurately enough. "Have we met before?"

"I, uh, um, er, not exactly," she said, luxuriating in the

warmth of his handsome gaze. The roses fell from her flac-
cid fingers and rambled rapidly away, as was their nature.
Her wits landed amidst them.

He bent down to help her collect her scattered wits.
"Then allow me to introduce myself," he said as he handed
them back to her. "I am Magician Trent."

Cynthia wanted to crank up her persuasive powers and
ask him to go away. Instead she said "I'm Cynthia. How
may I help you, Magician?"

He smiled roguishly, and she realized that her present
leaned-over posture was giving him rather too much of a
glimpse down her bodice. She was after all not all *that* far
from the innocence of childhood, and could almost feel the
censorious eyes of the Adult Conspiracy following his eyes
to exactly the same place. She nearly dropped her wits
again, this time down into her nice new cleavage. Fortunately she managed to straighten up without too much of a
blush.

"I would appreciate it if you would give me directions to
the nearest good river," he said.

Cynthia, being naturally sweet and innocent, clung to her
recovered wits and sweetly and innocently misdirected him.
If he followed her directions, he would wind up on the rail
that rode strangers right out of town.

Magician Trent gazed at her. "Are you sure?" he inquired
gently.

"Well, maybe I got it confused," she confessed, fearing
that he was suspicious. So she gave him directions to the
nearest love spring instead. If he drank from that, he would
fall hopelessly in love with the next female creature he encountered, like maybe a warty hog.

"Are you sure?" he inquired again.

"Quite sure," she said, stifling her impulse to confess all
and maybe kiss him for good measure.

"I am sorry for that," he said. "You see, I happen to
know this region. You have just directed me to a hostile
rail and to a too-friendly love spring. I fear I shall have to

deal with you, for such betrayal irks me. But I shall not interfere with your youthful beauty." Then before she could attempt to protest, he gestured with one manly hand.

Cynthia knew she was in trouble. She tried to flee, but already her body was changing. Her squeezable torso unsqueezed, stretched, expanded, and distorted. She became grotesquely huge. Her (for want of a nicer term) rump pushed out behind monstrously and sprouted a long hair tail. From somewhere in the center of her body four new appendages grew. Two were legs, but they didn't have feet; they had heavy black horny terminations. The other two were behind, and were white, feathery, and grotesquely convoluted. Her body turned mostly brown and hairy, with knobby knees and a belly as big as a barrel. Only her scant surviving bit of human torso remained clothed; her nether section had burst out of her skirt and was now devastatingly naked. Oh, utter horrors! She had become a complete monster. And the Evil Magician had tortured her further by claiming not to interfere with her beauty!

Properly appalled, Cynthia cried out in despair and humiliation and ran off as fast as her four cowlike legs could carry her. She knew she could never return to her home like *this*. But where could she go? What could she do? No use to ask the Evil Magician who had transformed her; he would just say, "Frankly, my dear, I don't give a dam." As if anyone could give or take anything as massive and watery as a dam. She would just have to hide until she could make her way out of Xanth and never be heard from again.

She was getting breathless, so had to slow to a trot. But she kept going as far as she could, hoping to get far enough away so that no one would know of her. But she couldn't go forever; the day was getting late.

She found a barn. Maybe she could hide there for the night, then sneak off early in the morning when few people were up and about. Maybe she could find a burlap bag to put over her head so she could not be recognized. Because she could tell by the feel of her face that it had not been changed; the Magician had done her the ultimate indignity of leaving her most recognizable aspects untouched, so that everyone would know her shame. There just seemed to be no end to the exquisite refinement of his vengeance on her.

She went to the back door, opened it, and wedged her ungainly body in. She was thirsty; maybe she could find some water here. She was also tired; maybe she could find some hay to lie in. Assuming she could lie down, with this clumsy contraption of a body.

"Who's there?"

Oh! She had thought this barn was empty. Cynthia tried to back out, but her huge hairy rump banged into the doorpost, making a crash that could be heard throughout. She tried to turn around so she could flee headfirst, but there wasn't room in this narrow passage. She was stuck, as the farmer tramped toward her from elsewhere in the barn.

He appeared around a corner. "Speak up, or I'll jab you with my pitchfork," he said gruffly, squinting into the gloom of her corner.

"Oh please, sir, don't hurt me!' she pleaded. "I'm trying to get out of your barn!"

"Why, it's a girl," he said, surprised.

"No, it's a monster. Please just let me go and I'll never bother you again."

"You sure sound like a girl. Let me get a look at you."

"No, please! Don't look at me! I'm all hairy and awful." She tried to hide her face, though that wasn't the hairy part.

The farmer appeared before her. He stared. "Why, you're a centaur filly! What's your kind doing here?"

Cynthia paused. "A what?"

"A centaur. Don't you know your own kind? What do you want in my old barn?"

A centaur! Suddenly she realized it was so. The four furred legs with their hoofed feet. The hairy tail. The massive belly. The human head and upper torso. "I didn't realize," she said. "The Evil Magician transformed me into a centaur. Except—what are these?" She spread the folded white feathery appendages on her backside. They promptly banged into the walls, and she had to stop.

"Why, those are wings," the farmer said. "You're a flying centaur!"

"So even the centaurs won't accept me," she said, realizing how completely the Magician had punished her. She would be an outcast from both human and centaur folk, because there was no other creature of this kind in all of Xanth.

"The Evil Magician did this to you? Why?"

"I tried to deceive him, because I didn't want him taking over our land. But he wasn't fooled, and he transformed me. I'll never be able to live it down."

The farmer nodded. "I guess I'd feel the same way. Very well, you can spend the night here. I've got a stall I'm not using. I'll bring you some food. There's water in the stall." He showed the way to the central part of the barn.

She found a bucket of fresh cool water, and used her hands to dip some out to drink. It was wonderfully refreshing. Then the farmer returned with some wry bread. The chunk was warped, with a twisted expression, but that was the nature of this variety. She bit eagerly into it, and it was very good.

"Oh, sir, how can I ever thank you?" she asked gratefully, belatedly remembering her manners.

"What are you good at?"

"I used to be good with children. I was apparent: children saw me as a parent, so I could baby-sit."

"Well, I have a little boy, but he's such a handful that no one wants to take care of him. His talent is making things go awry. I think it's because he ate too much wry bread. This is a wry farm; it's what we grow, so we use it."

"All children get into mischief," Cynthia said. "I'm used to that."

"I have to go into town tomorrow for supplies. The wife's away visiting her endless relatives. If you could watch him tomorrow—"

"I'd be glad to."

So she slept on the soft hay, getting the hang of her new body. The horse section had no trouble, but it took her a while to get her human portion comfortable, because it couldn't lie flat the way it had before. She finally propped it against a wall, resting her head against her braced forearms. In the morning she combed some of the tangles out of her hair and washed her face. She wished she could change her shirt, but it was the only one she had. She knew that centaurs normally went bare-breasted, but she couldn't bring herself to be so exposive.

The nice farmer brought her a bowl of wry pudding. Then he brought out the boy, who seemed to be about six years old, and toe-headed. That was not a concern; children normally grew out of the toes as they matured.

"This is Wryly," the farmer said. "Wryly, this is Cynthia Centaur, who will watch you while I'm gone."

"Gee, a centaur!" the boy said, pleased. "I'll ride her all around."

Cynthia hadn't thought of that. The notion did not especially appeal. "Maybe later," she said.

"See if you can manage him," the farmer said.

Cynthia tried her talent on the boy. But she realized almost immediately that something was wrong. Wryly didn't change; he looked just as mischievous as ever. But the farmer seemed to go into a trance. His jaw went slack and his eyes stared fixedly.

She waved a hand before his face. Nothing happened.

Cynthia worked herself into a worry. She put her hands on his shoulders and shook him. "Snap out of it!"

The farmer blinked once, then again to be certain he had the motion right. "Wh—where am I?"

"You're here in your barn, about to go into town," Cynthia reminded him.

He looked around in bafflement, then wandered off in the rough direction of his house. The boy, bored with such activities, reached into his pocket and pulled out what appeared to be the rest of his last night's supper of chicken and wrys. He chewed on that while pondering what new mischief he could get into.

Cynthia was not stupid as girls went, though she wasn't sure that was also true as filly centaurs went. She assessed the situation. When she had tried to use her talent on the lad, his father had gone into a daze. A dim bulb flashed over her head.

"Oh, no!" she exclaimed, laying a hand on her fair cheek. "My talent—it's gone trance-parent! I send parents into trances!"

She realized that the boy's mischievous talent had affected her. It had gone awry.

She ran after the farmer, who was slowly recovering his common sense. "I can't use my talent on your son," she said. "It just messes up. But I think I can watch him while you go into town. Then I'll have to be on my own way."

He nodded. He was used to this. "There's wrys pudding in the kitchen for lunch," he said. "I'll be back as soon as I can."

It turned out to be a real chore, keeping Wryly out of mischief, but somehow she managed without invoking her useless talent. She was able to clean up most of the pudding the boy had thrown before the farmer got back, and had found enough water to put out the fire before it burned up the barn. But it was definitely time to be on her way. The boy was too eager to live the life of Wryly, which could be the death of Cynthia.

"You know, if you're looking for a place to be out of circulation," the farmer said, "what about the Brain Coral's pool?"

"The what?"

He explained how deep in the underworld there was supposed to be this really intelligent coral that lived in a pool and collected things. "I hear it's not a bad creature," he concluded. "It just likes to keep things a while, and let them go later. Maybe you could stay there until folk have forgotten about you."

The notion appealed. So Cynthia went in search of the Brain Coral. But that was a separate adventure, along with how she learned to use her new wings to fly. The odd thing was that when that happened, she lost her baby-sitting talent. She realized, when she thought about it, that a creature could have only one magic talent, and hers was now flying. Maybe she would get back her old talent if she ever got back into full human form. Meanwhile, she had to confess, flying was rather fun, and really handy when there was a rushing river or nickelpede-infested chasm to cross.

"And now I guess a couple of years have passed, and you've been exiled to the Brain Coral's pool too, Evil Magician," she concluded brightly. "I guess I can't really blame you for transforming me, because I did try to deceive you. And you have transformed another girl, to another winged form, but this time you got caught. So it must be all even."

Trent exchanged a rather wary glance with Gloha. Cynthia had the wrong idea!

"It's not quite that way," Gloha said. "Maybe I can explain. I'm natural. That is, I'm the product of the first goblin/harpy romance in several centuries. I'm looking for a man of my kind, that is, a winged goblin; my brother Harglo doesn't count, and Magician Trent is helping me. We came to take you back to Xanth, if you want to go."

"Goblin/harpy romance? I never heard of that," Cynthia said. "I thought they were enemies."

"Well, it happened after you came here. They're still enemies, mostly. But that's changing, because there's a lady goblin chief now, my cousin Gwendolyn."

"But you must be as old as I am. There hasn't been time to—to notify the stork and grow up."

"I am nineteen," Gloha said.

Cynthia was amazed. "You mean it's been twenty years? I had no idea!"

"Even longer," Trent murmured.

"Impossible! You don't look any older than you were when you transformed me. You're still as evilly handsome as ever."

Trent looked somewhat helplessly at Gloha. Gloha realized that she was better equipped to handle this particular revelation. "Do you know how winged monsters never lie to each other?" she asked Cynthia.

"Yes, that's in the *Big Book of Rules*. I encountered a winged dragon in that part of my adventure I didn't cover, and he told me that winged monsters might fight among themselves, but that they had to unite against ground creatures, and they never deceived each other. He also told me that I was a winged monster, and that was a compliment, not an insult, because he thought I was luscious." She switched her tail thoughtfully. "I believed him, because he didn't chomp me. Maybe he just wasn't hungry at the time."

Gloha wasn't quite sure of the logic, but let it pass. "Then I'm telling you as one winged monster to another that seventy-two years have passed since your transformation."

Cynthia's pretty mouth dropped open in astonishment.

"And Evil Magician Trent was exiled to Mundania, and later returned and was king of Xanth, and now his daughter is queen of Xanth, and he's not called evil any more. He is now ninety-six, and just took youth elixir to restore his youth so he could help me in my quest. Xanth has changed a lot since you left it."

"And I apologize for transforming you," Trent said. "I will be glad to transform you back to your original form. But your family is gone, and your friends will be gone or very old. So I am afraid I have done you a greater evil than I ever intended, and I wish I could make it up to you."

Cynthia looked at Gloha. Gloha nodded. "It is the truth. Winged monster honor."

"I—I can't go back?" Cynthia asked plaintively. "Then what will become of me?"

Trent looked as if he were about to say, "Frankly, my dear," and go on about dams, but he stifled it.

"I—we thought you might prefer to remain a winged centaur," Gloha said.

"As the only one of my kind? I'd rather stay in the pool!"

"There is another now. A family of winged centaurs, in fact. Cheiron and Chex Centaur, and their foal Che. He—you—we thought maybe—"

"A male winged centaur!" Cynthia said. "How old is he?"

"Well, he's young yet, but—"

"How old?"

"Eight. But he gets older every year."

"You expect a sixteen-year-old girl to go with an eight-year-old boy?"

Gloha saw how foolish it was. "I guess it was a bad idea. I'm not interested in any eight-year-old goblin boy."

"There is an answer," Trent said.

Both girls looked at him.

"As you can see, the elixir of the Fountain of Youth can reduce a person's physical age. There is some available. So if you—"

"I don't want to be eight years old again."

"Then maybe if Che were made older—"

"He would still be a child in a grown body."

"Then I can transform you back to your original form," Trent said. "You are a pretty girl with an appealing age; I'm sure you'll be able to make your way in the human realm."

But Cynthia was having a second thought. "This centaur boy—what's he like?"

"Oh, he's very special," Gloha said. "All the winged monsters are sworn to protect him, because he is destined to change Xanth. We don't know exactly how, but already he has helped Gwenny Goblin be the first female goblin chief, and that's changing Xanth for the better. He is her official

Companion, which means he's away from home a lot, and his folks—but of course they understand about that."

"His folks miss having a child at home," Cynthia said. "I can guess how that must be."

"Yes. Gwenny and Jenny Elf lived with them for two years, but then Gwenny had to be chief, so—"

"Maybe I will take that youth elixir," Cynthia said. "I have a whole lot to learn about Xanth, and I'll just stumble around and get in trouble on my own. But if I could stay with a family of my own kind for a few years—"

"Oh, I'm sure they'd welcome you!" Gloha said.

"Then maybe if you are willing to see me safely there, and get me that youth elixir—"

"Certainly," Trent said. "It is the least I can do to make up for what I did. Come with us now, and this is the way it will be."

"Agreed." Cynthia Centaur extended her dainty hand. Magician Trent took it.

Gloha thought she might be mistaken, but she had the innocent little impression that Cynthia was rather taken with Magician Trent, whom she had never known as an old man.

Then the three of them walked up out of the Brain Coral's pool. They were about to be on their way.

4
ESCAPE

In due course the four of them set out: Gloha, Trent, Cynthia, and Swiftmud, whom Trent had transformed into a lightning bug to help light their way. This wasn't ideal country for a creature of Swiftmud's natural size. The other human folk were comfortably ensconced in the Brain Coral's pool, awaiting that seemingly timeless interval when Trent would return for the fade-away party. Tandy had decided to wait with the elders, because this might be her last chance to visit her parents before they faded out. Gloha had promised to deliver a message to Smash Ogre, so he would know what was keeping Tandy, if he noticed.

They had Tandy's pass, which had been duly authenticated by the demons, goblins, water monsters, and such, because she was related to legitimate underworld denizens. In times past there had been strife between the various factions, but in recent decades they had settled into their own regions and left each other mostly alone. So there shouldn't be a problem; not too many folk wanted war to break out because of a silly border incident.

The passage was marked by green glow. As long as they stayed on that, they would be left alone. It was like an enchanted path, on the surface. There would be camping sites with food and potable water. Gloha had been a bit distressed by the description of the water, until Trent explained that this meant a clean drinking pot, not the other kind of pot.

The first checkpoint they came to was in demon country. There was a demon at a desk. He had a broad-brimmed blue hat and huge flat feet. "Whatcha business?" he demanded from the side of his mouth.

"We're going to the surface," Trent replied.

The demon surveyed them. There was barely room for his gaze to get out from under his visor. "Oh yeah, manface?"

Trent gave the correct answer according to the protocol: "Yeah."

"I haven't seen any of you before."

"We haven't seen you before either."

The demon considered that. "You wouldn't know me, because I'd have been in a different form." He puffed into a swirl of smoke to illustrate the point.

"But you'd have known *us*, if you'd seen us."

The demon re-formed, hat and all. "Right." He did not seem to be the smartest of his kind. "Pass, then. Just keep your noses clean."

"My nose isn't dirty," Gloha protested.

The demon merely looked at her as if she had said something stupid. That made her suspect she had.

They went on through the demon settlement. Demons didn't need houses, because they had no set mortal forms, and didn't need food, because they didn't eat, but they did have a culture of a sort. Gloha understood that there was even a Demon University where magic was taught, and of course the demons operated the Companions Game, which allowed selected Mundanes to visit Xanth if they didn't bother regular folk. But exactly what their culture was, no one could be sure. Maybe it was all pretense, to deceive observers. Demons sometimes amused themselves by fooling mortals. So when colored balloons floated by and popped into smoke that formed into faces with glistening tongues and teeth that then threatened to bite the heads off the travelers, Gloha knew to ignore them. When the path ahead became a writhing mass of serpent coils with dirty noses on each loop, Gloha walked on without hesitation, though conscious of the tease. When giant eyes opened on the floor, looking up and winking, she hesitated; she was still wearing her skirt. Suppose a demon announced the color of her panties?

"Oh, are you concerned about the footing on the stareway?" Trent inquired. "That's readily taken care of." He picked up a handful of sand and threw it across the floor. The eyes blinked madly, turned red, teared, and finally had to close and fade out. "Now I'm sure the footing is better."

"It is, thank you," she replied with a smile.

There was a swirl of vapor. It formed into a rather pretty nude human female figure. "Why, I'd almost think that was Magician Trent, except for the age," the demoness said. "But it couldn't be, because Trent is mortal, and just about ready to kick the cask."

"The what?" Gloha asked.

"Basin, tub, pail, vessel, can, receptacle—"

"Bucket?" Trent offered helpfully.

"Whatever," the demoness said crossly. "What are you several mortal creatures doing here in the demon realm?"

"You must be Metria!" Gloha exclaimed. "I've heard of you!"

"Of course I'm Metria," the demoness replied. "I always have been and always will be, except when I'm not. How did you hear of me?"

"Crombie told me how he knew you when he was young. He said you wouldn't show him your panties."

"Well of course I wouldn't!" Metria said indignantly. "Do you think I'm a perverse?"

"You're a what?"

"Contrary, obstinate, balky, willfull, disagreeable, intract-able—"

"I think you mean you're not abusive of family conventions," Trent said.

"Whatever," she agreed crossly. "Would *you* show a child your panty?"

"I would not," Trent said with a remarkably uncurved complexion.

"Or an antlery teenage male?"

"By no means."

"So there." A matching skirt and blouse outfit appeared on her body, and sure enough, no panty ever showed. "So who are you, really?"

"Why do you want to know?" he asked in return.

"I'm chronically curious. Why else?"

"I am Magician Trent."

"But I explained why you aren't him, didn't I?"

"I took youth elixir."

"But only the Good Magician Humfrey and some unicorns know where the Fountain of Youth is, and they'll never tell."

"Humfrey gave me some elixir."

"I don't believe it. He's too grumpy. Transform somebody."

Trent gestured. The demoness became a blue toad with green warts.

The toad puffed into smoke. "I didn't mean *me*!" the smoke protested. In a moment the nude human figure was back, without panties. "But I suppose I can take your identity on faith. Who are these winged monsters?"

"I am Gloha Harpy-Goblin."

"And I am Cynthia Centaur."

The demoness squinted at them. "I don't think I've seen many of your kind before. Just Che Centaur's family."

"Is it a nice family?" Cynthia asked.

"You don't know? That's interesting." The demoness faded out.

"She's somewhat of a nuisance," Trent remarked. "But there's nothing to be done about her. She seldom does actual harm, at least."

"I thought she had been locked into the Companions Game," Gloha said, remembering something she had once heard.

A puff of smoke reappeared. "I served my time and got out on parole." It disappeared.

Gloha made a mental note: one could never be quite certain that a demon wasn't still around.

They walked on out of the demon realm. There were no more odd events. Evidently the demons had gotten bored with them. That was a relief.

The fungus along the marked route turned brownish. The air became chill. Gloha closed her wings closely around her body, insulating it with the feathers. Cynthia suffered less, because she had more furry mass, but she did take a jacket out of her backpack and put it on over her shirt to protect her maidenly human torso. Evidently she had never adopted the centaur mode of undress after gaining some experience with the form, and had retained some of her clothing in case of need. Trent, already competently garbed, seemed to have no problem.

The air proceeded from chill to frigid. Patches of frost appeared. The three stepped up the pace so as to warm themselves by the vigor of their exertion. Gloha would have been concerned if she didn't see that the trail-marking fungus continued, though now dark and dormant.

They turned a corner, entered a moderately large chamber—and came fact-to-snoot with a dragon. The creature had antennae instead of eyes, which made sense down here, but in other respects seemed formidable enough. It had dragonly form and mass, metallic overlapping dark gray–green scales, stoutly taloned feet, one and a half squintillion teeth, and an attitude. It moved forward, inhaling, growling inwardly.

"Wait!" Trent cried, advancing to meet it. "We have a pass for this path."

Too late. The dragon exhaled. A surge of snowy vapor blew him back. Ice crystallized on his body. He fell back into the girls, completely iced.

"It's a snow dragon!" Gloha exclaimed, appalled as the two of them automatically caught him before he hit the floor and shattered. "I thought all of them were white and in the winter mountains."

"Don't worry about that," Cynthia said. "Just get him back to safety and get him thawed."

She was right. They dragged the ice man back the way they had come, away from the dragon. Cynthia did most of the work, being much larger than Gloha. When they were around the corner and in a section of the tunnel too small for the bulk of the dragon, they laid him carefully on the floor. "Is he—?" Gloha asked, appalled.

"Not if we act promptly," Cynthia said. "The ice is on the outside. If we chip it off immediately, he shouldn't freeze inside."

They chipped at his body, and chunks of ice fell to the floor with tinkling sounds. "But his face—we must clear that so he can breathe," Gloha said. "But we can't just pound off the ice; we'd chip off his nose and lips too."

"You're right. We need to apply fast, gentle warmth. I think this means I have a pretext to do what I would have liked to do a year—I mean, seventy-one or -two years ago."

Gloha was bemused. "You mean—?"

"Yes," she said with naughty determination. "I'm going to kiss him. It's in a decent cause, even if it's not completely nice."

Cynthia suited action to word. She reached down, put her hands on the Magician's shoulders, and hauled him up with the kind of strength a centaur could muster. He rose board-stiff, his feet still on the floor. Then she put her head down, aligned her face with his, and planted her lips very firmly on his for a wild wet kiss.

After a moment she lifted her head. "Hy hips are hrozen," she gasped.

In a quarter of a moment Gloha made sense of this. "Your lips are frozen," she repeated. "I'd better take over while you recover."

"Hyes." The layer of ice was flaking off Cynthia's face, but her lips remained attractively blue.

Gloha stood on tiptoe to reach the Magician's angled face, and planted her warm lips against his slightly thawed ones. She kissed him as firmly as she could. The cold struck through, but as her lips congealed she felt his softening. It was working! When she felt she had no more warmth in that region to give, she withdrew, and was gratified to see a thin trace of vapor issue from his mouth. He was starting to breathe again!

Meanwhile Cynthia had been breathing hard and smacking her lips together to get them warmed. She couldn't use her hands because they were holding Trent up for the kissing. "I think I can go another round now," she said bravely. She put her mouth to his mouth again.

Gloha's hands were free, and she used them to waggle her lips and flake the ice off them. Then she flexed them and breathed rapidly, using the warm air to complete the job. By the time her mouth had recovered, Cynthia's had iced up again.

But now Trent's mouth was clear of ice and his breath was pluming nicely. So Gloha tackled his right eye instead, which was frozen shut. She kissed it, and as the warmth loosened the ice, she licked it off. When it finally opened and blinked she knew it was thawed. But her mouth had congealed again, and her tongue wasn't speaking to her.

"Good idea," Cynthia said. "His mouth is done, and part of his tongue, but he needs his eyes too." She kissed the left eye.

His tongue? Gloha didn't inquire.

After that they worked on his nose, and his ears, and finally his face was done. Then they worked on the remainder of his body, taking turns hugging him close and chipping away the rest of the ice as it thawed. His clothing was hardly even wet; they had managed to get most of the ice off before it did more than melt around the edges.

Trent moved. "Hthank you, hladies," he said somewhat coldly. But the coldness was of the body, not of the heart. "There are whorse things than being khissed and hugged to lhife by two lhovely young lhadies."

Gloha and Cynthia exchanged a solid glance and a half. Then they exchanged a half-body flush. That was a significant achievement for each of them, because the centaur's clothing and fur normally concealed any such expression, and Gloha's skin was goblin dark. But in a moment steam was rising from both their faces.

"Don't waste that heat!" Trent cried. "I'm still cold." Indeed, he was shivering.

"In for a nickel, in for a dime," Cynthia said through her burning chagrin. She was referring to archaic Mundane coins reported to have the magic properties of getting things started or suddenly stopped.

They hauled the Magician up again and hugged him from either side, giving him the heat of their embarrassment. Soon enough he had been warmed. "I thank you both for saving my life," he said. "But perhaps we won't speak of this elsewhere. Others might not properly understand."

They emphatically agreed. It would be their secret. But even more secret was Gloha's private feeling. She had never actually kissed a man of any kind before, not directly on the mouth like that, and certainly had never done anything like licking off his face. Trent, rejuvenated as he was, had the body of a handsome young man. Now she realized that she had, on some suitably hidden level, rather liked the experience. She suspected that Cynthia had also, for she had admitted to being flustered by the Magician's aspect when she had first encountered him. She might be a centaur now, but she retained her origin and upper front section as a human maiden. So perhaps she had had her revenge on Trent, if that was what it was. This had perhaps given each of them a taste of what it would be like to get really friendly with males of their own kind.

"But now," Trent continued, evincing the quality of leadership that made him a man, not to mention a former Magician–King, "we need to deal with that dragon.

"Yes," they agreed together, evincing the quality of agreeability that made them innocent maidens, however much that innocence had been stained by the recent event.

"I can of course transform it into something harmless, being now warned about its nature. But I don't want to do mischief by acting hastily. I did enough of that when I was as young as I now look." He glanced significantly at Cynthia, who then demonstrated that she had not expended quite all of her color before. "Do you think it was a misunderstanding, and the dragon iced me before realizing that we had a pass?"

Gloha considered. "I think the dragon could have sent another cold draft down this tunnel, and frozen us all, if it had wanted to. So maybe it *was* a misunderstanding."

"Yes, that makes sense," Cynthia agreed. "Maybe we should give it another chance."

"But if it inhales, I'll transform it," Trent said grimly.

They advanced tentatively around the corner again. The dragon was there. "I say, old chap—we have a pass, you know," the Magician said.

The dragon nodded. Its snoot was not crafted for apology, but it was evidently making the effort.

"So if you will just let us pass without molestation, we'll just forget this little misunderstanding," Trent continued.

The dragon nodded again. So the three of them approached it. But Gloha noted that the Magician's hand was ready to gesture, just in case. She doubted that it was the gesture that did it; probably the motion was just to get his hand within transformation range of the target. But it was clear that Trent was not one to be caught twice the same way. He might look young, but he had the better part of a century's experience. Which might be the reason Crombie's magic had pointed him out to help on this quest: Gloha was a trifle short on experience, and this more than made up the difference.

The dragon did not try to frost them again, so Trent did not transform it. They passed it and entered a new network of tunnels. But the dormant green glow fungus still marked the trail, and the farther they got beyond the snow dragon's lair, the warmer the air got and the healthier the fungus became.

In fact the environment went from chill to warm to sweaty. Cynthia removed her jacket and packed it away, retaining the shirt. True centaurs were of course completely unself-conscious about their bodies, and showed things and did things openly that the Adult Conspiracy forbade to straight humans. But as a transformee Cynthia had more of the human foibles than did most centaurs, or she would not have been embarrassed about having to kiss the Magician back to life. Gloha, as a first-generation crossbreed, was uncertain exactly what social hang-ups she was expected to have, so followed the human ones until she had reason otherwise.

The air got downright hot. Both Cynthia and Gloha flapped their wings to keep their bodies cool, and Trent looked as if he would have liked to remove some clothing. If this got any worse, they would have to have a discussion about whether there were special cases where nudity was tolerable. Were they walking into the lair of a firedrake dragon?

No, it turned out to be a fire pit without a dragon. Dark liquid bubbled up from nether crevices, and formed burning pools. The marked path skirted it by digging a small ledge into the side of the wall. But there was room in the cavern for Gloha and Cynthia to fly, so they had no trouble. Trent was the one who had to navigate the inadequate trail.

"If only you could transform yourself, the way Dolph can," Gloha told him.

"Dolph?" Cynthia inquired.

"His grandson, Prince Dolph, who can change to any living form he wishes," Gloha explained. "He's the same age I am, but he's already married, and they have twins." She tried to keep the envy out of her voice, without a whole lot of success.

"So Magician Trent is a great-grandfather."

"Yes. But I don't think anyone we meet will believe that." They both laughed as they hovered. It was good to be flying again, however briefly. That was another thing that Cynthia had clearly learned to do before she retired to the Brain Coral's pool. Maybe that was why she had decided to remain in this form; it did have an ability that her original form had lacked. Gloha could not imagine life without flight; she would rather die than lose her wings.

Meanwhile the man was trying to stay on the tiny path, with diminishing success. There just wasn't enough room for his shoes. He was too likely to fall off it and roll down the steep slope of the wall right into the fire.

He paused. "How do you fly, Cynthia?" he called.

"You transformed me, and you don't know? I just flap my wings and take off."

"The reason I inquire is that I have heard that the other winged centaur family has the magic of making things light by flicking them with their tails. When they flick flies, the flies become too light to stay perched, and fly away. When they flick themselves, they become light enough for their relatively small wings to lift. When they flick a person, that person becomes light enough to be carried. If you can do that with me, you can carry me across his hot cavern."

"No, I don't flick myself, except to tag flies, and that's not to make them light but to knock them off," Cynthia said. "I never get light, and can't make anything else light. I just fly."

"Perhaps we should verify this." He got down off the

path and quickly retreated to the end of the cavern before his feet got too burningly hot from the stone.

Cynthia flicked him with her tail. He did not get light. Then he tried holding on to her as she tried to fly, but she couldn't get aloft. Her wings sent a powerful draft of air down, enough to lift her, but not enough to lift very much else. It was evident that her magic was different from that of the other winged centaurs. Her magic was in the power of the downdraft she made, to lift her up.

"That's interesting," Gloha remarked. "He transformed you, and must have given you the magic to fly, yet he didn't know how it worked."

"That is the case," Trent agreed. "I don't understand my talent, I just invoke it. But this leaves me with a problem; I just don't see how I can use that little walkway."

"Maybe if you flew alongside him, and pushed him against the wall," Gloha suggested. "So he couldn't fall."

They tried it, but it was problematical, because Cynthia needed room for her wings. She tried facing away from the wall, so that her rump could brace Trent, and that worked, but then she couldn't fly sideways to pace him across the cavern. Gloha was too small to help at all.

"Could you transform one of us into a form that would be able to help?" Gloha asked.

"Would you want to be transformed?" he countered. "You know, you could find your ideal man quite readily if I transformed you to a suitable form."

"Oh, no, I like the way I am!" she protested. "I don't want to change, I want to succeed in life *my* way. But for just a temporary time, I maybe could stand it."

A cloud of smoke appeared before her. A mouth opened on its vague surface. "You fool."

"I didn't ask you, Metria," Gloha retorted, beginning to understand how a person could become annoyed with the demoness.

"Then I won't tell you how to get him safely by," the smoke said, and dissipated.

"How about a vine?" Trent asked. "You could take root at one end, and Cynthia could hold the tip of the vine at the other end, and I could use it as a rail to hold."

"A plant?" Gloha asked, dismayed. She hadn't thought of that, and probably never would have.

"The rock's too hot," Cynthia pointed out. "The plant would wilt."

"A flame vine wouldn't."

"That's right," Cynthia agreed, surprised.

Both of them looked at Gloha. She really didn't care for the notion, but saw no polite way out. She was about to say a grudging yes, when a realization saved her. "You can't transform me when I'm out of your reach, right? But I have to be all the way across the cavern."

"No, you could be this side, and I could fly you to the other side," Cynthia said helpfully.

"Or you could carry her to the other side to take root," Trent said. "Make sure there is a suitable place first."

The centaur flew across. "Yes, there's even some nice warm dirt here," she reported. "It looks quite rich. Maybe bats have enhanced it."

"Bats!" Gloha exclaimed indignantly. But she realized that she was stuck for it. "All right," she murmured, hoping she wouldn't be heard.

No such luck. Trent reached toward her, and suddenly she was a thing of flames and tentacles and leaves. She felt very insecure, because her roots didn't have much purchase. She was, indeed, a flame vine. She wasn't actually burning; she was merely fire-colored, with the capacity to generate small flames at the tips of her leaves if she chose.

Then Cynthia picked her up and carried her across the cavern. It was pleasantly warm in the center, then cool again at the edge. The centaur set her down on a patch of what her roots tasted as volcanic soil. That was ideal. She sank her roots deep and proceeded to grow. She focused on one long vine, sending it along the wall above the path. Wherever she found a crevice she ran a tendril in, anchoring it.

She put out regularly spaced leaves to take in the radiation of the fire along the cavern floor. It tasted almost as good as the soil. This was fun!

Soon she was all the way across, solidly anchored all the way. She didn't need Cynthia to hold her end; no one was going to pull her off that wall until she let go of it herself. For one thing, there were tasty minerals in that wall.

She waved a tendril at the Magician: get on with it!

He set out again along the path. He put a hand on her vine—and quickly removed it. He dug into his own pack and fetched out a pair of heavy gloves. Then, wearing these, he tried again, and this time was able to maintain a grip on her hot vine.

Toward the center where the ledge got thinnest he had to hold on quite firmly, but she strengthened her tendril anchors and stayed firm. Then he reached the near side. "Thank you, Gloha," he said. "Now I will change you back. But first we must get you all together, because otherwise parts of you may be stuck to the wall."

Gloha saw the logic. Cynthia flew back and carefully pulled the long vine out as Gloha released her tendril grip, stage by stage. Cynthia collected the vine in a bundle and flew slowly back with it as more was released. Gloha hated to do it, because there was still plenty of nutritious mineral there, but she suspected that her winged goblin form would be annoyed if she didn't. Of course why anyone would want to be a goblin when she could be a flame vine—

Then she was herself again, complete with her blouse and skirt in place. She quailed at the thought of remaining a flame vine; obviously a winged goblin was better. Yet now she could appreciate the differing perspective of the plant. Each form of life found itself marvelously compatible, and distrusted all others. Perhaps she should try to remember that lesson of life, if she didn't get distracted by more important things.

They moved on, following the passage generally down. It didn't seem to be in any great hurry to reach the surface.

Now they entered a region of stalag—stalac—those pointed pillarlike things that lived in caves.

"Stalagmites and stalactites," Trent said. "My, these are very thick—and look where the path goes!"

"How can you remember the difference?" Cynthia asked him. "I mean, between the ones that cling to the ceiling and the ones that grow up from the ground?"

The Magician laughed. "You have solved the riddle already! The ceiling-clinging ones are spelled with a *c* for *ceiling*, and the ground-growing ones with a *g* for *ground*. StalaCtite and stalaGmite. I think the other distinguishing letters, *t* and *m*, also indicate it; *t* is for *top*, but I forget what *m* is for."

The ball of smoke appeared. "Moron?" it inquired. He batted a hand through it, and it dissipated, leaving a dirty smell. It seemed that the demoness had not quite lost interest in them, and naturally she couldn't get the word.

"Mound," Cynthia suggested.

"Whatever," Gloha agreed, trying to look cross. But the effect was spoiled when they both giggled.

But they had a more serious problem to concern them. The C tites and G mites were so thickly spread that it was impossible to squeeze between them. The fungus path went across the points, coating the upward-and downward-pointing tips. There was room between them for the girls to fly, but Trent was out of luck again.

"I am beginning to wonder what the advantage is to being human," he remarked.

"The problem is not in being human," Gloha said. "It is in being wingless. If you had wings, you'd be all right."

"Thank you," he said. She realized that there was more than one way her statement could be taken, and she felt another faint flush trying to form. Fortunately she hadn't enough left to embarrass her.

"Maybe I can clear a path through these," Cynthia said. She faced away from the wall of G mites, then let fly with a well-placed kick. The nearest mite broke off and toppled, crashing down between the others.

But almost immediately there was a shower of spearlike C tites from above. The three mortal creatures barely got out of the way in time to avoid getting skewered.

"I think we would never be able to clear that path," Trent said. "This cave protects its own."

"Maybe we can find another way," Gloha said. She flew up and between the needlelike tips of the upper and lower fields of stalacs and stalags (or whatever), careful not to touch any of them. But all she found beyond was a passage angling up to a medium-small river going merrily about its own business. There was no other exit; the passage continued along the river.

She flew back and reported. "I am beginning to wonder whether we are on the right trail," she concluded. "This one seems entirely too difficult for human folk to manage. It's hard to believe that Tandy traveled this way alone."

"I suspect she had her ogre husband along before," Trent said. "These hazards would not have dared to interfere with an ogre."

That seemed to make sense. But meanwhile what were they going to do? This cave seemed to be even less passable than the others.

"You say there's a river?" Cynthia asked. "Do you suppose it could be diverted?"

"It seemed pretty self-absorbed. Oh, you mean, to change its channel? I suppose that's possible; one bank was sandy. But that would just make it flow into this cave, and fill it up."

"Yes. Then maybe Trent could swim between the tites and mites without disturbing any of them."

Trent considered. "Do you know, you may be almost as smart as you are pretty. I think it could be done."

Cynthia's powers of coloration had evidently regenerated without impairment. She might once have been the Magician's enemy, but that was a long time ago. Now it was clear that she found him rather intriguing. Gloha found it easy to appreciate the feeling. Trent was handsome, intelligent, experienced, disciplined, and had one of the strongest magic talents in Xanth. There wasn't a lot more required of a man.

Gloha flew back to the river. She landed on its bank and used her fine little feet to scuff a channel in the sand. The water flowed eagerly through it, and plunged down into the cave. It widened the channel as it went, so that more water could follow. Soon the entire river was headed for this interesting new region, forming an expanding pool around the base of the G mites.

She flew back. "I have diverted the river, and it seems to be quite entertained," she reported.

"We suspected as much," Trent said dryly, which was a good trick because he was standing knee-deep in the pool.

The river disported itself mightily, and the level of the pool steadily rose. Gloha and Cynthia hovered over it. "Are you going to be all right?" Gloha asked the Magician.

"Oh, certainly; I can swim. You girls go ahead and wait on dry land; I'll be along in due course."

They did as bid, for hovering soon enough became tiring. "He's a brave man," Cynthia said as they flew.

"And a marvelous Magician," Gloha agreed. "It's hard to imagine that they ever called him evil."

"Oh, that was because he was trying to take over Xanth before the Storm King was ready to fade out. And he was transforming a lot of people. But I gather he was a good king, when he finally got the office.

"Yes, Xanth has prospered. Bink's son Dor and Trent's daughter Irene have done well too. I guess it shows that you never can tell how things will turn out."

"You never can tell," Cynthia agreed wistfully.

They landed on the dry part of the bank, then watched the water rise around the G mites. Every so often one of them flew back to check on the Magician, who was doing what he called treading water, though it looked exactly like swimming in place.

At last the water covered the tip-tops of the G mites, so that only the descending points of the C tites showed above it. Now the cave looked like a dragon's mouth half full of saliva. But Gloha wasn't entirely comfortable with that image, so let it go.

Trent came swimming along, having no trouble. Only at the end did one of his feet accidentally kick a hidden G mite. The pool shook, and several C tites dropped into the water with menacing splashes. But Trent had already gotten clear.

They moved on again. The river path deserted the river, having no loyalty, and wended its way up to another large cave. This one was dome-shaped, with a single massive stalagmite in the center. There was neither dragon nor fire here; the floor was bare. But there was also no exit. The glow-fungus path went to the center and stopped.

They looked all around, but the wall was solid. The only hole in it was the one through which they had entered. The circular wall was painted with pictures of assorted creatures: dragons, griffins, chimerae, sea serpents, sphinxes, and the like; nothing really unusual. Here and there were even some men with spears.

"Do you know, this must be an ancient cave," Trent said. "These are the creatures the early men of Xanth hunted. They painted pictures of them to be sure of the magic necessary to bring them down. Or perhaps it was opposite: they were working magic to protect themselves from such predators. Either way, this is a historic artifact."

"How could they hunt such creatures down here?" Gloha asked. "All we've seen are dragons."

"Perhaps they hunted all the others to extinction."

"Or perhaps the dragons hunted the humans to extinction," Cynthia said. "Because no men seem to live here now."

"You have a sobering point," he agreed.

"But how are we going to get out of here before *we're* extinct?" Gloha asked plaintively.

Trent grimaced. "That is a somewhat better question than I feel competent to address at the moment."

Then Cynthia noticed something. "The glow-fungus path doesn't stop here. It circles up the stalagmite!"

They looked, and found it was so. The fungus spiraled right up toward the distant ceiling. And there, at the very top, was a hole. The G mite poked a short way into it.

"And there's our exit," the Magician said. "And once again I feel inadequate to the need. I don't believe I can climb that smooth column, and this time there is no water to float me up."

"But this time you can use your talent," Cynthia said. "Simply transform me into something huge enough to lift you up there, then transform me back to this form."

"I can if you wish this," he agreed. "You have been most generous in your attitude toward me, considering our prior experience, and I have not wished to impose on you by transforming you again."

"Well, a lot has happened since then, and we're not on opposite sides any more," she said with a smile that might in some other circumstance have seemed ingratiating. "Now we have to work together to get through."

"We do, at that," he agreed. "Very well, I'll transform you to a roc, which should be strong enough to carry me there. But we shall need to calculate this carefully, for if I then transform you back before you are through the hole, you could fall."

And such a fall could kill her, Gloha realized. Then she realized that she had fallen into a mental trap: a flying centaur wouldn't fall, she would just fly away. But the hole looked way too small for such a creature to squeeze through, so there was still a problem. But she had an answer: "Then you transform her to a little bird, who can fly on up through the hole. *Then* back to centaur form, when she is safe."

"You, too, are uncommonly clever," Trent told her. Gloha discovered that she had not after all used up her own store of blush.

Then the Magician gestured, and the centaur became a truly monstrous bird. The roc took the suddenly tiny-seeming man in its ferociously huge beak, spread its giant pinions, and launched into the air. Now, there was an act of trust, Gloha realized: the bird could cut the man in half simply by closing its beak. It flew up, circling the stalagmite, until it reached the top. Then it flipped its head, opened its beak, and the man sailed up through the hole. He didn't fall out again, so he must have landed somewhere.

Now the roc flew as close to the hole in the ceiling as possible without colliding with the stalagmite. The tip of one wing brushed past the hole—and the big bird vanished. In its place was a tiny hummingbird.

Gloha had been halfway keeping pace, staying clear of the immense downdraft from the roc's wings. Now she flew up through the hole herself.

There were Trent and Cynthia, waiting for her. "See? It was routine," the centaur filly said nonchalantly as she let go of the man. He must have held her steady as he transformed her, or perhaps she had clung to him for balance as she adjusted.

Trent smiled obliquely. "Routine," he agreed.

But Gloha was seriously wondering how many more such tricky transitions they would be able to make. This did not strike her as a safe or easy route. It was more like trying to gain entry to the Good Magician's castle. But she didn't want to alarm the others, so she kept her meek little mouth shut. About that and whatever else she might conjecture about that wasn't her business.

They moved on again. This time the passage led to a snoozing goblin. "Ahem," Trent said.

The goblin rolled over on his mat. "Go away, dunderhead," he muttered without opening his eyes.

"I presume this is the goblin checkpoint," Trent said.

"We want you to be sure you know that we have a safe conduct pass."

The goblins forced open an eye. Then suddenly both eyes wedged wide. "What are you creatures doing here?"

"We are on our way out of the underworld," Trent said evenly. "We are following the established exit route, for which we have a pass." He showed the pass.

"But that's impossible! We changed the route so nobody could get through."

Trent, Gloha, and Cynthia shared three halves of a glance. Suddenly something was making sense. Goblin mischief.

The Magician turned back to the goblin. "And why would you change the path?" he inquired with truly deceptive mildness.

"Because we don't honor any deals made by the crappy saps who ran this region before we got here, but we didn't want to say so outright before we got really well established. So we could claim that travelers just got lost or something, in case the demons snooped."

"And the regular path is easier to travel?"

"Of course it is, yokel. It just winds straight up past the checkpoints to the surface. But now we'll erase that, and eat any more travelers who come, pass or not."

"That could plunge the underworld into war, after decades of peace."

"Yeah," the goblin said zestfully. "So now get ready for the pot, because we're going to stew you three for supper. Better take off your packs and clothes; they don't boil well." He squinted at them. "One dumb human man, one stupid winged goblin girl—oh, we'll have fun with you before we cut off those wings!—and one idiotic winged centaur filly." Then the goblin did a double take. "A winged centaur! We *hate* winged centaurs! Ever since that little snoop came to Goblin Mountain and made it possible for a girl to be chief. What a pain! We real he-man goblins just had to get the Hades out of there and find a place to regroup. Oh, we'll pull out your feathers one by one, and make you hurt worse and worse, until you're just begging to be dumped into the boiling pot! What a treat we have coming!"

Gloha felt an awful chill, and she could tell that Cynthia was experiencing the same ugly draft. But the Magician seemed oddly unconcerned. Gloha was pretty sure that was misleading, she hoped.

"And this path now goes straight on up to the surface?" Trent inquired conversationally. "No more hazards?"

"Sure. But you won't be taking it, man-puss, because we're closing the gate. You might as well eat that pass before we feed it to you."

"And you are the only goblin guarding this path?"

"Right." The goblin paused. "Except for the other hundred that moved in while we were talking." He waved, and suddenly the passage beyond was crammed with goblins carrying spears and clubs. "You thought maybe you'd just run over me and be gone, meat-man? You're even dumber than you look."

Gloha felt a worse chill. Suddenly they were faced with bad faith—because of bad goblins who had fled the enlightened female chiefship of cousin-once-removed Gwenny and come here to establish their evil order. She knew the three could expect no mercy, because she knew what goblin men were like in their natural state. This was doom.

"I take it that you don't know who I am," Trent said, seeming unperturbed.

"Human scum, I am proud to tell you I have no idea who you are, and don't care to soil my mind learning. You'll taste just as good as anyone else, once we add the spices. Now get those clothes off before we hack them off."

"I am Magician Trent. Perhaps you have heard of me."

"Of course I never heard of you, crapbrain! And even if I had, I—" He paused. "Who?"

"The Magician of Transformation."

The goblin began to sidle away. "It don't mean nothing to me! You're probably lying anyway."

Trent strode forward, gesturing. The goblin became a large purple snake with venom dripping from its fangs. "Now go greet your comrades," Trent said.

But the snake did not flee. Instead it slithered toward the Magician. Gloha realized that the change of form did not stop it from being an enemy, any more than her change of form had stopped her from being a friend. Trent's magic could not change personality.

The purple snake became a pink elephant, the kind of monster that drunks dreamed of. But the passage was not large enough for it, so it filled the space completely, blocking off the other goblins. But it also blocked off the easy escape route to the single-G-mite chamber.

"We need another exit," the Magician said mildly. "Gloha, can you find your way through goblin tunnels?"

"Yes. But there will be enemy goblins in them. They'll attack us from ambush before you can transform them. They'll throw stones from beyond your range. I don't think we can get through them."

"What about some passage they won't use?"

"They can go anywhere we can, because you can't fly." She hated to bring that liability up to him again, but it was unfortunately true.

"Then find a passage you two can use and they can't. I'll keep them from following, if they make the attempt."

He was offering to sacrifice himself so that the two of them could escape. Gloha knew she wouldn't accept that, and she thought Cynthia wouldn't either. In fact she was pretty almost certainly sure Cynthia wouldn't. But there was no point in arguing about that right now. She peered down the passages that debouched from this region. Already she heard the sounds of goblins running through passages, closing in on this one by devious routes.

Then she spied a goblin sign. "I see a forbidden tunnel!" she cried. "This way!" She ran toward it.

"Why is it forbidden?" Cynthia asked as she trotted after her.

"I don't know. But it means that goblins won't use it, and that's what we want."

They entered the tunnel as goblins appeared in the one behind them. This one was well lighted by fungus and big enough for them all to use comfortably, which made Gloha wonder, because both the man and the centaur were twice the height of any goblin. Why should such a large tunnel be forbidden? If they were afraid to use it, why hadn't they blocked it off?

It led fairly directly to another large cavern whose base was filled with water. That was all; there was no offshoot passages. Just the quiet pool.

"The goblins are afraid of this?" Cynthia asked, perplexed.

"Yes," Gloha said. "I don't understand why. If there were any really bad monster here, they would have blocked off the tunnel, so that it couldn't come out after them. Instead they merely marked it forbidden. This is distinctly odd. But it doesn't mean that it's safe for us, or that it is any way out. Just that they won't be coming in here."

Cynthia peered across the dark water. "I think I see something."

They all peered. "It looks furry," Gloha said.

The thing came toward them. Indeed it was furry; in fact it seemed to be a big ball of fur. But when it got close, it opened a furry mouth that seemed somewhat bigger than it was, and snapped with large furry teeth. Sparks flew as the teeth clashed together.

"This is not a place to swim," Trent said. "I gather the fur monster does not leave the water. That means that the goblins don't need to fear it coming after them. They just have to stay clear of its pool."

"Yes, that would explain the simple warning sign," Gloha agreed. "Goblins are lazy; they don't do anything they don't have to. If there's no need to block off a tunnel, they won't bother. So they just posted the warning and let it be."

"But this doesn't look like enough to back off a whole

goblin tribe," Cynthia said. "The creature is hardly half as massive as I am. That's enough to gobble up any goblin that might fall in the water—"

"Or be thrown in," Trent suggested.

"But the tribe could gather and throw a barrage of spears at it from the edge," Gloha finished. "You're right; goblins are lazy, but in a case like this their meanness should make up for it. They should take pleasure in attacking it from the safety of the shore, just because it's there. There must be something more."

"And we had better find out what it is," Trent said, his mildness fading now that there was no one close by who needed deceiving. "Now I can transform this creature into something innocuous. But I don't know whether it's the only one, or what else may be lurking near. I am not comfortable with this."

The man was a master of understatement! "I suppose you could transform me into something that shouldn't fear the furball," Gloha said. "Like maybe an allegory. Then I could explore the depths of the pool to see if there's any exit from it. There doesn't seem to be any above or around it."

"Let's not act too quickly, if we don't have to," Trent said. "I have learned to be careful about what I don't understand. There is a mystery about this pool that the presence of a monster doesn't satisfactorily explain."

Cynthia leaned forward over the water and dipped the tip of a finger. Immediately the furball shot through the water and snapped at her hand. "Oh!" she cried, whipping it away.

"That thing is fast," Gloha said.

"It's not that. That water stings." She brought her finger to her mouth.

"Don't do that!" Trent snapped, startling her. "That water may be poison."

"Oh!" she repeated, staring at her hurting finger.

Gloha brought out a handkerchief. "There is a bit of healing elixir in this," she said. She used it to wipe off the finger, which she saw was already blistering. Poison indeed!

"Oh thank you," Cynthia said. "That feels so much better."

"So now we know another reason why the goblins avoid this pool," Trent said. "It is poison water. The fur monster must be specially adapted to it. Still I'm not sure we have fathomed the whole of this unpleasant mystery—and I think we shall have to, if we want to pass through this pool to escape this region."

"How can we know there is any way out under the pool?" Gloha asked. "There might be underwater caves that don't go anywhere."

"I see no water dripping down from the dome above it. Yet the pool is not brackish or cloudy. It seems to be fresh water, such as it is. That suggests that there is a wellspring somewhere below the surface. If we find that inlet, it may be our outlet."

"I suppose," Gloha said dubiously. "We certainly don't seem to have any other way out."

"But we can't go through poisoned water," Cynthia protested.

"I wonder," Trent said thoughtfully. "It seems unlikely that it would be poisoned by contact with the local rock, because then other waters in the region should suffer a similar effect, and we have not noted this. That river we diverted was quite pure. I think the goblins would not have poisoned it, because that just makes it useless to them. That suggests that this pool is magically poisoned."

"Magically poisoned!" Gloha exclaimed. "You mean, like some pools are love springs, and some are hate springs, and some are youth springs, or healing springs, and so on—this one is a poison spring?"

"Something like that," he agreed. "If it did not wish to be molested by goblins, this device would be effective."

"It certainly would!" Gloha agreed. "But that stops *us* from molesting it too."

"But perhaps we can make a deal with it. Sometimes the inanimate has special desires."

"You mean things that aren't alive, like pools, want things?" Cynthia asked.

"My son-in-law Dor has the ability to talk with the inanimate. It is clear from his experience that inanimate things have concerns, just as animate ones do. We lack the ability to communicate as he does, unfortunately, but maybe we can handle it."

"We can talk to water?" Gloha asked, as doubtful as Cynthia. Stones might be considered individual entities, but water was just fluid.

"Perhaps. I suspect that the fur monster understands the pool, and perhaps it will tell us what the pool desires that we might provide."

Both girls looked at him, not trusting this.

"Suppose I transform one of you into a similar furball, also immune to the poison," he said. "I can do this, despite not really knowing its nature, because my talent takes care of the details. Then you could communicate with it, get some answers, and perhaps make a deal."

"You transformed Cynthia last time," Gloha said. "It's my turn." She hardly believed that this would work, but what other hope was there?

The Magician approached her and gestured. Suddenly she was a hairy furball. She rolled into the pool with a satisfying splash. The water felt wonderful.

The other furball charged aggressively across, its teeth leading the way. "Wait, furface!" she cried in its language, which wasn't exactly verbal but which came naturally to her. "I'm your kind. Let's talk."

"You're female!" the other said, amazed. "I'm male. Let's—"

"Talk first!" she insisted. She hadn't expected this particular complication.

"What about?" he demanded impatiently.

"About this pool. Is it magically poisoned?"

"Of course. Isn't it great? No one else bothers me. Of course I do get lonely. So let's—"

"Can the magic be nullified? So regular creatures could pass through it without getting dissolved?"

"Sure, if Aqui wants. But what's the point? Now let's—"

"That's the pool? Aqui?"

"Sure. And I'm Fur. We get along great, but we get bored with just each other's company, you know? So let's—"

Gloha realized that Fur had a one-track mind. She probably wouldn't get much help from him until she got his concern settled. Well, she was of age. It was more of a sacrifice than she had anticipated, but they did have to find a way out of the underworld. "Exactly what is it you want to do?" she asked guardedly.

"I want to play, of course. I haven't had a playmate in years. Neither has Aqui. We're getting bored with each other."

"Play? Just how do you mean?"

"You know. Racing around the pool. Splashing each other. Playing hide-and-peek down below. All that fun stuff."

Gloha realized that though she was of age, Fur wasn't. He was still a child, and wanted childish play. She could readily oblige him in that. "Catch me if you can!" she cried, and took off through the water at a zoom. She didn't know exactly how she did it, as she had no arms or legs or tail; she just moved.

"Great!" he responded, and zoomed after her.

She dived. Immediately she saw that there *was* an exit: water was flowing in from a hole well below the surface, and filtering out through a lattice on the opposite side. This was indeed fresh water, that surely was as fresh and pure as ever, the moment it left the magic ambience of the pool. Trent had been right about it. He seemed to be right about most things.

But she should make sure. So as Fur was about to catch up with her, she dodged to the side and shot into the spring.

"Hey, no fair!" he cried.

She paused in the current. "Why?"

"Because that doesn't go anywhere fun. Just straight up to the outside world. I don't want to go there."

"I'm sorry," she said apologetically. "I didn't realize." She shot back down with the current so swiftly that Fur wasn't able to tag her before she was past him. "Pokey Fur! Pokey Fur!" she cried.

"Am not! Am not!" he retorted. "Anyway, you're worse."

"How?"

"Because you're a gurl!" The term was neither written nor verbal, but he managed to misspell it anyway.

She paused as if stricken. "Oh, my, you're right! How can I ever live it down?"

He was immediately contrite. "Aw, I didn't mean it. You can't help it. I'm sorry."

"That's okay," she said generously. Then, seizing the moment: "If you two had a nice new playmate to stay here, would you let three funny creatures go by?"

"A playmate to stay? Gee, yes!"

"Then check with Aqui, while I check with my folks," she said. She realized that it was best to be positive and assertive when dealing with children and the inanimate.

"Okay." Fur zoomed somewhere down in the depths of the pool while she zoomed for the surface.

She went to the edge. "Transform me back," she cried.

But she saw the Magician hesitate. Then she realized why. He didn't know which fur monster she was. So she moved in a pattern across the water. G-L-O-H-A she spelled, then zoomed back.

This time there was no hesitation. The Magician gestured, and she was the winged goblin girl again.

"We can make a deal!" she gasped. "There's a river out! Right to the surface. But we need to give them a playmate to keep. I was thinking maybe you could transform an ant or something into another furball, and—"

"We may not need to do that," Trent said. "We have with us a creature who loves fresh water in what he wishes to be his natural form."

"We do?" she asked blankly.

"Swiftmud!" Cynthia exclaimed. "I had almost forgotten him."

"But he's not the same species," Gloha said.

Trent looked around. "We three are of different species, or even five or six species, depending how we count it, yet we get along. Swiftmud is quite a character in his natural form, when you get to know him. Let's inquire." He brought out the lightning bug, set it carefully on the floor, and suddenly the giant mud bank was there, taking up the tunnel behind them. "Swiftie, we have a lonely Aqui pool and a lonely kid furball," he said. "If you can get along with Aqui and Fur you may stay here, your service to us done."

Swiftmud promptly slid into the pool without making a splash. He seemed to have no trouble with the poison.

Fur appeared. The two would have sniffed noses, if either had a nose. Then they began frolicking in the water. Swiftmud, no longer constrained by having to stay on the surface carrying other folk, dived and swirled, became a cloud of dirty water, then formed back into a mud bank. Fur circled around him, then rolled over him and splashed back into the water on the other side. The ball was having a ball.

"I think we have our answer," the Magician said. "Of course we'll have to make our way by foot and wing when we reach the surface. But I had told Swiftmud that if he served us loyally, I would see that he found a compatible situation. He really does like fresh water. He'd take all of it if he could."

"How will we get through the lake and the underground river?" Cynthia asked. "Our wings won't be effective, and we won't be able to breathe."

"You two will have no trouble; I'll change you to fish. It is myself I am worried about."

"Maybe we could help you, if we were the right kind of fish," Gloha said. "Lungfish, maybe, for breathing."

"Lungfish," he agreed. "That would do it." He leaned

down and touched his finger to the water. "It is safe now; Aqui is satisfied with the deal."

Gloha and Cynthia verified that the water was no longer poisonous. Then Trent transformed them both to lungfish and they flopped into the water.

Gloha discovered that she liked this form, too. Each form that she assumed had its own virtues, and there was much to be said for being a fish in water. Cynthia seemed similarly satisfied.

Then Trent dived into the pool. He swam down to the river hole, and into it, the two fish showing the way. Then Cynthia swam up to his face and put her mouth to his. It looked like a very solid kiss, and maybe Cynthia thought of it that way, but it was more. She used her lungs to breathe some fresh air into him. Her gills were enough for herself.

They swam on upstream. Gloha took her turn, planting her mouth on the man's mouth and giving him another lungful of air. She found it was fun thinking of it as a deep kiss. Of course she would never admit to enjoying such illicit contact with a male of another species, any more than Cynthia would. But its secret nature added to its appeal.

In this manner they continued until the light of day showed ahead, and the Magician reached the surface.

He clambered out, then reached over the water to transform them to their regular forms. They came out, shaking their wings dry. Their clothing would take longer.

They were by a small river that tunneled into a gully. Now they knew where it was going. Meanwhile they were back on the surface of Xanth. It was wonderful.

5

Xxxxxxx

"I've lost my direction," Gloha said, dismayed, as they dried in the sun. They had agreed that technically they were of three different species, so need have no concern about each other's exposure; nevertheless, they studiously avoided looking. Gloha's sneak peeks indicated that Trent, at least, was honoring that tacit agreement. "I got all turned around on the way out of the underworld, and don't know which way Crombie pointed."

"It was southeast," Trent said. "Back toward Lake Ogre-Chobee."

"Oh—maybe that's why he pointed you out to help me," she said. "Because you would remember."

"That must be it," he agreed with part of a smile.

"Then this must be where we part company," Cynthia said, seeming not completely pleased. "Because I must go find the winged centaur family."

"Not yet," the Magician said. "I undertook to get you safely to a compatible situation. Since I know where that is,

I believe I should complete that task before seeing to Gloha's more mysterious quest."

"Yes," Gloha said quickly. She liked Cynthia and wanted to be sure she was all right. Also, she was a bit wary of her quest, and not as eager to get on with it as she thought she should be. She wasn't quite sure she should travel alone with Trent, and this wasn't because she thought he would do anything untoward. Not at all. So this was an excellent pretext for delay.

"You are very kind," Cynthia said. She would have been clearly relieved, but her eyes were tearing a bit, so she was cloudily relieved.

"It is the least I can do, for someone who has kissed me as often and firmly as you have."

Cynthia seemed to be learning how to handle his teasing, because her flush progressed to no more than pale pink this time, and no farther down than her (temporarily) bare breasts. Gloha was glad the remark hadn't been directed at her, so she didn't have to flush similarly despite being as guilty of such kissing as Cynthia.

"The winged centaur family is north of the Gap Chasm," Gloha said. "The two of us could fly there, but that won't work for you, Magician."

"I regret being such a drag on this party," Trent said. "It reminds me of when I traveled with Bink and Chameleon, when they were young. I rather interfered with their progress too, for a while."

"Well, you were evil then, weren't you?" Cynthia inquired.

"So I was called. But I think I don't need to hold you folk back. I can transform one of you into a roc again, and you can carry me there." He glanced at the sky. "It's about noon now; I lost track of time below, but we can make better progress now and be there before the day is out."

Cynthia sent a wavering glance out. Gloha intercepted it and sent it back. Suddenly she realized that neither one of them was quite ready to end this segment of their journey.

It wasn't exactly uncertainty about their respective futures, though that helped, and not exactly that the youthened Magician Trent was pleasant company, though that also helped. They just weren't yet ready to end this interlude, for reasons that were surely best left unfathomed.

"Let's just remain with our own forms for a while," Gloha said. "Cynthia needs practice in today's Xanth."

"As you wish," he agreed. "I merely did not wish to delay either of you. We can proceed north at my limited pace."

In due course their clothing was mostly dry, and they took turns dressing while the others tried not to peek too much. Their packs remained damp, but would probably survive.

They set off, following the stream, which moved generally north and northwest. Cynthia and Gloha remained on the ground, since they were the ones who had declined the chance to become big enough to carry the Magician through the air. There turned out to be interesting things down here, such as colored stones in the streambed and pretty flowers along the bank. Each of them picked a pink flower to put in her hair; then they picked two blue flowers for Trent's hair. "So no one will confuse you with a girl," Gloha explained, lightly kissing his left ear to make the flower stay in place.

"Or a winged monster," Cynthia added, kissing his right ear, for a similar reason.

"If I did not know better, I'd suspect one of you of flirting with me," he responded. "Unfortunately I can't tell which one."

"We'll never tell," they said together, not even bothering to blush.

The stream climbed a hill, then relaxed by filling in a pool. There by a ledgelike bank in the pool were three young female human heads. One was blond, with her long fair tresses artfully obliterating her right eye on their way down. One was red, with her hair spreading out across the ledge in front. The third was dark gray-brown, with hanks of hair swirling tantalizingly across her heaving bosom. All three had eyes as deep and blue as the very freshest water.

"Eeeek! People!" the blond screamed cutely, not sounding frightened.

Then, as Gloha and Cynthia crested the hill, the redhead clarified it. "Two half people. Female. I can tell by their pink flowers." She sounded disappointed.

"And one straight human man," the brunette said. "I can tell by his blue flowers." She sounded interested.

"And who are you?" Trent inquired in friendly fashion. But Gloha saw that he was casually moving to within transformation range. He was not the most trusting person, which was just as well.

"Merely three beautifully bored mermaids," the blonde said as the three lifted their tails behind them. "Ash, Cedar, and Mahogany. I'm Ash, of course. Who are you, who come to us with your ears kissed?"

"Trent, Gloha, and Cynthia," the Magician said. "I'm Trent."

"You are named for trees?" Gloha asked.

"For colors," Cedar said, making an appealing moue. "The local wood nymphs got all the water colors, so we had to take wood colors."

"We would love to give you a wonderful time, Trent man, but you seem to be already well attended," Mahogany said. "We see that your mouth has been rather soundly kissed, too. However, should you too be bored with overly familiar things—"

"We are just rapidly passing through," Cynthia said, just possibly not quite pleased by the presence of three more pretty crossbreeds.

"Still, diversions are seldom and slow," Ash said. "Can we not persuade you to dally a moment?" She gave Trent a wonderfully liquid look as she lowered her tail and lifted her marvelously full bare breasts from the water.

"Only if you have something interesting or useful to offer," Gloha said somewhat disparagingly. Her tone was sheer bluff, because she knew that never in her wildest fantasy dreams would she have a bosom as globular as that.

Water folk were able to wear more flesh than air folk, because it helped them float and didn't help them fly. That was one of the unfairness of reality.

"Well, we do have one talent between the three of us," Cedar said, performing a similar maneuver with slightly better exposure. "As your brightly kissed eyes may see, if you wish." She inhaled.

"But do you have a magic talent?" Cynthia inquired, knowing that crossbreeds often did not, and if they did, it was likely to be related to their survival as crossbreeds. Such as flying, for the winged ones.

"Why, yes," Mahogany said, taking her turn at the maneuver and managing a truly double-barreled (as it were) display. All three of them were distressingly well endowed in that particular respect. "We read titles."

"Titles?" Trent asked. He had, perhaps diplomatically, stayed clear of much of the prior dialogue, though he had kept a firm eye on the proceedings. Most of the firmness had been elsewhere, however.

"Whatever title is written, we can read," Ash explained. "The three of us have to do it together, and we can't read any more than the title, but it can nevertheless be interesting."

Trent shook his head. "We are more interested in making progress toward our destination than in reading titles."

But now Gloha, perversely, was intrigued. "What kind of adventures are we in for?" she inquired.

Trent considered. "It's hard to know, since none of us happen to have a talent for seeing the future."

"But sometimes you can get a hint by checking the chapter title of the Muse of History's ongoing series on the history of Xanth, can't you? If we could glimpse the current chapter, it might save us some complications."

The Magician seemed bemused. "In theory, yes. But that presumes that she has already written the chapter. I suspect she waits until the action has been finished before describing it."

"But maybe she describes it, and then the action happens," Gloha said. "Doesn't an event have to be scripted before it can happen?"

He shrugged. "We can try." He faced the three mermaids, who inhaled in unison at that moment, perhaps coincidentally. "Can you read the title of the current chapter of the current volume of history?"

"We can try," one or more of them echoed with a winning smile. They swam together, linked hands, closed their eyes, and concentrated with perfect coordination. Their three flukes lifted and slapped the water as one.

In a moment they separated. They swam back to their ledge bank and resumed their former display. They fixed the Magician with three well-tempered gazes.

"Did you find the right volume?" he asked after a moment.

"Yes," Ash breathed fetchingly. Gloha sent half a glance of disgust to Cynthia.

"And did you read the right title?"

"Yes," Cedar agreed as the surface of the water formed a marvelously rounded decolletage. Cynthia's returning glance was tinged with envy.

"And will you tell us what it is?"

"That depends," Mahogany murmured as innocent little currents in the water managed to carry her decorative tresses away from her heaving bosom so that nothing obscured the view. Neither Gloha's nor Cynthia's glance was able to nudge those tresses back into place.

"And on what does it depend?" Trent asked, hardly seeming to be bothered by such irrelevancies as breathing or tresses.

"On how long you care to stay to hear it," Ash said, propping her chin on her right hand without interfering half a whit with the view of her left upper quarter.

"That certainly sounds like fun," the Magician said. "But I feel I should advise you that I am somewhat older than I may appear."

"We like mature males," Cedar said, her pupils alluringly large.

"In fact I am an old man, recently youthened by youth elixir."

Mahogany began to grow cautious. "How old?" The wayward currents were now carrying her hair back into place.

"Ninety-six."

All three heads descended into the water before the mermaids recovered equilibrium. They emerged with their lustrous hair somewhat matted and their expressions somewhat dissolved. "True?" Ash asked.

"True," Gloha and Cynthia said together.

The mermaids' torsos seemed to deflate. "The title is meaningless," Cedar said.

"How so?" Trent asked, seeming as oblivious of their deflation as he was of their prior inflation.

"It's just 'Xxxxxxx,' no words," Mahogany explained.

Trent shook his head. "I was afraid of this. It's like trying to inquire about Bink's talent. Something always interferes. The Muse evidently knew we would look at the title, so left it blank."

"We are so sorry you have to go so soon," Ash said.

"Yes, so sorry," Cedar agreed.

"Why couldn't you have been younger?" Mahogany asked rhetorically.

"I didn't realize I would be meeting three such intriguing females," Trent said, walking on past the pool.

"Just as well," Cynthia muttered.

Gloha could only agree.

They followed the stream onward. It wound around as if trying to lose them, but wasn't successful. Then a small mean dragon emerged from the brush. It eyed them hungrily, breathing rapidly to stoke up its fires.

"Dragon, allow me to show you something," the Magician said. He gestured at a small burr-weed that was about to stick a burr in his sock. It became a cacklebird. The bird, almost as astonished as it was dismayed, took flight without even remembering to cackle.

"Now your turn, if you wish," Trent said. He strode purposefully toward the dragon.

The dragon reversed course so suddenly it almost left its tail behind. In only part of a fraction of a moment it was gone.

"But that dragon could have given you an awful hotfoot before you got within transformation range," Gloha said.

"The aspect of confidence can be deceptive," the Magician remarked mildly.

After a time the stream changed its mind about running in gullies or valleys and diverged up into a mountain pass. But there was a suitable path through the forest which seemed interested in getting somewhere. As evening thought about setting in they found a pleasant glade. "I think we should camp for the night here," Trent said. "Perhaps tomorrow we shall reach an enchanted path and make better progress."

Then they saw a crude shelter under a nut and bolt tree, with a fire by it. "Someone else is here," Gloha said, alarmed.

"It's a centaur!" Cynthia exclaimed, quickly touching up her hair.

It turned out to be two people: a male centaur and a female human. They were glad to share their accommodations in return for some pie from the pie tree Trent made by transformation. They ate pies by the fire and agreed to exchange stories.

"I am Braille," the centaur asserted. "I have a forbidden love."

"I am Jana," the young woman confided. "I am that love."

"You met at a love spring?" Gloha asked, surprised.

"No, we just happened to get to know each other, living nearby," Jana said. "His magic talent is transcribing documents, so that those who can't read can sense their meaning. He did some work for us, and I got to know him, and I realized that no man I know was half the creature of this centaur."

"Of course intellectually I knew this was folly," Braille said. "But emotionally I found no centaur to match the qualities of Jana. The situation is distinctly awkward." He glanced at Cynthia. "I gather you are in a similar situation."

Cynthia blushed halfway between pink and red. "Oh, this man and I are not a couple! We are merely traveling together."

"Same for me," Gloha said quickly. "I am looking for a male of my kind, and Magician Trent is helping me search. Cynthia is going to join a winged centaur family."

"You're a Magician?" Jana asked, awed. "What's your talent?"

"I transform living things," Trent said. "Didn't you see me change the weed into the pie tree?"

"Oh, I thought that was all of it," she said, embarrassed. "I mean, that you made pie trees, nothing else."

"By no means. I can if you wish transform you into a centaur filly, or Braille into a human man."

The two looked at each other. "But I'm not interested in a human man!" Jana protested. "I love your centaurly qualities."

"And I love your humanly aspects," Braille said.

"We are going to ask the Good Magician for a solution to our problem," Jana said.

That did seem best.

In the morning Jana got on Braille's back and they moved smartly west. Trent, Cynthia, and Gloha proceeded north. "You know," Cynthia remarked, "I could probably carry you, Magician, in similar manner, on the ground. That might speed our progress."

"I could transform a fly to a horse and require it to carry me," Trent replied. "I haven't felt the need, unless you are in a hurry. My rationale is that you need to learn the current ways of Xanth by slow experience, and I can protect you from most hazards as long as we travel together, so time is not of the essence. I must admit, however, that I am enjoying this experience myself, as a reminder of what ordinary life is like for the young. Once I am done with my missions, I will return to my wife and friends, resume my actual age, and we shall fade away as planned. Somehow I feel less urgency about that than I did before."

"I feel similarly little urgency about settling in with strangers," Cynthia agreed. "But of course this is just a diversion from Gloha's mission, so we shouldn't delay her."

"Let's face it," Gloha said. "I'm looking for a male of my own crossbreed species, when as far as I know there isn't one. That suggests that the faster I complete my mission, the sooner I will be disappointed. I'm not in any great rush for that."

"I could transform some other male into a male of your kind," the Magician said. "That may be why Crombie pointed to me. In which case—"

"No!" Gloha cried more sharply than her caring little concern warranted. "It wouldn't be the same. Just the way Braille and Jana didn't want each other transformed. Some other creature wouldn't have grown up as a product of the harpy and goblin cultures, and wouldn't understand what it feels like. I don't want an artificial man." Yet there was a tiny little trace of doubt, for she remembered how comfortable she had felt being a flame vine or a furball or a lungfish; the sentiments of the species had come with the form. Did she really have a case?

"So it seems that none of us have much motive to hurry," Trent said. "For reasons that are sufficient for ourselves. So we might as well proceed as we have been doing until we have reason to change."

"Yes," Cynthia said. "I feel easier about that."

"So do I," Gloha agreed.

They continued roughly north, because that was the way the best path insisted on going. When anything threatened them, Trent discourage it either by drawing his sword or by transforming it to something harmless.

Then they came to a several-way fork in the path. There was a sign:

DRAW WELL   STEPPES   PIER   COM PEWTER

"I am getting thirsty," Trent said. "I would be happy to pause for fresh well water."

Cynthia and Gloha agreed. The Magician had conjured watermelons along the way, but they were ready for straight natural water.

They took that path. It led to a round stone structure whose top was a large flat panel. As they approached, a jointed stick unfolded before the panel and made rapid movements.

Trent put his hand on his sword. But the weird thing did not seem threatening. It was just doing its own thing, whatever that was. There was no sign of water.

Then Gloha realized what was happening. "It's drawing a picture!" she exclaimed.

Indeed, the thing was sketching a picture of the three of them: a human man, a winged centaur filly, and a winged goblin girl. It was an excellent group portrait done in black and white.

"It's a draw well," Cynthia said. "Just as represented."

The appendage caught the edge of the panel, and tore off a sheet of paper. It threw it aside, then commenced drawing Cynthia alone. Apparently it oriented on whoever moved or spoke, and drew a picture of that person. It didn't care what happened to its pictures; it was just interested in drawing them well.

Trent shook his head. "I would have settled for nice cold water."

The appendage ripped off the centaur picture and drew one of Trent drinking a beaded goblet of water. Gloha laughed. So naturally it drew one of her laughing. She salvaged that drawing as it got ripped off.

There was nothing to do but retrace their steps, as the path ended here. They returned to the fork and went along the STEPPES path. "Steppes are broad grassy plains with few trees, easy to travel across," Trent remarked.

But instead the path fed into an isolated mountain completely covered with stairs. Some of them were dainty small, others gigantic huge, and still others were ornate and decorated. "What's this?" Cynthia asked.

Again Gloha figured it out. "The steppes! Many steps."

"Xanth is made mostly of puns," Trent said. "We seem to have walked into a zone of them."

"I don't remember encountering this sort of thing in the North Village," Cynthia said.

Gloha glanced at her paper. She discovered to her surprise that it had changed. It was now a picture of a sleepy dull village.

"This is because the North Village has always been the staidest place in Xanth," Trent explained. "That is why we retired there. It is very conservative, with little humor and not a great amount of imagination. The wild effects are mostly elsewhere. Even Fracto finds it too boring for a storm."

"Fracto?" Cynthia asked.

"Xanth's meanest cloud," Gloha explained. "Wherever folk are having fun, Cumulo Fracto Nimbus goes to drown it out. You don't want to run afoul of him; he's not bright, but he's all wet."

Meanwhile the paper was a picture of a mean-spirited cloud gleefully raining out a picnic.

"I don't suppose that well knew what kind of adventure we're going to be having next," Gloha said.

The picture was of an assemblage of junk in a cave, with a piece of glass projecting from its center. Across the glass was printed the word CURSES.

Trent and Gloha laughed, while Cynthia looked blank. "That's Com Pewter," Trent told her. "Formerly Xanth's second worst scourge, until Lacuna tricked him into reprogramming as a nice machine. He has the power to change reality in his vicinity. But I really wasn't thinking of going there."

"So we'll have to try the pier next," Gloha said.

They returned down the path as the picture was of a lake with a dock.

They returned to the fork and took the path labeled PIER.

This led to a small lake where there was indeed a dock. But there was something odd about it. It didn't actually enter the water; instead it was along the bank. It was made of boards, and the boards did not lie still; they moved. One would jump over the others, laying itself down at the head of the line; then another would jump, getting ahead of the first. In fact they were walking by themselves, making their way around the lake.

"That's the first time I've seen a board walk," Trent said wryly. They watched the boards walk until they came to a small river entering the lake. There was a rickety little bridge across it. The boards laid themselves down on this, starting across.

"Get off there!" someone cried. "Shoo! Shoo!"

It turned out to be an ugly greenish troll. Trent's hand hovered near his sword again. "We mean no harm," he said. "We are merely looking for a fair way northwest."

The troll's head turned. "I wasn't talking to you," he said. "It's these confounded walking boards. They think they can walk all over everything. I'm trying to protect the bridge from their traffic."

"They don't seem to be doing any harm," Cynthia said.

"Well, they don't actually harm it. But it's my job to keep this bridge clear. Suppose someone came to use it, and it was all cluttered with moving boards? This would make a very bad impression."

"Where does the bridge lead?" Gloha asked.

"Nowhere. It's just there. This is a useless sinecure. But what am I to do? I'm a troll. Trolls guard bridges, and this is mine."

"Perhaps we should introduce ourselves," Trent said. "I am Magician Trent, and these are Cynthia Centaur and Gloha Goblin-Harpy. We are on a quest or two to find compatible situations."

"I am Tristan Troll. I was banished to the sticks after betraying my village. But the sticks turned out to be boards, and now I'm bored stiff."

"Bored with boards," Cynthia said. "I can appreciate that."

"How did you betray your village?" Gloha asked.

"We had a raid on a human village, and I let a little human girl go instead of bringing her in to be boiled for dinner. I was supposed to have a really bad dream for that, but Grace'l Ossein, the walking skeleton, messed it up and got in trouble herself. It was a bad scene."

"Oh, you are that troll!" Trent said. "My grandson Dolph defended Grace'l in her trial. She was found to be too nice for bad dreams, and she married Marrow Bones."

"Who?" Cynthia asked.

"Another walking skeleton from the realm of bad dreams," Gloha said. "It's a long story. He's a nice person."

"But he must be a dead person!"

"As I said, it's a long story. This is a troll we know of; he's decent, for a troll."

"Things certainly have changed! In my days trolls were all horrible."

"They still are," Gloha said. "Except for Tristan."

"Who was punished for his unbad deed," Trent reminded her. "And the troll tribe was not wrong in doing so, by the standards of its culture."

"Why don't you just walk away from this boring job?" Gloha asked the troll.

"Several reasons. For one thing, the other trolls would catch me and bring me back, or give me an even worse assignment. For another, it isn't easy for a troll to find a job. Bridges are about it. I would expire of boredom if I didn't have something useful to do."

Gloha got a glancing little glimmer of a notion. If this path went nowhere, they would have to take the next one, and fulfill the well's prediction of an encounter with Com Pewter. Meanwhile here was a decent troll with a problem. This might not be coincidence. "What would you do if you had your choice?" she asked Tristan.

"I'd like to get into one of the forward-looking bridge jobs, like information processing," Tristan said. "A bridge to knowledge. But who would pay attention to the mind of a troll?"

"So it's your mind you wish to exercise, rather than your body."

"Who would remain with a troll's body, if he had a choice?" Tristan asked rhetorically. "But of course I'm stuck with the way I am. I'm surprised that you handsome folk are even talking to me."

"Well, we're sort of having an adventure, without being in a hurry to conclude it," Gloha said. "I think we just might be able to do something nice for you."

"Don't risk it!" he said, alarmed. "Favors can become expensive."

"But sometimes worthwhile even in their expense," Trent said, glancing briefly at the two females. "What was that glib little glimmer of a notion I saw flickering through your head, Gloha?"

"That maybe Tristan could work with Com Pewter. Pewter's supposed to be a clean machine now, and maybe he could use an assistant. Someone interested in his sort of business."

"And we are going to have to take Pewter's path after all," he agreed. "That machine may no longer be evil, but he could still be mischievous. We just might be able to trade favors with him."

"We'd have to do him a favor so he would take Tristan?"

Trent smiled. "Pewter would have to do *us* a favor if we gave him Tristan."

Gloha felt her mouth forming an orotund little O. "Oh," she said.

Trent turned back to the troll. "I am a transformer. I can render you into a different shape. Then we can take you to Com Pewter and inquire whether he can use an assistant. What form would you like to assume?"

"Oh, anything would do. Even a bug."

"Very well. I shall transform you into a humbug for now,

and we can decide on a final form later." He reached toward the troll, and Tristan abruptly became a small bug.

"Now find a suitable place to ride on one of us," Trent said. "And don't fly away, because if we lose you, I will be unable to transform you again."

The bug considered. Then it hummed and flew up and perched on Gloha's hair. "Hhhummmm?" it inquired.

"That's all right," Gloha said. "I don't mind if you ride there, as long as you don't—" She hesitated, not wishing to speak of anything as dirty as bug excretion.

"Nnnummmm!" the bug hummed negatively. It wouldn't do anything like that on such nice hair.

They left the walking boards and returned once more to the fork. This time they took the path leading to Com Pewter.

It turned out to be an enchanted path, leading them almost immediately to the machine's den, though it was supposedly some distance.

But as they approached the entrance to the cave, there was a terrible shaking of the ground. "Eeek!" Cynthia screamed. "A ground quake!"

"No, I think it's the invisible giant," Trent said. "He works for the machine."

Sure enough, a monstrous footprint appeared in the ground nearby, squishing two trees and a boulder into two toothpicks and a grain of sand.

"We're going to get squished into mites!" Gloha cried, alarmed.

"I don't think so," Trent said. "His purpose is to herd clients into Pewter's cave, in case any should be hesitant. Fly up to the region of his head and tell him we're coming voluntarily."

"But I can't see his head!"

"You don't need to. Fly up until you smell his breath. His head will be in that vicinity."

Gloha flew up. So did Cynthia, who was just about as nervous about the ground near those footprints as Gloha was.

Way up above treetop range they encountered an awful

wind. Not only did it blow them off course, it smelled like a wagonload of cabbage that had sickened and died before managing to rot. The humbug on Gloha's head coughed and choked.

"I think we've found his breath," Cynthia gasped, her hair blowing out sideways from her head as if trying to flee the odor. "I'm losing control." She glided erratically away. Fortunately she was able to recover somewhat as she got out of the wind; Gloha saw her gliding safely back down toward the forest.

Gloha nerved herself, held her neat little nose, and flew into the putrid breeze. She had a smaller nose than Cynthia did, so it didn't take in as much of the stench. When she banged into an invisible cable she grabbed onto it. This was a strand of the giant's hair. She worked her way down to an ear. "Hey, don't step on us!" she shouted. "We're coming to see Com Pewter anyway!"

"OOOOGAA!" the giant responded deafeningly.

"Pump down the volume!" Gloha screamed.

"What did you say?" the giant whispered.

"I said that we're coming to see Com Pewter anyway," she shouted. "So you shouldn't step on us."

"Okay." There was a stir as something huge moved. He was turning his head. "Say, you're a pretty little creature."

"Thank you," she gasped.

"But your nose is swollen."

"That's because I can barely breathe."

"Why is that? Are you ill?"

Gloha pondered perhaps five of her moments, but only a quarter of a giant moment. She decided to tell the truth. "It's your breath," she shouted. "It's awful."

"That's nothing. You should smell my cousin's breath. It can knock over an ogre at fifty paces."

"Well, I'll go away now, so I can recover," Gloha said. But then, so as not to be impolite, she introduced herself. "I'm Gloha Goblin-Harpy."

"I'm Greatbow," he replied. "Nice to meet you."

Gloha couldn't honestly express pleasure at encountering the giant, so she evaded the issue by asking a question. "Why is your cousin's breath so bad?"

"My cousin Graeboe? He's ailing. He has some sickness. He's even turned visible, which means he's not much longer for happy stomping."

"How horrible," Gloha said. "Well, I must be gone." She let herself drop, which wasn't at all difficult at this point. Only when she got down near the trees did her breathing begin to clear. Surely a person could not blame the giants for being as big in odor as they were in person, but the dialogue had been a strain. She had at least accomplished her purpose: the giant was no longer stomping. They should now be able to enter the cave safely.

Cynthia had reached the ground, and joined Trent at the mouth of the cave. "I'm so sorry I couldn't stay up there," Cynthia called as Gloha glided in. "I just couldn't—"

"I understand," Gloha said. "Maybe my experience with goblins and harpies gave me strength to endure it. Or maybe my smallness enabled me to take smaller breaths."

Trent and Cynthia exchanged a generous glance. "Or perhaps your spirit is larger than your body," Trent said. "Shall we tackle the next incidental challenge?"

Gloha felt a chill, though she had been in a sweat when bathed in the giant's breath. Just how safe was this venture? "I suppose, if there is no other path."

They entered the dark cave. There was just enough light for them to see the one route forward into the mountain. Com Pewter was supposed to be a nice machine now, but his record as an evil machine was much longer, and Gloha had, if not a doubt, certainly a qualm.

They came to a chamber with a collection of junk on the floor. One pane of glass was propped up in the center. WELCOME, USERS appeared on that surface.

Trent strode forward to stand over it. "I am Magician Trent; perhaps you know of me."

YOU CAN'T TRANSFORM INANIMATE CREA-
TURES, the screen said, flickering worriedly.

Trent smiled. "I have not come to quarrel with you, Com-
mie. The only viable path led here, so I thought I would pay
you a call. If you don't attempt to change my reality un-
pleasantly, I won't transform this creature to a sphinx who
will sit on you." He indicated Gloha.

AGREED. The screen brightened with surprise. YOU
LOOK YOUNG, MAGICIAN.

"Youth elixir subtracted seventy years. I will return to my
real age when this mission is done."

WHO ELSE IS WITH YOU?

"Gloha Goblin-Harpy, whom I am helping to find her
ideal man. Cynthia Centaur, whom I transformed some time
ago, and am now escorting to the single winged centaur
family of Xanth. And Tristan Troll, whom I have transformed to a bug."

A BUG! the screen printed, alarmed. DON'T LET IT
NEAR MY PROGRAM.

Trent nodded. "As I remember, you have been known to
have a problem with a virus. I can appreciate your caution.
But I come not to bury you but to do you a favor."

I DON'T BELIEVE IN FAVORS.

Gloha was impressed. It was evident that the machine was
quite wary of the Magician, and there were surely very few
people or creatures in Xanth who commanded such respect.

"Naturally I expect a return favor," Trent continued
smoothly.

OH. NOW YOU ARE MAKING SENSE. WHAT DO
YOU WANT?

"Nothing difficult. Merely a clear, pleasant, and safe path
from here to the residence of Cheiron Centaur."

The screen dimmed a moment as Com Pewter pondered.
THERE IS ONE TO WHICH I CAN DIRECT YOU. IT
CROSSES THE GAP CHASM VIA THE INVISIBLE
BRIDGE AND PAUSES AT THE RESIDENCE OF
GRUNDY GOLEM. WILL THIS BE SATISFACTORY?

"Certainly. Grundy isn't much, but his wife Rapunzel is delightful."

WHAT RETURN FAVOR DO YOU OFFER?

"It happens that Tristan Troll is a thoughtful and decent creature, unlike many of his kind, who seeks employment as an information processor. It occurred to me that you could use an assistant."

I DON'T WANT A TROLL! THE LAST ONE I ENCOUNTERED TOOK MY WHEATSTONE BRIDGE.

"Well, perhaps if he had another form. Such as a cat—"

NO.

"Or perhaps a mouse."

The screen blinked. A MOUSE!

Trent shrugged. "Of course if you're not interested, he could be a spring chicken."

THE MOUSE WILL DO!

Gloha stifled a laugh. Spring chickens were notorious for aging rapidly and ceasing to be attractive. They were almost like harpies in that respect. But what would Pewter want with a mouse?

Trent reached toward Gloha. The humbug jumped from her head to his hand. Then it became a cute mouse. Trent set the mouse down before the screen. It ran around, and the path of its motion was traced by a line on the screen.

AH, YES, PERFECT: YES. ~~NO~~.

"Now if you care to show us the path," Trent suggested.

WATCH THE MOUSE.

And the mouse ran to the wall—where there was an opening Gloha had not seen before. She could almost have sworn it hadn't been there a moment ago, but of course she was a nice girl who would never swear.

They entered the new passage. The mouse sat up and squeaked. Gloha squatted down. "Thank you, Tristan," she said. "I hope you are happy here." She extended one finger to stroke his head.

"Just exactly what does a mouse have to do with a funny machine?" Cynthia inquired as they moved on.

"I understand it is very useful in helping people relate to the machine, perhaps because they prefer to have a living interface," Trent said. "With a mouse, much more information can be processed in a simpler way. It's a special kind of magic that few in Xanth understand, but I knew that Pewter would. Of course there are those who don't like mice, with or without a machine. That won't bother Pewter; he'll be happy to have his mouse spook them, while remaining nominally nice."

Now Gloha understood better. Pewter surely wasn't happy having to be nice all the time. Now he could be nasty while seeming nice.

The tunnel led directly out of the mountain—and there before them was the great gulf of the Gap Chasm. "So soon?" Gloha asked, astonished, as they peered down on the top of a small cloud that happened to be slumming.

"Com Pewter changes reality in his vicinity," Trent reminded her. "He gave us a direct path."

"He certainly did!" She was almost disappointed, because she was rather enjoying this journey with Cynthia and wasn't eager for it to end quickly.

Trent followed the path to the brink and put one foot cautiously over the edge. "Yes, it's here," he said, and walked out into air.

"Eeeek!" Cynthia screamed, jamming a good four *e*'s into her ek.

"It's the invisible bridge," Gloha reminded her.

"I thought that was a joke."

"I believe it was built after your time," Trent said cheerily from midair.

Cynthia flew near him and reached out to touch the invisible structure. "It's there!" she exclaimed. "It's really there."

"All the same, I'll fly across," Gloha said. "The troll's bridge and invisible giant were bad enough; I don't need to trust an invisible bridge."

"Me too," Cynthia agreed. "I'm glad for my wings." Then, suffering a second thought, she added: "Thanks to you, Magician. I would no longer be comfortable as a human maiden, or even a regular centaur. What made you choose this form for me?"

"You were so pretty, I didn't want to spoil it. But I didn't want you joining the centaurs, who can be as difficult as straight human folk. It was a spur-of-the-moment compromise. He glanced up at her as she hovered close by. "I think it was a good decision, given the exigencies of the moment. I would not do such a thing today, but I believe you remain as pretty as you were then."

Cynthia blushed again. She flew on ahead, so as to hide her face. Gloha knew why: Cynthia still found the Magician insidiously attractive. Gloha understood the feeling, because she felt that attraction herself. She had been trying to deny it, but it would not be denied. But like Cynthia, she would not care to be transformed to a full human woman, even if the Magician were interested in her, or unmarried, or actually as young as he looked. She liked her own form too well. But it didn't stop her half-witted little heart from having naughty little notions.

Trent completed his crossing. Gloha was relieved; she knew the invisible bridge was sturdy, but it was still easy to imagine him plummeting into the chasm. Perhaps if she had gotten on the bridge herself, and kept her hands on the handrails, she would have had more confidence. That was another reason she never wanted to be without wings: the groundbound human form was so limited by mountains and chasms.

The way led north through the forest. Now that they had crossed the bridge, she knew it was an enchanted path, free from menace by dragons, griffins, basilisks, mean men, and other ilk. That was a relief; she hoped never to meet an ilk. But she had to admit that their small encounters along the other route had been interesting. Maybe they would have been less so if there hadn't been a Magician along to protect the innocent maidens. Yet they wouldn't have had to stay down on the ground if he hadn't been along, so wouldn't have needed protection. So her impressions were sort of mixed up.

Soon they came to a giant club stuck endwise in the ground, the thorny business end up. As they came close, it quivered, as if about to lift itself up and take a swing at them. The thing was so massive that a single blow would crush any of them.

"Does the enchantment still hold?" Gloha asked in a nervous whisper.

"It should," Trent said. "But sometimes there are flaws in the magic, and something gets through. It is best not to take any threat for granted."

"Let me fly by it first; I don't think it could move fast enough to hit me," she said. "If it comes out of the ground and chases me, then we'll know."

"I'll agree only if you fly along the path. The club may be dangerous to anything that strays off the path, and merely threaten whoever passes on it."

"That would make sense," Cynthia said. "It might make a feint, scaring someone off the path. Then it could smash that poor person, because the enchantment doesn't extend beyond the path. The enchantment can't protect someone from foolishness."

Trent nodded. "That's probably its ploy. So if we simply refuse to react, we'll be safe. Nevertheless, I think you had better test it. If it actually strikes in the pathway, I'll transform Cynthia into a giantess who can grab it by the handle and tame it."

Gloha flew swiftly by the club, while the Magician and centaur waited behind. The club quivered, working its way out of the ground, about to take off.

"Gloha!" someone cried.

Gloha spun around in the air, looking back. There was a tiny man standing on top of the club. "Grundy!" she called back. "What are you doing here?"

"I'm home. This is my clubhouse. Don't worry; it doesn't bother friends. I came out the moment it started to shake." He tapped his foot on the wood. "At ease, house. Gloha's okay." The club stopped moving.

"You had better introduce it to my friends, too," Gloha said, indicating Trent and Cynthia.

Grundy turned to look. "A winged centaur!" he exclaimed. "But she's too young to be Chex."

"Actually she's older than Chex," Gloha said. "Remember, Chex is only a year older than I am. She matured rapidly."

Grundy squinted. "Still, this one looks only about sixteen."

"She was delivered in the year 1005."

"She's eighty-eight years old? You're pulling my little leg, harpy-wings. Next you're going to tell me that young man beside her is ninety-six!"

"Right. He's Magician Trent."

"Sure, and let's see him transform something."

Trent squatted and pointed to an ant on the path. Suddenly it became a gi-ant, a humongous creature the size of a unicorn. It looked around as if startled to see the world become so much smaller, vibrated its antennae, and made ready to chomp someone with its mandibles.

Trent transformed it to a pink bunny. The bunny hopped toward the forest.

"That's not nice," someone called. "Change it back to its natural form before it gets lost and hurt."

Trent went after the bunny and transformed it back into a small ant.

"That's Magician Trent, all right," Grundy agreed. "But what's he doing so young, and with you folk?"

"He's helping me find my ideal man," Gloha explained. "And the centaur is Cynthia, whom he transformed long ago; she's been in the Brain Coral's pool until now."

"So she's not really all that old!" Grundy said. "She was in suspended animation."

"Yes. Now we're taking her to join the winged centaur family."

The golem nodded. "But she's a bit old for Che."

"Magician Trent has some more youth elixir."

"Gotcha." Grundy looked around. "I heard my wife a

moment ago—ah, there she is. Come on out, dear, and meet these folk."

The tiny woman came out of the tiny door in the clubhouse. Suddenly she was full human size, with a head of dark hair that reached to the ground and then some, turning brown, red, blond, and eventually white on the way, despite being braided and bound. She was lovely in a dress covered with ads for places and things.

Grundy jumped down to her extended hand. "My wife Rapunzel, wearing her address," he introduced. "I call her the hairy monster."

Rapunzel lifted him to her face, made as if to bite his tiny head off, and kissed his face instead—his whole face at once.

"One of these days she's going to be inhaling when she does that, and I'll be gone," Grundy said ruefully.

Rapunzel shook hands with them all. Then she reached to the clubhouse again. "Let me introduce our daughter, Surprise," she said.

A figure even smaller than Grundy came to the doorway and stepped into Rapunzel's hand, joining Grundy. "Here she is," he said proudly. "Delivered by surprise six months ago." He turned to the child. "Say hi to the nice folk, kid."

"Hi, nice folk," the girl said.

Gloha's jarred little jaw dropped. So did Cynthia's. "I thought you said she was six months old," Gloha said.

"That isn't what he said," Rapunzel said, smiling. "He said she was delivered six months ago."

"But she's talking!"

"Yes, she talks a lot," Rapunzel agreed. "She's five years old."

Even Trent looked startled at this. "How can she be that old, only half a year after being delivered?"

"It was a surprise," Grundy admitted. "So we named her—"

"That I think I understand," Trent said. "Still—"

"We think the stork got lost on the way," Rapunzel explained. "We had ordered her some time ago, and kept expecting her, but somehow she never arrived. Then, when we least expected it, there she was. The stork didn't speak to us; he just flew quickly away, as if greatly relieved."

Trent shook his head, acting for all of them. "I thought I had seen some unusual things in my day, but this does surprise me. Does she have a talent?"

Grundy and Rapunzel exchanged several fragments of a glance. "Not exactly," Grundy said, looking uncomfortable.

"Talent!" the tiny child exclaimed. Suddenly she was full human child sized, with a sweet smile and a headful of curly black hair. Rapunzel had to set her quickly on the ground, almost spilling Grundy in the process.

"Size changing!" Gloha exclaimed. "How nice. But of course it must run in the family."

"Not exactly," Rapunzel said with the same uncomfortable look Grundy had had a moment before. "We don't like to mention it, because—"

"Not mention a fine talent like that?" Gloha asked. "But why not?"

"Talent!" Surprise repeated. Suddenly her hair was growing. It curled down around her shoulders, turning dark brown. It extended to her waist, becoming light brown. Then it reached to her knees, becoming red. Finally it touched her feet, blond.

Rapunzel quickly gathered it up before it could drag in the dirt. She borrowed several pins from her own tresses to fasten it in place, while the child played idly with a pebble she found on the ground.

"*Two?*" Gloha asked. "I thought no one in Xanth had that!"

"Well, one may not be a—I mean, both these things take after her mother, sort of," Grundy said.

"But that's still amazing! Maybe she does have two talents."

"Talent!" Surprise said a third time, evidently picking it up from their discussion. She held up the pebble—and it became a dragon's tooth.

This time Trent's jaw dropped as far as the others' did. "Shape-changing of objects!" he said. "A third—" He cut himself off as both parents looked about to faint.

"This *is* a surprise," Gloha said. "How many—whatevers—does she have?"

"Just one, we think," Grundy said. "One at a time, that is. We never know ahead of time which one it will be."

"Or whether we've seen it before," Rapunzel added. "It's very unnerving."

Gloha appreciated the situation. "I can see why you named her Surprise."

"Surprise!" the child cried, and vanished.

This time the jaws of Grundy and Rapunzel dropped. "Oops," he said.

"This is a new one," she said.

"Is she invisible, or elsewhere?" he asked.

Rapunzel reached out to where the little girl had been standing. "Invisible," she said with relief.

"She never acted up in company before," Grundy said, looking wary.

"Perhaps we are a disruptive influence," Trent said diplomatically. "We have to move on anyway."

"Yes, we should reach the winged centaur family by nightfall," Gloha said. Actually they had no schedule, and weren't rushing it, but if they were inciting Surprise to mischief, they needed to depart quickly, before anything really bad happened.

"Nightfall!" the childish voice cried happily. Suddenly it was night. Not blackness, but actual night: the stars were shining down.

"Farewell," Trent said, somewhat hollowly. "We'll just shoot on out of here along the path. The stars give us enough light."

"Shoot! Star!"

One of the stars moved from its place in the sky. It came swiftly toward them, leaving a trail of light behind. "Did somebody say my name?" it demanded. "I'll plug him dead!" A bolt of thin lightning zapped out.

"All we needed," Trent muttered. "A shooting star."

"With an attitude," Gloha agreed.

"I think it's cute," Cynthia said.

The star paused, brightening. "You do? Well now." It shot back to its place, pleased.

Before long the region turned reddish-dawn-colored, and then the light of the day returned. They paused and looked back. They were still on the path, having felt its smooth surface underfoot, and nothing was threatening them. But behind was the black blob of night, covering the clubhouse and its neighborhood.

"That child will be a handful," Trent muttered. "That's at least five talents she's shown, and some border on Magician class. I wish we could help them, but I think they'll just have to work things out themselves."

"Yes," Gloha agreed. It hadn't occurred to her that a strong talent could be a problem. But that child had too much talent at too young an age; she had learned how to invoke it, erratically, but lacked the responsibility that went with such magic.

They followed the path north, and in a surprisingly short time came to a pleasant glade with a large thatch cottage in the shape of a stall. Before it was an anvil where horseshoes might be hammered. Com Pewter had been true to his part of the bargain, giving them a direct route to the centaur residence. It probably would have taken a lot longer, and been much more difficult, otherwise.

Trent paused, turning to Cynthia. "I think now is the time to use the Fountain of Youth elixir Magician Humfrey gave me."

Cynthia looked doubtful. "I don't want to deceive anyone, especially centaurs. I'm really not a child."

"You're really not sixteen, either," he pointed out. "In Xanth, appearance counts for most of reality. We are not going to deceive anyone. We'll simply adjust your age as appropriate to the situation."

Still she hesitated. "My body may be young, but my mind will still be almost seventeen. I wouldn't blame them for objecting to that."

"My mind is ninety-six," he said evenly. "Has that bothered you?"

"Oh, no! You have been marvelously knowledgeable and helpful."

"Were I really twenty-six, I doubt I would have acted always with propriety, especially when you uncovered your upper torso, or when you were kissing me back to warmth. There are advantages of age and experience."

"I suppose," she agreed uncertainly. "Too bad you weren't really that age. I might have given you man thoughts to match my woman thoughts."

Trent's lips pursed, but he managed to ignore the remark. He turned to Gloha. "We seem to have a difference here. What do you say?"

"I think you should youthen her, and let the centaurs decide. If they don't want her, she can stay with us."

"But I'll be nine years old!" Cynthia protested.

"Your mind will be sixteen."

"It's not the same."

Trent shrugged. "Then let's meet the family now, and use the elixir later, if it seems warranted."

"Yes," Cynthia said, relieved.

They went to the house. Trent knocked on the door, which was double, opening in the middle and hinged at the outsides, as with a barn. A woman's face appeared in the window panel, looking surprised. Then the door opened. A mature winged centaur filly stood there, magnificently barebreasted. "I recognize Gloha," she said. "but not the man or the—oh, my!" For now she had seen Cynthia's wings.

"Chex, I am Magician Trent, youthened for the time being. I am accompanying Gloha on her quest to find her ideal man.

This is Cynthia, whom I transformed to this form in my youth. She has been in the Brain Coral's pool since. She—"

"She wanted to meet the only other winged centaurs in Xanth!" Chex said. "Oh, I'm so sorry she isn't younger!" Then she put her hand to her mouth, embarrassed. "I shouldn't have said that. It's just that—"

"Why would you want her younger?" Trent inquired, as if merely curious.

"I had this foolish notion—our foal Che—it was a wild presumption, for which I apologize. I was just so startled to see another winged centaur."

Trent didn't even need to swap glances with Cynthia. "We have some youth elixir. She can readily become a decade younger, physically."

"But why? She's already been through her childhood. She would hardly want to do it again."

"She might, if she could be with her own kind."

Chex looked at Cynthia. "You were human, before you were transformed?"

"Yes," Cynthia said. "I was sixteen. I've been a centaur less than a year, in living time. I learned to fly. But I was the only one of my kind. The real centaurs—they—" She clouded up, evidently suffering an unpleasant memory.

Chex stepped quickly forward. She put an arm about Cynthia's shoulders. "I know the feeling. They reject crossbreeds. Even my own grandsire and granddam refused to associate with me, at first. If you would like to join us—"

"Yes!"

"Do you know centaur lore?"

"I'm afraid I really don't," Cynthia said, abashed.

"Would you be willing to learn it? It would take several years. You see, a human being of your age is the equivalent of a centaur of eight or nine, intellectually. Our foal Che is eight."

"I want very much to learn it."

"Che isn't here now; he's at Goblin Mountain. We—" Chex looked momentarily pensive. "We miss the children."

Cynthia looked at Trent. He held out the tiny vial of elixir. She took it, opened it, and gulped down its few drops of liquid.

Suddenly she was a physical eight year old. The dose had halved her age. In a unicorn that would have been full grown, but centaurs paralleled humans, and she was half grown. Her jacket hung baggily on her. "Oh!" she exclaimed faintly. "I didn't realize it would be so quick."

"First centaur lesson," Chex said. "You don't need clothing, unless the weather requires it. As you see, I have no concern about exposing my body." She helped the filly remove the material. In a moment Cynthia stood bare. Her formerly ample breasts had vanished, leaving her human section boylike, but they would grow again in due course. Her hair had dwindled into a ponytail.

"I think our business here is done," Trent said.

"I guess it is," Gloha agreed. She flew up to give Cynthia a parting hug, for the centaur child was now just about the height of a grown goblin girl. "Maybe we'll meet again soon."

"Oh, I hope so!" the young Cynthia agreed. "We have known each other for half of my life."

Gloha had to laugh through her tears. The statement was perhaps technically correct in a way that most others would not understand. Cynthia had lost half the age she had been during their acquaintance. Then they separated.

Cynthia looked at Trent. There was something in her demeanor that suggested that she had not entirely forgotten her adult feelings, but she did not speak. Gloha remembered Jana and Braille Centaur, for some irrelevant reason.

The Magician pretended to be oblivious. "Farewell, centaur filly," he said.

"Thank you—for whatever," she replied.

Chex led Cynthia into the house. The door closed. Gloha knew that this clean break was best. She turned resolutely away. There would be other times. Meanwhile she had her own quest to fulfill.

6

MARROW

They walked back the way they had come, away from the house. Gloha saw Cynthia's hoofprints and blinked back tears of nostalgia. It had been only an interim episode, but she liked the winged centaur filly and missed her already.

"This isn't the same path," Trent remarked.

"But it has to be, because we're retracing our steps."

"The scenery's different. We're no longer on Com Pewter's magically direct route. See, there's a volcano."

"A what?"

"A mountain that magically catches fire and dumps its ashes all around." He gestured, indicating the oddity.

She looked, and saw it. The thing was cone-shaped, with smoke issuing from its narrow tip. As she watched, it belched out a cloud, and the cloud spread out and settled across the landscape. Gray particles drifted down like snow. She put out a hand to catch one. Sure enough, it was a bit of ash. "Marvelous," she said.

"That depends on the volcano's attitude. If it doesn't like us passing too close, we'll have to find another path."

"But we don't want to leave the enchanted path. We wouldn't be safe then."

"We may not be safe now," he said. "This may no longer be an enchanted path."

That seemed odd to her. "Let's follow it anyway. If it gets dangerous, then we can look for another."

"I can't transform an inanimate threat," he reminded her. "I would be helpless against that mountain, if it got angry."

"Then we'll just have to hope it doesn't get angry," she said, hardly concerned. Imagine a mountain with a temper!

The mountain rumbled warningly. More smoke plumed from its top. But Gloha still couldn't take it seriously. Mountains were inanimate, after all; they couldn't have feelings. They couldn't resent anyone passing close to them. Maybe stones had personalities when King Dor talked to them, but a mountain was a feature of the landscape. So the rumble was coincidence.

"I think this is Mount Pin-A-Tuba," Trent said. "I heard of it once. When it gets mad, it breathes out so much ash and vapor that it shades the whole of Xanth so the sun can't get through, and the land cools."

"What a weird name for a mountain," she remarked.

The path was headed right to the base of the volcano. Trent was right: this wasn't the way they had come. Cynthia's hoofprints no longer showed. The way had magically changed. With magic, anything could happen, but this was slightly strange. She must have spent too much time in the air, so had never become properly familiar with the routes of the land. Of course she could fly away at any time, but Trent couldn't so it was easiest just to stay aground.

There was another rumble, and more smoke. This time the ground itself shook. It did seem as if the mountain were reacting like an irritable sphinx. Yet that had to be her imagination.

"I don't like this," Trent muttered.

"Could you transform a creature into something that could carry us swiftly past it?"

He looked around. "There don't seem to be any living creatures or plants within range." Indeed, the region was covered by a layer of gray ash, like off-color snow.

"Then maybe transform me into a roc bird, and I'll carry you over it."

"That would be even more dangerous. I believe that mountain dislikes big birds, and fires hot boulders at them with unpleasant accuracy."

There was a larger rumble. A boulder shot out of the mountain's mouth. It arced high through the sky, and landed with a thunk to the side. More and thicker smoke poured out, blotting out much of the sky. The ashfall became stronger. Ash was getting in her hair and coating her wings. She was increasingly uncomfortable.

"I guess you're right," she said. "We'd better go back and find another path."

"It may be too late for that." It was unusual to see him so gloomy.

"Let's hurry," she said, as yet another rumble built up inside the mountain, getting ready to come out.

They turned and started away from the volcano. But the rumble only built up power and vigor, and burst forth in a cloud of swirling black smoke. The day darkened, and ash descended so thickly it was hard to see and breathe.

They tried to run, but the ground shook so violently that it was hard to keep their footing. Gloha spread her wings to fly, but hot ash came down to burn them speck by speck and feather by feather, and gusts of hot wind threatened to blow her away. She quickly folded them again, so as to minimize exposure. She was stuck on the ground, for now.

Then a boulder crashed into the path ahead, gouging out a crater. "It's got our range," Trent said.

"Oh, I'm sorry I didn't listen to you before!" she cried with a certain dismal little dismay.

"I didn't think it would be this bad. We'll have to change

our course erratically, so it can't catch us." He dodged off
the path to the side, running through the thickening layer of
ash. His forming tracks were almost immediately covered
by newly falling ash.

Gloha followed. The swirling winds buffeted her, and the
gloom and ash almost made her lose sight of him. Then he
ducked back and caught her by the wrist. "I can transform
you to something safe, at least," he said.

"But that won't help *you*!" she protested.

"Maybe I don't deserve help."

"What?" she demanded, appalled.

"Never mind. Just keep clear of falling boulders."

She didn't need to worry about that, as he was hauling
her along, preventing her from getting lost in the terrible ash
storm. "Why don't you deserve it?"

"Because I was reacting in a manner unbecoming for my
age and marital status."

"What are you talking about?" Another shower of ash
came down, but most of it missed them. The volcano
couldn't catch them as long as they kept moving erratically.
"You have behaved perfectly throughout."

"I wanted to transform Cynthia back into a human
woman."

So he had not been impervious to her interest! Gloha, half
human herself, though without a human parent, had understood enough of Cynthia's feelings to perhaps comprehend
Trent's. More than enough! "Handsome and pretty people
find each other attractive," she yelled over the ash wind.
"It's what they do that counts."

"Not what they feel?"

She found she couldn't debate that. "Maybe there is some
guilt. But you did the right thing. You maybe wronged her
when you transformed her to a winged centaur, but you
righted her when you didn't change her back. She'll be
happy now, with her new kind. And I just know Che Centaur will like her, when he meets her. Maybe you are help-

ing him to achieve his destiny, which is to change the history of Xanth."

"Perhaps," he said, seeming slightly more positive.

She had reassured him. But it was odd, because he had surely had many times her total experience with male/female interest, in his life that was five times as long as hers. He had been married twice, and had at least one child. He had to know volumes about love and passion. How could her limited perspective help him in any way?

There was a series of boomings behind them. Mount Pin-A-Tuba was sounding off almost musically. But it wasn't musical business; Gloha knew that it was spitting out more boulders and ash. If they didn't get out of its range quickly, one of those rocks might score.

"Well, now."

Gloha looked. There was a swirl of smoke that wasn't quite like that of the mountain. "Metria!"

"You mortals have a funny idea of entertainment," the demoness observed.

"We are not amused," Trent said. "We're trying to get out of range of the volcano."

"You can't," Metria said confidently. "You'd do better to get under cover."

"If I thought you knew of any close cover, I'd ask you," Trent said contemptuously. His urbane manner was deteriorating under the pressure of this threat that was beyond his ability to handle. For the first time she was seeing him unguarded. For what obscure reason she couldn't fathom, she found she liked him better for it.

"I do too know of it," the demoness retorted, becoming smoky and getting her vapors riled.

"I don't believe it," he said. Gloha was appalled; why was he vexing the demoness right when they needed her help?

"Right in the next unclean," Metria said.

Suddenly Gloha caught on. The demoness meant to tease

them, but Trent was making her give them the information. "The next what?" she asked.

"Dirty, smirch, sully, violate reputation, character assassination—"

"Defile?" Trent asked.

"Whatever," Metria said crossly, fading into the swirling ash.

"We must find that sully," Trent said. "I mean gully." He forged on, still hauling Gloha along. She felt his male man strength as she practically flew behind him, but his grip on her arm was not painful; he was being careful not to hurt her despite his aggravation. This, too, impressed her.

"But a gully will just fill up faster with ash," Gloha protested. "And boulders will roll down into it."

"Metria always speaks the truth, in her fashion," he replied. "There's shelter of some sort nearby. We just have to find it."

"I hope so," she agreed weakly.

They crossed a rise, but the depression beyond seemed to be filled only with more choking smoke and the sound of falling rocks.

Then she saw something. She blinked, trying to get her aching little eyes clear of ash dust. "I think I saw a house made of bones," she said.

"Must be the remains of an animal who perished here," Trent said.

"Must be. Maybe I'm hallucinating."

"Where did you see it?"

"Over there." She pointed blindly.

He leaned into the awful wind and tramped in that direction. Suddenly he stopped. "You're right! A bone house!"

"Please don't tease me," she begged. "I'm already miserable enough."

He moved forward again. Abruptly the bones loomed close. There really was such a house!

"Anybody home?" Trent called.

A door opened. A skeleton stood there. "Flesh folk!" it exclaimed.

"Marrow Bones," Trent said. "It must be you. I'm Magician Trent, and this is Gloha Goblin-Harpy. We need shelter."

"Then come in," Marrow said. He extended a bone-hand to help. In a moment they were both inside, and the tumult of the flying ash cut off as the door closed.

Gradually Gloha's eyes watered clear, and she got a good look at the interior of the house. It really was made of bones. They were so cunningly fitted together, and so securely bound with tendon, that the walls and roof were ash-tight. The demoness had been right: this was the cover they had needed.

"Thank you, Marrow," Trent said. "It is fortunate for us that your dwelling was here."

"What are you two fleshy creatures doing in a fleshless region like this?" the skeleton inquired.

"Gloha is on a quest to find her ideal man, and I'm helping her."

"That is nice of you." The skull angled, the eye sockets peering at him. "I must say you look younger than I expected. Aren't you Prince Dolph's grandfather?"

"I am. I am old, but under the influence of youth elixir at the moment. I appreciated the way you helped him on his quest to find the Good Magician, even if he succeeded only in getting himself betrothed to two girls at once."

"He was young," Marrow said. "The young can have maladjustments of emotion."

"So can the rejuvenated," Trent murmured.

"But he had excellent magic," the skeleton continued. "Similar in respect to yours, I believe."

"Yes. I am proud of my grandson, and of my granddaughter, the Sorceress Ivy."

"What are you doing here, Marrow?" Gloha asked. "I thought you had a family now."

"I do, I do," the skeleton agreed. "I married Grace'l Ossein, and we have two little bone-buckets, Joy'nt and Picka Bone. But I do not have a soul, and without it I shall shortly fade away, for I am a creature of the dream realm. So I agreed to participate in the demons' Game of Companions if they would give me some indication how I could acquire a soul. I was not selected to be a Companion, but for my service the Demon Professor Grossclout told me that though my head lacked even mush, I might acquire half a soul if I camped beside the volcano long enough. So while I waited here, I foraged for animal bones and made this house, because I didn't like being constantly pelted with pieces of ash. Do you happen to know how I might acquire half a soul?"

Trent considered. "I have heard of the Demon Grossclout. He's so arrogantly intelligent that not even many demons can stand him. But he always knows what he's talking about. I suspect he meant that you could get half a soul from some mortal passerby. I would offer you half of mine, as they normally regenerate if properly treated, but it is so old and withered that I fear the halves would fall apart and do neither of us any good."

"I suppose you could have half of mine," Gloha said doubtfully. "Does it hurt to lose half your soul?"

"It does not," Marrow said. "But I couldn't take yours. It would serve only briefly, because you are female. I need half a young, vital male soul, if it is to be healthy.

"Then we do not seem to be the ones you have been waiting for," Trent said. "Yet your presence here has helped us, and we appreciate it, and would like to repay the favor. Is there any way to do that?"

"I don't think so. Your kind and mine do not have a great deal in common. But I thank you for the offer."

"Maybe there is a way," Gloha said. "Maybe what the Demon Professor meant is that if you were here, and you helped someone, that person would then help you to find a soul somewhere else."

"This is possible," Marrow agreed, surprised. "Certainly this region seems inhospitable to souled folk."

"So maybe you should come with us, and along the way there will be a chance for your own quest," she said. "At least it's worth a try."

"Perhaps it is," the skeleton said. "If you do not object to my company."

"Any friend of my grandson's a friend of mine," Trent said.

"And you are a friend of Chex Centaur too, aren't you?" Gloha asked. "It seems to me I heard something like that."

"We have interacted compatibly on occasion," Marrow agreed with gaunt conservatism.

"Then let's travel together, at least until you find a suitable lead on getting half-souled." Gloha was a small little wee bit surprised at herself for making the offer, because she had never before associated with a walking skeleton. But she was still in the early pangs of loneliness after losing Cynthia Centaur as a companion, and she knew that Marrow had not merely been a companion for Prince Dolph, he had been a truly good and dedicated adult at a time when a nine-year-old boy really needed guidance. Gloha had encountered Prince Dolph often enough in the interim, being the same age, and had had the story from him. It should even be fun, because the skeletons had unusual powers that could be quite helpful at times, especially to an already groundbound companion.

"Is there any living thing here?" Trent inquired, combing the last ash out of his hair.

"Only a bone flea, which I have been unable to eject," Marrow said. "I try to let living things be, but I must confess that bone fleas make me nervous."

"How could a flea hurt you, when you have no flesh?" Gloha inquired.

"A bone flea eats bone," Marrow explained. "It tries to drill into the center, where my marrow-essence is, and gorge on that. Without my marrow, I would fade immediately away from this realm. I find the prospect uncomfortable."

"Then you won't mind if I transform that flea to something else?" Trent inquired.

"I should be most satisfied to see it transformed."

"Where is it?"

Marrow pointed a bone-finger to a slightly chewed section of the bone wall. There was a tiny creature chomping blithely away.

Trent moved his hand close to the flea. Suddenly there was a fair-sized pot pie bush, growing from a pot, bearing a steamingly ripe pie. "Oh, wonderful!" Gloha exclaimed, realizing how hungry she had become. "But it looks too hot for us to touch."

"I have utensils," Marrow said. He produced several long thin bone slivers. "I chopped these up to use to seal crevices, but they may also be serviceable for your purpose."

"Ah, chopsticks," Trent agreed. He took two and held them with the fingers of one hand.

"You can eat with those?" Gloha asked, perplexed.

"With a little practice, so can you," Trent said. "Marrow, if you will be so kind as to harvest that pot pie and set it on your table for us, we shall dine."

Marrow plucked the hot pot pie with his bare fingerbones and set it on his bone table. Trent drew up a bone chair, and Gloha, being much smaller and lighter, perched on the edge of the table, the other side of the pie.

"Thus," Trent said, demonstrating with his chopsticks. He poked into the pie and brought out a chunk of something that looked and smelled good, pinned between the two ends. He lifted it to his mouth.

Gloha took up two suitably sized bone slivers and tried to hold them the way he did. When she moved them, they flipped out of her less than gainly little grasp. She tried again, and began to get part of the hang of it. In due course she was able to spear a chunk of vegetable.

So they shared the pie. Trent ate most of it, because he was far more massive, but Gloha had all she wanted.

It had gotten dark. Marrow started a bone fire with some otherwise useless bone fragments. Its light and warmth were small, but the need was similarly small. They were comfortable.

"I think we had best rest here the night," Trent said. "Perhaps by morning the volcano will have forgotten us."

"Why should it matter?" Marrow asked. "When I go out, I merely make myself resemble a clog of ashes, and it doesn't recognize me."

"Why didn't we think of that!" Gloha exclaimed.

"You have less space in your skull," Marrow said diplomatically. "All that living meat gets in the way of thought."

"That must be it," Trent agreed before Gloha could organize her reaction. "We living folk are at a disadvantage compared to you fantasy folk. I am surprised that you wish to join our number by acquiring a soul. Don't you know it will make you mortal?"

"Half a soul should not go that far," Marrow said. "A living person can regenerate a full soul from half a soul, but that will not be the case with my kind. My half soul will merely endure, enabling me to reside permanently in exterior Xanth. That is all I want from it."

"You may discover that it provides you more than you want," Trent remarked.

"Then I shall politely decline what else it offers," Marrow said. "I need only permanence in this realm."

Trent's gaze crossed Gloha's gaze briefly, not really establishing a glance. She knew what he was thinking: the skeleton, never having had any part of a soul, did not understand the consequence of being souled. Perhaps it would not be possible to explain.

But something else occurred to her. "What about your family?" she asked. "Will they survive without souls?"

"By no means. But it is my hope that I will be able to share my half soul with them, so that each of us has a fragment, and then Grace'l Joy'nt, and Picka Bone will endure with me satisfactorily ever after in Xanth proper."

Gloha nodded. It was a good answer.

Trent transformed the pot pie plant into a blanket bush, and each of them harvested a nice warm blanket. They lay down in separate corners. Gloha found the blanket on bones, cushioned by her sturdy wings, to be surprisingly comfortable, but something was lacking. She focused her minute little mind, which tried to hide its thought from her, and finally ran it down. She was dissatisfied because she was sleeping alone. She wished she could be snug beside a winged goblin man. So she tried to picture one. The odd thing was that he seemed to have the face and form of Magician Trent. She knew that was foolish, but didn't quite get around to changing the image. She relaxed, and slept so quickly that it was as if the morning came before the evening ended.

In that morning she got up, stretched her wings, and tried the knee-knob on the bone door. The door swung open on smooth joints, and she looked out across the ashy vista.

It was lovely in its fashion. All the irregularities of the landscape had been smoothed over. It was like a gently surging sea, frozen in place. The mountain itself was quiet, with only some scatters of white cloud drifting near its peak. It looked peaceful.

"I made you hats," Marrow said from within.

Gloha turned, startled. She had forgotten that he didn't sleep. "Thank you." She accepted the broad woven bone hat he proffered and put it on her head. It was decorated with ash on top, so that from above it should look like a piece of ash.

She stepped outside. The ash was knee-deep on her, so she spread her wings and flew above it. The mountain did not react, so either the hat was still effective, or Pin-A-Tuba was asleep. She found a suitable gully, landed, and caught up on a function or two that was best done privately. Then she flew back to the bone cabin.

Trent's tracks led around to the back of the house. She would not be so uncouth as to conjecture, of course, but it was possible that he was in quest of a similar gully.

She entered the bone house. There was a sugarplum bush. How thoughtful of the Magician! She plucked the sweetest plum and ate it for breakfast.

They set out, wearing their ash hats. Marrow looked funny in his, because of the incongruity of a skeleton wearing anything. The volcano did not seem to be too smart, because it didn't notice them. They crossed to the original path, and followed it on toward the mountain, because that was really about the only way to go.

Pin-A-Tuba blew a few resounding bass notes as they came close, and puffed up some smoke. But this was a mere turning over in its sleep; their ash hats concealed them well enough so that the mountain was not roused from its slumber. They skirted its base—the skirt was made of fallen ash, of course—and proceeded on south.

"Phew!" Gloha said. "I was afraid old Pun-A-Tub would catch on and dump more ash on us."

The ground shuddered. An awakening rumble traveled up the cone of the mountain. An irate column of smoke shot up.

"Oops," Gloha said. "It heard me."

"Let's move," Trent said.

They hurried along the path. But they were not far enough away from the mountain. The rumbling became horrendous, and a great ugly crack of a vent opened along the side of the cone. Roiling purple gas rose out of it and rolled down toward them.

"I think you living folk would do well to avoid that vapor," Marrow said politely. "On occasion I have seen it encompass creatures."

"Oh! What happened?" Gloha inquired.

"That is where I got the fresh bones for my house, after the vapor passed."

"Point made," Trent said, breaking into a run. But the

path was bearing downhill, and the ball of gas was rolling faster than he could run. It would soon catch them.

Gloha spread her wings and flew. She could rise above the gas. But she knew that wouldn't do Trent much good.

"It will not harm me, of course," Marrow said, keeping the pace. "But if you have any emergency procedures, this would seem to be the time to invoke them."

"I'll have to transform you," Trent puffed to Gloha. "Then you can carry us both away from here."

"All right, if you wish," she said, flying down close to him, to get within his range. "What kind of creature do you—*squawk, squawk, squawk*?" she concluded from her big bird's beak. She had become a roc.

The gasball was almost upon them. She reached down with two feet and caught both man and skeleton. She closed her talons carefully, so that they formed a kind of round barred cage instead of transfixing or crushing anyone. Then she pumped her wings and heaved into the sky.

The ball rolled underneath her. The draft from her wings beat at it, battering it apart. It lost cohesion, and became a sinking pool of ugh-colored ick. Served it right, as far as she was concerned.

The mountain, balked, shot out a furious blast of ash. The fragments were so hot they glowed as they arced toward Gloha's wings. They would set her on fire if they caught her! But she was at the fringe of the volcano's immediate range, and was able to fly clear before the burning bits reached her. Now she truly appreciated the Magician's prior caution; indeed, no big bird was safe near that deadly cone.

She looked for a good place to land, but the terrain was too rough for a bird this size. She needed a reasonably level region clear of trees. So she flew on south—and in a surprisingly brief time she spied the yawning gape of the Gap Chasm. She realized two or maybe three things: she had reached it so rapidly because big strong rocs flew with much bigger wing-strokes than did little weak-winged goblin girls. It was yawning because this was still morning and it hadn't had time to wake properly up yet. And if she could travel this readily and swiftly, she might as well continue until they reached their starting point above Crombie's cave. Then they could head southeast, the direction he had indicated.

As she flew, she had a daydream. In it, she was turning the pages of a big book. The pages were filled with text, but she was unable to read it. Then she came to one that said "Chapter 5: Xxxxxxx." She recognized that title: it was her story! So she turned more pages, until in the middle of the following chapter the pages turned blank. The chapters were numbered through 12, but there was nothing written in the last six. Which meant, of course, that her story was as yet unfinished. Then there was the flick of an invisible tail, and Mare Imbri, the bringer of daydreams, galloped off to her next assignment.

Gloha was surprised to realize that almost half her story had been told, and she hadn't yet started the main part of her quest. It was high time to get on with it, so a little velocity here wouldn't hurt at all.

But where exactly was Crombie's cave? She had come to it mostly by water before, and underground. She had returned to the surface through a convoluted system of caves that left her with no idea where she had been. She didn't know how to identify its location from here.

Well, maybe she should return to the place where they had emerged. That should be somewhere in the right vicinity. Maybe Magician Trent or Marrow Bones would have a notion how to proceed from there.

She found that in this form she had a fine eye for details on the ground. She saw where Com Pewter's cave was, and the board walk, and the pool of the three mermaids. Well, maybe that was close enough, and would do for a landing place; there were no trees in the middle of the pool.

She glided down. She swooped low and slow over the pool, and let the two figures go. They dropped into the pool with two splashes. She knew that the mermaids would rescue Trent if he had any trouble, and the skeleton could simply sink to the bottom and walk out, as he didn't need to breathe.

She climbed again, and saw that it was as she had surmised: Trent was surrounded by the three lovelies. Then one of them went to rescue Marrow Bones—and changed her mind. Maybe she hadn't seen him clearly before. It must have been a shock to recognize his nature. Gloha somehow wasn't too sorry.

She descended again, and this time splashed into the water herself. It had a wonderfully cushioning effect, but wasn't as deep as she had thought; her feet touched bottom. Then she realized that it had been deep but was so no longer; her entry had splashed most of the water out. The three mermaids were stranded by the suddenly dry shoreline, their once-lovely hairdos matted, glaring in perfect harmony.

Gloha waded out. When she reached Trent, she returned to her natural form. "Sorry about that," she said with as much apology as she could muster.

"Quite all right," Ash said through gritted teeth. "It will fill again any week now. We shall surely flounder through in sufficient style."

"Perhaps sooner," Trent said. He gestured, and a stranded fish near him became a very large watermelon vine with a number of huge fruits. He poked a melon, and it burst, its water flowing into the pool.

"Oho!" Cedar exclaimed, catching on. She poked another fruit, adding its water to the pool.

Trent slogged on around the depression, turning fish and weeds into more watermelon plants. The others followed, poking the fruits. All this water, added to what was flowing back from the higher slopes, soon had the pool about half full again. There was enough for the mermaidens to swim in, and for Marrow and Gloha to wash in. Trent, thoroughly splashed by the bursting melons, was pretty well clean anyway.

"Thank you," Mahogany said. 'I suppose if you wanted to put your clothes out to dry and dally a bit in the water, Magician, we just might manage to forget exactly how old you claim to be." She smiled reasonably winningly from amidst her bedraggled dark tresses.

"I fear we have to move on," the Magician said. "But I thank you for the consideration."

The mermaids did not press the issue, evidently being not completely forgiving of the splash. The encounter was less than ideal. For that Gloha was privately thankful.

They followed the stream down to where it entered the mountain. Then they looked for some way southeast from there. Beyond the river's gully was a mountain. There was a path that seemed to lead around the obstruction, but it did not look entirely healthy. There were bits of bone and feather strewn along it, and it smelled of dragon's breath. "I could become the roc bird again, and carry you over to the other side," Gloha suggested.

"We're not sure exactly where Crombie's residence is," Trent reminded her. "It might be under this very mountain. If we skip the mountain, we might already be beyond it, and the farther we went, the less likely we would be to fulfill your quest."

She nodded. "But I hope it has nothing to do with the dragon who maybe lives near this path."

"I'll transform the beast if necessary."

They set off afoot. Gloha couldn't have flown ahead to check, but the path wound under such a dense canopy of foliage that it was impossible to see from above. So she kept her wings ready, but remained low.

There was indeed a dragon. A big one. It was snoozing with its head across the path. Its dragon ears perked up at their approach, and wafts of smoke surged from its nostrils.

"A smoker," Trent said grimly. "We won't be able to get close enough to it for me to transform it."

Gloha understood why. The most feared dragons were fire breathers, but smokers could be devastating too in close quarters. Their smoke surrounded and suffocated the prey, and when it cleared, the dragon could chomp victims at leisure. Here under the close canopy the travelers would have no chance.

"We'll have to go back and look for another path," she said.

"I see no reason for that," Marrow said, striding forward.

"But the smoke—" she cried warningly.

He walked on, straight at the dragon. The dragon was as surprised as they were. It huffed and it puffed and it shot twin jets of smoke from its nostrils that looked almost thick enough to walk on. The smoke bathed the skeleton—who plowed on through it, unaffected.

"He doesn't breathe!" Gloha murmured, remembering. "He can't choke!"

"He has no eyes," Trent agreed. "He can't be blinded. And he's immune to any heat that isn't high enough to burn bone."

"But what can he do to stop the dragon from simply chomping him into bonemeal?"

"That I am not sure. But he seems confident."

The dragon's big eyes grew larger as he saw the skeleton emerge from the bath of smoke. He inhaled again, getting ready to send out a worse blast. But Marrow jumped forward and grabbed onto the dragon's nose!

"He'll get himself chomped to splinters!" Gloha cried, appalled. For the dragon's head was larger than Marrow's whole body.

"Maybe not," Trent said appraisingly. "He has changed his form."

"That's right—they can do that," she agreed. "They can disassemble their bones and put them together in strings or other combinations. He looks like one big clamp now."

Indeed, the long bones of what were Marrow's legs had become man-sized pincers, clamping the dragon's nose closed. The dragon tried to paw Marrow off, but immediately the clamp tightened painfully, forcing the creature to desist. The skull, perched at the top, looked around and spied them. "You may pass safely," Marrow called. "He can't breathe smoke through his mouth, only his nose."

"He's right," Trent said appreciatively. "That dragon is largely helpless. Certainly I can now approach near enough to transform it. But I think I don't need to."

They walked by, almost close enough to touch the dragon's huge nose. The creature looked as if he really wanted to chomp them, but that clamp tightened warningly and he had to relax.

"But won't he chomp you the moment you let go?" Gloha asked.

"It will take him a moment to get reoriented," the skull said. "In any event, I don't taste very good. There's no meat on me."

So they went on by. Once they were safely out of smoke range, they called, and heard a muffled whomp as the clamp let go and the dragon resumed stoking smoke. In a moment Marrow appeared, striding nonchalantly as if this were routine.

"This is a creature to be respected," Trent murmured, not referring to the dragon. Gloha could only agree.

The path continued on around the mountain. There were no other dragons or other dangerous creatures. This was not surprising, because no smaller predator would dare to encroach on the territory of the big one.

The path finally left the deep forest and debouched into a halfway open valley. A village nestled within it, and there seemed to be a fair amount of activity therein. From the far side a cloud of dust or smoke wafted up into the sky.

"What are they doing?" Gloha asked.

"I believe this is the Magic Dust Village," Marrow said. "They mine the magic dust and blow it into the air so that it will circulate throughout Xanth, enhancing the magic everywhere."

"The Magic Dust Village!" she exclaimed. "Of course! I have heard of it. The most magical place in Xanth."

"Why, that's right," Trent agreed. "I should have realized; this is indeed the area. I shall have to be extremely careful about performing transformations, because the extra potency of magic in this region can be dangerous."

They walked on down to the village. An elderly troll moved to intercept them. "As far as I know, the natives are friendly," Trent murmured. "They have members of many crossbreed humanoid species living and working in harmony, including goblins and trolls. But perhaps you, Gloha, should stay behind me until we are sure."

Gloha was glad to agree. They had encountered one friendly troll, but that was a rarity. Another would be pulling on their luck.

"Hail, man, goblin, skeleton!" the troll cried. "Do you come in peace?"

"We do, if left in peace," Trent agreed.

"Then I must warn you that our village is about to become inhospitable. You must move on, lest you be exposed to hazard."

"We have had a moderately arduous day's journey, and were looking forward to a relaxed night," Trent said. "We are also on a quest, and it is possible that the object of that quest is to be found here. Let us exchange introductions and see whether it is possible for us to do each other any good."

"By all means. I am Pa, the eldest troll of Magic Dust Village. I am too old to work well, so I walk around and warn away strangers."

"Glad to meet you, Pa Troll. I am Magician Trent, formerly the transformer king of Xanth. This is Marrow Bones, formerly of the dream realm, and this is Gloha Goblin-Harpy, whose quest we are supporting."

"Magician Trent!" Pa exclaimed. "Perhaps you are the one we are waiting for." He paused. "Wait—you are far too young. You must be an impostor."

"I have been temporarily youthened," Trent explained. "I will demonstrate." He pointed to a tiny flowering plant beside the path. It became a monstrous spreading acorn tree whose trunk obliterated that path, shoving them into the surrounding brush. "Oops—I forgot the intensity of magic! That was supposed to be a medium-small acorn tree."

Pa Troll touched the massive trunk. "So it's not illusion. I apologize for doubting you, Magician." He glanced at Gloha. "And a crossbreed harpy—this is most interesting. Come to the village, and we shall see. I am most excited." Indeed, he was quivering in a manner trolls normally reserved for the anticipation of some truly dastardly deed. Gloha didn't need Trent's additional caution to remain on guard.

Trent restored the tree to its original state, this time getting it right. They came to the village square. A throng of crossbreeds of every description quickly gathered there. Not merely trolls, but elves, fairies, ogres, a small giant or two, goblins, gnomes, centaurs, griffins, masked basilisks, and other creatures too numerous or confusing to mention. "Ho, you rabble of low degree!" Pa Troll cried. "Maybe we have our salvation, and maybe not. This is Magician Trent, in the company of a walking skeleton and a honey of a harpy crossbreed." He indicated the three.

There was a muted ooooh of appreciation. Gloha was surprised and discomfited to find most eyes focusing on her. She realized that there were no harpies here, oddly.

"You see, we have a problem," Pa Troll continued, now speaking to the three visitors. "We have been told to carry on until Harpy Time, but no harpy has appeared, and we have only a day or two left before disaster. So if you are not able to help us, the village and all Xanth will be in deep dung."

"Exactly what is the nature of your problem?" Trent inquired. "And how do you think a harpy could solve it?"

"First you must understand the nature of our village mission," Pa said. "This is the site where the magic rock wells up from the unknown depths of magic. We pound it into dust, and our roc bird flaps his wings to blow it high into the sky, where it spreads and circulates and sifts down across all of Xanth. Without this service we render, the Land of Xanth would slowly lose its magic and revert to— pardon the expression—mundane nature. This is why we all work together despite having in our number creatures who otherwise would prefer to quarrel with each other and eat strangers." He glanced at Gloha again and licked his thin troll lips in a reminiscent manner that made half a shiver scramble up her back. "We use little magic, preferring to do the job by hand and foot, because the use of magic is dangerous in this vicinity."

He took a breath. "But recently a new vent opened in a nearby mountain. From it issues not magic stone, but poisonous thick fluid that slowly courses down toward the village, destroying all life in its path. We can not remove or divert it, because the fumes of its surface are also lethal. Our only resort is to remain well away from it. But soon it will ooze into the village itself, and begin to pool here, and then we shall have to flee, our labor will no longer be accomplished. The magic of Xanth will begin to fade, and in time our entire land will be as dreary as the drear region beyond." There was another ooooh from the villagers. Gloha had to agree; the prospect was appalling.

"So we sent a representative to the Good Magician Humfrey, to inquire how we can prevent this disaster. She is now serving her year's Service with him. But we can't say that we are entirely satisfied with his response."

"Whom did you send?" Gloha asked, unable to restrain her irrelevant curiosity.

"A winged monster, of another type than yourself. A glyph."

"I met her!" Gloha cried with dear little delight. "A nice horse/dragon crossbreed. She was one of my challenges on the way in."

"I hope they are treating her well," Pa said in paternal fashion.

"Oh, yes. At first I thought they weren't, but that was part of the challenge. She's really quite happy there."

"What was your Answer?" Trent inquired, more relevantly. "To carry on until Harpy Time?"

"Precisely. I must say that the Good Magician's Answers leave something to be desired, considering their expense."

"But they are always accurate and relevant," Trent reminded him.

Pa glanced at Gloha, this time refraining from licking his lips. "Were you satisfied with your own Answer?"

"Well, no. Actually, he didn't give me an Answer, exactly, so I didn't have to do any Service."

"So you can no doubt appreciate our dissatisfaction."

"Yes, I think I can. And I have to say that I don't think I'm the harpy you're looking for. About my only harpy aspect is my wings; apart from that I mostly resemble a goblin, unlike my brother Harglo. I have no idea how to stop that poisonous flow, because it would affect me too."

"And it is not something I can transform," Trent said. "But why didn't you make a dam to stop its advance?"

"We did, but it oozes between the stones and dissolves them, seeping on along its destined course. The only way we can stop it is to plug its source—if any of us could only get close enough."

"Could a roc bird drop a boulder on it?"

"No. It issues from a fissure in the steep slope. It should be fairly easy to plug, if only any of us could approach it. But our every effort has led only to disaster."

Then something occurred to Gloha. "Marrow, you were immune to the dragon's choking smoke. Would you be able to approach a poison vent?"

"Why, I see no reason why not," the skeleton said.

"Then you are the ones we have waited for!" Pa Troll cried. "You signal the Harpy Time."

"Perhaps," Trent said. "However, it should be clarified that Marrow Bones is also on a quest. He needs half a soul, so that he can remain indefinitely here in Xanth proper. If anyone here cares to—"

It was amazing how quickly the crowd dissipated. It

seemed that the dedication of none of the villagers extended quite that far. Even Pa Troll had somehow found elsewhere to be. The three of them were left standing in the center of an apparently deserted village.

"These creatures have too much human nature," Trent remarked sourly.

"Yet their need is genuine," Marrow said. "Xanth will profit. I will plug that vent." He set off in the direction Pa Troll had looked when he spoke of the encroaching poison.

Trent shook his head, watching the departing skeleton. "I could almost swear he already has at least half a soul."

"Certainly he doesn't seem to need more than he has," Gloha agreed. "I had a lesson in decency not too long ago. This reminds me of it."

"It may be that souls aren't what they used to be."

"Maybe I'd better see if I can help him." She spread her wings.

"Not too close," he warned. "If you smell anything at all, get away from wherever you are."

"I will," she assured him. She pumped her wings and lifted into the air.

It was good to be flying again, in her own form. Her limber little legs had gotten worn with all that walking, while she was afraid her wings would dissolve with disuse. So maybe her decision to try to help Marrow was as much selfish as unselfish.

In a moment she saw the poison flow. It was like a messy black river flowing from a nearby mountain right toward the village. Every so often it jogged, and she realized that those were the places they had put up rock dams that hadn't quite done the job. No plants grew near it; everything within smelling distance was barren. It seemed to be aiming for the village as if guided by some malignant will. She would have dismissed that notion, except for her memory of how the inanimate things reacted when King Dor talked to them. They tended to be shallow, but they did have opinions and feelings. And of course Marrow Bones was not alive, being an-

imated by magic, and he had an objective and a code of
behavior. Then there was Pin-A-Tuba, the angry volcano
who tried to stop folk from approaching it closely. So why
shouldn't a poisonous flow have an objective too?

In fact, she realized now, that poison was from Pin-A-
Tuba! That was the volcano's other slope. They had circled
around it without catching on that it could have nasty vents
on both sides, or that these could issue either noxious gas or
nasty fluid. So they hadn't finished with this evil mountain.

Meanwhile Marrow was walking up the ruined slope toward the vent. But Gloha saw that he wasn't going to be
able to reach it, because there was a small cliff in the way.
The black poison goo had no trouble dribbling slowly down
it, but there was no way for a person to climb up it. However, there was an indirect route, clear only from above.

She flew down to tell Marrow. But he was walking right
beside the poison flow, supremely unaffected. The moment
she started to think of getting faintly close, her breath began
to choke and her vision blurred and her wings got shaky and
weak. She plunged away to the side, so she wasn't directly
above the flow, and recovered her equilibrium. No, she
couldn't go and tell him directly.

But maybe she could signal him from afar. She flew back
and forth before him, waving her arms. "Marrow!" she
called, sure he couldn't hear her from this distance.

But in a moment he noticed her. He waved a bony arm.

"Go that way!" she cried, zooming to the mountain's
right side. "There's a path!"

But he couldn't understand. He moved on beside the
flow.

Was there any other way to get through to him? She
racked her blank little brain but dredged up nothing. So
she just followed along, hoping to be able to help when
there was a chance.

He finally trekked to the cliff and stood looking up. It
was obvious that he couldn't climb it. He looked around.

Now was the time. She flew to the right again and hovered there, beckoning him. This time he caught on. He walked that way, away from the flow. She led him to the place where a ledge angled erratically up the steep slope. From there it moved back across to the top of the cliff, and the way was followable.

Marrow found it, and made his way up. He was carrying something, and she realized that it was a piece of stone he hoped to use as a plug. It seemed to be an old stalactite that some cave had discarded.

She watched from afar as he went all the way to the vent. He studied the situation, then lifted his stalactite and rammed it straight down into the center of the vent, where the poison started flowing. It went partway in. Then he lifted off his skull—Gloha did a double take at about that point—and used it to pound in the spike.

That was it. He replaced his skull and walked away. Gloha saw that the flow was clearing near the top. It remained below, but there was no more coming out of the vent. He had plugged it.

Gloha thought of something else. Marrow had been too close to the poison. He probably reeked of it now, so that it wouldn't be safe for anybody else to get near him. He would have to get clean before he returned to the village.

She flew back and forth, signaling him as she had before. Then she headed for the nearest stream that didn't originate on Mount Pin-A-Tuba. He followed. The foliage on either side of his route wilted as he passed. The stream was far enough away so that she was able to land beside it. But when Marrow approached, sure enough, he reeked of poison, and she had to fly away before she fainted. "Wash! Wash!" she cried, pointing at the water. Then, afraid he couldn't hear her, she made vigorous scrubbing motions along her body.

He caught on, and waded into the water. He disappeared in it. The plants downstream began to wilt. Gloha was sorry for them, but at least it showed that the water was carrying the poison away from his body. Before too long it should get so diluted that it wouldn't hurt anyone anymore.

She hovered at a safe distance until he emerged. He walked downstream, and when he got beyond the wilted region, there seemed to be no further wilting in his vicinity. So she risked a closer approach. There were no deadly fumes. Finally she landed before him. "You're clean," she announced.

"Thank you for advising me," he said. "It had not occurred to me that I might have become unsanitary, but when you signaled I realized that life in my vicinity was perishing."

"Yes. That poison is very strong."

They returned to the village. Trent had evidently been at work there, because there was now a large pile of fresh food from plants and creatures he must have transformed. The villagers were aware that the poison was no longer flowing. That meant that the existing stream should slowly dry up or sink into the ground, leaving the village clear. They would be able to continue their business.

"I have talked with the villagers, and ascertained that there are no winged goblins here, nor have they even seen any before you," Trent advised her. "As far as they know, you are unique."

"I'm afraid I am," she agreed. "But Crombie wouldn't have pointed a direction if there weren't an answer. It just means it isn't here."

"True. We can rest here the night, and continue southeast in the morning." He hesitated. "I wouldn't judge the villagers too harshly with respect to their unwillingness to yield half a soul. Many are female, making them imperfect for this purpose, or old. Others are simply frightened. There are a number of misconceptions about souls that are hard to eradicate."

"I know," Gloha agreed, remembering her own concern about losing half of hers.

"I would not care to take half a soul from someone who did not freely wish to give it," Marrow said.

"We'll keep looking," Gloha said.

They had a good meal, really a feast, and the villagers were very appreciative of the service Marrow had done for them. "You have benefited all Xanth," Pa Troll said, with an emphasis that hinted that maybe it was all Xanth who owed Marrow the half soul, not the local village.

There was a nice house for them to use for the night, left by a family that had moved out recently in anticipation of a complete evacuation. Gloha had the pleasure of a private room with a nice soft bed. She slept well, despite still wishing that she had a perfect man with warm feet to share it with. She realized that the Good Magician had been right about a harpy (or part harpy) helping to save the village at the last moment. Maybe his son was right about the direction of the solution to her own quest. Meanwhile, she did feel slightly useful.

$$\overline{7}$$

MADNESS

In the morning they resumed their travel to the southeast. However, Pa Troll had a warning for them: "The wind currents carry the magic dust everywhere, but they are thickest immediately downwind from the village. Usually this is to our southwest, but at the moment it is to our southeast. Your route may take you through the fringe of it. You would be well advised to avoid that direction, at least until the wind changes and some of the dust can clear."

Trent looked at Gloha. "This is good advice."

She knew it was. She had heard stories about the effects of magic madness. "But is it possible that my perfect man and Marrow's half-soul donor will be found within the Region of Madness?"

"It is possible," he agreed. "I suppose if such quests seem unlikely to succeed in normal Xanth, the abnormal should be tried. But I'm not sure you appreciate just how weird the Region of Madness is likely to be."

"Oh, pooh! It can't be worse than Mount Pun-A-Tub was."

"Which threat you also doubted, at first," he reminded her evenly.

She knew he was making sense, and that she was being an unreasonable teen crossbreed female. Somehow that didn't cause her to become more reasonable. It didn't help that she wished she could make an impression on him as an intriguing adult female, for no legitimate reason, and didn't know how. So her fouled-up little feelings just made things difficult. "Anyway, I'm curious to see just what's so weird about it."

His gaze remained straight, yet somehow she had the impression he was rolling his eyes. "As you wish."

Marrow Bones tilted his skull. His nonexistent eyes were rolling too.

They proceeded southeast. Downwind. There was no problem. The country consisted of rolling hills covered by forest and fields, with an occasional river wandering through. Trent was about to wade through the first river, but the skeleton stopped him. "Kick me," he said.

"Thank you," Trent said.

Gloha thought they were joking, though neither creature had been much for humor before. But Marrow bent over, and Trent delivered a fine kick to the skeleton's hipbone. Marrow flew apart. The bones landed in a pile—in the shape of a small boat. Trent pushed the boat into the water, where it floated despite not seeming to be watertight, then stepped into it and sat down. The craft then moved across the water under its own power. Trent got out on the far bank, then kicked the boat, and the bones flew apart and landed back in Marrow's natural form.

Gloha finally got her gape hinged. She had known that the walking skeletons could change the arrangement of their bones, but hadn't realize how neat and useful this could be. After all, Marrow had changed to clamp the dragon's nose.

Trent's kicks had merely facilitated the effort. She flew across the river herself. They resumed walking.

"We seem to be skirting the Region of Madness," Trent remarked. "Perhaps the folk of the Magic Dust Village were operating at reduced efficiency the past few days as the poison flow approached, so the dust level is not high. But now they are likely to be back at full efficiency, and we are apt to encounter more of the effect."

"I believe you are correct," Marrow agreed, his skull turning. "There may be a waft of it approaching now."

"Well, I don't see any madness yet," Gloha remarked impertinently. She shouldn't have.

Gloha sucked and licked at the sticky ends of her fingers. She was too old for Aunt Grobigatail's honey flummery, but a taste of honey always whetted her appetite for more. She sighed, her joy mixed with a little bit of sadness. She was, at the age of eighteen, getting more than a bit long in the tooth, too old for sweet treats. But she was still too young for goblin garbage rituals. Now she was too bored doing her usual good job of baby-sitting her obnoxious little brother Harglo. He might be her sibling, but he wasn't her kind; he had the head and legs of a goblin, but the full-feathered body of a harpy complete with tail, and no hands. He was a stronger flyer than she was, and a stronger runner too, but couldn't do much delicate handling of things with just his wings. He made up for that by having an excellent command of harpy vocabulary; already at age nine he could make some foliage wilt when he swore, and he was still confined to non–Adult Conspiracy words.

But today she was free of him, having a day off while he took flying lessons (and probably illicit cussing lessons) from Aunt Fowlmouth. So she could relax and enjoy herself. So why wasn't she happy? She tasted her fingers again, but this time her scalding-hot salty tears caused her fingers to hurt like the singing stinging threads of sea wasps. The problem was that today she had time to appreciate just how much it hurt being a half-and-half crossbreed, never quite fitting in with either the goblins or the harpies. So now she was caught up in her self-pity party. She had stopped grooming herself; her wing feathers were droopy and creased, her hooded blue bio-luminescent eyes were dull, and her glorious blue-black glossy hair hung in salty honey-sticky twisted loops.

Harpies flew overhead, hooting and hurling a golden cop-rolite about. This was a gold-plated fossilized ball of dragon dung that they caught in their claws and tossed up again. Whoever could get out the longest and foulest string of cussing before the next harpy touched the flying ball was winner for the moment. Harglo loved that game, and longed for the day he could play it; Gloha had never even tried, as she could not even begin to understand the implications of its most basic terms without going into a terminal blush.

These were good days in Xanth, in the harpy caves and goblin dens, when things went medium to bad instead of bad to worse. But from time to thyme a demonic, shot-fowl (or maybe foul-shot) rogue-awful day sneaked in, and this seemed to be one of them. So instead of enjoying her rest from spite, her respite, she was having Xanth's most miserable little mood.

It had started with dawn, which had lifted its brooding mists to reveal a bleary red-eyed sun surrounded by bruised purple clouds whose only desire was to make an acid rain and wet on someone's head. Then had come the snarling, whining, grunting, screaming rush to the breakfast cave, aptly termed the mess hall, where her dozens of aunts fought for the juiciest dripping raw bleeding morsels. Gloha had found herself wedged between Aunt Hoary Harributtes and the Grand Harridan Queen-Chief of this branch of the family clan, each of whom could screech more piercingly than the other. Gloha managed to plead difficulty clinging to the perch, so she took her quivering chunk of whatever to a separate bench where she could sit in what was disparagingly termed human style. Then someone had accidentally dropped a splash of hot coffee down her back, never mind that harpies never dropped anything they had ever snatched up unless they meant to. Gloha had had to flee to her personal nest to change clothes and put salve on her burn.

She had tried to cheer herself by dressing up. She donned her festival outfit: mock-leather jerkin, thongs of molten golden color trimmed in a musical pattern with mellow golden bells, brazen Hell's Bells, and icy crystal stars. A really nice outfit always made her feel so good. But then her tutor, Magpie, had told her not to wear it, because harpies didn't wear clothing and she would be a laughingstock.

"But I'm a laughingstock anyway!" she protested.

"Nonsense. You just haven't found your place yet."

"What do you know about it?" Gloha flared rebelliously. "You aren't really a harpy at all! You're just an unlikely kindly demoness."

"But I have worked with quite a number of mortals," Magpie said with an evenness impossible to mortals. "Okra Ogress thought her life was hopeless, and now she's a Major Character. Rose of Roogna thought she'd never find a good husband, and then she married the Good Magician and had a lovely daughter. I could list others."

Gloha knew she could. At length. So she didn't ask. Instead she went into Routine #2: a terrible little tantrum. "Don't tell me what to do!" she screamed with a great deal of hair tossing and foot stomping. Her show frightened several nearby birds, who flew under the bed to hide, disturbing the snoozing monster there.

But Magpie had seen it all before, and was unmoved. In the end Gloha had to remove her finery and return to her dull ordinary state. Her dreary life continued unabated.

Gloha shook her heavy little head. She was back in the forest with Magician Trent and Marrow Bones. What had happened?

"I had supposed your life was happy," Trent said, surprised. "But I realize now that no one living among harpies could be satisfied."

"You saw my flashback?" Gloha asked, amazed.

"It appeared before us," Trent said.

"I am not expert in the ways of living folk," Marrow said. "But it seems to me that it was not nice of that harpy to spill hot black liquid down your back."

"You really did see it? In wild living color? Even when I threw my—"

"I averted my gaze when you changed clothing," the Magician said. "I thought you might consider that private."

She had been going to say "tantrum," but now she realized that she had more to be concerned about. She had relived an episode of her past life, and they had seen it unfold exactly as she had. Including her temporarily bared body. What madness was this?

Then she realized the rest of it. This was the Region of Madness, with the intense magic of the concentrated magic dust making even memories become visible. She hadn't realized that it would be like this. She wasn't at all sure she liked it. "Let's get quickly out of here," she suggested.

"What, when the fun is just beginning?" a voice demanded.

"Who is that?" Gloha asked, alarmed.

Smoke swirled. "Nothing to concern you, antiseptic goblin girl."

"What kind of goblin girl?"

"Unpolluted, sanitary, unadulterated, immaculate, faultless—"

"Innocent?" Trent suggested.

"Whatever," the smoke said crossly.

"What are you doing here, Metria?" Gloha asked a brief little bit crossly herself.

"I poke around wherever anything interesting is happening. Anyone fool enough to blunder into the Region of Madness is bound to be interesting."

"Well, my past life is about as uninteresting as anything can get, so you might as well go away."

"Oh, I don't know about that. Magpie always takes the interesting characters to work with."

"You know Magpie?"

"She's a demoness, isn't she? She knows when something's going to happen, and she's always there to nursemaid it through."

"Well, nothing's going to happen right now, so—"

"That's what you think. Here comes another waft of madness."

"I don't believe it," Gloha said. "You're just saying it to tease—"

. . . and long lonely hours had been spent conducting endless imagined conversations with her adversary, that harpy flying tiger, her Aunt Hoary.

"Chaos and coffee!" Hoary Harpy screeched as she used one soiled wing to sweep strands of slop, glop, and flop out of the mess hall and into the fire pits. She clutched a teaming mug of brew in one claw while standing on the other scrawny leg. She vaguely resembled a black-feathered desultory stork, her red eyes glowing like soiled coals in the dusky purple shadows of the messy hall. She swept long dirty strands of feathery black hair back from her stony alabaster brow and glowered at her niece.

Gloha's sensitive little stomach knotted and burned, her heart cramped, and her hair wanted to wriggle out of sight. How had she gotten into this dill picklement?

"I said, what game are you playing?" a low whispery voice repeated, which was somehow worse than the usual screech.

With an icy start Gloha realized that the subject of her worries was now focusing her formidable annoyance at her. She blushed, which of course only made things worse, making her seem even more guilty that she probably was. "Auntie?"

"You politely requested this early morning interview, which showed how unharpyish you are," the harpy said. "You should have demanded it in the foulest vernacular. Now what in the name of idiocy do you want?"

Gloha somehow nerved herself enough to speak her muted little mind. "Auntie Hoary, I've been made sick and tired by living a dull and middle-of-the-road life amidst creatures who aren't exactly like me. We all know what happens when you stay in the middle of anything: you get run over. Auntie, I want to be an alchemist, a geo-alchemist on a wizard's team. I think a person without a dream becomes mired in our st—st—" She faltered, unable to get the ugly word out.

"Stinking!" Hoary screeched. "S-T-I-N-K-I-N-G! Where's your harpy vocabulary? Girl, you need to learn to swear, if you're going to get along. Now try it again."

Gloha made an effete little effort. "M-mired in our st-stinking pig pit," she managed to eke out. "Over and over I dream a bad dream brought by a night mare, that I can no longer fly—that I am a crippled broken-winged bird. Let me leave the nest—"

"What kind of nest?" Hoary screeched.

"The st-stinking nest, and go to seek—"

"What in the hell is the hurry?" Hoary demanded. "Leave the safety of the flock when you still don't know how to swear? You'd really break your wings then! The nest is best for chicks."

"But I'm eighteen, Auntie," Gloha reminded her.

"And have the vocabulary of a dirty bird half your age," Hoary pointed out, cleaning gore from her teeth with a dagger like claw. "If a monster came to eat you, you wouldn't even be able to give it a toothache with either your voice or your hygiene. You'd be one mouthwatering little morsel."

All too true. But Gloha, knowing that she'd never get up the courage to broach this subject again, tried to see it through. "Couldn't you let me fly with a proper escort to pay a professional visit to the castle of the Good Magician

Humfrey, there to ask my one Question and give my year's Service for his Answer? Oh, please, Auntie Hoary! I would do anything if only I could—"

"Harpies never plead!" Hoary snapped, disgusted by this weakness. "Show me that you can let out one incendiary oath, and I'll let you go."

Gloha tried. "Darn!" she cried. "Help! Ship!"

Hoary sighed. "You're improving; at least you are taking aim at the words. But you're off by one letter in each case. That nullifies it. There's not even a stir of fire in the air. Now pay attention: this is the proper mode of harpy expression." She took a breath. "*%#@ƒ$!!"

Gloha managed to cover her ears just in time. Even so, she felt the heat of the terrible blast. The air shimmered and burned, and scorch marks appeared on the table. A fiery smell wafted outward.

As fresh air moved in, making it possible to breathe again, Hoary resumed normal screeching. "Now can you do that, chick?"

"M-maybe in time," Gloha said, knowing it was impossible.

"In harpy thyme, maybe," Hoary said with resignation. "Gloha, you are still wet behind the ear feathers. It would be folly to let you go out alone or in incompetent company. Do you even know where the Seeds of Destruction are kept? Can you do an aerial survey and map or organize things according to the harpy thyme line? We, the horrid harpies, the stinking untouchables, the ultimate fowl-mouths, we have that knowledge and keep the temple of hope for Xanth until the time we choose to assume the mantle of dominance for ourselves. Our time is not yet, but drawing nigh. Once we have the harpy thyme—"

She broke off, realizing that she was saying too much. "Anyway, you must at least learn to swear effectively before you can safely go out on your own. When you can do that, perhaps I will let you go."

That was it. The discussion was at an end. Aunt Hoary

had made what was by harpy definition a reasonable and moderate requirement. But how would Gloha ever be able to learn to swear like that? Her mild little mouth couldn't even begin to form the awful configurations necessary.

Gloha blinked. She was back in the forest. The waft of madness had passed. "Now that's a sensible harridan," Metria said approvingly.

"You saw—heard Aunt Hoary Harpy?" Gloha asked, embarrassed.

"Saw her? I *was* her!" the demoness said. "Look at the foliage."

Gloha looked. The leaves nearby were wilted, and some even burned, as if blasted by a truly ferocious oath. "But how could that be?"

"Those aren't mere memories," Trent explained. "The rest of us get caught up in the parts. The magic governs us."

"Then we must get away from here before something awful happens," Gloha cried, appalled. "Some of my memories are not nice."

"I don't think we can escape until your memories are resolved," he replied. "Something is bothering you, and until that is brought out and alleviated, we shall be locked in."

"Oh, I never wanted to get into this," Gloha wailed.

"You were an arrogant little snit," Metria said. "You thought the madness wouldn't take you."

"I was wrong!" Gloha cried in anguish. "I'll flee it!" She started running, but already she saw a slight wavering of the landscape, as if its level of reality were shifting. The effect was coming right toward her. There was a rushing sound, as of swiftly flowing water. Oh, no!

Behind the kitchen herb garden Gloha could hear Chrysalis Crystal Creek before she could see it. Hugely swollen by the weird weather, with consecutive drenchpours, the creek waters had taken the bit in their wet teeth and were in a dangerous mood. They were surging at boulders, trying to rip them out of the soil, and rushing at any living thing that dared approach. Whatever they caught they were carrying away, tossing about, and finally pounding to quivering bits. This was no safe place for an antiseptic, uh, innocent winged goblin girl.

Almost blinded by her rampaging feelings and tears, Gloha half ran, half flew down the very muddy, irregular, treacherous path to the very edge of the stream. Nearby monsters woke and stirred, sniffing the air, aware of the lingering odor of juicy, tender, young winged girl. Slowly they rose and moved toward her, blocking off her escape.

Affrighted, Gloha spread her wings, about to take flight. But the violent water signaled the air, and the air stirred, whirling itself into a deadly cone that reached for Gloha's winsome little wings. She did not dare take flight now, lest her feathers be plucked, leaving her truly helpless. She had to stay grounded.

But now she saw something even worse: silvery, slithering, slinky nickelpedes, going for her tender little tootsies. Tendrils were reaching out of the ground, casting about to catch her feet and hold her there while they burrowed into the flesh. She had blundered into a truly awful trap. How was she ever to escape?

She tried to run along the only path she saw, not knowing where it led. But a tendril caught a foot, sending her into a headlong fall to the ground. Her knocked little knee twisted on the way down, making her scream with pain. "Help!" she cried. But the roar of the water drowned her out, and she knew that no one would hear or come to her rescue.

The tendrils found her body and curled over it, anchoring her so that they could drill into her succulent little shape. The nickelpedes scuttled to arrive in time to gouge out their coin-sized chunks before the plants shriveled her body too far. The hungry shadow of a larger monster loomed close.

Gloha screamed. This time it was no meek little mock effort. It was a double-throated piercing ululation at ultrasonic and ultraviolet levels containing a suggestion of the vocabulary Aunt Hoary had been trying to teach her. The tendrils, momentarily stunned, writhed back away from her. The nickelpedes clicked their pincers, briefly disoriented. The looming monster hesitated a third of a moment, or perhaps nine tenths of an instant.

Then all three threats recovered and converged. But in that meager instant Gloha made an exhausted little effort to fight for what hopeless little hope remained to save her lost little life. She heaved herself somewhere else.

She fell down a long sandy shaft of dirt, wings over heels. She was aware of wild glowing molds, bugs, and many intriguing shades of dirt touching barely mentionable parts of her body along the way. Then she fetched up against the ragged cobweb-covered gape of a hidden hole. She plunged heedlessly into it and discovered a dark tunnel leading she knew-not and hesitated-to-inquire where. It just had to be less unsafe than what was behind.

The tunnel twisted around as if trying to dislodge her, but she followed it through every convolution, not daring to delay. Finally it gave up and let her into a faintly flowing small, forgotten, long-unused set of carved stone caves hiding under the harpy hutch caves. Against all odds, she had found a secret place that almost seemed to be safe. She stumbled under rocky crevices holding poisonous-looking twining clumps of vines glowing in brilliant vegetable green, ultraviolet, Luna white, and blood-red, growing among broken sculptures of gargoyles, through rotting logs, and across the faces of prehistoric rocky ruins. She crawled over a perilous, crumbling, narrow, rotting wooden bridge across a gaping dark chasm filled with a horrible deep menacing rustling. As she passed it, it gave way, and collapsed behind her into the depths. She listened, but never heard the sound of its landing below.

At long last the magic path ended in a pool of sinister mist. She didn't quite trust this, so she grasped a tough root growing from a crevice in a ruin. After several timid little tries she managed to haul herself through muck and mud up to a higher level. She was, she hoped, safe for a while.

"How I wish I could fly, fly, fly up to the stars once more," she breathed. But she was too tired to fly, even if she hadn't been caught in a deep dank gloomy cave unimaginably far below anywhere she cared to be. So she did the sensible thing and let herself collapse into sleep.

After a time she had no idea when she woke. the Demi-Luna moon's silvery beams were streaming in through a network of cracks in the cave's ceiling. She lay quietly beneath her spread cape, barely breathing as she sought answers to the questions that squeezed into her helpless little head at too rapid a pace.

"Where am I?" she murmured, momentarily disoriented.

"In a long-forgotten cave," came a whisper, perhaps from a stony face. Somehow this did not seem unusual. She was probably imagining it anyway.

"Am I alone?" she asked.

"Yes and no," came the cold whisper. The stone face didn't move, so that wasn't it. In any event she knew stone didn't speak. Whence came the windy voice, since there seemed to be no one else in the cave?

Maybe this was sleep, and this was a dream a night mare brought. So all she had to do was wake up. She pinched herself cruelly on the arm, but though it hurt, nothing else changed. Except that now she became aware of her feet. Something was nibbling on her tasty little toes.

She moved her head, looking about. She lay with her head in a nest of egg-shaped stones and her feet in a circulating pool of chill water. There were indeed cute little fish tasting her toes, though they weren't actually biting. Maybe they were just trying to alert her to her situation.

She sat up, wrapped her cape around her, and climbed to her feet. She shouldn't have. She screamed with pain. Her right knee was swollen as big as a globular little gourd, and it hurt twice as large. She quickly sat down again. She was hungry, she was thirsty, and she missed her mother Glory

Goblin and her father Hardy Harpy and her tutor Magpie ever so much. Why had she ever come to a place like this?

She took sober little stock. Well, she could do something for the thirst. Carefully she lowered her face to the cold, crystal-pure pool of water and touched it with her lips. She sucked in several greedy little gulps, and her raging thirst eased.

Now, with her face close to the pool, she paid attention to the gold and scarlet shapes in it. They were three tame Coy fish she knew from her occasional swims on the surface. She recognized their distinctive patterns. They weren't trying to eat her; they just wanted company.

She reached down with one hand. "I won't hurt you," she said. "I'm in the same position you are. Come, let me tickle you, and I'll share my life-and-death struggle with you." They wiggled appreciatively, and played faint music on their scales.

Suddenly the presence of the fish unnerved her. They gave her hope, and that frightened her. Maybe she could give them a message to take to the harpies, to come and rescue her. So she couldn't just give up and peacefully expire.

"Go, friends, and tell my folk where I am," she said. "Especially Magpie, if you can find her." Because Magpie, as one of the few caring demonesses, would surely have the will and ability to help.

The fish played another little melody and scooted away.

Gloha lay down again, trying to return to sleep, as there wasn't much else to do except suffer. It took her only eight long minutes and two or three short ones to realize that sleep was unlikely to come. She just lay there, cold, hungry, wretched, and rigid on the bed of egg stones, wishing it were made of ruffled feathers, though she had never been exactly comfortable on those either. The stones glowed in pretty colors, but remained uncomfortable.

So she got up, putting her weight on her swollen knee very carefully so that the pain was almost bearable. She walked to the largest crack in the cave wall. She looked at each stony detail with a reasonably clear and open little orb or two. If this were harpy thyme for her, so be it. She would make it as pensively little pleasant as she could.

She made her way to the center of the ruins in the cave, hummed to herself, and thought about Magpie. If the fish found her, she would come. If not—

Gloha tapped a column. It rang with a somber note. She tapped another. Its note was different. She found several other notes. She organized them into a tune, and sang along with it, setting the golden motes to dancing in the shards of sunlight which now fell through the jagged cave cracks. The rays of light vibrated like the strings of a harp, changing color, touching different places on the sandstone slab. The effort warmed her body, and perhaps the stone too. Each ruined runic surface seemed to resonate to her music, becoming friendlier. The spirits of the stones whispered counterpoint to her song, and clustered around a breach in the wall she hadn't seen before. She went there, and lo, it was a window to another world that might be part of the surface of Xanth, or might lead to it. This could be her way home. If she could just somehow wedge her battered little body through the crack and follow the new chamber up and out.

Her awareness of the surroundings increased, and she heard the whispering voices of the stoned gathering of gargoyles. Now she knew their identity, and what had happened to them. "Some day your story will be known, O gargoyles," she said. Then their faint voices increased, becoming an incoherent babble, as if the air were being sucked out of the cave. The cavern began to shake, and stone fragments flaked off the ruins. The crevice before her yawned wider.

Afraid that the cavern was collapsing on her, Gloha screamed and with a dreadful little determination jammed herself through the crack, out of the cave, and into the next. She fell down slippery shale and slid to the base of the scene.

Was she truly free, or was this but a tantalizing dream?

She would soon enough find out. She half ran, half flew, taking as much weight off her bad knee as she could without rising up to bang into the rough ceiling. She followed the steep trail up and around—and it opened on the surface, in sight of the harpy caves. She ran out, and the scene changed. She tripped, almost falling, and turned around.

There were no ruins behind her, no caves. Just Xanthly forest. So had it all been a bad dream? She wasn't sure.

Gloha blinked, realizing that another wave of madness had passed, leaving her damp but no longer immersed. She had relived the time she got lost in the nether caves—the ones the harpies claimed didn't exist. She knew better, and perhaps some day she would be able to prove it.

"So there are ancient ruins with gargoyles," Trent remarked. "Someone should excavate them and restore them to their original grandeur."

"You could see to that," Gloha reminded him, "if you decided not to fade away yet."

He smiled. "There will be others after me. It would be no good for us old folk to remain too long, cluttering the later history of Xanth. That's one reason the Good Magician keeps the secret of the Fountain of Youth."

She thought of something else. "Why is it *my* madness that keeps being explored? Doesn't anyone else have any bad memories?"

"Not I," the Demoness Metria said. "I'm infernal. I have no soul, therefore no conscience. My past doesn't bother me, so I would not have any bad memories or dreams even if I cared."

"I have no soul either," Marrow said. "But I would like to have one. Then perhaps I could suffer sieges of madness too."

"Which leaves me," Trent said. "I suppose if I stood upwind of you, I would feel the next wave of madness first, and perhaps then it would be my bad memories that animated."

Gloha hastily moved downwind from him. "Be my guest, Magician!"

Metria formed her smoky features into a huge sneer. "Twenty-five years of kingship—that must be a horrible memory!"

"From 1042 to 1067, when Magician Dor assumed the throne," Trent agreed. "However, the twenty years before that I spent in Mundania. You might consider that a terrible memory."

"Ugh, yes," Gloha agreed.

"What is so bad about Mundania?" Marrow asked.

"Everybody knows it's the dreariest place imaginable," Gloha said. "Because it has no magic. No wonder Magician Trent was desperate to return to Xanth."

"Not necessarily," Trent demurred. "Mundania just needs understanding."

"Here comes another wave," Metria said with relish.

Gloha found herself on the bank of a river. A solid stone bridge with a wooden drawbridge crossed it, and a group of women were washing clothing nearby in the shallow edge of the water. A two-wheeled covered cart drawn by a single unicorn—no, a horse, because it had no horn—was just crossing the bridge.

She looked down at herself. She was a child of five or six, wingless, in a human skirt and jacket, sitting on the bank above the women.

She looked to the other side, and saw a man standing not far off. He was sort of thin-haired, looking almost bald, with a short reddish beard and brown eyes. He had a funny little stand with a board on it, and he was facing it and looking every so often at the women and the bridge. Then she realized that he was painting the scene. So she got up and started toward him, to see what his painting looked like.

"Child!" one of the women screamed. It was the girl's mother; she just knew that without remembering it. "Stay away from that man! He's mad!"

So Gloha had to reverse course. Regretfully she went toward the bridge. The cart had gone on, but now a single man was walking across it. He was oddly dressed, and seemed to be somewhat confused. But he was somehow familiar.

He was Magician Trent! Looking much the way he did now, in his youthened state. But she knew that this was the original young Trent—and this must be Mundania, because it certainly wasn't Xanth. She was sharing his madness vision of his past.

She tried to call to him, but could not. The child she animated just watched. He crossed the bridge, then looked around. He saw Gloha but seemed not to recognize her. This wasn't surprising, because she wasn't herself at the moment. Then his eye fixed on the painter. He left the road and walked across to approach the man.

Gloha wanted to listen to their conversation, but knew her Mundane mother would forbid her getting close. So she busied herself on the bank, chasing down a bug, going one way and another, just sort of coincidentally getting closer to the painter. Finally she sat on the bank, and managed to scoot a bit nearer yet.

But she was disappointed. Trent tried to talk to the painter, but the man seemed not to understand him at all. Gloha realized what the problem was: Trent was speaking Xanthian, which came naturally to all residents, while the painter was speaking Mundanian. With different languages they could not communicate with each other very well.

Finally Trent gave up and went on. Gloha wanted to follow, but couldn't; the girl just was not going that way. She wrenched herself, trying to prevail. To her surprise, it worked, maybe. Something happened.

Then she was in an orchard. The fruit trees were flowering beautifully. They seemed to have hardly any leaves, but were completely covered with flowers. The painter was out there, painting the scene. She was unable to approach him again, because the woman she occupied was just walking by, but at least she could tell that this was a different day and different place.

However, it was Trent she wanted to see, not the painter. She wrenched again, and this time found herself in another body, watching him. He was somewhat ragged now; time must have passed, and he had had a hard time foraging for food in this strange country. But now he had found work at a farmstead, doing menial work, and seemed to be learning the language. Food and shelter seemed to be part of the deal; he might have to sleep in the loft of the barn with the chickens, but right now he was being served a wooden bowl of gruel by a plain young woman who must be the farmer's daughter. There was something familiar about her—

"Metria!" Gloha tried to exclaim, but of course nothing came out. She was just another farm child snooping on others' business. She was also—oops—male. A farm boy. Part of his body was weird. So she wrenched out of there and went to watch the mad painter. Well, he wasn't mad, of course; she just thought of him that way because this was a scene in the wave of madness, and he was the first man she had seen here. Still, the way her body glanced glancingly at him suggested that this native considered the painter highly eccentric if not outright crazy. But his painting was nice enough; it was of a wheat field, with a city in the background, and there was a sort of soft rounded quality to the wheat plants. And—he was animated by Marrow Bones. He didn't look like Marrow, but there was just something about the way he moved and the shape of his skull that made her certain. So he was a significant character of some sort, and it behooved her to keep an eye on him until she discovered how this sequence played out.

She found that she could control her wrenches better with practice. Each one took her approximately where she wanted to go, but always forward in time. She could see the season advancing with each jump. She had started in early spring; now it was summer.

Trent's relationship with the farmer's daughter improved.

She evidently liked him, but was shy because she wasn't
pretty. She was lean and homely, but of good character.
Something was definitely developing there.

Meanwhile the mad painter was everywhere. Each day he
tramped out to establish his position, and then he just stood
there and painted. On rainy days he did "still lifes"—tables
with fruit and pottery. But most days he was out painting
the town in all its aspects. Trees, flowers, fields, clouds,
houses, the sea, boats, and people. All of them had his
rounded, sometimes slightly fuzzy flair, but all were pretty
and realistic in their mad way. It was amazing how much
variety he could find in what had seemed to Gloha like a
pretty dull Mundane town. He never seemed to do anything
with the paintings; they just got stacked up and forgotten.
No one else seemed to want them.

Trent married the farmer's daughter. Gloha was gradually
learning how to understand the weird Mundane language
and writing, seeing it through the eyes of those she occupied, so now she was able to understand the information on
the wedding paper: this was a place called Arles in a region
called France at a time called 1888. All of that was meaningless to Gloha, but since she was here now she might as
well know it.

The mad painter kept right on painting as the season
progressed. Sometimes he painted at night and slept in the
day. Sometimes he went inside and painted piles of books,
or a pair of shoes, or chairs, or people eating at tables. But
mostly he painted fields and houses and people going
among them. Often he made sketches, and then completed
the painting later. As winter came he painted flowers in
pots. He seemed to be satisfied only when he was actually
in the process of painting; the rest of his life was blah. But
he really was mad, because he got into a fight with another
painter-friend, then cut off part of his own ear, and took it
to a house where a number of women lived. Their profes-
sion was something Gloha was not competent to fathom; it
seemed to relate to making men happy for short periods.

They weren't bad women; in fact they understood the mad painter about as well as anyone did, and showed him some sympathy. They had him taken to a place where folk got repaired and bandaged so that he wouldn't bleed to death. That slowed down his painting.

Trent was doing better. He came to know the painter, perhaps because both of them were considered mad in their ways, and now they were able to talk. If Trent told the man of the wonders of his homeland, no one would believe it if the painter spoke of it elsewhere. Maybe he did, and that only increased his seeming madness, because in the spring the painter went to a special place for the mad folk. He kept on painting, and when he couldn't go out he painted pictures of himself and others there, or even invented figures. Gloha was startled to see him paint a picture of her, with her wings, though she had none here. Either Trent had told—no, he couldn't have, because this was before Gloha had ever existed!—or the mad painter somehow saw without seeing.

Trent's wife ordered a baby the Mundane way, which Gloha found so weird that she didn't watch. There was no stork; instead—never mind. In the Mundane year 1889 it arrived, a boy, and on occasion Gloha animated it. But she also wrenched out to watch the mad painter, who was really more interesting right now. He finally left the madhouse and went to another town where a Mundane healer called a doctor tried to take care of him. That didn't seem to help much, but the painter did like the healer's slender sweet daughter. Suddenly Gloha was animating the girl, who was exactly her age of nineteen, and the painter painted her in a garden, and as she was playing a music machine called a piano. Then, suddenly, he killed himself.

Gloha, shocked, returned to Trent's family. This was proceeding normally. She watched the little boy grow older. But this lacked flair; she had become distracted by the mad painter, and now that he was gone she just wanted to get out of this scene. So she jumped ahead as fast as she could, seeing the boy become a teenager, almost a man—and suddenly a bad illness came, and Trent's wife and son died.

"Oh!" Gloha cried. "That was awful!"

"Yes," Trent agreed. "She was the only woman I ever loved, and the only son. There was nothing to do but to return to Xanth, where I had more power. But that was a separate story."

"The mad painter—" she said.

"I liked him too. He was named——" He paused, working to remember it after all this time. "Go. Van Go. Something like that. I think people got interested in his paintings after he died. But they all thought him mad while he lived. He wasn't; he merely had strong artistic passions. He understood about Xanth; he was the only one who believed me. That's why I liked him." He sighed.

"And the girl he painted, near the end? Who played the music."

"The doctor's daughter, Marguerite. A nice girl. Like you."

"This is odd," Marrow said. "I have never been a mad Mundane painter before. If I were capable of such emotion, I would have considerable sympathy for the man."

"He warranted sympathy," Trent agreed. "Had he lived in Xanth, magic could have helped him. He might have been successful and happy here. Instead he had to face life in Mundania."

"And he couldn't face it," Marrow said.

"I don't know how anyone faces drear Mundania," Metria said. "No magic—my kind doesn't even exist there." She hesitated. "Yet there was a certain ambiguity of feeling."

"A certain what?" Gloha asked.

"Doubt, uncertainty, indefiniteness, vagueness, equivocation—"

"I believe she had the right word the first time," Marrow said.

"Whatever," the demoness agreed crossly.

Trent glanced at her. "You animated my wife for a summarized period of fifteen years," he said. "I must say that if you did not feel emotion, you emulated it well enough to fool me."

"I felt it," Metria said, looking unusually pensive. "Understand, in real life I think you're an impossibly rejuvenated over-the-hill mortal human man, a fit object for endless scorn. But in that mad vision, I—she—" Something very like a tear glistened in her eye. "She did love you, didn't she?"

Gloha understood how that could be.

"And I loved her, and my son," Trent agreed. "Others called her unlovely, but in her spirit she was beautiful, and I think as time passed that came to be reflected in her physical aspect. She did not understand me as the painter did, but she treated me well from the outset, and taught me the language and ways of that land, and when we came to love each other, I learned responsibility in a way I had never known before. She made me what I was when I returned to Xanth."

"And you made her lovely," Metria said. "And she got you a fine son. Then that evil magic came—"

"A plague," he agreed. "An illness that swept across that land of France, and other lands, taking its toll of folk each time. I don't know why it spared me. I sold the farm we had inherited to finance an expedition to Xanth, which I happened to know how to reach, and recruited soldiers of fortune, trained them, prepared them to face magic, and then had the irony of achieving the kingship of Xanth without conquering it. But I would never have returned, if I had not lost those I loved." There seemed to be a tear in his own eye. The mad scene had shaken him. That, too, Gloha understood.

Meanwhile, she was also amazed. She was learning aspects of the Magician's history she had never suspected. "Didn't you love Queen Iris?" she asked.

"No. That was a marriage of convenience. We both understood the necessity."

"And your daughter, the Sorceress Irene?"

"Her, yes. And my grandchildren. Which is why I am ready to fade out of the picture and leave Xanth to them. My day is past."

Still Metria was unusually hesitant. Now she assumed the form of the woman she had animated in the vision, of mature age, with her hair tied back in a bun. She was not laughing at them or dissolving into smoke. She just gazed at Trent without speaking again.

"Please don't tease me with that form," Trent said mildly. But Gloha remembered how deceptive his mildness could be. His true emotion was not far from expression.

"I—I know it is the madness," Metria said. "But I never felt feeling before. Would you—"

The Magician evidently didn't trust this. "Would I what?"

The demoness actually fidgeted. "Would you—kiss me?"

Trent stared at her, then exchanged glances with Marrow and Gloha, who were just about as surprised. Then Gloha looked at Marrow, and decided. "Go ahead. I don't think she's teasing you."

"Agreed," the skeleton said.

"This *is* madness," Trent murmured. Then he took the image of his first wife in his arms and kissed her. It turned out to be a long and feeling kiss.

"Thank you," Metria said when he released her. There was definitely a tear on her face. "I wish it could have been real." Then she slowly faded out.

Magician Trent stood where he was, thinking his own thoughts. Then he spoke in a whisper. "Thank you, Demoness, even if it was only a game to you."

"I think she meant it," Gloha said. "The madness touched her."

"As it touched all of us," Marrow agreed. "More than ever now, I want a soul."

"Nevertheless, I think we had better get out of this region," Trent said, shaking off the mood. "I understand that the madness can strike in many ways, and many are not pleasant."

The others were glad to agree. They started walking at a swift pace, with Gloha flying ahead every so often to spy out the path. But several more waves of madness caught them anyway, though not as intense as the first ones; they were getting out of the worst of it.

During one siege Gloha returned to her harpy home and resumed her normal life—but somehow after her experience in the secret cave, that life was less satisfying than ever. In another siege the focus was on Marrow Bones, who got spooked in the boneyard by a rampaging monster—Gloha recognized Smash Ogre—and fled, only to get lost on the Lost Path. He was finally found by Esk Ogre, son of the ogre who had spooked him. Fortunately Esk was only quarter ogre, so they got along well enough. They even found another lost denizen of the gourd, Bria Brassie, who was so pleased to be found that she married Esk and set about living happily ever after. But Marrow never returned to the original boneyard, which was why he was now looking for half a soul. In that sequence Trent animated Esk's image and Gloha animated Bria's image. At one point Bria inadvertently embarrassed Esk, so she apologized in the gourd realm manner, by kissing him passionately. That was probably what led to their later marriage. But this time it was Trent and Gloha kissing. Oh well, Gloha thought as the madness faded; it wasn't as if it were the first time she had infringed on matters best left to the Adult Conspiracy.

In another siege Gloha was farmed out to harpy relatives on the Gold Coast. There she caught a rare illness. They were afraid it was the purple-hulled pink eye, whose cure would have required her to be dipped into a snakepit filled with a mixture of poultry poop and peanut hulls. Fortunately Magpie learned that it was something else, and all that was required was a foul-tasting potion. What a relief, even if the potion did taste like the contents of that snakepit. Marrow played the doctor who had made the misdiagnosis, and Metria returned to play Magpie. That was an easy role for another demoness to assume.

At last they won free of it, and came to the shore of Lake Ogre-Chobee. There were ordinary houses and gardens, not the creations of memory or horror. The madness was over. Gloha was glad they had passed through only the fringe, where it came in waves rather than solidly; more of a dose would have been troublesome indeed. Now all they had to face were the Curse Fiends.

"Let's go say hello to the neighbors," Gloha said. "Just to be sure they're real." Trent and Marrow nodded.

8
PLAY

They approached the first house. It was a neat cottage set amidst a yard with clusters of pretty mushrooms, with a little box on a post outside. On the box was neatly printed the words RICHARD C. WHITE.

"What's that?" Gloha asked.

Trent's lips pursed. "We may not be clear of the madness after all," he murmured. "That is a Mundane mailbox. See, the man's name is on it. They commonly use two or three names there."

"They keep men in little boxes in Mundania?" Marrow inquired.

Trent smiled. "No. Only letters, which are delivered each day."

"Delivered?" Gloha asked. "You mean the storks carry letters there?"

"No, there is a somewhat more cumbersome mechanism which varies from place to place and time to time. My concern is not about that, but because of the Mundane nature of it. My madness memories concerned Mundania."

"Do you remember a house like this?"

"No. So perhaps the similarity is mere coincidence."

The door of the house opened and a man emerged. He seemed to be in his mid-forties. "Hello," he called. "Are you folks lost?"

"We hope not," Trent answered. "We have just passed through a Region of Madness, and we hope this is not more of the same. Are you Richard White?"

"Yes. And I understand about the madness. I came through it myself, last year, on the way here. It was an awful experience, yet tinged with longing. I had my house built right at the edge, so I could return through it if I ever decide to. Usually the madness stays within bounds, though it has spread somewhat the past few days." He paused. "But I'm being insensitive. You folk are surely tired and confused after your experience. Come in and relax. Did you pass through the worst of it?"

"Only the fringe," Trent said. "Fortunately. I am Magician Trent, and this is Gloha Goblin-Harpy, and this is Marrow Bones. None of us are hostile folk." They followed Richard into the house.

"I have read of you, Magician Trent," Richard said. "But I thought you had faded out. And, if I may say so, you look remarkably young."

"I have been temporarily youthened for this adventure," Trent explained. "When it is done, I will fade out."

Richard brought out a bowl of oddly thin slices of something. Gloha wasn't sure what they were for. Trent took one, smiling. "I believe these are potato chips, a Mundane delicacy in some regions." He put one to his mouth, and it crackled as he chewed it. "You are recently from Mundania?" he asked Richard.

"Yes, I arrived about a year ago, though of course that may not relate well to Mundane time. The folk of the Black Wave and the Curse Friends helped me build my house.

Now I put in septic tanks for them." He smiled at Gloha's blank expression. "Those are big containers I install underground. They take the refuse from the families' privies and turn it into soil for their plants."

"Oh, magic," Gloha said, understanding. "We could use some of those for the harpy dung heaps."

"Perhaps I shall be able to do business with them, when I catch up here," Richard said. "I like making Xanth cleaner and healthier, though it is really much better than Mundania."

Gloha finally got up courage to bite into a potato chip. It crunched for her too. "It's good!" she exclaimed, surprised.

"I am not yet fully acclimatized," Richard said. "I like it in Xanth, and I'm glad to be here, but there were some Mundane things I missed. So I tried to have them duplicated here. These aren't the best potato chips, but my technique is improving."

Marrow was looking at a picture on the wall. "Is that your home?"

Richard laughed. "No, that's my effort to show Jenny Elf's home in the World of Two Moons. I hope to meet her some day. We have something in common, in the way we—" But he broke off, evidently suffering a painful memory.

"You seem to know a lot about Xanth, for a Mundane," Trent remarked. "How did you come here?"

"I always liked Xanth," Richard said. "When things soured at home, I—well, it's a story I'd prefer to leave in the Region of Madness. I'm just glad that I managed to find my way here, instead of getting lost."

"Few Mundanes are able to get here," Trent agreed. He looked around. We thank you for the food and dialogue. We have to go on about our quest now. Gloha and Marrow are looking for things we hope to find somewhere along this route."

"I understand. Some day perhaps I will travel, hoping to find a good companion." He showed them out.

"How did you get such pretty mushrooms?" Gloha asked, admiring the many clumps.

"I had some Mundane paper money with me when I arrived," Richard explained. "I knew it was useless here, so I buried it in jars for safekeeping, in case I should ever go back to visit my sister. But my hiding place turned out to be no good, because the mushrooms sprouted over each jar."

"Leave them there," Gloha said. "It's Xanth's way of keeping you here."

"It must be," he agreed. He glanced in the direction they were going. "I've never been down that way. I've heard there's a giant there, and I don't want to run afoul of him."

"Giants aren't necessarily hostile," Trent said. "But we appreciate the warning. We'll be careful."

They walked on, refreshed, waving goodbye to the nice man. They found a convenient path around a small hill. There was a tree house: someone had cut a door and windows into an old beerbarrel tree and made it into a house. There was no longer any smell of beer, so the tree must have drained some time before. It was surrounded by fancy iris flowers. Nearby were assorted fruit trees, and one spreading nut, bolt, and washer tree.

A woman of about thirty-three was just fetching in some edible washers as their party passed. She had harvested those that were in reach, and was trying to get her fingers on one that was just beyond. She was standing on tiptoes, somewhat unsteadily.

"Let me help you," Marrow said, stepping close.

She turned and saw him. "Eeeeek!" she screamed, putting a good five *e*'s into it. "Death!"

Gloha hurried forward, understanding the confusion. "No, merely a friendly walking skeleton," she said quickly. "He means you no harm."

The woman took heart. "A sweet little goblin girl," she said. Then her eyes went beyond. "And a young man."

"I'm Gloha," Gloha said. She introduced the others, giving only their first names. "We're on a private quest."

"I'm Janet," the woman said. "Janet Hines. I haven't been here long. I'm sorry I screamed. I have been told there is a giant in the vicinity, so I'm a bit nervous."

Marrow reached up and brought down the washer. He handed it to Janet. "In the realm of bad dreams, where I originated, it was my job to frighten folk," he said. "I apologize for coming upon you so suddenly."

"No, that's all right," Janet said. "I have heard of your kind. I shouldn't have reacted. Thank you for helping."

"How did you come here?" Gloha asked.

"It is a dull story. I wouldn't want to bore you."

"We recently emerged from the Region of Madness," Trent said. "We are relieved to find ourselves among ordinary folk."

"Well, it started when I was fourteen, in Mundania," Janet said. "I got sick. I was a pretty girl, some said, but this wasting disease—"

"You are still a handsome woman," Trent said, accurately enough. Gloha wasn't sure that anyone over the age of twenty could actually be pretty, but he hadn't used that word.

"It took away my ability to move, and blinded me, so that all I could do was listen, and blink my eyes to respond. But my mother read books to me, and wrote letters for me. I even had a nice new iris named after me—and I found it growing here, so I knew this was where I belonged, when I left Mundania."

That explained the irises. "But what do you do, most of the time?" Gloha asked.

"I've just been learning how to use my body again. It was a shock when I began to see, and I still don't see very well, but it's a little better each day. I had to get used to all the sights. At first I had to crawl out to pick up fruits and nuts and bolts that dropped from the trees, but later I learned to walk again. I think I'm almost normal now."

"But don't you get lonely, living alone?" Gloha asked,

and was sorry the moment she said it, realizing that it wasn't a proper question.

"I do miss my mother, who took care of me all those years," Janet admitted. "But I don't think I can go back. I'm a little afraid to meet any other people. I haven't had the courage to go far from this house I found."

"How long were you ill?" Trent asked.

"Nineteen years," she said sadly.

"Then you never had an adult life," Gloha said. "No friends, no—" She stopped herself, realizing that she was going wrong again.

"I had friends," Janet said. "They came in and read to me. But I suppose it was rather limited."

"Maybe you should take a walk around the hill," Gloha said. "There's a nice man there you might like to meet. He's from Mundania too."

"Oh? I didn't realize. Perhaps I will."

They left Janet and went on to the southeast. But soon they came up against the shore of the lake.

"But are the Curse Fiends directly on the line Crombie pointed?" Trent inquired. "My impression is that it transects the lake, but not the center where the fiends live. Perhaps we can avoid them. They are not known for their friendliness to strangers."

"Oh, pooh!" a voice exclaimed. "I was hoping you wouldn't realize that you didn't have to brace the Curse Fiends. It would have been so much more interesting."

Trent exchanged a three-way glance with Gloha and Marrow: the demoness had just confirmed his suspicion.

"In that case we might as well walk around the lake," Gloha said, relieved. "Which end does the line cross?"

"The south end, I think. So we can walk south around it."

"Curses, foiled again," Metria's voice came.

Gloha wondered about that. She was afraid that there was something they were about to encounter that the demoness would find interesting, so Metria was trying to make them think the opposite. But that was only a suspicion, and in any event, they had to circle the lake one way or the other, or make a boat. Walking around seemed less likely to trigger an encounter with the Curse Fiends.

However, they encountered something else: an ant engagement. There seemed to be an ant war on, for an army of combatAnts were laying siege to a giAnt hill. Each ant was huge, and most looked formidable. "I think we had best detour around this," Trent murmured. "It seems that the warnings about the presence of a giant were well taken; we just didn't understand what kind. I could transform those ants that come close, but they could overwhelm us if they charged in from all sides."

An Antenna quivered. The head turned toward them. "That looks like a defendAnt," Marrow remarked. "See the Antagonistic mandibles."

"Let's get out of here," Gloha said. "We don't have an Antidote to getting chomped up."

They retreated. But then they heard the ant's Anthem, carrying to the distAnt wings of the formation. They were summoning their throng for an Anticipated attack. The sound was triumphAnt.

"I think we had better hurry," Marrow said. "They may see us as cliAnts."

"I think we need an inherAnt defense," Trent said. "They are already surrounding us."

Gloha saw that they were. "I'm not conversAnt with their tactics," she said. "What's relevAnt? A roc bird? If you transform me, so I can carry you away—"

"No. They have Antiaircraft artillery." He pointed to where several antis had great long snoots suitable for blowing rocks out with great force. "It is importAnt to select the right creature."

"Then what?" she asked, becoming alarmed.

"An Antelope," he said, reaching toward her. Suddenly she was a huge four-legged creature with big Antlers. Trent and Marrow got on her back.

The ants stopped closing in. Gloha wondered why, because she did not seem to be a really unusual creature. "You are now the Antithesis of the ants," Trent explained. "The equivalAnt of something they can't handle. Just walk on by them."

Gloha, nervously, did so. Soon she saw that the ants gave way before her. Magician Trent had known what type of creature to use.

Only one ant remained close. She saw that it had a clipboard, on whose paper it was making a note. "Merely an accountAnt," Trent said. "Tallying the ones that got away, I suspect."

Good riddance, she thought.

Once they were safely past the ant activity, Trent transformed her back to her natural form. They continued skirting the lake.

A cloud passed. It peered down at them. Then it huffed and puffed, making itself bigger and darker.

"That's Fracto!" Gloha cried. "What ill luck!"

A nebulous mouth formed on the cloud. "Ho ho ho!" it breathed, its breath forming new cloudlets.

"We'd better find a dry place to camp," Trent said. "I think we won't be getting much farther today."

They hurried on, looking for a place. The cloud continued to build, eager to catch them in the open.

"You think you've gotten past the Curse Fiends without trouble," a smoke-filled voice said. "But you haven't. Look there." A dusky arm appeared, pointing.

"Oh, no!" Gloha muttered. "Metria's back."

"But there is something there," Marrow said.

Ahead of them was a huge building. It seemed to be made of stone and brick below, with a dome-shaped roof above. It was right across the general region of their line to the southeast. A prominent sign before it said THUNDER-DOME. But there was no thunder; all was quiet, except for Fracto's rising winds.

"Could there be a winged goblin male in there?" Marrow inquired.

"I doubt it," Trent replied. "As far as I know, there are still no such males. But we shall have to investigate."

"At least maybe it will be dry inside," Gloha said. The cloud was just about ready to rain on them. Then a nagging thought nagged her. "Do you think Fracto's trying to drive us into that building, because he knows there's something nasty in there?"

"Close," Metria said, her top half appearing. "It's Curse Fiend property. They had it built recently, hoping to catch something in it."

The building nevertheless seemed to be deserted. "Halooo!" Trent called. "Anybody home?" There was no reply.

They entered, as the door was open. They passed through a cavelike labyrinth of passages and emerged in a great central chamber that seemed to take up most of the building, extending right up to the dome. There were tiers of benches all around, making the chamber resemble a monstrous covered bowl.

And there, lying curled on the floor, was a giant, asleep. So the rumors had been true after all.

"How did he get in here?" Gloha asked. "He's way too big for the passage we used."

"He must have lifted up the lid and stepped in," Marrow conjectured. "Perhaps he was looking for a dry place to sleep."

"As we are," Trent agreed. "Let's hope he is friendly."

"I suppose we had better find out," Gloha said. "Maybe we should wake him, and if he tries to eat us, you can transform him into something harmless."

"Agreed," Trent said.

They advanced cautiously on the sleeping creature. They stood by his ear. The air near him was foul, and Gloha realized that it was his putrid breath. But maybe they could stay clear of the giant, once they ascertained his nature.

"Giant," she said carefully into the ear. "Please wake up and tell us whether you are friendly to regular folk."

The giant snorted. The air grew even worse. His eyes opened. He turned his head on the ground and peered at them. "Oh, hello," he said, his breath nearly knocking them over both by its physical force and its stench. "I am Graeboe Giant."

"Graeboe!" Gloha gasped. "I met your brother!"

"I don't have a brother," he protested.

"Greatbow," she said, trying her brave little best not to choke impolitely. "He said you were ailing."

"Ah, my cousin! Yes, I have an unconscionable malady, and can no longer maintain my invisibility. I did not realize you were here, or I would not have intruded upon you. My apology. I shall depart, for I know my presence is uncomfortable for normal folk."

"No, we intruded on you," she protested. "You were here first. We should be the ones to go."

"As you wish," he said. "Stand back, please, for I shall now lift my head."

They retreated as the giant lifted his head and propped it with a hand. He was too big to sit up in the building. It was obvious that Graeboe was not unfriendly. But his breath—!

Marrow met them at the edge of the passage out. "I have just checked the exterior," he announced. "It is raining canines and felines, and lightning is striking every available target. I think it will not be convenient to depart these premises for the nonce."

"But there's a foul-smelling giant in there," Gloha said.

"Perhaps we can do something about that," Trent said. "Metria?"

"Why should I help you deal with the stink?" the demoness inquired, appearing. "I enjoy seeing you mortals sweat."

"Because we shall be unable to remain here unless we can breathe," he responded evenly. "So we shall have to go elsewhere, and you will not have the dubious pleasure of snooping on our otherwise surely interesting dialogue with the giant."

"You can't go elsewhere. Its raining bovines and equines."

"Dogs and cats," Gloha said.

"Whatever. You're stuck here."

"Not if I transform Gloha to a creature that likes water, such as a gargoyle."

Metria considered. "Um. You could do that. Very well, what do you want?"

"A sprig of parsley."

She vanished, and reappeared a moment later with the sprig. "I wouldn't let you manage me like this, if you hadn't kissed me," she said.

"Surely true," he agreed, taking the parsley. "I wouldn't have asked you, if I hadn't kissed you."

Metria looked stunned. That, too, Gloha was coming to understand. Trent had that effect on women who came to know him. Even demon women, it seemed.

He walked to Graeboe. "Here is a sprig of parsley. It has the magic property of purifying breath. If you will eat it, it may solve a problem."

"I didn't know that!" Graeboe exclaimed, pleased. He moved a huge hand and tried to take the sprig, but it was much too small.

"I shall stick it under your fingernail," Trent said. He fitted the sprig into the massive crevice. The giant lifted his hand and sucked the sprig from the finger.

The air cleared. "Thank you," Graeboe said. "Even I can smell the difference."

"Well, it wasn't really your fault," Gloha said. "You can't be blamed for your illness."

"It is kind of you to say that," the giant said. Now his breath smelled like new-mown hay. "I really don't like being objectionable, so I have tried to stay away from other creatures."

"Exactly what is your ailment?" Marrow asked.

"I am not entirely clear about that," Graeboe said. "It came on me gradually. I went to ask the Good Magician, but he refused to talk to me, understandably. He merely sent word that help would come if I remained in this region long enough."

Gloha took note; that was the word Marrow had received.

"What are the symptoms of your malady, apart from the breath?" Trent asked.

"Increasing general weakness and susceptibility to illnesses. I sleep much more than I used to, yet remain tired. I fear I will not be able to remain in Xanth much longer."

"Oh? Where will you go?" Gloha asked before she thought.

The giant smiled sadly. "To fertilize the trees, I think, lovely little lass. At least I shall then be able to do something some good." He glanced around. "I can hear thunder outside. This dome seems to attract it. I think you will not want to go out soon. I have food; do you care to share it?"

"Yes," Gloha said. She liked the giant, now that she could breathe freely near him. Possibly his compliment had something to do with it.

Graeboe brought out a snack from his purse: a gross of pickle pies and a keg of green wine. They accepted tiny portions, which were all they could eat, and settled down on the floor beside him.

It remained light in the dome, though it was dark outside. "Perhaps we could play a game, or something, to pass the time," Gloha suggested politely.

Graeboe brightened. "Do you like angry word puzzles?"

"I love them," Gloha said.

So they drew lines in the dust and alternated filling them in with words, and it was fun. The giant was ill and weak and somewhat homely, but not stupid; he had a good vocabulary and a fair sense of humor. Gloha realized that just because a person was different did not mean he was necessarily unpleasant. Then they settled down to sleep, hoping that the storm would be through by morning. Trent spied a flea and transformed it into a pillow bush, so they had plenty of pillows, including a huge pile of them for the giant's head.

Gloha woke to the sound of a general stirring or rustling, as of an enormous throng of people getting ready to witness some rare event, or maybe just a flock of birds cleaning bugs from a spreading acorn tree. She opened her eyes— and saw that her first impression was the correct one. The tiered benches of the bowl chamber were filling with people.

Startled, she looked at her companions. Magician Trent and the Giant Graeboe were still asleep, but Marrow, who didn't need sleep, was alert. "What's happening?" she whispered to the skeleton.

"The Curse Fiends are assembling," he replied.

"Oh, they must be getting ready to put on a play. We must depart before we get in their way."

"Adipose chance," a ball of smoke said.

"What kind of chance, Metria?"

The smoke expanded into the nether portion of an extremely well endowed woman. "Corpulent, obese, fleshy, potbellied, rotund, blubbery—"

"Fat?"

The top half of the figure formed. "Whatever," the face said crossly as the overall figure slimmed down. "They have latched down the dome and magically sealed the premises, so we can't get out."

"They can trap a demon?" Gloha asked, surprised.

"I don't quite understand about that," Metria said, disgruntled. "I've been having weird effects, since associating with you folk." Her eye fell on Trent. "Since the Madness."

Gloha got another glimmer. She remembered how intrigued Cynthia had become with the handsome Magician, and had felt the attraction herself. Metria had played the part of the one woman Trent had loved, and it had affected her. Maybe she didn't really want to depart just yet. But of course she wouldn't admit to having anything that could be seriously mistaken for human feeling. So containing magic that ordinarily might not restrain her now had greater force. At least it was a pretext to stay near Trent.

But that was an incidental concern. Gloha addressed the major one. "What do they want of us?"

"I suspect we shall discover that in one and a half moments," Marrow said. "One of them is approaching."

Sure enough, in one and a half moments the man reached them. Trent and Graeboe woke to the sound of his footsteps. Neither spoke, evidently realizing that they needed more information before reacting.

"Who is responsible for this intrusion of our premises?" the man demanded.

Metria huffed into harridan form. "Listen, oinkface—" she started.

Gloha realized that this would never do. "Cumulo Fracto Nimbus," she said quickly, realizing why the nasty cloud had chosen to harass them. "He blew up a storm last night, and we had to hurry to cover. This building seemed to be unoccupied, so we camped here for the night. We'll be glad to get on our way—"

"Chubby chance," he said sourly. "You have intruded on our demesnes, and must pay the penalty."

Gloha felt like huffing into harridan form herself. "Penalty? Just because we came in out of the rain?"

"Perhaps we should exchange introductions," Marrow said diplomatically.

"Certainly. I am Contumelo Curse Friend, Playmaster for the Thunderdome."

"I am Gloha Goblin-Harpy, and these are Marrow Bones, the Demoness Metria, Graeboe Giant, and Magician Trent."

She had thought that the last name would faze the man, but it didn't. Maybe the Curse Fiends were too insular to be aware of who was who in the rest of Xanth. "Well, strangers, you have usurped our stage for a play, disrupting our scheduled event. You must therefore provide us with equal measure before departing the premises."

Gloha looked around, but none of the others seemed inclined to argue this case. They were leaving it to her. Probably Marrow was too polite to argue with anyone, and Trent was biding his time in case he should have to transform someone. "What kind of measure?"

"A play, of course. The people have made the arduous journey across the lake to come to our new theater, and they must be entertained. If you ilk hadn't occupied our stage, preventing our scheduled company from setting up its props—"

"Ilk?" Metria said. She was all too ready to argue, but would probably just get them all into more trouble. "I'll show you ilk, you o'erweening wretch!" She began to huff into a truly awful configuration.

"What kind of wretch?" Contumelo inquired.

The smoky shape paused in mid-huff. "Pompous, insolent, swaggering, presumptuous, haughty, o'erbearing—"

"Arrogant?"

"Whatever," the half shape agreed crossly. "Oh, now look what you've done! I've forgotten what I was huffing into."

"Perhaps a frog," Contumelo suggested, almost smiling.

"Thank you." A huge green frog formed. "Hey, wait half a moment!" the frog exclaimed. "That wasn't it. I have three quarters of a mind to—"

"Really? I would have taken it for half a wit."

The frog seemed about to explode into a mushroom-shaped cloud.

"What kind of play did you have in mind?" Gloha asked quickly.

"Something we just might find useful in our repertoire," Contumelo replied. "Of course we would have to rewrite any abysmal effort that such poor players as you might essay, but after you strut and fret your hour upon the stage you will be heard no more. Sometimes we glean inspiration from the unlikeliest sources." A sneer hovered somewhere in his vicinity without quite getting established.

Even Marrow was beginning to look annoyed, which was an unusual effect considering the bony blankness of his countenance. Graeboe, who had been completely amiable hitherto, was starting to frown. Only Trent continued to look mild—which might be the worst sign of all.

"So if we put on a play for you—something that maybe makes you laugh—then you'll let us go in peace?" Gloha asked, hoping to avert what was threatening to be an ugly scene.

"Your mere attempt will surely make us laugh. What we require is something useful, as I just informed you."

Gloha sent a somewhat disheveled gaze across the others. "Then maybe we should try to do that," she said uncertainly.

Now Trent spoke. "We shall need props and scenery."

"You should have thought of that before you intruded, bumpkin," Contumelo said.

Trent started to gesture toward the man, but Graeboe spoke. "I think some folk are not aware of the impression they make on others. It was some time before I realized why folk were avoiding me, as my illness developed."

The Magician glanced at him and nodded. Gloha relaxed; Contumelo had just been spared a transformation he surely wouldn't have liked. "Perhaps we can provide our own props," Trent said.

"I should hope so," the Curse Fiend said. "We shall give you half an hour to prepare. Then we shall expect you to perform. Of course all five of you must have significant parts; we don't tolerate slackards." He spun neatly about on heel and toe and stalked away.

"Half an hour!" Gloha exclaimed. She would have snorted, but she didn't have the nose for it. "How can they expect us to get a play ready when we have no chance to make up scenery, to write a play, to rehearse—when we've never done anything like this before?"

"They don't," Marrow said. "They expect us to fail, and be their laughingstock."

"Yes, I remember now," Metria said. "They hired the Black Wave to complete this stadium, and they like to lure strangers in and make them perform. Then they punish the strangers when they don't do well enough. It's how they relieve the dullness of their routine lives."

"And Fracto is in on it!" Gloha said, realizing.

"Of course."

"How do they punish the failures?" Marrow asked.

"They hit them with one of their massed curses. It so dazes the victims that they can barely wander away, and it may be a long time before they are able to function normally again."

Trent frowned. "I think the Curse Fiends are about due for a reckoning."

"Yet it is no worse than what dragons or goblins do to those they catch," Graeboe pointed out. He glanced at Gloha. "Present company excepted."

Trent nodded again. "Your tolerance becomes you. Yet if we are unable to put on a play that satisfies them, given what I deem to be unfairly short notice. I shall not sit still for a curse. I shall have to take action."

"Such as turning one of them into a sphinx who will then tromp the rest of them to pulp," Metria said enthusiastically.

""Oh, no, that would not be kind," Graeboe protested. "We must simply avoid the issue by putting on a suitable play."

"I never saw a giant as peaceful as you," the demoness said, not meaning it as a compliment.

"That is because the other giants are invisible; you have seen none of them," he pointed out reasonably enough. "Most of us do not wish to cause small folk any inconvenience. That is why we do not tread on their villages or fields. We wish only to exist in mutual harmony."

The more Gloha learned about the giants, the more respect she had for them. However, there was no time for incidental dialogue. "What kind of play can we do in a hurry? That puts all five of us into significant roles? I have no idea."

"Something simple, I think," Trent said. "Perhaps we

should adapt a well-known fable or story. There should be one that provides suitable roles for all of us."

"For a giant?" Graeboe asked, interested.

"Jack and the Beanstalk!" Gloha cried. "Except that it's a mean giant."

"Well, perhaps I could portray such a giant, as long as it is only in a play."

"But there's no demoness in that story," Metria protested.

"Then maybe Aladdin and the Magic Lamp," Gloha said. "You could be the genie. Trent could play Aladdin."

"Or the Genie in the Bottle," the demoness agreed with relish. "With a female genie. Every time he uncorks the bottle, she smokes out and kisses him." She formed into smoke with a huge pair of lips.

"But there's no giant in those ones," Graeboe said.

"And no goblin girls in any of them," Gloha added.

"And no walking skeletons," Marrow said.

Trent scratched his head. "Can anyone think of a tale that includes a giant, a demon, a man, a skeleton, and a winged goblin?"

None of them could. "I suppose I could be some other kind of girl," Gloha said. "A fairy, perhaps, or even a human girl, if I pretended my wings were a white cloak."

"Or a princess," Graeboe said. "Many tales have princesses. And the demoness could assume some other form, such as a frog, for the Frog Prince."

"Say, yes," Metria agreed. "Maybe the Frog Princess, who marries the Little Prince." She looked at Trent again.

"But what form can I assume?" Marrow asked somewhat plaintively.

"Death," Graeboe suggested.

"Say, yes," Gloha agreed. "The same role your kind plays in dreams."

"In the Frog Prince?"

"We keep running into that problem," Gloha said. "No single tale works."

"But a medley might," Graeboe said.

"A medley?"

"A mixture of tales," Trent explained. "We can put them together, so as to have all the characters we need."

"But what about the scenery?" Gloha asked. "The costumes and things?"

"We'll just have to play ourselves, as it were," Graeboe said. "I'm dressed as a giant, you're dressed as a girl, Marrow's a skeleton, and Trent is a man. Metria can assume any form. We'd better concentrate on the story line."

"And the scenery," Marrow said. "That will be difficult to make in the small time remaining."

"I can transform local bugs into things like wallflowers and paintbrush flowers," Trent said. "We can make scenes from them."

Contumelo approached. "You have five minutes to curtain call," he said with evident satisfaction.

"We had better get organized," Trent said. "I suggest that we separate into committees. Metria and I can devise scenery, and Gloha and Graeboe can organize the plot."

"But what of me?" Marrow asked.

"You are perhaps our most objective member. You can coordinate the two committees, and make the announcements."

"But they won't pay attention to a skeleton!"

"Yes they will, if you're in costume." Trent spied a bug on the ground, and reached toward it. Suddenly it was hat tree. "Pick a suitable hat and wear it for announcements."

Marrow selected a tall stovepipe hat and donned it. Suddenly he looked very official.

Gloha flew up to perch on Graeboe's lifted hand, so she could talk to him conveniently. "We must assemble several tales into one in a hurry," she said. "I hope your imagination is bigger than mine right now."

"My head is larger, at any rate." He considered briefly. "Perhaps if we start with Jack and the Beanstalk, to get the man and giant, and then bring in a captive princess—"

"Yes! He wants to eat her—"

Graeboe winced. "Oh, I hope not. That wouldn't be nice."

"But this is only a play. The giant has to be mean, or it won't be exciting."

"But in the real tale, the giant valued precious things, like a hen to lay golden eggs, and a magic harp—"

"How about a magic harpy?" she asked, laughing. "And the giant doesn't want to kill her, he wants to marry her, but of course she'd rather be eaten, so—"

Marrow approached. "What scenery and props will be needed?"

"A magic bean to grow into a beanstalk," Gloha said. "A land up on a cloud. A castle for the giant—"

"That's enough to start," the skeleton said, and went to the other committee.

In a moment he was back. "Perhaps if I knew the story, I could narrate the interstices."

"Wonderful idea," she agreed. She described what they were working out.

Two more minutes of hectic coordination brought them to curtain time. Trent had transformed bugs to various things: several large wallflowers, a giant bedbug, pillow and blanket bushes, a big box elder tree with red, black, and yellow slats, and assorted other things stored within that box. They were perched around Graeboe's curled body, which actually took up most of the stage. Gloha's confused little cranium was spinning. Could they possibly make this work?

"Are you ready to perform?" Contumelo inquired with grim relish.

Marrow stepped up, donning his tall hat. "Indeed. Please get out of our way, functionary."

Gloha would have laughed at the expression on the Curse Fiend's face, if she hadn't been so nervous about whether their scatterbrained assemblage would work. She retreated to hide in the box elder until her turn came to be onstage. In a round theater like this there really was no way to go offstage, but the box served well enough.

A hush descended across the audience, which now pretty well filled the theater. Gloha was surprised by the number of Curse Fiends there were. Then she saw that a number of faces were black; the Black Wavers were attending too. They looked more friendly.

Marrow Bones stepped to the center of the arena. "Greetings, or should I say, curses to you," he said grandly, doffing his impressive hat for a moment. There was a murmur; Gloha wasn't sure whether it was of approval, mystery, or outrage. "We, the Haphazard Players, are pleased to present *The Princess and the Giant*."

He turned, making a grand sweep of one bony arm. "Once upon a thyme—" And a thyme plant appeared beside him. Gloha was startled, until she realized that it wasn't real; Metria had assumed the form. She saw with satisfaction that the audience was surprised too.

Marrow waited for the reaction to fade out. Then he resumed. "There was a handsome young man named Jack."

Trent walked out from the box and stood in the center of the stage, which was defined by the giant's curled body. He looked exactly as described.

"Jack was poor but honest," Marrow said. "His family had fallen on hard thymes—" Here "Jack" tripped over the thyme plant. There was a squeak from the depths of the audience; someone almost thought the joke was funny, but had managed to stifle the laugh.

"So Jack had to take the family bovine to town to sell for coins to live on," Marrow continued. Suddenly the thyme plant was a holy cow, seemingly none the worse for the huge holes through her body. Metria had changed form again.

Jack took hold of the cow's ear and led her in a circle around the field, which was that portion of the arena outside the giant's body. "Mooooo!" she complained loudly.

"But on the way to town Jack encountered a suspicious character," Marrow continued. He removed his announcer hat, put on a sleazy hat, and stepped up to meet Jack. This time there was a laugh; it was from Contumelo, who just couldn't resist the description of Marrow as suspicious.

"And where are you going, my fine innocent young mark?" the sleaze inquired.

"I am taking our family cow to town to sell for coins so we can eat," Jack replied innocently.

"Ah, I have something better than coins," the sleaze said. "I have this magic bean, which I will sell you for your holy cow, because I like your attitude."

"Gee, that's nice of you," Jack said naively.

The play took them through the exchange, and Jack went home to the box carrying the bean, which had appeared when the cow disappeared. He entered the box. "Mother, dearest, see what a good bargain I have made," he called from the box.

"A magic bean?" Gloha screeched in her best emulation of harpy mode, speaking for the unseen mother. "You %#¢*!! idiot!" She was rather proud of that word; it wasn't of full harpy cuss-quality, but it was within hailing distance of nasty. She took the bean and threw it back out onto the main stage.

"Jack's mother was not entirely pleased," the narrator said with fine understatement. "She threw the seed out the window, and Jack had to go to bed without his supper. However, it really was a magic bean, and in the night it sprouted and grew somewhat."

The bean sprouted on the stage, and grew rapidly into a giant green vine. That was Metria again, changing her shape. The vine grew up high, becoming as large as a tree, though somewhat more diffuse.

"In fact it grew right up to the clouds," Marrow said. The vine fogged, becoming a cloud that obscured the stage, giant and all. "And in the morning, when Jack saw that, he decided to see what he might find up in that cloud. So he climbed the beanstalk, and emerged on top of the cloud."

The cloud onstage cleared in one section, and there was

Jack, just standing up, as if he had come up from below. He put up his hand to shade his eyes, as if looking around.

"And there on the cloud was a giant castle," Marrow narrated. More of the cloud thinned, to reveal an impromptu castle with walls made from wallflowers and a main turret formed by the box elder. Most of the structure was perched on Graeboe, as if he were the foundation. It was really fairly impressive, considering.

"So Jack went to the castle to see what he could find," Marrow said. Jack walked to it and pulled open a swinging wallflower to show the interior. "Fortunately the giant was sleeping at the moment." And there was Graeboe's face before him, stretched out across several bedbug beds, snoring hugely.

Jack tiptoed around the sleeping face, and there on a pile of twenty feather quilts on the giant's hand sat Gloha, looking despondent.

"There in the giant castle he found the giant's captive, a princess," the narrator continued. "She was tied to her bed, and not at all happy about it."

"Who are you?" Jack asked.

"I am a captive princess," Gloha replied. "As you can tell by my fancy feather robe." She moved her wings a trifle.

"What's a nice princess like you doing in a place like this?"

"The giant wants to marry me, and of course I would rather be chopped up into little quivering pieces," she replied. "So he has tied me to this fiendishly uncomfortable bed." She gestured at the pile of quilts.

"But those look very soft," Jack protested.

"They are. But under them he put a bean. I might have tolerated half a pea, with an effort, but a whole magic bean was just too much. See, I'm all black-and-blue."

There was a snigger from the audience, because of course Gloha's natural body was goblin dark.

"But I outsmarted him, I think," she continued. "I managed to bounce around enough so that the bean rolled out, and fell to the ground below this cloud. So now I can sleep more comfortably. But of course I still groan every so often, so that the mean giant will think I'm still being tortured."

"So that was the bean I traded my holy cow for!" Jack exclaimed.

"Shhh! You'll wake the giant."

Indeed, the giant's face stirred and snorted. Both Jack and Princess were desperately quiet, and after a moment the snoring resumed.

"I must rescue you from this face, uh, fate," Jack said gallantly. "Let me untie you and take you home with me."

"Oh, you can't untie me," the princess said. "This is a magic cord." She lifted her wrist, showing the cord looped loosely around it. "Only the giant can untie it, and of course he won't, unless I agree to marry him."

"Then how can I rescue you?" Jack asked, perplexed.

"You must get the frog to help you."

"The frog?"

"The frog can fetch out a precious golden bottle that contains the only thing that the giant fears," she explained. "That's why he threw it in the cistern, thinking that nobody would ever find it there. But the frog knows."

Marrow stepped out again. "So Jack went to the rear of the castle," he announced while Jack did that, walking around to Graeboe's rear. "Where the frog lived in a deep cistern."

And there was a huge green frog: Metria in another role. "Croak?" the frog inquired.

"I need a precious golden bottle that lies in the bottom of the cistern," Jack said. "Because it contains the only thing that the giant fears. Can you fetch it out for me?"

"Certainly I can, manface," the frog agreed.

There was a pause. "Well?" Jack asked after a bit.

"Well, what?"

"Will you fetch out the bottle for me?"

"Oh, you asked only whether I could, not whether I would. Certainly I will, peasant man."

There was another pause. "Well?"

"You asked whether I would. You did not say whether you wished this."

Jack began to get impatient. "Listen, frogface—" Then he thought the better of it. "Yes, I wish this."

"That is good to know, mammal creature."

There was a pause. "Well, why don't you?" Jack asked.

"You did not say please."

"*Please* fetch out the bottle for me."

"What's in it for me, toothmouth?"

"Oh, you mean you want something in return?"

"Do I look like a charity outfit? Of course I want something in return!"

"What do you want?"

"I want you to take me to your leader."

"Huh?"

"You're not the brightest character, are you?" the frog observed.

Jack, evidently somewhat nettled, nevertheless managed to remain mild. "Why do you want to go to my leader? I mean, I should think you'd prefer to remain in your nice chill puddle or something."

"You're a peasant, right? So your leader is a prince or king, right? I need to be kissed by one of those."

"Kissed by a prince? Why?"

"Because I am not an ordinary frog. I am an enchanted princess, doomed to remain a frog until kissed by a prince or king. If you were a prince, I'd have you kiss me. Since you're just a peasant, you're no good to me. But if you take me to your prince, he can kiss me. Then the enchantment will be broken, and I will return to my glorious natural form and can go home to my fabulous kingdom, okay?"

"Oh. I see. Okay, I'll take you with me. But it may be a while before I reach the king's castle."

"I'll wait," the frog said. Then she dived down to the bottom of the cistern and fetched up the golden bottle from where it sat at the edge of the stage.

Jack took it. Then he headed back to the castle.

"Hey, wait for me!" the frog cried. But he was already out of hearing.

He brought the bottle to the princess. "Now what?" he asked her. "I don't see anything in there."

"I don't know what's in it," she said. "Only that whatever it is, is what the giant fears."

There was a thumping at the wall-door. "Croak!"

"What's that?" the princess asked, alarmed.

"Oh, that's just the stupid frog wanting to come in."

"Why does it want to come in?"

"Because I told it I'd take it with me, so it could kiss a prince some day."

"Well, then, you made a deal, and you must honor it," the princess said sternly. "Let the frog in. Besides, it will wake the giant otherwise, with all that thumping." Indeed, one of the giant's eyelids quivered.

So Jack went out and let the frog in. It hopped up on the twenty-quilt bed. "Oh, this is comfy," it said. "But there's a discontinuity. There must have been a pea underneath, not long ago."

"There was a nasty old magic bean," the princess said. "How did you know?"

"I'm a princess. My skin is very sensitive. I felt the ripple left by that erstwhile bean."

"Oh, that explains it. Now what do we do with the bottle?"

"The peasant must take it to where the giant is sleeping, and open it. It contains a bad dream that will frighten him. He fears nothing in the world, but the dream realm is something else."

"So Jack took the bottle to the sleeping giant," the narrator said, as Jack did so. "He opened the bottle, and out poured a menacing vapor."

Indeed, the vapor swirled and thickened, then thinned to reveal—the narrator, in a pointed horror-hat. He did the "Danse Macabre," rattling his bones. "I am Death," the white skull said. "I have come to take you away with me, Giant!"

"Who?" the giant inquired blankly.

"Death. I was locked in that bottle, but now the deadlock has been unlocked and I am free to resume my business. When I take a dryad from her tree I leave only deadwood behind. Now I have come for you. So make yourself ready for your dead end."

"Oooh!" the giant groaned. Then he burst into tears. "Oh, I'm glad my mother the Queen of Giants can't see me now, bless her royal bones! All I wanted to do was make her happy by not marrying below my station, and now I'm going away with Death instead. Oh, woe is me!"

"He's a prince?" the princess and the frog asked together.

"So it seems," Jack said. "But don't worry. Death is reducing him to a quivering nonentity, and we shall soon be rid of him."

"Not so fast, Mack," the frog said.

"That's Jack."

"Not so fast, Jack. I want him to kiss me first."

"And I'm sorry we made him cry," the princess said. "I didn't know he was royal. Hey, Prince Giant! Would it make you feel better if I agreed to marry you after all?"

The giant woke. "Oh, yes," he agreed, immediately cheering up.

"But first kiss me," the frog said.

"Wait," the princess said. "If he kisses you, and you return to princessly format, he might want to marry you instead of me."

"Are you kidding?" the frog demanded. "I've got a princely boyfriend back home. My father doesn't like him, so he enchanted me to keep me from marrying my boyfriend. He figured my boyfriend would never find me and kiss me back to femininity before I got old an unattractive. Now we'll elope before my father catches on, and it'll be too late for any more enchantment."

"But I wanted to marry the princess," Jack protested.

Both princess and frog burst out laughing. "You? A peasant? Marry a princess? Just what fantasy world do you live in, Mack?" the frog asked.

"Well, I should have something for my trouble," Jack said, out of sorts.

"Oh, take a bag of money and get out of here," the giant said, tossing down a tiny bag that was nevertheless all Jack could carry.

Death doffed his hat, and the narrator donned his hat. "And so the giant kissed the frog," he said, as the giant did so, and the frog puffed into an extremely voluptuous princess with a remarkably low decolletage. "And then freed the other princess, and she kissed the giant," as Gloha flew up to perch on Graeboe's lower lip so as to kiss his upper lip. "And they married and lived happily almost ever after. Jack took his bag of gold home to his mother, who was fairly pleased, considering that it wasn't a bigger bag, and so were the village peasant girls, who suddenly discovered qualities in Jack they had somehow overlooked when he was poor. And Death, freed from imprisonment in the bottle, resumed business as usual, as many of you will discover in due course." He bowed to the audience. "We trust you have enjoyed our presentation," he concluded with a lipless grin.

The cynical Curse Fiends tried to retain their aloofness. Then it cracked. One of the members of the Black contingent started applauding, and then a few more. Gloha saw that the first one was Sherlock, whom she had met when riding on Swiftmud with Magician Trent's party. Others around him joined in, and finally some of the Curse Fiends. Not a majority, but a fair minority. She wondered whether Sherlock supported her because he recognized her and Trent, or because her goblin skin was as dark as his, or because he simply liked the play. She hoped it was the last reason.

Contumelo grimaced. "The applause meter said your effort qualifies, barely. We should be able to rewrite your play and make it into something presentable to ignorant children. You are free to go now."

"About time, curseface," the Frog Princess said.

Then Graeboe slowly heaved himself to a hunched sitting position, lifted up the edge of the dome, stood, and stepped out of the building. Gloha, Trent, and Marrow exited the arena in more conventional manner. Metria popped out of sight with a rude noise, leaving only a foul waft of smoke behind to annoy the Curse Fiends.

They saw the giant standing outside. He looked lonely. "What's the matter?" Gloha called to him.

"Well, I don't have anywhere to go," he replied. "Geographically or in life."

"Would you like to come along with us?" Gloha asked before she thought.

"Why, yes," he agreed. "I enjoyed our brief association, and would like to extend it. Perhaps I can be of some further service to you, before I expire."

"Fool!" Metria's voice came from the air beside her. "Your soft girlish human heart is going to get you into trouble sometime."

Gloha wasn't sure how they were going to manage with a sick giant along, but Graeboe was a nice person, so she didn't really regret her impulse. And it was possible that he would be able to help them out in some way, such as if they had to cross a mighty river, chasm, or desert.

Trent and Marrow didn't comment.

9

NYMPHO

They walked on along the invisible line Crombie had pointed out, southeast of Lake Ogre-Chobee. There were routine problems like rivers, dragons, cliffs, and unfriendly B's, but they were able to handle these with the giant's big hand and a little imagination.

Then as they were looking for a suitable place to camp for the night, where there was room for the giant to sleep, Gloha spied a creature flying in. For half an instant she was afraid it was a dragon or griffon, but then she saw that it was a crossbreed. It wasn't exactly a harpy, because the body was wrong, but it wasn't a griffon either. "Hey!" she called.

Startled, the creature hesitated. Then it flew away.

"Wait!" Gloha cried, flying after it. "I'm not an enemy! I'm a crossbreed. A winged monster. Like you."

The other creature paused, allowing Gloha to catch up. It turned out to be female. "Oh, so you are," she said. "I was afraid you were a man with a bow and arrow or something."

Gloha hovered near her. "No, I'm a unique creature. I think maybe you are too. What are you?"

"I'm half girl, half griffon. My name's Amanda." She blushed faintly. She seemed to be somewhat younger than Gloha. Her shoulder-length yellow hair was tied back with a blue ribbon that matched the hue of her wings. "My parents met at a love spring. They don't speak of it often."

Gloha appreciated that. "I'm Gloha Goblin-Harpy."

They shook hands, hovering.

"I'm looking for my species," Amanda said. "But I haven't found any others quite like me. I don't know what I should call myself."

"You look like a girlfon to me," Gloha said.

"A girlfon! That's perfect. Well, I had better get on home before Mom misses me."

"Bye," Gloha called as the girlfon flew away. She was somewhat sorry that it hadn't turned out to be a male winged goblin. Still, if there were a love spring nearby, there might be such a goblin. That could be why Crombie's finger had pointed this way. So maybe this was an encouraging sign.

She returned to their campsite. "It wasn't the one I was looking for," she said regretfully.

"Perhaps next time," Graeboe said. He was now sitting carefully beside their campsite. "You're such a nice girl, there must be a boy for you somewhere."

"Thank you," she said, flattered.

Trent had meanwhile transformed a small plant into a big tent caterpillar. The tent had room for himself, Gloha, Marrow, Metria, and the giant's face. The rest of Graeboe was covered by several other tents. Cushions from a transformed pillow bush served for their beds and Graeboe's head.

They feasted on berry pies, because pie plants were the easiest way for transformations to provide food. There were also pods of milk from milkweeds, and chocolate from a chocolate plant. Metria and Marrow did not need to eat, so contented themselves with exploring the surrounding region. Graeboe, oddly, did not eat any more than Trent did.

"Are you sure it's enough?" Gloha asked him, concerned.

"My illness diminishes my hunger," the giant replied. "Have no concern."

"But I *am* concerned. You can't do giantly things if you don't eat like a giant."

"True. I am weak and worsening. I know I am not the best of company. I appreciate your willingness to have me with your party. This gives me some valued solace."

"Don't you know anything about your malady? Maybe you could find a cure, if you had a name for it."

"I know only that it is a disease of the blood. My body does not make blood quite the way it should. As a result, I have less and less of it, and that makes me weaker each day. I would have trouble keeping up, were you folk not so much smaller than I am."

"Maybe Magician Trent could transform you to some other form, that doesn't need as much blood," she suggested.

"That would not help," Trent said. "That form would have the same illness. I can change folk's forms, but can't heal them."

"Maybe if we found a bloodroot—"

"No," Graeboe said gently. "My body can use only the blood it makes itself. It comes from my bones. But please do not dismay yourself on my account; I have no wish to cause you any discomfort, lovely little creature."

Gloha was flattered again. She wasn't at all sure she deserved the good opinion the giant had of her. Probably he was merely thankful for someone to talk to. "The Good Magician must have had reason to send you to this region, just as he indirectly sent me here. Maybe there are answers for both of us, just a little farther along."

"It is nice to think so," he agreed wanly.

Then Marrow and Metria returned. "What's this?" the demoness exclaimed. "Making out in a tent?"

"What passes for your mind is in a rut," Trent informed her. "Graeboe and Gloha have merely been talking."

"Then we were doing better than you," Metria retorted.

Gloha knew that this was supposed to arouse her curiosity and force her to inquire. She stifled it as long as she could, but it was too much for her to contain. "What were you doing?" she asked.

The demoness looked at her triumphantly. "I thought you'd never ask! We were summoning the stork."

Gloha, Trent, and Graeboe choked, almost together. "But—" Gloha managed to speak.

"She kissed me," Marrow explained. "That is not quite the same."

"It's close enough," Metria said stoutly.

"Walking skeletons do not summon the stork," Marrow said. "We assemble our little ones from spare bones. But in any event, I would not choose to summon or construct with a demoness. I am a married skeleton."

"Oh, pooh!" Metria said. "What's so special about marriage? The stork listens regardless."

"You are a demoness," Trent reminded her. "You have no soul, and therefore no conscience. You can't love. You have no basis for understanding."

"But I'd like to understand," Metria said, frustrated.

"Why?" Gloha asked, curious.

"In the Madness Region I was Trent's wife, for a time," the demoness said. "There was something there. It seemed interesting. I don't like missing out on anything interesting. I want to know what love is."

Graeboe shook his head slightly; any greater motion would have knocked down the tent. "I would like to know what love is too. Possession of a soul does not guarantee love."

"That's right," Gloha agreed. "I have never known stork-variety love."

"Because you're the only one of your type," Metria said.

"When you find a winged goblin man, you'll get into stork language quickly enough."

"To answer your question," Trent said. "marriage is, to those with souls, a sacred contract. The parties to it agree to love only each other, and to summon the stork with no other people. It is possible to summon the stork outside of marriage, but this is generally frowned on. You, as a demoness, can assume any form you wish. You can go through the motions, of summoning the stork, simply by showing some naive man your panties and encouraging him to proceed. But that isn't marriage or love."

"Maybe if I married someone, I'd find out about love," she said.

"I doubt it. You could go through the ceremony, but it wouldn't mean anything to you. The only demoness I know of who was able to love was Dara, who married Magician Humfrey a long time ago. But she had a soul. As soon as she lost her soul, she reverted to form and left him in the lurch."

"But she came back," Metria said.

"A hundred and thirty-six years later," he reminded her. "Because she was bored. She doesn't actually love him now. She merely emulates the mood. However, you might ask her what it was like when she did love him."

"I have. She said I would never understand."

"So there you are. Maybe you should give it up, Metria, and let us proceed on our various quests without your kibitzing."

"No, I want to know what love is. You're my closest approach. Maybe if I watch you close enough, I'll learn."

"Not by trying to seduce married skeletons," he said.

Metria pondered briefly. Then her clothing began to fuzz away.

"Or married Magicians," Trent added, closing his eyes.

"Curses! Foiled again," the demoness muttered, dissolving into smoke.

Gloha closed her own eyes. She had a certain sympathy with Metria's frustration. It was not too far from her own.

In the morning they moved on. Gloha wasn't sure whether it was her imagination, but she had the impression that Graeboe Giant was weaker. It took him some time to get to his feet, and then he seemed unsteady. But it might simply be that he was always a bit fuzzy in the morning. So she flew up to inquire.

"Graeboe, are you all right?" she asked as she landed on his shoulder near his face. "I mean, apart from your malady?"

"Please do not concern yourself, pretty thing," he replied.

"Now stop that!" she said with an annoyed little irritation. "You did it last night. You think that because I'm so small, I must be childlike, and you're patronizing me. I *am* concerned."

"Oh, no, Gloha," he protested. "I don't see you as a child at all. You're a lovely person, in body and mind. I merely do not wish to burden you with any problem of mine."

"Well, tell me anyway," she said, mollified.

He sighed. "I am weaker each day. I think I shall be able to keep on my feet only a few more days. When I fear I will not be able to get up again, I shall make my way to some desolate wilderness and there expire, as I have said."

"But you're supposed to find help here, and it must be us who can help you, somehow. You can't just give up."

"Perhaps so," he agreed, not debating the matter.

"It *must* be so," she said firmly. She walked along his shoulder, came to his giant ear, spread her wings, and flew up to kiss his earlobe. Then she flew back down to ground level.

They proceeded southeast in their assorted fashions. Graeboe took huge slow steps, setting his feet down carefully so as not to crush any houses or trees. Metria smoked out at one place and smoked in again at another. Gloha made short flights. Trent and Marrow simply walked. No more monsters bothered them, perhaps having caught on that a party including a giant and a Magician made poor prospects for prey.

Then they came to the Faun & Nymph Retreat. They could tell, because there was a sign by the path saying that. It turned out to be a small mountain by a lake, where the fauns and nymphs cavorted happily all day long. The fauns were human in form except for their cute little horns and goat's feet, while the nymphs were completely human except for their attitude: when chased, they screamed fetchingly, kicked their feet, and flung their hair about. When caught, they—

Gloha looked around, nervous that children might be in the vicinity. Fortunately there were none, so no violation of the Adult Conspiracy to Keep Children Ignorant of Interesting Things was occurring. She understood that Princess Ida had grown up in this general vicinity, but she had been too innocent to know that she wasn't supposed to see such activity. Because what they were doing was stork summoning, constantly. The odd thing was that the storks seldom if ever responded to these constant signals. Maybe they knew that fauns and nymphs could not raise children, because they didn't have families. They were unable to remember anything overnight, so no enduring relationships existed.

"I wonder where new fauns and nymphs come from?" Gloha said musingly as they watched the activity of the Retreat. "I mean, if the storks don't come here—"

"They are immortal, I believe," Trent replied. "At least until some few of them become mortal. Remember, Jewel the Nymph didn't begin to age until she fell in love and married."

"Jewel was always a special nymph," Gloha said. "She put the gemstones in the ground for prospectors to find. She had a soul. I think she was able to remember things even before she married."

"Yes, she was special. She may have been on the way to womanhood, which was why she was capable of love. Now that she's retiring, a new nymph from this region is being trained to do the job, and no doubt she is starting to remember things too. But here they have no need for memory. It may be that any who leave the Retreat start to assume normal human qualities."

Marrow was tilting his skull, looking here and there. Metria noticed this. "You are interested in peeking at stork summoning?" she inquired snidely.

"No, I think for them that is mere entertainment," the skeleton replied. "What concerns me is the apparent imbalance in the numbers."

Now the others were curious. "Imbalance?" Gloha asked. "It looks to me as if they are doing it in the usual ratio: one faun to one nymph at a time."

"But see how many fauns are left over," Marrow said. "In fact lines of fauns are forming near each nymph. I had understood that the numbers were supposed to be approximately equal. That seems not to be the case."

He was right. There were about three times as many fauns as nymphs. As a result, the nymphs were considerably busier than the fauns. That did not seem to bother the nymphs, but the fauns seemed to be somewhat unfaunly out of sorts. It was evident that each would really have preferred to have one or more nymphs to himself.

"Perhaps we should inquire," Trent said with a third of a smile.

So Gloha stepped up to the nearest faun. "Why aren't there as many nymphs as fauns here?"

He looked at her. "A tiny winged clothed nymph!" he exclaimed. "I didn't know you existed. Come play with me!" He reached for her.

Marrow extended a bone-arm to block the faun. "This is not a nymph," he said. "Merely a foreign visitor. Answer her question."

"Oh." The faun stifled his disappointment. "I don't know why there aren't enough nymphs. There just aren't, is all." He ran off in pursuit of a nymph who was momentarily free.

"That of course is the problem," Trent remarked. "They don't remember. Something must have happened to a number of the nymphs."

"A dragon ate them?" Gloha asked, horrified.

"Dragons and other predators are impartial about the sex of their prey," Trent said thoughtfully. "They should take out about as many fauns as nymphs. There must be some other explanation."

"Men, maybe," Metria said. "Human men really like nymphs, I understand, while human women don't care as much for fauns."

"True," Trent agreed. "But human men are discouraged from raiding this Retreat."

"Oh?" Gloha asked. "How? I don't see any discouragement."

"Do you see that bed in the center of the Retreat?" Trent asked her.

"Yes, but no one's on it."

"It's what's under it that counts. Snortimer is there, I believe."

"Who?"

"Snortimer. My granddaughter Ivy's monster under the bed. He took the place of Stanley Steamer Dragon, protecting the fauns and nymphs. He can't leave the bed by day, of course, but any intruding men soon try to lie on it with a nymph or two, and that's when Snortimer grabs their ankles and scares them away."

"But adults don't believe in monsters under the bed," Gloha protested.

"They do when Snortimer grabs them," he replied. "This region is special, as the presence of the fauns and nymphs suggests. They have no trouble believing in him, being childlike. With so many believing in him, he has much more power than his kind usually does. Also, Ivy Enhanced him before she left, so he's unusual. I understand he does an excellent job."

"I find this hard to believe," Gloha said, shaking her head.

"Naturally, because you're an adult. Only children and old folk about to fade out recognize the validity of monsters under beds."

"I recognize it," Marrow said.

"So do I," Metria said.

"You folk are from the dream and demon realms; you don't count."

"I recognize it," Graeboe said, squatting down to join the conversation.

"Giants don't count either," Trent said with a good two-thirds of a smile. "Only normal run-of-the-mill close-to-human folk count in this respect. And I think you, Gloha, will be able to believe, if you make the effort, because you aren't exactly of that description."

Gloha made the effort. "Maybe, around the edges, I can believe," she said.

"But we must proceed to more serious concerns," Trent continued. "This Retreat is on the line we are following, which suggests that this could be where we shall find the solutions to one or more of our problems. We should explore it carefully before going beyond. I believe there are mainly the Ever Glades farther in the direction we are going, which we would prefer not to face if we don't have to."

Gloha had heard of the Ever Glades, which went on forever and ever. She hoped they would not have to go there. "I don't think I'm likely to find a suitable man here, and I don't think the fauns and nymphs have souls to share with anyone. I don't see anything to help Graeboe either." In fact she was feeling a tiny little tad discouraged.

"The ways of magic can be strange," Trent said. "We shall just have to explore this until we are certain that our answers aren't here."

He was making sense, which was the problem. Gloha wasn't eager to remain in this region of constant dubious activity. The male members of the party seemed to find it interesting, which also bothered her on some hidden level.

"Let's camp out of sight of the Retreat," Metria suggested.

At times Gloha could almost think of beginning to start to like the demoness. "Yes, let's," she agreed.

"As you wish," Trent said with the suggestion of a significant fraction of a smile.

So they camped by a stream that was hurrying to find the lake, and set up with tents and pies and such. There was still time in the day, so they explored the vicinity, especially along the invisible line that Crombie had pointed out. Graeboe stood and looked far in all directions, but spied nothing special. Metria puffed in and out to all intermediate directions, but also spied nothing special. Marrow walked fearlessly in all near directions, spooking stray plants and creatures, but he too spied nothing special. Trent lay back on a bedbug and pondered.

"What are you pondering?" Gloha inquired.

"I am trying to decide whether the mystery of the missing nymphs bears any relation to our several quests."

"How could it?" she asked listlessly.

"That is a mystery in itself. But suppose that whatever is causing the loss of nymphs also represents the solution to our problems? What do you suppose that might be?"

She focused her alert little attention on the question. "Something with half a soul to give Marrow, and a cure to give Graeboe, and an ideal man to give me."

"Something about that last bothers me," Trent said. "Suppose we do find a winged goblin male. How can you be sure that he will be your ideal partner?"

"Why," she said, flustered, "he would have to be, wouldn't he? The only other member of my crossbreed species."

"Yet I have encountered very few goblin males whom I would care to know."

A goblin male. Gloha felt a pang of apprehension. The

average goblin male was ugly, brutish, bad-tempered, violent, and somewhat stupid. Much like the average harpy female. Why should a winged one be any better? And why should she ever want to marry such a man?

"Oh," she said, distraught. "I've been seeking a fantasy!"

"Not necessarily," the Magician said. "It just may mean that the answer to your quest is not precisely what you have supposed. Perhaps it is not a winged goblin you seek, but self-discovery."

"I don't understand that at all!" she cried, and ran out of the tent. She knew that she couldn't actually run physically away from the truth, but she needed time to figure things out for herself.

She found herself walking toward the Retreat. But as she did she couldn't stop herself from mulling it over. What did she want? A nice, handsome, intelligent, thoughtful, considerate, loving, winged goblin man. And no goblin man was like that. Why should a winged one be any different? She was a fool to suppose that such an ideal man existed or could ever exist.

Yet Crombie had pointed out a direction. That suggested that there *was* such a man. How could that be reconciled?

She shook her perplexed little perception, wishing she could find an answer where she feared there was none. So Magician Trent thought she needed self-discovery. But she was satisfied with herself; it was her prospects that needed fixing. Didn't Trent know that? What good was self-discovery if she had to spend the rest of her lamentable little life alone? She'd much rather spend it with someone like Trent himself. He answered all of the description except for his size and lack of wings.

She spied something ahead, lying on the ground near the edge of the open region that was the Retreat. It looked like a piece of popcorn, but it was the wrong color. Popcorn was supposed to be buttery yellow, or caramel tan. This was bright red.

She came up to it and picked it up. It certainly looked

like popped corn. She put it to her nose. It smelled like popcorn. She tasted it. It *was* popcorn.

She looked around. She spied another piece, right at the edge of the faun/nymph glade. This one was blue. She picked it up and ate it too. It was definitely popcorn, and very good. If she closed her eyes, she would not be able to tell what color it was; it tasted exactly like regular-colored popcorn, freshly made.

Now she stood at the edge of the Retreat. The fauns and nymphs were still at it, chasing each other down and striving enthusiastically to summon every stork in Xanth. Odd that they hadn't caught on that it wasn't working. But of course it took time for the stork to make a delivery, and these creatures remembered only the day they were in, so never learned better. That explained that, but didn't explain why so many nymphs were missing. Trent thought that mystery might be related to Gloha's quest for the ideal man. How could it? Maybe Trent's real age was making him senile, despite his greatly youthened body.

There were no more colored popcorns. Too bad; they had been delicious, as well as diverting her briefly from her private concerns.

She turned, about to go back to the camp. Then she saw another popcorn, this time a green one. And beyond it, a purple one. There was actually a trail of them; she had intersected it at an angle, so had seen only the last two.

She went to pick up and eat the green and purple pops, finding them as delicious as the first two. Then she followed the trail along the divergent path through the forest. How had these brightly colored morsels come here? Had someone been carrying a bag of them, and some had spilled out, leaving a trail? If so, she should catch up and tell that person to close up the hole before he lost the whole bagful.

She passed under a hugely spreading acorn tree, intent on the continuing trail. Suddenly a net dropped over her. She was so surprised she forgot even to scream. She just stood there stupidly wondering what had happened. Then she tried to spread her wings to fly away, but of course they were fouled in the net.

An ugly man dropped down beside her. He reached for her. His hands were huge and gnarled.

Now she remembered to scream. She inhaled, opening her mouth. "Ee—"

He clapped a hand over her mouth, stifling her scream before more than two *e*'s were out. Then he wrapped a bandanna around her face, covering her mouth so she couldn't get out any more of her scream. He picked her up, still swathed in the net, and carried her away.

Belatedly, Gloha realized how stupid she had been. She had wandered away from her companions, and foolishly followed a trail of popcorns, until she was well away from camp. Now she was the captive of some brutish man, and whatever was to become of her?

Meanwhile the man was tramping along a path of his own. It led to a dirty pond, and in the pond was a dusky island, and on the island was a battered old castle. The man got into a sodden boat, dumped her down, and paddled across to the castle. When he reached the island he hefted her up again, and carried her to the great dark wooden door. He hauled out a big metal key, put it in the keyhole, turned it, and then pulled the door open. He entered, then paused to close and lock the door behind him.

He carried her down a dark passage to a central chamber. She heard a faint whimpering. Then she saw where it came from: a small barred cell they were passing. There was a nymph in it, looking unnymphly unhappy. No wonder; nymphs lived to cavort in the open with the others of their kind. They couldn't stand being alone in a closed cell.

Now she realized that there were other cells along the way, containing other nymphs. She was beginning to understand where the nymphs had gone. They had followed trails of colored popcorn, and been netted and nymphnapped and brought here. Just as Gloha herself had been.

He set her down before an altar and drew off the net.

Gloha immediately spread her wings and flew up out of his reach.

"Hey, you aren't supposed to do that," the man protested.

"You abducted me against my will and hauled me in here and you say I can't fly away from you?" she demanded, a taut little tinge of outrage coloring her fear.

"That doesn't matter. You're supposed to marry me."

Gloha had been opening her maidenly little mouth for a paragraph of protests, but his last two words sidetracked that. "*Marry* you?" she squeaked.

"Yes. Let's get on with it. Stand before the altar and say, 'I, so and so, hereby take you, Veleno, to be my husband, by the law of the Notar Republic.' I will say much the same, taking you as my wife. Then we'll go to the bedroom for the consummation." He glanced at her. "You're somewhat small, but I can live with that."

Gloha's mouthful got sidetracked again. "Just like that?" was all she could get out.

"It's very efficient," he agreed.

"I'm getting out of here," she said. She flew to the hall, and down it to the front door. But the door was still locked, and it was far too massive for her to open even if it had been unlocked. There seemed to be no windows on this level, and the stairs were closed off by other locked doors. She was trapped in the castle.

She looked at the cells along the hall. Most contained dejected nymphs. She knew better than to ask any of them about anything; they would have no memory of their abductions or of the layout of the castle. But she was getting the picture on her own, and it was so unpretty that her pretty little perspective could hardly compass it.

She flew back to the main chamber, because there was more room there. "You're a nymphomaniac!" she cried accusingly at Veleno. "You're obsessed with nymphs!"

"Well sure," he agreed. "That's all I can find here. But I never saw a winged nymph before. And you're smaller than the others, and you have clothing. Why is that?"

"Because I'm *not* a nymph," she said. "I'm a winged goblin-harpy crossbreed. I have better things to do than run around naked all day screaming, kicking my feet, and flinging my hair around."

"Oh? What things?"

"Like searching for my ideal man to marry."

"No problem. You'll marry me."

"Marry you! You insufferable—" Gloha discovered that she lacked the appropriate vocabulary. She really should have heeded her aunt's advice and learned to speak the burning word. So she settled for a succinct substitute. "No."

"No?" he asked, surprised. "Why not?"

"Because I don't know you, don't love you, and don't think you're anyone's ideal man, certainly not mine." Even without proper harpy vocabulary, that seemed to cover the situation.

Meanwhile he was picking up on her prior statement. "You're not a nymph!" he said, excited. "You can remember from day to day."

"I certainly can," she agreed angrily. "And I don't think I'll ever forget how you kidnapped me."

"So you're definitely the one I must marry."

This was getting to be a bit much for her. "Huh?" she inquired intelligently.

"I need to marry a girl who can remember she's married."

"Well, I'm not the one," she said with a certain firm little firmness. "Now let me go before my friends come to rescue me, or you'll be in trouble."

"You have friends?" he asked, surprised again.

"Of course I do!" she said indignantly. "Don't you?"

"No."

This put her offtrack yet again. "What, none?"

"No, none."

She couldn't believe it. "What, none?" she repeated.

"Well, once I had a pet poison toad, but I don't think he counts, because he hopped away once he got to know me."

She was beginning to realize that this was not an ordinary

evil abductor. There were complications. "How did you come here to this castle?" she inquired. Maybe some background would help.

"That's a brief and dull story," he said. "Now why don't you come down here and marry me, so we can get on with the consummation."

"I'm not going to marry you, let alone consum—" But her nervous little nature would not allow her to say such a suggestive word. "Anyway, what makes you think you can just grab a girl and marry her?"

"That's what I've been doing. Each day I net a new nymph, and marry her, and consummate it, and next morning she doesn't remember. Then I have to start all over with another nymph. It's very frustrating."

"Well, let's hear your brief dull story," she said. If he was willing to be distracted from his disastrous ambition, she was willing to encourage him in that. "And be sure to include how you got this castle and why you call it a republic and why you're marrying anyone. Meanwhile I'll just stay well out of your reach, if you don't mind."

"I don't mind," he said. "It's nice to have some halfway intelligent dialogue for a change."

If all he had had to converse with was nymphs, whose minds were pretty much mindless, on the theory that no creature with a nymphly body needed a mind, then he might indeed miss the dialogue of a real person. Gloha settled down to the floor behind a chair, ready to fly instantly away if he tried to get near enough to grab her again. Meanwhile she listened to his history.

Once upon a thyme in the mists of antiquity—maybe thirty years ago—there lived an old crone. She was a weaver, and worked hard at her trade from morning till night to earn a living for herself and her innocent young daughter. She scarcely gave herself and her child a chance to rest. However, as busy and industrious as this crone was, she loved her daughter, and took time one day to give her good advice.

"Heather, my dear daughter, when the time of Rut comes over a young man, there is a failure on his part to act in a Timely and Responsive manner. Do you understand?"

"No, Mother dear," innocent Heather replied, exactly as a good girl should.

"No? Look, such a young man is so Hot to Trot that even the village sheep aren't safe. Do you understand now?"

"No, Mother dear," Heather said, embarrassed because she didn't like perplexing her mother.

"No? Well, do you have any notion of how to summon the stork?"

"No, Mother Dear," Heather said. "That's in the Adult Conspiracy, so naturally I never heard of the stork. Why are you telling me this?"

"Because once I was as ignorant as you, and that's how I came to summon the stork that brought you, Daughter dear. I don't want you to make the same mistakes."

"But how could you summon the stork, if you didn't know how, Mother dear?" Heather asked, doubly perplexed. "I can't do anything I don't know how to do."

"By the ogres and night mares of Xanth, Heather—just say No!!"

Heather was really impressed, because she had never heard a double exclamation point before. She took the lesson to heart, and saved up her very most positive No for the occasion when she should encounter a young man being Untimely and Unresponsive, or mistreating sheep.

However, as she became a teenager she became aware of certain social proprieties. She saw that her mother wore work clothes all the time, and labored with her hands, which were callused and gnarled, and she became ashamed of the old crone. So she did what any teen in such an insufferable situation did. She screamed at her mother, called her vile names like "Hag," "Witch," and "Harridan," in fact everything except the accurate term of "Crone," and to really make her point she ran away with Shadows, the village idiot. This man did not know the meaning of Timely or Responsive, and he was unconscionably mean to sheep, shearing them every spring, so this really broke the old crone's heart.

Naturally the idiot knew nothing of stork summoning either. So the two of them just had a good time. But by some curious coincidence a stork got the notion that this couple deserved a baby. This was obviously a confusion, because Heather, who had once had a figure reminiscent of a minute glass, seemed to be adding sand. She got fatter daily, and hardly seemed to be in shape to handle a baby. In any event she didn't know about the stork's notion. For a long while she pretended that she had no appetite, and she ate no food other than a few black and blue berries stolen from neighboring gardens, and some cookies. She said that these were nicer and tasted better than her mother's good soups and stews and homemade peasant bread. Shadows made her several gunky yellow banana slug stews, but they just caused her to toss her cookies. He resented this, because he didn't like seeing the cookies get wasted. That showed what an idiot he was, she reminded him frequently.

Finally there came a day when Heather was as displeased with Shadows as she had been with her cronish mother. As she lay in the dark one night, cold and hungry, her impatience with her situation boiled over in a chilly way. "Well, I've done more than enough suffering for humanity in the last nine months. I want my mother, even if she is a crone. If that idiot Shadows doesn't like it, he can go jump in the Kiss-Mee Lake with some other damsel." Because she realized now that her health had started its reversal soon after the two of them had swum in Lake Kiss-Mee and in consequence done a whole lot of kissing. Maybe the water was also fattening.

So one fine morning a not-so-fine Heather left the idiot's sandy driftwood hut and walked home, leaving her accumulation of self-pity behind. She found her mother, the village midwife, and the stork standing at the front door, wringing their hands or whatever. They wept when they saw her.

"Why are you so sad to see me?" Heather asked as she pushed impatiently over to her dear little clean lavender-smelling bed. "Didn't you say I'd be back?"

It turned out that they weren't sad, they were glad, though their emotions seemed to be stuck in reverse. The stork was especially relieved, having feared it had come to the wrong address. It dumped a baby boy in the cradle and took off. In its haste it dropped a thyme seed that had been intended for another delivery. The seed landed in the garden, and from it grew a first plant which didn't do well, and a second plant, which in the course of sixty seconds became a minute plant, and in sixty minutes became an hour plant, and in a year it was an annual, and it continued to age with the obvious intention of finally maturing into a century plant. Since that would take some time, it had a brilliant crystal on top to mark its place in space-time. The crone ignored it, being too busy, thinking it didn't matter. She probably shouldn't have done that.

After seven days the village elders came to participate in the baby's naming ceremony. Heather named him Veleno, which she understood meant Poisoned Gift. The elders sprinkled Heather with rainbow rose water and declared that, in the light of recent events, she was no longer a child but an adult.

Immediately the weight of adult responsibility descended on her. She realized how she had summoned the stork during that time when she had done just a smidgen more than kissing. She was properly appalled, and resolved never to do that again. Heather joined her mother at the loom, never to leave it for the rest of her life, and concentrated on becoming a crone herself. From then on the little stone dwelling was known as "The House of Two Weavers."

Seven or eight years crawled by, and the baby boy managed to become a boy child. He was quiet, a loner, and he displayed his magic talent early. He changed plain white popcorn into rainbow-colored popcorn. This followed naturally from his mother's talent of changing plain white roses into rainbow-colored roses. She didn't use her talent much, because she seldom encountered a white rose, but at least she had the magic. No one ever found out what talent Veleno's father had, other than idiocy; Veleno never met the man.

Veleno's small world embraced his mother, grandmother, and the nearer region of his village. One day he woke from his midday summer nap under his favorite fringed umbrella tree, took a dip in the conservative gold-water pool to the right of the village, dressed himself in his cool white well-worn cotton clothes, and headed for home. But he found everybody in great disarray standing around the village fountain. They were screaming, tearing their hair, wringing their hands, and weeping bitterly.

"What's the matter?" he asked in a faltering whisper, fearing that something was amiss. After all, it wasn't comfortable to have one's hair torn, and was painful to put one's hands through the wringer, which tended to flatten them.

"A dreadful fiery dragon is approaching the village," a man with golden orange hair replied. His name was Menthol, but that had no significance and probably shouldn't have been mentioned. "It seems that nothing can stop it from massacring everyone here."

"But why are they so upset?" the boy asked, perplexed.

The man studied the boy for a moment. Then he nodded, as if coming to a private decision. "What is your name, little boy?"

"Veleno."

"What a nice name. What does it mean?"

"Poisoned Gift."

Menthol nodded again, as if he had just confirmed a suspicion. "Ah. Does an eight-year-young century plant grow in your yard, by any chance, helping your family keep thyme?"

"Yes."

"Well, Veleno, your mother doesn't want you right now. In fact she wants you to take a walk with me. Do everything I tell you to do, and I will give you a whole bowl full of boiled sweets."

"Great!" Veleno agreed.

So Menthol took Veleno by the hand and led him away. As it just coincidentally happened, Menthol was a child stealer. He recognized Veleno as a child marked by the demons for their eventual entertainment, so he brought him to the demons for a reward.

"And so the demons put me in this isolated castle," Veleno concluded. "And told me that I would have my every desire in life supplied except one: love. I can achieve that only by marrying a woman who will marry me and share her love with me. What they didn't tell me was that the only human-seeming females in reach would be nymphs. They are incapable of love, and can't remember anything from one day to the next. But the demons did mention that hidden among them might be one who could remember and love. So from the time I grew old enough to join the Adult Conspiracy I have used my colored popcorn to lure one nymph at a time away from the mountain. I have married her and tried to summon the stork with her, hoping that she will remember in the morning. But so far every nymph has forgotten, though she has been enthusiastically cooperative in making the effort to signal the stork. Thus our marriage has been dissolved, and I have had to try again."

"But why do you keep them prisoner in the castle?" Gloha asked. "They are naturally careless creatures, but they can not be happy in confinement."

"Because I can't tell one nymph from another. If I let them go after marrying them, I might catch the same one again, wasting my time. The only way I can be sure each one is new is by holding the old ones out from the group."

It was starting to make sense. But Gloha still didn't like it. "Well, I'm not going to marry you, and I shall be neither

enthusiastic nor cooperative about—about whatever. And I
will never love you. No, not in the time it takes that century
plant to mature. So you might as well let me go."

"Oh, no, I have to marry you, because you can remember.
You are the one who can love me, and with whom I can at
last experience love. Then I will be free of the demons' enchantment, and can live like a normal man."

Veleno did not seem to be paying very close attention to
her declaration. Was there some other way to discourage
him? Gloha remembered something about demons. "Are
they watching this?"

"Oh, yes, of course. It's how they entertain themselves.
But if I find love, they'll know it immediately, and their
amusement will be over. They'll dissolve this castle into
smoke, and I will return with my bride to my village, where
we can live ever after as peasants scrounging a mean living
from the reluctant soil."

"That's certainly a modest ambition," Gloha said. "And I
wish you well with it. But it isn't going to be with me. I am
not going to marry you, and that's that."

"Then I shall have to lock you in a chamber until you
change your mind," Veleno said. "Because you may be my
only chance for love, and I would be a fool to let you escape."

Gloha realized that the man was not going to be reasonable about this. So she flew away, seeking some other exit
from the castle. She found a stairway that wasn't closed off
and flew upstairs, but all the windows were barred, and
most of the chambers were locked, with whimpering nude
nymphs inside. Escape seemed to be hopeless.

Then she spied one dark passage she had missed in her
prior haste. It was low and narrow, so she had to come to
the floor and walk along it. It led to a winding stairway
leading up. A secret exit to the roof?

She came to a small door. She tugged at its handle, and
because it was small she was able to move it. Beyond was
a closed little chamber with several barred windows. This

must be the castle's highest turret, from which there was no exterior way down. The kind used to imprison reluctant damsels. But if she could get one of those windows open, or pry out a bar, she could leap from the window. She wouldn't fall to her death; she would merely fly away. The builders of this castle hadn't reckoned with a winged goblin girl.

She entered the chamber, crossed to the far window, and peered out. She was right: this was way high up in the sky, with glorious naked air all around. She took hold of a bar. It rattled—and there was a curious little click behind her. She turned nervously, and saw that the door had swung itself closed.

Alarmed, she ran back to the door, to make sure it hadn't locked—and found that it had. It absolutely would not budge. She was trapped.

And she heard Veleno's footsteps climbing the stair. The nymphomaniac was coming for her, and he thought her to be a satisfactory substitute nymph.

What could she do? She did it. She put her frantic little face to the window and let out Xanth's most strident little scream.

10
GRAEBOE

Graeboe's giant ears perked. That was a faint distant scream! Could it be Gloha?

He peered in that direction, but all he saw was forested mountains. If Gloha was there, she would have to scream repeatedly before he would be able to find her.

He squatted, carefully, so that in his weakness he wouldn't lose his balance, fall over, and crush a fair section of forest and maybe a friend or two. He put his face near the tent. "I heard a scream."

The Demoness Metria popped into smoky solidity just under his nose. "You did? Where?"

"North of Nymph Mountain. All I saw was mountains and trees."

She faded out. In a moment she was back. "I have told Trent and Marrow. They'll hurry here. Can you carry them to that region?"

"Yes, I still have strength enough for that, I think."

"Meanwhile, stand up and show me exactly where it came from. Maybe I can investigate first."

Graeboe stood, unsteadily, breathing deeply to ease the dizziness he felt as his body straightened. He was a poor shadow of a giant! Then he pointed toward the mountains. "But it was faint, and I can't be sure it was Gloha," he cautioned her. "All maidenly screams sound alike to me."

"That's why I'm checking," she said, and with a *Zzzrrpp!* she was gone.

He slowly squatted again. Soon the Magician and the skeleton arrived. He repeated his news to them.

"Take us there," Trent said.

Graeboe opened his left hand and laid it palm-up on the ground. Trent and Marrow climbed on. Graeboe lifted them up to head height, then tramped delicately toward the mountains.

They had been at first perplexed, then alarmed at Gloha's disappearance. She had been right there, walking on the path to the Retreat, and then she hadn't returned. Trent had been the first one to be concerned, because it was his job to see that no harm came to the cute little creature. She might have taken a side path to address a call of nature, so they did not rush to seek her, but when time passed they realized that something was wrong. She was definitely gone.

She hadn't been caught by a tangle tree, because they had zeroed in all such threats in the vicinity, and Gloha knew better than to go near any. The same was true for dragons and other land monsters. Gloha didn't have to worry about winged monsters, being one herself. Graeboe had to smile at that; the girl was completely unconcerned about the term, not considering it to be anything other than a description. Trent was a human man, Graeboe was a human giant, Marrow Bones was a walking skeleton, Metria was a demoness, and Gloha was a winged monster. Such lack of affectation was one of her many endearing qualities. She was also pretty, nice, sensible, and caring. The man she finally found would be extremely fortunate.

He remembered how she had kissed him, in the play they had put on for the Curse Fiends. The notion of a tiny princess marrying a giant was ludicrous, but the play had been for entertainment rather than realism. For the finale she had walked up to his face and planted a delicious little kiss somewhere on his upper lip. There had been a laugh from the audience, but he had really liked that kiss.

In fact he really liked Gloha, and would be devastated if anything untoward happened to her. He would do everything he could to rescue her if she were in some dire strait. But first they had to find her. He tried to suppress the thought that it might be too late to help her. He had to hope that that scant little scream was hers, so that they could save her from whatever pit she had fallen into.

Metria reappeared, floating in front of him. "I assumed smoke form and drifted through the woods," she reported. "I found a few straight goblins, but no winged ones. I don't think she's there."

"We'll just have to hope she screams again," Trent said.

"If that really was her scream," the demoness said with demonly logic. "If the giant wasn't just imagining it."

"It is our best lead at the moment," Trent replied, seeming unconcerned. But Graeboe had come to realize that when the Magician seemed least affected, he was controlling his reactions. If someone assumed that this mild-mannered man was to be ignored or shoved aside, that person was likely to find himself transformed into a stink horn. The Magician was actually a very old man, youthened for this quest, and he had the experience and control of age. Graeboe respected him.

Graeboe came to stand beside the mountains. They were only a bit taller than he was, but they were more massive. He looked down at the carpet of forest covering them. It was quiet. Had he been mistaken about the direction of the scream? *Had* he imagined it? Could he have led Gloha's friends to the wrong place, while she was in some awful trouble elsewhere? He would never forgive himself, if—

The scream came again. This time they all heard it. It was from beyond the mountains, in the same direction they had been going.

"Score one for giantly imagination," Marrow remarked. The skeleton, too, was a good person, and Graeboe hoped he was successful in his quest for half a soul. Graeboe had a notion about that, because he knew of a soul that would before long become available. But right now was not the time to discuss that. Gloha was the immediate concern.

He looked for bare sections on the mountains, so he could climb over them. Slowly he stepped up, his head rising above the peaks so that he could see beyond them.

And there, in the valley beyond, was a castle. And from a window in its highest turret flew a colorful little pennant. It looked like Gloha's blouse.

Metria vanished so suddenly there was a pop. She was going to investigate. Meanwhile Graeboe told the man and skeleton what he had seen, and lifted them up high enough to see it themselves. His judgment about the scream had been vindicated. He was relieved, because now they could see about rescuing Gloha from her evident captivity.

Step by step he navigated the mountain range, treading over the peaks, and starting down the other side. The castle loomed larger and clearer. It was about as tall as Graeboe's shin, sitting on an islet in a muddy pond. A path led from it through a pass toward the Faun/Nymph Retreat. Graeboe began to get a glimmer of a suspicion.

Metria reappeared. "Gloha's captive, all right," she reported. "Along with a fraction of a squintillion sad nymphs. Seems this oafish man's a nymphomaniac; he's obsessed with nymphs, and keeps nymphnapping them for his one-night stands. Then he locks them into cells and goes for more. He thought Gloha was a nymph when he netted her."

Trent's expression became mildly grim. "Gloha is not a nymph, and he shall not hold her prisoner. I am not at all sure that he should be holding any nymphs captive either."

There was that dangerous mildness again. That nymphomaniac was surely in trouble. Graeboe wished he could speak with such deadly understatement. But he knew himself to be no more than an ordinary giant, even after allowing for his illness. If he were Trent's size, he would be of no consequence whatever.

"Perhaps we should rescue Gloha, then reason with the man about the nymphs," Marrow suggested.

"Yes. I want to take no chances with Gloha." Trent turned to Graeboe, which wasn't hard to do while standing on Graeboe's hand. "Are you able to lift off the roof of that turret, so she can fly out?"

"I will try," Graeboe agreed. He stepped toward the castle, kneeled beside it, reached forth, and put his thumb and forefinger on the conical tower roof. He lifted, but the roof was firmly secured. "I fear I lack the strength," he said with regret. "There was once a time when this would have been no problem. I might bash it back and forth to loosen it, but that might harm Gloha inside."

"Don't risk it," Trent said quickly. He turned to Metria, who was hovering nearby. "Can you form yourself into a key to unlock the door, so that Gloha can escape confinement and perhaps exit the castle by another route?"

"I thought you'd never ask!" She puffed out of sight.

But in a moment she was back, looking somewhat shamefaced for a demoness. "That's an enchanted castle! I can't touch any part of it."

"Can't touch it?" Trent asked, surprised.

"It's as if it's smoke to me," she said. "When I try to touch it, my hand and body pass right through it, as if I'm not real, though I am in solid form. I recognize it now as being demon-constructed. I can enter it and see what's happening, and talk with folk, but I can't actually touch the castle of any of its artifacts. It's frustrating."

Trent considered. "I could transform some creature into a monster that would attack the castle, but I have some cautions. The monster might harm the nymphs and Gloha too. And I would not have control over it. I deem this to be too risky, since the monster would be out of my reach when it entered the castle. I need to transform a friendly person or creature, to be assured that no inadvertent harm would be done."

"Perhaps I could enter the castle," Marrow said. "The barred windows would not stop me, if I could get my skull through, and I could climb the wall to reach such a window."

"The bars are set too close for your skull," Metria said. "I checked. And you may find the walls to slippery to climb. Enchanted castles aren't easy to handle, by no coincidence."

The skeleton nodded. "True. I fear that I too am defeated. If I could get inside it, someone might use one of my long bones to wedge the bars apart. But if Gloha can not get out, I can not get in."

"Then it must be up to me," Trent said. "I'm not surprised. Until this point Gloha has done as much to help me as I have to help her, but Crombie's pointings are always accurate. Now I shall do what I am here to do. She's a fine girl and certainly worth the effort. Graeboe, if you would be so kind as to set me on the roof of the main castle, I shall see about rescuing the princess."

Graeboe smiled. This endeavor did seem to be coming to resemble aspects of their Beanstalk play. He lifted Trent and Marrow to the castle roof and laid his hand flat so that Trent could dismount.

Marrow Bones also slid off. "But you don't need to risk yourself this way," Trent protested to the skeleton.

"Yes I do," Marrow replied.

Trent didn't argue. Graeboe withdrew his hand and watched from a reasonable distance. He would never say so, of course, but he was tired from carrying the two, small as they were, and needed to rest. What mischief this downward-spiraling ailment was!

Trent cast about on the roof, and found a tiny beetle-bug. He transformed this into a saw-fish. Marrow picked up the fish, for its serrated edges weren't as hard on his hands as they were on flesh. He carried it to the locked roof door. He put the fish's saw-toothed nose to the edge of the door frame, held it firmly, and let it saw through the frame and into the door itself. The fish sawed right around the locking mechanism, and when that fell out, the door could be opened. Then Trent transformed the fish back to a bug and returned it to the place he had found it. Graeboe found that interesting; the Magician was taking pains to do no unnecessary mischief, even to incidental bugs.

The two went into the castle. Graeboe traced their progress as they passed by the upper windows. They were in an unused wing, and there was another locked door between it and the main castle. So Marrow had to go back to fetch the beetle-bug, for transformation again, because it seemed that there were no bugs inside the castle. It appeared to be a sterile place.

"Hey, get a load of Veleno," Metria said in his ear, startling him. "He's headed up to the high turret with a costume."

Graeboe shifted position, trying to orient on the man. Night was looming, and lights were illuminating the castle. No one turned them on; they just did it, glowing in every room. In fact there seemed to be no servants or defenders in the castle. It was empty, except for Veleno and the captive nymphs. It seemed to run itself automatically. Since the demons had made it, according to Metria, they didn't bother with human servitors. There seemed to be a few pie trees growing in the central courtyard, which probably provided Veleno with his daily nourishment, and that was about it. It was a self-sufficient castle.

At least the lights made it easier to see what was going on inside, while Veleno couldn't see Graeboe outside, if he cared. The castle wasn't made of glass, but might as well have been in some sections, because of the view through the upper windows. Only the bottom story was completely opaque.

Veleno went on up to the turret chamber while Trent and Marrow were making their way past the second locked door. The man didn't seem to be aware of the intrusion. Maybe he had lived so long in this secure castle that it didn't occur to him that any invasion was possible. He came at last to the chamber. Graeboe put his ear down close so that he could overhear what was said.

"I have brought you a wedding dress in your size, so you can marry me in proper style," Veleno informed her.

"I told you before, I'm not marrying you," Gloha retorted. "My friends are about to rescue me from your fell clutches."

"No one can rescue you here. This castle is invincible to mortals. Now take this dress, put it on, and come down to the main chamber so that we can be married."

"What is it with you?" she demanded incredulously. "I just told you that I won't marry you. Aren't you listening?"

Veleno frowned. "You are a real girl, not a nymph," he said. "Therefore you can remember from day to day. That means that our marriage will not automatically dissolve tomorrow. At last I shall have fulfilled the requirement, and I shall know love, and be able to go home."

"You said all that before," she reminded him. "And I said before that I wouldn't do it. I am no nymph, and I'll never marry you. Now take back your stupid dress and let me go, and I'll just forget about this and go my way."

Graeboe shook his head. What a lovely little spirited creature she was! She wasn't taking any guff from her captor.

"If you don't come down and marry me," Veleno said evenly, "I shall bring you no food. Since you are real, you must eat. I think that when you get hungry enough, you will agree that it is better to be married and eat."

"You're trying to starve me into marrying you?" she demanded, aghast.

"Yes. Now are you ready?"

"No!"

"I regret this," Veleno said. "I had hoped to have a pleasant evening of consummation. But I suppose I can wait." He set down the dress between the bars of the door.

"Consummation!" Gloha cried. "Never!" She stamped her fine little foot for emphasis.

Graeboe sighed with admiration. Gloha did not buckle under pressure. And soon she would be rescued, so her resistance would indeed save her the grief of an unkind marriage.

Veleno went back down the stair. Metria appeared before him. "She'll never marry you, you clod of dragon dung," she said triumphantly.

"What are you, a rogue demoness?" he demanded. "Get out of my way." And he walked right through her.

Metria's face showed fury, but she stifled her retort. She couldn't affect Veleno or the castle, being unreal to them except in appearance. So she popped up to Gloha's chamber. "You told him," she said. "Good for you, goblin girl."

"I am getting hungry," Gloha confessed. "I haven't eaten anything since those colored popcorns."

"You'll be rescued soon. Trent and Marrow are making their way into the castle."

"Oh, that's such a relief to know," Gloha said. "I'm frightened of that man Veleno. I'm afraid he might—"

"Afraid of what?" the demoness asked.

"That he might try to—to consummate even without marriage."

"I hadn't thought of that," Metria said. "I suppose he might." She faded thoughtfully out.

Graeboe felt a surge of anger at the demoness. Instead of reassuring Gloha, she had made her feel worse. Demons had no human feelings, and it showed.

Meanwhile Marrow and Trent were sawing through the second door. But by the time they succeeded, Veleno was downstairs again, well out of hearing. Had he heard them, and come to investigate, Trent could have transformed him, making the rescue much easier.

Well, now they could go on in and up to the turret chamber, where Trent could transform Gloha into something small enough to get out of her cell. Then he could transform her back to her normal nice form, and she could fly away.

The two came to a third locked door, blocking a passage that ran beside an outer wall. Marrow turned back to fetch the bug again, but this time another door swung closed behind him, preventing him from getting there. The bars were too closely set to allow Marrow to get his skull through, just as Metria had said.

"Uh-oh," Trent murmured mildly.

Graeboe echoed the sentiment. In fact, the two of them were trapped, and couldn't get free because there was nothing to transform into a useful tool. The castle had outsmarted them, in its passive way.

"You could kick me, and I could assume another configuration," Marrow suggested.

"But your skull still would not be able to get out, and without it, the rest of your body could not function independently," Trent pointed out.

"True. I regret being inadequate to the occasion."

Metria appeared. "Now what picklement have you boys gotten yourselves into?" she demanded.

"We acted stupidly," Trent said mildly. "We are paying the price of our folly."

Metria reached up and tore two hanks of her hair out. "How can a mere stupid castle defeat us all?" she demanded rhetorically. "I'm just a soulless demoness, but I expected better of you, Magician." She let go of the torn hanks, and they dissolved into smoke and rejoined her body.

"You are right to be annoyed," Trent said, even more mildly.

Graeboe knew it was time for him to act. He leaned toward the just-formed cell. "Transform me, Magician," he said. "Make me be something small enough to get inside the castle, and large enough to be of some help."

Trent nodded. "I will render you into a mouse, so as to

get in here, and then an elf so as to be able to search out a set of keys to unlock the doors."

Graeboe reached for the cell, his finger touching the bars outside. Magician Trent reached through and touched him, pinching his skin in tiny fashion. Then suddenly Graeboe was a mouse, dangling by one foot from Trent's pinched fingers.

Trent brought him inside before he could fall, and set him on the floor. Graeboe tried to walk, and discovered that he had to coordinate four feet instead of two. So he walked carefully on hands and feet, and that worked. He went somewhat awkwardly to the door that barred the way to the forward passage. He slipped through, then turned around to face the Magician. This was the first time he had been transformed, and it was a weird experience.

Worse, it was a depleting experience. Graeboe felt weaker than ever. He hadn't thought of this complication; how weak could he get, and still be able to function? He wouldn't be any help if he couldn't move around sensibly.

The Magician's huge hand came down. Was this the way that he, the giant, appeared to ordinary folk? That hand could squish him in an instant! Then Graeboe found himself in the body of an elf. He was even dressed like an elf. That was just as well; he would not have wanted to appear naked. That was powerful magic the Magician had.

But he was also staggeringly weak. The second transformation had taken another dollop of energy from his meager supply. He had to grab onto the bars to keep from falling.

"Graeboe," Marrow said solicitously. "Are you in discomfort?"

"No, just very weak," Graeboe said weakly. "I—I fear I am not up to another transformation."

"I did not realize," Trent said. "I would not have transformed you, had I known it would hurt you. I apologize."

"Not hurt—just weakened," Graeboe gasped. "I will proceed in a moment."

"But I may have taken days away from your remaining life," Trent said. "That was not a kind thing to do."

"A few days hardly matter. Just so long as I am able to accomplish my purpose, and get you and Gloha free."

Trent and Marrow exchanged a glance, but did not remark on the situation further. "Rest," Trent suggested. "Recover some strength. Then Metria will show you where the castle keys are."

Graeboe rested, and after a bit he did feel slightly more stable, or at least acclimatized to his new form and state of energy depletion. "I am ready," he said.

Metria appeared. "Follow me," she said, and walked down the passage.

Graeboe tried, but with the first stride he fell against the wall. He pushed himself upright and took a tottering step before falling against the wall again.

"Oh for pity's sake," the demoness said, disgusted. "Can't you move any better than that? We'll be all night."

"He is weak from his ailment and the recent transformations," Trent called. "It behooves you to be more understanding."

"Why?" she asked, beginning to fuzz into smoke.

"Because it would make you emulate the attitude of a person with a soul, who is capable of love."

The smoke froze in mid-swirl. "Understanding would help me grasp love?" Then the smoke resumed swirling, and the demoness reappeared. "Say, I heard myself just then. I do need to practice understanding. Very well; I'll try. What do I do now?"

"Were I standing where you are," Trent said mildly, "I would try to help him to move, by lending what physical and verbal support I could."

She considered that. Then she walked across to the elf. "Let me help you," she said. "I'm sure you can accomplish your task with a little encouragement and support."

Graeboe remembered that he was the elf. He had halfway

disassociated, listening to their dialogue. It was strange being so small! "Thank you," he agreed.

She put one arm out to support him. But she was normal human size, while he was elf size: one-quarter her height. So her hand barely reached down to his head.

"Hm," she said. Then she swirled into smoke again, and reappeared as an elf girl. He was surprised at how pretty she was in that form. But of course she could assume any form she chose, and her demonly vanity encouraged her to be attractively packaged. She reached out to put one arm around his waist and drew him in snug. "Come on, hold on to me," she said. "We've got to get moving—I mean, I'm sure you will be more comfortable that way."

He put his arm around her lovely slim and supple waist. This was certainly more comfortable, but perhaps not in quite the way she intended. They walked together, down the passage and around a corner, and when he faltered, she drew him in yet more snugly. He found his hand crossing a region it probably shouldn't.

"Oh, this isn't working," she said in a flash of impatience.

"I apologize," he said. "I did not mean to touch—"

"Oh, I don't care where you touch me," she snapped. "You're of age, aren't you? You can even see my panties, if you want to." Her clothing fogged out, leaving her nymphly naked except for a bright pink panty on which his hand now rested. "I mean this is too slow. I'll just carry you."

She smoked, and his hand fell right through her naughty panty and whatever flesh might be beneath it. Then she reformed in full human size, and his hand was resting on her shapely calf. She reached down to pick him up in her arms. Now his body was wedged against her large soft bosom. "Onward," she said, and marched swiftly down the passage.

Graeboe decided not to protest. The truth was that he had not had much experience with women, whether of the giant, human, or demon persuasion, and was somewhat at a loss about the protocol. So he let his weak head rest against her pleasantly soft bosom and let her take him where she chose. There were, he concluded, worse ways to travel, and this was probably the only occasion he would have to experience this mode before he died.

Metria carried him swiftly down to the ground floor, evidently having familiarized herself with the castle. She could walk firmly enough on its floors; she just couldn't affect it in any way. Since he was not part of the castle, she could affect him, and that was fortunate. He doubted that he could have walked this far alone.

Along the way they passed many cells, and in most of these were nymphs. "Oh please, kind folk, let us out!" the nymphs cried to them. "We know not how we came here, or what will become of us. We live only to cavort and be happy, but we are not happy here."

"We've got to free these poor creatures!" Graeboe said.

"Why?" the demoness asked.

She really didn't understand! "Because shallow as they may be, they do not deserve to be penned unhappily," he said carefully. "Every creature should be allowed to live its own life in its own way, so long as it does not interfere with the lives of others."

"Well, I'm looking for love, and this doesn't reference."

"Doesn't what?"

"Pertain, associate, connect, attach, belong, apply—"

"Relate?"

"Whatever," she agreed crossly.

"Yes, it does relate," he insisted. "Love is not simply the feeling of one person for one of the opposite sex. It is a generalized condition applying to the whole of existence. Only a person who is sensitive to the welfare of others in general is capable of truly loving any one other person."

"But isn't that a whole lot of trouble?"

"Sometimes it is. But that is a liability of the condition of being a person who can love and be loved."

"So if I cared what happens to those stupid nymphs, I could love a man?"

"I think the two are linked, yes. Because you are inhuman and lack love, you care neither about the plight of others nor about any particular man."

She was silent, evidently thinking it over.

They came to a small chamber just inside the main door where there was a hook, and on the hook hung a ring with a single key: the key to the castle. Veleno probably took it with him when he went out, or when he went to lock up a nymph, and kept it here betweentimes.

Metria set Graeboe down. He reached for the key, but it was too high. Metria reached for it, impatiently, but her hand passed right through it. "Oh, stink horns!" she swore. "I keep forgetting." Then she put her hands under Graeboe's shoulders and lifted him up so that he could get the key.

It was heavy, but not too much for him to handle. He got the key ring down. "Now we must go free Trent, Marrow, and Gloha," he said, pleased. "Thank you, Metria."

"Why bother thanking me?" she asked. "I'm only helping you because Trent told me to try to be understanding."

"Because I am a living, feeling creature, capable of love, and I appreciate being helped," he explained. "Especially in my extremities of diminished size and strength."

"You mean I have to act wimpish, if I want to learn love?" she asked indignantly.

He smiled. "No. Just have feelings, and show them on occasion."

"I have feelings. I get impatient with slow humans all the time, and I think it's funny when they mess up. And I love tantalizing them with my body." Her torso became wrapped in a bright, very tight red dress whose decolletage seemed to cover only the outer quadrants of her bulging breasts and whose short skirt had to struggle valiantly to keep her panties out of sight. She took a breath. "See? Your eyes are bugging."

Graeboe blinked, getting his eyes back into shape. "True.

You craft a most impressive body. I compliment you on that."

She paused. "How would a feeling person react to that remark?"

"She would turn just the mere suggestion of a shade of pink, cast down her gaze demurely, and say 'Thank you' as if it were a matter of little importance. Inside, she would be pleased at the compliment. At least such is my judgment based on my limited observation of the gender."

The demoness turned a faint shade of pink, looked down demurely, and said "Thank you." Then she looked up again. "Like that?"

"Exactly. You learn very quickly."

She turned another faint shade of pink, looked down again, and repeated "Thank you."

Letter-perfect—and still without true feeling. Graeboe decided not to make an issue of the matter. "We had better get moving." He stepped out of the chamber, having recovered a bit of strength.

The nymphs in the nearest cells spied them. "Oh please let us out!" they chorused pitifully.

Graeboe hesitated. It would be unkind to leave them locked up, but if he took time to free them, the delay might prevent him from freeing his friends. He compromised. "I will return for you, as soon as I have accomplished my business," he told them.

"But you may never return!" they cried.

That was true. He sighed. And compromised. "I will free one of you, and she can look for another key to free the rest of you."

He went to the nearest cell and reached for the lock. Metria had to lift him up. He put the key in the keyhole and tried to turn it. It was too stiff for him. So Metria held him up against her extremely plush front with one arm across his body, and used her freed hand to brace his little hand, adding considerable power to his effort. The key turned and the lock clicked.

"Oh thank you, kind sir!" the nymph exclaimed. She pushed on the door, and it swung open. She stepped out in her pert nakedness, leaned forward, and kissed Graeboe on the forehead. He was still aloft, because Metria had not yet set him down.

"Is that a variant of a proper reaction?" the demoness inquired.

"Yes," Graeboe agreed, yanking his gaze from the nymphly assets. Small size was having unexpected benefits! "I did her a favor, so she thanked me in a nice way, though she is a soulless creature."

"Well, let's get moving," Metria said. She adjusted her grip so as to carry him as she had before, and started down the hall.

"Ho!" someone called. It was Veleno.

Metria paused, and the nymph screamed. "Eeek!" She kicked her feet and her hair flung about as she sought some hiding place—which turned out to be back in her cell.

"Well, I'm not waiting for this," Metria said. She strode right toward Veleno, whose eyes were glazing slightly as he took in her configuration and motion. Graeboe had a notion how the man felt. The effect would have been even stronger, had Graeboe himself not been covering the most eye-popping section of her body, by being carried against it.

"You can't escape," Veleno said, reaching out to grab the demoness.

There was a collision. Not with Metria. With Graeboe. The demoness, unable to interact with the things of the castle, passed right through Veleno's body and out the other side. Graeboe was left in Veleno's arms, because he was a real creature, and therefore solid to the castle. The demoness must have lost cohesion with respect to his body when it collided with the man's body.

The two looked at each other. "Ugh!" they said together. Veleno dropped Graeboe, who was able to land on his feet without too much of a jar. He discovered that his small size made him light, so that a fall that could have killed him in

giant form didn't hurt him in elf form. He staggered to the
side, where a nymph reached between the bars to catch him
and help support him.

Veleno turned and stared after Metria, who was well
worth staring after. "You're a demoness!" he exclaimed, disappointed.

"So?" she demanded, turning impressively so that her full
display was functioning. "You're no prize yourself, nym-
pho."

"If only you'd been mortal," he said. "You'd be ten times
as good to marry as that freaky little winged goblin."

Metria turned a faint shade of pink. She cast down her
demure gaze. "Thank you," she breathed, the top contours
of her dress dipping slightly to facilitate the effort.

Veleno seemed about to lose his balance. That wasn't surprising, as Graeboe would have lost his own footing had the
nymph not been steadying him.

"What's she got that we haven't got?" the nymph inquired, evidently not impressed in quite the same manner.

"Clothing," Graeboe answered. "It adds mystery, as well
as support and, uh, uplift."

"Oh, pooh! We could don clothing if we wanted to."

"She can also doff her clothing when she wants to," he
replied. "With no hands."

But their dialogue was merely incidental. The main interest was in the center of the hall.

"What are you doing carrying an elf in here?" Veleno demanded of Metria.

"What are you doing immuring nymphs?" she retorted.

"Doing what to nymphs?"

"Penning, committing, jailing, impounding, imprison-
ing—"

"Incarcerating?"

"Whatever," she agreed crossly.

"I'm looking for the one who will love me."

"Well, you're a dung beetle, and you'd better—" She
paused. "To do what to you?"

"To love me."

"I thought you just wanted a body to maul." She adjusted her position, and inhaled more deeply. Her decolletage, overmatched, would have given up, had it had any common sense.

"That too," he agreed. "When I find love, I'll be free of all this." He gestured at the castle around them.

"Why don't you let the nymphs go, once you know they don't love you?"

"I told you that before."

"Not me you didn't."

He sighed. "Because I can't tell one from another. So I have to save all the used ones."

Metria shook herself, remembering something. Her dress was definitely supernatural; nothing less would have survived that motion. Then she walked back through Veleno, who seemed dazed. She picked Graeboe up again and headed down the passage.

"Hay, wait!" Veleno cried, trying to recover some notion of initiative. "You can't take that elf! He's got my key!"

"He sure has," she agreed, accelerating. Graeboe actually bounced against her bosom. Fortunately it was so soft that he suffered no harm.

"No you don't!" Veleno said, starting after them.

"Yes I do," Metria retorted, breaking into a full run. She came to a stairway, clambered up it, turned at the landing, and was ascending the second flight as Veleno reached the first.

He glanced up, and lost his stride. Graeboe realized that the man must have caught a glimpse of demonly panties from the angle, and been suitably stunned. Metria was really using her assets.

But in a moment they heard the pursuit resuming. Veleno could no longer see what he should not be seeing, so was able to remember what he was supposed to be doing. However, Metria now had a good lead, and she continued to move swiftly.

"I wish I could be a souled creature, just for an hour," she said. "Just long enough to find out what love is."

"I wish you could too, Metria," Graeboe said. "For whatever reason, you are really helping me, and I appreciate it. I wish there were some way to reward you."

"Me too. But I think I just have to learn love by myself."

"I think you do. Maybe you will find the way."

They came to the upper section. This was the level where Trent and Marrow were confined. But there was a problem: Metria in her haste had taken another route back, and they were in another passage. One that did not pass that cell. Metria cast about, trying to find the way, but there seemed to be none. Meanwhile Veleno was catching up.

"Free us! Oh free us!" the confined nymphs there chanted in unison. But the demoness ignored them, searching for the connection.

"Where the funk *is* it?" Metria demanded. "I didn't explore this floor carefully before. I could pop right over there, but only you can carry the key."

"Maybe this way leads on up to Gloha's cell," Graeboe said. "We can release her first, then see about the others."

Veleno came into sight. "Ha!" he cried. "Got you trapped!"

"Never, you creep," Metria cried. She kicked her feet, turning around, and her hair flung out in almost nymphly fashion as she oriented on the passage ahead and got up velocity. She found the circling stairway and zoomed up it, bounce by bounce. Graeboe just hung on to the key.

They reached the top. There was Gloha's cell. "We've got the key!" Graeboe gasped as Metria came to a sudden stop almost against the door.

"Oh, wonderful!" Gloha cried. "But who are you?"

Graeboe realized that she did not know about his transformation. "I am Graeboe Giant. Trent and Marrow were captured trying to rescue you, but I reached out to Trent and he transformed me to this form so I could get the keys."

"Graeboe!" she echoed, astonished. "How you've changed!" She peered at him more closely. "But you do have his features. I mean your features."

"Homely," he agreed without depreciation. 'It usually doesn't matter how an invisible giant looks."

Metria held him up while he put the key in the lock. Then she helped him turn it, as before. The lock clicked.

Graeboe pulled on the door, and Metria pulled on him, and it swung open. "Oh thank you, both of you!" Gloha cried, impulsively hugging Graeboe. She, as a goblin, was about twice his elf height, instead of Metria's quadruple. She just sort of leaned down and picked him up in her embrace. It was a delightful experience, because she, unlike Metria, was sincerely caring.

"Ha!" It was Veleno. He charged up to the cell and pushed the door shut. The demoness tried to block him off, but he ran right through her, as before.

"The key!" Graeboe cried, remembering, as Gloha set him down. "It's still in the lock!"

"Not any more," Veleno said with grim satisfaction. He turned the key, locking the door again, and drew it out.

"Let go of it!" Metria cried, trying to grab the key from him. But her hand passed through it and him. She was completely ineffective. "Oh, fudge!" she swore.

"What kind of confection?" Veleno inquired snidely.

"Oh, go fry an eyeball!"

He faced the cell. "Let me know when you are ready to marry me, goblin girl. I will check on you every few hours. I suspect you will grow hungry and thirsty before too long, as will your elf friend."

"Never!" Gloha cried as he departed.

Outraged, the demoness puffed into smoke and dissipated.

"Wait, Metria!" Graeboe cried desperately, thinking of something.

She reappeared inside the cell. "I can't do anything for

you," she said. "I can't touch him or the key. So I guess I'd better go amuse myself elsewhere."

That was what he had been afraid of. "Metria, you have really made progress in learning human emotion. Now perhaps you can make more. You can do the generous thing and get help for us."

"Why should I bother?" she asked.

"Because it's the kind of thing a feeling person would do. You do have some feelings, as you explained before. Maybe you can get the one you want, if you just keep acting the way a person who had such feeling would."

She considered. "All right. I'll give it one more shot. What do you want this time?"

"Pop over to Gloha's relatives and tell them where she is, and how she is about to be married against her will. Then lead them here."

Metria considered further. "That *would* be a feeling thing to do, wouldn't it?" she mused.

"Very feeling," Gloha agreed, catching on to the ploy. "Maybe tell the winged centaurs too. And the giants."

"You're asking for a lot!" the demoness said, bridling.

"Yes. Only a really generous and feeling person would consider it," Graeboe said.

"Oh, all *right!*" Metria agreed crossly. She vanished.

There was a silence. Then Gloha turned shy. "Are you really Graeboe?" she asked. "Not just an elf in his image?"

"I really am. I confess it is strange being this size, but it is what seemed necessary." He looked around. "Do you mind if I sit down? I am very weak."

"I'd offer you a cushion, if I had one," she said. "I'm afraid the stone floor will have to do."

"Thank you." He sat, leaning against the wall. "I'm sorry I didn't succeed in rescuing you."

"But it was nice of you to try."

"I should have remembered to take the key out," he said, angry at himself. "What a stupid mistake."

"No more so than my getting myself caught like this," she said. "You really didn't have to risk yourself like that."

"Yes I did."

She smiled. "I think your decency is as big as you are. In your natural size, I mean."

"No, it wasn't that. I'd have done it anyway."

"Why?"

"I—" Suddenly he realized why, and knew he couldn't say it. What was the point, when they existed on two different scales, and he was so soon to die anyway? "It was just the right thing to do."

"No, I was foolish, and should pay for it. It's not right to get you and Trent and Marrow in trouble because of me." She paused, angling her head in thought. "Maybe I should agree to marry him, if he'll let the rest of you and the nymphs go."

"No!" he cried, stricken.

She looked at him in surprise at his vehemence. Then she changed the subject. "What is it like to be a giant?"

"Big," he said succinctly.

She laughed again. He thrilled when she did that. "How true! But I mean, what do you do? How did your breed come to be? To be so big, and invisible too?"

"That's not much of a story," he said, fidgeting.

"Are you uncomfortable about it? I'm sorry; I shouldn't pry. I was just curious."

"Oh, it isn't that," he protested. "I'll be happy to tell you our history. I'm fidgeting because I'm very weak and the stone is very hard."

"Oh, yes, it is, isn't it?" she agreed. "But maybe I can do something about that. Let me hold you."

He thought he had misheard. "I—think I don't understand."

"I am larger than you now, and softer. I can handle the stone. Let me hold you, and shield you from its hardness."

"Oh, that wouldn't be right," he protested.

"Why not?"

"Because I—" Again he had to stifle it. Because he would so very much like to be so close to her.

She cocked her head again. "Are you going to give me a reason, Graeboe?"

"No."

"Then come on," she said. "You have been a friend to me when you didn't have to be, and I will be a friend to you. It is little enough, considering our situation."

He found that he wasn't able to demur when she phrased it that way. He tried to get to his feet, but had difficulty.

"Oh, you really are weak," she said solicitously. "I keep forgetting. It carried right through from your other size. Here, I'll get you." She got readily to her feet, stepped across the cell to him, sat beside him, reached across, and heaved him onto her lap in a sitting posture. She put her arms around him, holding him steady. His head came up just to her petite bosom. "Is that better?"

"I feel like a child," he said.

She laughed once more, rocking him with the expression. "That's the way I usually feel, when dealing with regular human folk. It's about time I made somebody else feel that way." She settled back against the wall. "Now tell me about the giants."

Centuries ago, the ancestors of the giants were ordinary human folk. They lived in a village in central Xanth, and harvested not-holes from the local pining trees, which they traded to other villages for other goods. Wherever there was an unwanted hole, one of their special not-holes would eliminate it, without the necessity for any rebuilding. So there was a fairly steady demand, and the village got by, trading the holes for what else they needed.

But there were problems. There were a number of monsters in the vicinity, such as dragons, griffins, river serpents, ogres, and trolls. Any villager who wasn't careful was apt to discover himself in the stomach of a monster. This made them feel rather insecure. They wished that they didn't have to worry about monsters. Meanwhile, their numbers diminished, because the monsters were eating them faster than they could grow new children. At this rate, the day would come when no village was left.

Then one of them heard that a Magician, or at least a person with a very strong magic talent, was in need of assistance. It occurred to them that they might be able to make a deal with the Magician. If they helped him, maybe he would help them. So they sent a representative to negotiate. It turned out that the Magician's talent was making things very large. Huge, in fact. And suddenly they realized that if they were large, they wouldn't have to worry about dragons and whatnot; they would be big enough to throw the dragons away. This notion had considerable appeal. So they made the deal: they would build the mountain the Magician wanted, if he would make them too big for any dragon to devour.

They packed up their things and traveled to the Magician's place of residence. He touched the first man, and the man began to grow, enormously. He grew right out of his clothing, which was embarrassing; in fact his bare bottom was blushing. "Do not be concerned," the Magician said. "Your bodies will not show."

"They will show across the length and depth of Xanth!" a woman protested. "We must have giant clothing!"

"Just watch, and you will see," the Magician said, unperturbed.

"That's what's bothering us!" the woman said, covering the curious eyes of her children. "We are seeing too much. Those aren't exactly moons in the sky."

But as the man grew further, something weird happened. He began to become less visible. His body seemed to be thinning, in the manner of a demon turning to smoke. "He's fading away!" someone cried. "He's not mooning us anymore."

"No, he is merely becoming visually diffuse," the Magician said. "There is only so much to see in an ordinary person. When his body expands, that sight gets spread across a wider surface. Finally it expands so much that he can't be seen at all. But he is still solidly there."

They watched, amazed, as the first man became a virtual shadow of himself, a faintening outline, and finally nothing. But when they went up to where he had stood, they discovered his monstrous bare feet. He was indeed still there.

"We didn't agree to this!" someone said.

"Consider this sensibly," the Magician responded. "As big as you will be, you will have little if any need for clothing for warmth, because of an aspect of magic called the square cube ratio, and if you do need it, you can make it of suitable size. Meanwhile no one will stare at you or be concerned when you walk near, because no one will see you. Thus you have the ultimate privacy along with your size. This combination should work very well for you."

They considered, and the more they thought about it, the more sense it made. So they decided that it would be all right to be invisible, and they would communicate with each other by calling back and forth. They would make do.

So the Magician made the rest of them large. There was much blushing as they burst out of their clothes, and some glances of admiration before they faded out, and finally all of them, even the children, were huge and invisible. They could see perfectly well; they just couldn't be seen.

"You are fortunate that you aren't in Mundania," the Magician said. "Because there your invisibility would make it impossible for you to see, and you would be blind with the light passing right through your eyes and never stopping to give you the picture. But here in Xanth you don't have to be concerned about such confusions."

Then they got to work, and with their enormous bare hands they scraped up a big mound of earth and rock for the Magician, forming his mountain. When he was satisfied, they linked hands and walked away, seeking a region where they could dwell without stepping on anyone, because they were peaceful folk who did not like to make trouble. They found an isolated region, and there they settled. They found that indeed they did not need clothing, unless they wanted to become visible. When they did wear clothing, it tended to fade after a while, becoming invisible too, so there didn't seem to be much point in it. Anyway, they found they liked being invisible; it had a number of advantages.

After a time some giants left the community to find separate employment. Some just wandered around seeking good works to do, taking care where to set their feet so as to do no harm. Sometimes one would find that a storm had blown a big tree down on a normal person's house; he would quietly lift that tree away, so as to free the people trapped beneath, and the people would think that the wind had done it. Graeboe's cousin Greatbow found employment with Com Pewter, scaring folk into the evil machine's cave. But Greatbow himself was careful never to actually step on anyone or to do irreparable damage to the forest.

Another cousin, Girard, was so softhearted that he tried to water trees in a drought and to help injured animals. He took do-gooding to an extreme that became a fault. When he tried to help a little human boy, he wound up getting a bad dream that had been intended for the boy, and in that dream saw Gina Giantess, with whom he fell instantly in love. But she was only a figment crafted for the dream, making fulfillment of his love impossible. But finally he was able to find her anyway, in the dream realm of the hypnogourd.

Graeboe himself had not even gotten around to seeking love. His malady had come upon him, and slowly wasted him, so that his breath turned too bad for other giants to stand, he lost his invisibility (apparently there was after all a bit of magic involved in that), and he became increasingly weak. Yet the Good Magician seemed to think that there was an answer for him, and he had sought that answer. Now he realized that there was no answer, or he had lost it along the way. So he was satisfied to try to do what bit of good he could before he expired.

* * *

"Oh, but that's very sad," Gloha said, trying to comfort him. "You're such a nice person. You really deserve to live beyond your youth. Just how old are you?"

Graeboe counted on his fingers. "Just about coming onto my majority," he said. "I was found on a cabbage patch forty-eight years ago."

"But that's old!" she exclaimed, amazed.

"Not for a giant. Ordinarily we live to be two hundred or so. So I'm not yet a quarter through my scheduled life. In your terms I would be about—" He concentrated, trying to do long division on his fingers, but it wasn't working very well.

"About nineteen?" she asked.

"Yes, I think so," he agreed. "That sounds right. If I were to stay in this body, and live out my term, I would not live any longer than you would. But of course that's academic."

"There must be some way to save you," she said.

"I am more concerned with saving you," he said. "It would be intolerable to let Veleno have his way with you."

"Yes, you are here now because you tried to help me," she agreed. "Well, you rest for a while, Graeboe, and I shall see if I can think of any way to help any of us."

"Maybe Metria will get help."

"Maybe she will." She held him and rocked him, and he found himself fading into sleep. Her embrace was wonderfully comforting.

Graeboe expected to die without revealing it, but he could no longer hide the foolish truth from himself: He was by nature a giant, and she was a goblin-harpy crossbreed, but he loved her. All he could do was hope that Gloha escaped this prison and found her desire. Meanwhile he could not imagine a nicer way to fade out than this, being rocked in her arms.

$\overline{11}$
METRIA

Gloha held Graeboe while he slept. She felt so guilty for foolishly getting herself caught here, and thus leading her friends into captivity too. Trent had accompanied her to protect her, and he had tried to, but there were limits, and she had stretched them too far. Marrow had come along to see if perhaps his own quest for half a soul might be found, and he had been helpful, and now was also a prisoner. But Graeboe was the worst, because he had nothing to gain from them, yet had tried his best to help, and now had no chance to pursue his quest for life. It was interesting that in giant terms he was just about her own age. That was way too young to die!

There was a tramping on the stairs. Veleno appeared, carrying a lamp, for it was now dark. "Are you ready yet?" he inquired.

"Never," she said quietly, so as not to disturb Graeboe's sleep. The poor giant had enough trouble, without having his rest disturbed, and she was glad to do this much for him.

"You will change your mind eventually," he said. "I'll wait."

"And if I don't?"

"You're mortal. You'll expire."

"You wouldn't dare!" she exclaimed, too vehemently, for Graeboe stirred. She increased her rocking, hoping he would not awaken.

"Of course I would dare," he said. "I don't expect you to call my bluff. The hungrier and thirstier you get, the more reasonable my proposal will seem. And I think that goes double for your mortal friends. You won't want them to suffer unduly on your behalf."

Gloha stiffened. He was right. How could she do this to Trent and Graeboe? Graeboe might be about to die anyway, but Trent wasn't. She just couldn't let them pay such a horrible price for her defiance.

Yet the idea of being married to this gross man Veleno, who was twice her height and not remotely like the one she was looking for, forever ending what foolish dreams she might have had—that was too appalling to contemplate. If she had to marry a human man, it should be someone more like Magician Trent. That particular foolishness had considerable appeal. But she did know better.

What was she to do? She couldn't stand either alternative. So all that was left was for her to hope that the Demoness Metria succeeded in summoning help. So that she and her friends could be rescued from this fell man with his fell castle.

Veleno waited a moment, and when she didn't answer again, he turned and tramped back down the stairs. He was sure that time was on his side. Maybe—perish the thought!—he was right. Unless Metria—

A swirl of smoke appeared. "Well, I'm back," the demoness said.

"Did you summon help?"

"Not exactly. I consented them."

"You whatted them?"

"Whatted?"

"What did you do to them?"

"Oh. Agree, enlighten, apprise, acquaint, inform, notify—"

"You advised them?"

"Whatever," the demoness agreed crossly.

Gloha contained her temper, still trying not to disturb Graeboe. "Whom did you advise?"

"Oh, everyone. Your goblins, harpies, winged centaurs, giants—"

"Giants?"

"Graeboe's a giant, isn't he? When he's himself?"

Gloha glanced down at the elf she held. "Yes. If the invisible giants come, they can just lift off the roof and free us all. Good thinking, Metria."

The demoness turned faint pink, averted her gaze, and said, "Thank you."

Startled at this display of modesty, Gloha lost her chain of thought. However, it didn't fall far, and she was able to recover it. "So is anyone going to come to help? Did you tell them where we are?"

"Oh, sure. And I even told Smash Ogre that Tandy will be delayed returning, because you forgot to. He said that was okay for now. The others'll be here the day after tomorrow, maybe."

"The day after tomorrow!" Gloha exclaimed, then quickly rocked to lull Graeboe back to sleep. "We could starve of thirst by then!"

"Starve of what?"

"Never mind. I don't think Graeboe can last that long without food and water. We're going to have to do something sooner."

"Such as what?"

Gloha stifled her groan. "Such as marrying Veleno."

"What, me marry him?"

"No, me. I'm the one he wants to marry. I hate the notion, but I see no alternative."

But the demoness had caught hold of an idea that in-trigued her. "I wonder if I could marry him?"

"No way. You're a demoness. You can't love, remember? His enchantment won't be broken until someone loves him."

"And you can love him?"

Gloha stiffened again. "Oh, you're right. I may be capa-ble of love, but not with him. I can't stand him. So even if I married him, I wouldn't break the enchantment. It would be a wasted effort." That realization was actually a relief.

"Suppose I married him, and pretended to love him. If I fooled him, would that do it?"

That was a difficult question. "I don't think you could fool him, Metria."

The demoness bridled. "I can fool just about anyone, when I try. Anyone except Grossclout."

"Who?"

"The Demon Professor Grossclout. He's so smart he thinks everyone else's head is filled with mush. He proves it all the time. I tried to fool him with Woe Betide, but he saw right through her."

"Who?"

Metria disappeared. In her place stood the most darling, sweet, cute, innocent, huge-eyed forlorn little waif of a girl imaginable, dressed in rags. "Hi," she piped. "I'm Woe Be-tide. Buy a match?" She offered a tiny twig of wood.

Gloha was impressed. "That would fool me," she agreed.

The waif's face clouded tragically. "It didn't fool Grossclout. Nothing fools him. He's a terror."

Graeboe woke. "Who's that?" he asked, startled.

The ragamuffin turned her great sad orbs on him. "I'm just downtrodden Woe Betide, the poor little match girl. Ev-erybody gaits on me."

"Everybody what's on you?" he asked.

"Paces, struts, tracks, hobbles, shambles—"

"Steps?" he asked.

"Treads?" Gloha asked at almost the same time.

"Whatever," the waif said crossly.

Graeboe laughed weakly. "Hello, Metria."

Woe Betide puffed into smoke. "What gave me away?" the demoness inquired, re-forming in her full buxom edition.

"It was just a lucky guess," he said.

Metria sent him a suspicious glance, but didn't argue the case.

Gloha remained intrigued by the prior subject. "I wonder if you *could* feel Veleno?" she asked "Not that it would be ethical."

"Who cares whether it's ethical, so long as it works?" the demoness asked.

"Fool Veleno?" Graeboe asked.

"He wants to marry someone who will love him," Gloha explained. "Metria might marry him and pretend to love him."

"Why?"

"To get the rest of us free."

"Why?" he asked again.

"Because it would be a caring thing to do," Metria said shortly. "So I could learn to rapture."

"To what?" Gloha asked.

"Adoration, esteem, amour, passion, stork—"

"Oh, love," Gloha said.

"Oh, whatever," the demoness agreed crossly.

"I think I understand," Graeboe said. "Veleno wants to marry and love, and Metria wants to do something caring, so she might help us by making him think he had found love, so that he would release all the others."

"Might, schmight!" Metria said. "We'd make a deal: he releases them, or he gets no nookie."

Gloha wasn't familiar with the word, but decided not to inquire lest the correct word be troublesome. "I don't think it would be ethical," she repeated. "Therefore we can't do it, tempting as it is."

"You haven't said why ethics matters," Metria said.

"It matters to feeling folk," Graeboe said.

"Oh, why do you have to put it that way!" the demoness exclaimed, more than crossly.

"It's just very hard to explain feeling things to one who doesn't feel," Gloha said, somewhat at a loss.

"Let me get this straight: it's all right for him to capture folk and starve them to make them do what he wants, but it's not all right for them to fool him into letting his victims go?"

"Oh, my," Gloha said, taken aback. "Put that way—"

"Veleno is being unethical," Graeboe said. "But that does not give us leave to be unethical too. We prefer to be governed by the best standard, not the worst."

"Yes," Gloha agreed, appreciating his clarification.

"Okay, let's get practical. Suppose I tell him I'm a demoness and can't really love him, but I'll pretend to for a couple of days, so he can break his geis, and—"

"Break his what?" Graeboe asked.

"I got the right word," Metria said crossly. "Geis, pronounced *gaysh*, plural geasa, as in girl. No, that's not quite it; forget the plural. It's a magical obligation. He has to find love, so he can get out of here. That's his geis."

"A geis," Gloha said musingly. "That's interesting. I wonder if anyone else has such an obligation?"

"Oh, many do. You should hear about the geis of the gargoyle. But that's a whole nother story. So anyway, he wants something, you want something, I want something; why can't we make a deal?"

"Perhaps, if the terms are clearly understood and honored, it would be ethical," Graeboe agreed.

Gloha was moved to something like wonder. "You would do this, Metria, just to get the feeling of doing something generous?"

"Sure. You people seem to have all kinds of feelings I don't understand, and they make you do funny things. You seem to get a lot of fun out of love. I want to try it, once, just so I know what it is."

"But there is no guarantee that doing something nice for us will enable you to love," Gloha said.

The demoness shrugged. "There's no guarantee it won't."

Gloha thought about the ugly alternatives she faced. If this could free her of those . . .

"Perhaps it is worth trying," Graeboe said. "So long as you do speak truly, and do follow through."

"The follow-through is easy. Any demoness can make any man deliriously happy, if she chooses."

"I wouldn't say that," he demurred.

"Oh wouldn't you? How about when you were bouncing on my bosom? Didn't you like that? And what about sleeping on *her* bosom? Don't you like that even better?"

Both Gloha and Graeboe stiffened. He scrambled off her lap. "I—" he started, while Gloha tried not to flush.

"And you have to tell the truth, right? So tell me it isn't so. I could assume goblin girl form too, you know."

He was silent. Gloha managed to come to his rescue. "Real folk can make real folk happy," she said. "But that's not the same as a demoness doing it."

Metria fogged out, and reappeared as Woe Betide. "Maybe someone your size," she said to Graeboe. "Suppose I do a strip mine?" She began to dance, pulling off her innocent bonnet.

"What kind of—?" Graeboe began.

"Never mind!" Gloha said. "We'll grant that a demoness can—can do what you said, when she wants to. How can we be sure you'll tell Veleno the truth? So we aren't ethically compromised?"

"Suppose I do it right here? So you can listen?"

Gloha exchanged exactly one glance with Graeboe. "That seems fair," she agreed.

"Done! When he comes here to torment you again, I'll make the deal."

Gloha was hardly sure how she felt. If this was ethical, and it worked . . .

The demoness popped out, leaving them alone in the cell. Graeboe found a place to sit down against the wall.

"You don't have to go there," Gloha said.

"I think I do. I never wished to cause you any embarrassment."

"And you didn't. It was the demoness who did that."

"Still, I will not contribute to any problem for you, in any way I can prevent."

Something that had been hovering around the periphery of her thoughts came into focus. "You like me, don't you?"

"Well, that isn't relevant to our situation. Anyone would have tried to help you."

"No, I mean you—" She hesitated. "You *really* like me."

He brightened. "I—do. But I have no wish to cause you any distress, or to interfere in any way—"

"Yes, that's what you said. And you are such a good man. If only you weren't—"

"A giant," he finished wanly.

"No." For she was just now coming to understand something Magician Trent had said, about knowing her own mind. "If only you weren't dying. I think I could—could like you the same way. To be a friend to you as you have been a friend to me. But even if I get away from this castle, you can't get away from your fate. You'll never be a happy giant again, going your way, marrying a nice giantess, and living happily ever after."

Graeboe seemed to reconsider something, and to come to a painful conclusion. "Friends, yes," he agreed. "That is true. I am sorry I did not think far enough ahead to realize that it was not only pointless to make new friends at this time, it was cruel. To those friends. I was so hungry for company that I did not question it in the way I should have. I have done all of you a disservice."

She considered. "I see your logic, Graeboe, but not your feeling. I think I would not want never to have known you or Magician Trent, whatever happens. All this time I have been looking for a winged goblin, when I should have been looking for truly good friends. Friends like you."

"No, I am not truly good. I am ordinary in all but body, and even that is fading."

"And so am I. Ordinary, I mean, in spirit." She shook her head. "At least I have learned to look beyond the body. Much good may it do me."

They lapsed into silence. Gloha hoped that Trent and Marrow weren't feeling too despondent. Her guilt for their fate remained. If only she hadn't stupidly followed that popcorn! She had sidetracked their whole quest and gotten them all in trouble. Now their only hope was a demoness whose only reason for helping was infernal curiosity.

She heard the tramping of feet on the stairs. Was Veleno returning so soon? Or *was* it soon? It was hard to tell, in the dark. Maybe she had snoozed in the interim.

This time the man had brought a tray with food. "Are you ready to marry me?" he asked.

"No, but maybe someone else is," Gloha said.

"The nymphs don't count. None of them remember that they married me. You will remember."

"There is another who will remember. Who is willing, as I am not."

He showed interest. "Who?"

"Metria."

"Who?"

"The demoness."

"Oh. Demons count even less than nymphs do, because they can't interact with me or the castle."

Metria appeared. She was exquisitely garbed, showing less of her voluptuous body than usual. Her dress was of silk and gauze, and she wore a sparkling necklace, and a tiara in her glossy hair. "I have learned something about this castle of the Notar Republic," she said. "No demon can interact with you within it, but any demon can outside it. And anyone who marries you can interact with you in the castle, because it will then accept that person as its mistress."

"Why, that's true," Veleno said, surprised. "I had forgotten. I thought it didn't matter, because no demoness had any interest. Are you saying that you do?"

"Yes. I will marry you. For a price."

"A price?"

"Let all the captives go. All the nymphs, and the mortal folk, and the walking skeleton too."

"I told you before: I can't let the nymphs go until I find the right one."

Metria considered. "Well, when you're sure that I'm the right one."

"The moment I find love, none of them will matter. They'll all be freed automatically, and your friends too."

"Automatically?" Gloha asked.

"When this castle dissolves."

"Oh, the geis," Metria said. "Yes, that's right. So we don't have to worry about that. Still, we must bargain. I want you to feed everyone who needs it now. These two here, and Trent in the other cell."

"If you marry me tonight, they shall eat tonight."

"Deal. Let's do it."

Gloha cleared her throat.

"But there's something else I have to tell you," Metria added. "You know I'm a demoness. I can't really love anyone. But I can pretend to, and make it so good it will fool you. Maybe it will fool the castle too."

It was Veleno's turn to consider. "It seems worth a try. If it doesn't work, the castle won't dissolve, all the captives will remain, and the goblin girl will have to marry me next."

"Hey, I'm not agreeing to that!" Gloha protested.

"You don't need to. I'll simply start starving you and your friends again, until you change your mind."

"Your logic is inescapable," Gloha said cuttingly.

"So let's get with it," Metria said.

"Come down to the nuptial chamber."

"First feed my friends."

He sighed. "Very well. I have a tray here. I will fetch another."

Metria reconsidered. "I don't want a stupid simple chamber wedding. I want a full-scale bash."

"But that will take time."

"I can wait if you can." Metria's dress shifted, becoming a fancy wedding gown. "Don't you want to do it right, for once?"

"That would mean having witnesses and all that inconvenience."

"There can be witnesses. Let my friends attend. The nymphs too."

"But I'd have to let them out of their cells."

"So the castle's still tight, isn't it?"

"One's a Magician. He could change one of the others into a monster to devour me."

"He has a point," Graeboe said. "He has no reason to trust us."

"Make them take oaths of nonhostility," Metria said. "In this castle, all oaths are binding, even if the people who make them aren't honest."

"You *have* learned about it," Veleno said.

"Sure. The Notar Republic isn't really the castle, it's a situation. Anything it oversees has to be true. Wherever the castle is, that's a piece of the Republic, and its law governs. So the oaths will do it."

Veleno looked at Gloha and Graeboe. "Will you make the oath of nonhostility? That means you can't do anything hostile to me, such as trying to act against my interest. Such as trying to escape."

Gloha felt a chill. "Oh, I don't like this," she murmured.

"You don't have to swear to marry him," Graeboe pointed out. "Just not to hurt him."

It occurred to her that the freedom of the castle would be a lot more comfortable than confinement to this chamber. For one thing, she needed to get to the privy room. "All right."

"Then swear, and I'll give you the freedom of the castle," Veleno said.

Gloha closed her eyes, nerved herself, and spoke. "I hereby swear the oath of nonhostility to the proprietor of this castle." At that point she felt several loops of a silken cord settle around her and draw gently tight. She opened her eyes, surprised, but there was nothing to see. She realized that these were the ties of the binding oath; it bound her invisibly, but securely.

Graeboe took the oath. Then Veleno unlocked the door. He handed Gloha the key. "Let your other friends out—but only after they make the oath. I'll go see about more food, and arrangements for the wedding."

Surprised again, Gloha took the key. "You have this tray," she said to Graeboe. "I'll have the next. After I release Trent and Marrow."

"And I'll make sure of those wedding arrangements," Metria said with enthusiasm. "Oh, I'll make Xanth's most beautiful bride." She vanished.

Gloha followed Veleno down the stairs. Things had happened so swiftly she felt dizzy. But at least now there was a chance for things to work out better.

"That way," Veleno said, pointing to a side passage. He continued straight ahead.

She followed the passage, and came to the cell. "You got free!" Trent cried gladly.

"Not exactly. Metria is marrying Veleno, so he is giving us the freedom of the castle, provided we swear an oath of nonhostility. We can't try to harm him or to escape, until it is clear that the marriage is valid. Graeboe and I made the oath, and you must make it now."

"I am not ready to make that oath," Trent said mildly.

"Then I can't unlock your cell."

"This is interesting. Have you learned honor?"

"I thought I always had it. But it doesn't matter. When I made the oath, invisible bindings bound me, and I must honor it. It's a geis."

"An obligation of honor," he agreed. "If Metria's marriage doesn't work, what becomes of you?"

"Then I am back where I started. I haven't agreed to marry him, but I would get locked up and starved until I did agree. And so would you and Graeboe."

"Yet you honor your agreement, despite this risk?"

"Yes. Now are you going to make the oath? You will be fed anyway, but I can't let you out without that oath." She hesitated. "Please, Magician, I don't want to leave you confined." In fact she didn't want to leave him at all. She remembered how he had confessed his desire to transform Cynthia Centaur back to human form, for a reason he didn't need to state, considering Cynthia's interest in him. Gloha couldn't help wondering how it would be to be transformed to human woman form, at least for a night with him. Of course the Magician had no notion of her interest, and she would not tell him. She just—wished.

"I don't need to make the oath," Trent said. "Neither does Marrow."

"Yes you do. Because otherwise I can't let you out." The binding oath held her firmly, though she really wanted to free him so she wouldn't have to leave him here and go about her remaining business alone.

He smiled. "Let me explain. You meant well, but you came within transformation range just now. I could have changed you to a flea, and picked up the key ring as it fell to the floor. Then we would have been free without the oath."

"Oh!" Gloha said, stepping hastily back. She knew it was true. "Why didn't you?"

"Because part of what I learned during my exile from Xanth was honor. I have never since that time played false to any person or creature. It would not have been honorable to use your naivete to trick you into violating your oath. So though I am not entirely at ease with the compromise you made with the master of this castle, I must adhere to the deal you made, and may offer no hostility to him. My continued incarceration thus becomes **pointless**." He pushed on the door, and it swung open.

Gloha gaped. "How did that get unlocked?"

Marrow held up a crooked bone. "Skeleton key," he explained. "I have learned how to adapt. I wish I had thought of this before Graeboe got caught, but my hollow head isn't always efficient with thoughts. Once I did think of it, it seemed best to wait until we knew the full situation of the castle."

"You mean you could have gotten out without making the oath—if I hadn't made it?" Gloha asked, appalled.

"True," Trent said. "But it was your decision to make, as this is your quest we are on."

She shook her head. She could only hope that Metria's decision to marry Veleno worked out. Otherwise the demoness might have made more mischief than she knew.

They went downstairs. Gloha located the castle privy, then checked the rest of the main floor layout. It seemed to be a well-designed castle, but very quiet, because there were no servants. There in the castle dining room Veleno had laid out several more pies from his courtyard pie trees. The fare here was limited, but that couldn't be helped. They were hungry.

"I'll take mine up to eat with Graeboe," Gloha said. She would rather have remained with Trent, but the giant needed her company more. She laid the key ring on the table where Veleno would find it, and started off.

"I shall wait here for Veleno to reappear," Trent said, sitting down to attack his pie.

"I shall release the nymphs," Marrow said. "They don't need oaths either; they are harmless." He picked up the key ring. "And they surely appreciate weddings."

Gloha wasn't sure about that. Each nymph had been married to Veleno for one evening, and then suffered what must have been by Notar Republic rules an automatic annulment when she didn't remember it next morning. But she agreed that it wasn't right to leave them locked up.

Gloha followed the route to the highest chamber. Graeboe had hardly started eating his pie. It wasn't that he wasn't hungry, but that he was too weak. That was what she had been afraid of.

"Come on. I'll help you." She sat on the floor beside him. She didn't ask him if he wanted help, because then he would have remembered his pride. She just used the spoon that she had picked up with her pie. She fed him one mouthful after another. Betweentimes she ate bites of her own pie.

"Thank you," he said, seeming to recover somewhat. "I regret putting you to this trouble."

"I wish I could feed you something to make you strong again," she said wistfully.

"I am glad just to have known you."

"Thank you." She leaned down and kissed him on the ear.

When he had eaten as much as he could, she finished off her pie and his, then lifted him and carried him carefully down to the main floor. She wanted to be able to keep track of him, though she had no idea what she could do if he got worse.

Meanwhile, things were changing. Every chamber was lighted. Nymphs were all over the place, helping with the wedding preparations. Marrow Bones was directing the construction of benches for a number of folk to sit on. Metria was fogging in and out, giving spot instructions on decor. The demoness could not do anything physical herself, but seemed to enjoy directing all the others. The nymphs did not seem to find it unusual for a demoness and a skeleton to be supervising things. Since their memory did not extend back to yesterday, they probably thought that this was the way it always had been. Trent must have transformed one of the plants of the courtyard garden to a fabric tree, because nymphs were tearing brightly colored lengths of cloth and hanging them up as decorations. The castle was becoming festive, in strange contrast to its normal atmosphere.

Two more figures appeared. "Magpie!" Gloha exclaimed, stepping up to hug her old tutor. "What are you doing here?"

"Why, I came for the wedding, dear. And so did Dara."

Gloha looked at the other woman. She was elegantly formed and garbed, looking much like a queen. "You're Dara Demoness? Humfrey's first wife? I've heard so much about you," she said insincerely.

Dara smiled. "Not all of us are like Metria, as you should know from knowing Magpie."

Metria appeared, trailing smoke. "I heard that! You lost your soul, and *pzoop*! you were gone. That's just like me."

"But I reformed," Dara said evenly. "Now I act as if I have a soul, though I don't. That won't be a problem for you, I suspect."

"No problem at all," Metria agreed. "I'm only going to stay long enough to find out what love is. Then I'll be out of here."

"Oh, I don't think so, dear," Magpie said.

"Well, what do you know?" Metria demanded. "You've spent too much time being a servant to mortals. It was bad enough with that Princess Thorn—"

"Princess who?" Dara inquired.

"Prickle, spur, barb, spine, spike, nettle, cactus, blood-red, flower—"

"Rose?"

"Whatever," Metria agreed crossly. "Princess Rose. But then you got into lesser ones, even goblins and ogres like that Gumbo."

"Okra," Magpie said. "Okra Ogress."

"Whatever. You've lost your perspective."

"I doubt it," Magpie said, unperturbed. "I wouldn't miss this occasion for anything."

"Well, you might as well make yourself useful, then. The wedding's in only a time and a couple of moments."

"I shall be glad to," Magpie said. "The job might as well be done right." She vanished, to reappear elsewhere in the room just in time to prevent three nymphs from hanging a festoon upside down.

"And who is your young man?" Dara inquired, glancing at Graeboe.

Gloha realized that she was still carrying the elf. Hastily she set him down. "This is Graeboe Giant. He's not my—"

"A giant?" Dara said, surprised. She looked more closely. "Why, so he is. Is the Magician Trent in the vicinity, by any chance?"

"Yes, he transformed Graeboe. It's complicated."

"It certainly is. But it will soon simplify dramatically. I wish you every happiness together." She moved off to untangle several nymphs who had gotten themselves wrapped in material; shapely arms and legs were waving at odd angles and screams were starting to emerge.

Gloha turned to Graeboe, embarrassed. "She just assumed we were—"

"She just came on the scene," he said. "She doesn't know."

Another figure appeared before them. This was a portly elder demon with a frighteningly certain face. "Of course she knows," he said. "Are your heads full of mush? You would have seen the outcome yourselves if you had any wit at all."

Gloha made a wild guess. "Hello, Professor Grossclout," she said politely. "I am surprised to see you here too."

"I couldn't avoid it," Grossclout said. "I have to officiate." He glanced sourly around. "I must say, Metria holds the dubious distinction of being the worst of all the nitwitted, inattentive, mushminded students ever to disgrace my classes."

Metria reappeared. "I love you too, Professor." She kissed him on the cheek with a resounding smack.

"Stop that, you wretched creature!" he exclaimed, seeming almost ready to detonate.

"It's really nice of you to take the trouble," she said, unconcerned by his ferocity.

"I came only to make absolutely certain that you go through with it, you irresponsible inamorata."

"Irresponsible what?"

"Flame, lover, beloved, sweetheart, mistress, paramour, concubine—"

"Fiancée?" she asked.

"Whatever," he agreed crossly.

Metria colored faintly pink and averted her gaze. "Thank you," she said modestly.

He poked a chubby finger at her nose. "You are about to get what is coming to you, you infernal nuisance."

"Just so long as I learn love. That's something you never taught in your classes, Professor."

"I taught the love of knowledge, but you were incapable of learning it." He paused, reconsidering. "But indubitably you will learn something now," he added, obscurely gratified.

Metria vanished. Grossclout shook his head. "She is the most annoying female," he grumbled. "She definitely does not think like a scholar."

"But she is trying to do something decent," Gloha said.

"For the wrong reason." He focused disconcertingly on Gloha. "Whereas your case is far more positive. You deserve the joy you are about to achieve."

"Joy?" Gloha asked blankly. But the Demon Professor was already turning away.

"I really don't understand demons," Graeboe said.

"Metria says that he's the only one who can't be fooled," Gloha replied. "But if he thinks I face my prospects with joy, he's way out of touch."

Grossclout marched to the podium in front of the benches. "Take your seats, please," he said in a voice so fraught with authority that the timbers of the castle trembled. "The ceremony is about to commence."

Immediately the nymphs scrambled to perch cutely on the benches. Magpie appeared before Gloha. "You and Graeboe must sit at the front, as friends of the bride."

"We aren't exactly friends," Gloha said.

"All the better, dear. This way." She guided them to the place.

"All the better?" Graeboe whispered after they were seated.

"I don't understand this at all," Gloha confessed.

Magpie reappeared. "Oh, I'm sorry—I forgot. You are the maid of honor, Gloha."

"Me!" Gloha exclaimed, horrified. "I don't know anything about—"

"We demons can't interact with the castle directly, and in any event there needs to be a mortal contribution to the ceremony. It's important."

"But Veleno has been marrying a nymph every day, without any such fanfare."

"Yes. And none of those marriages lasted. This one will."

"It will?" Gloha asked, beginning to hope.

"If it is done correctly. Come."

So Gloha got up to follow Magpie, whose judgment she trusted. The demoness could not interact with Veleno or the things of the castle, but could touch Gloha. Quickly she fashioned a suitable maid-of-honor dress, complete with a dainty little hennin—a long conical hat with a bit of material descending from it. She guided Gloha to a mirror.

There stood a pretty goblin girl whose wings blended nicely with the gown. "Oh, I wish I could always look like this," Gloha breathed.

"You always do, to others," Magpie assured her. "They think of you as an angelic little angel. Now you must get out there for the ceremony."

"But I don't know what to do," she protested.

"Just be there to witness the ceremony, and to take the bouquet during the placing of the ring."

"That's all?"

"That's enough." Magpie urged her onward.

The ceremony was already under way. There was music from somewhere, not exactly an organ; it turned out to be

Marrow Bones, playing notes on his rib cage. The notes were surprisingly accurate; she recognized the Wedding March.

And there was Metria, in a splendiferously stunning gown and veil, marching down the center aisle with a phenomenal bouquet of flowers, She almost floated, which she certainly could do if she wished to. The nude nymphs went "Ooooo!" almost in unison, wishing they could dress like that.

Veleno waited at the front. He was almost handsome in his dark formal suit.

They came together—and there was Professor Grossclout, speaking words so solemn and full of import that Gloha was to wish ever after that she could remember what they were.

There was a pause. "The ring."

Trent stepped forward from the other side. He too was handsomely suited. He presented a little box. Gloha realized that the ring must also be of castle substance, so could not be handled by demons. So Trent was playing the part of best man. Gloha wondered if that wasn't taking nonhostility to an extreme. Yet why not? If the marriage actually worked, they would all be free without violence or deceit.

Veleno took out the ring. Metria looked for a place to put her bouquet. Gloha quickly stepped up to take it. But as she did, it puffed into smoke. Oh—it wasn't real; the demoness had formed it out of her own substance to add to the effect. Still, to maintain appearances someone had needed to take it at this stage of the ceremony.

Now came the critical part. Veleno lifted the ring, and Metria lifted her left hand. Would the ring fit on her, or would it pass right through her substance the way all the other things of the castle did?

The ring stayed. Metria held her hand up triumphantly, showing it off. She had become real to the castle.

"Man and wife," Gloha heard the Professor intone.

Then Veleno took her in his arms and kissed her. His hands did not pass through her, and neither did his lips. She was real to him too.

Satisfied, Professor Grossclout grandly faded out. So did Magpie and Dara, more petitely. They had done what they had come to do.

The scene dissolved into the wedding feast. The nymphs did not need to eat, but they nibbled at the assorted pies anyway. Gloha, Trent, and Graeboe had already eaten, but they also nibbled. Meanwhile the groom and bride disappeared into the nuptial chamber for the consummation, where Metria would make Veleno deliriously happy for an hour or so. Gloha knew it didn't mean anything; what counted was whether the bride remained solid and with her memory intact on the following morning. Until then, nobody could be released. That was the deal.

Meanwhile it was left to the rest of them to clean up. They all pitched in, restoring the castle to its previous condition, with one exception: they left the decorations. Why not be festive another day?

At last it was done. The nymphs retired to their cells to sleep, feeling most comfortable there. In the morning they would remember none of this. But their cells would no longer be locked, so they would be able to come out and deport or disport themselves as they wished. There weren't any fauns here, but perhaps the nymphs could run around and scream a little anyway.

Trent, Marrow, Graeboe, and Gloha sat at the kitchen table, unwinding. Soon they too would return to their cells to sleep, this time taking pillows with them to make it comfortable. Everything depended on the morrow. "Do you think it will take?" Trent asked.

"Oh, I hope so!" Gloha said fervently. "The demons seemed to think it would."

"I understand that the Professor Demon is never wrong," Marrow remarked.

"It is odd that he came to handle the service himself," Graeboe said. "Considering that he has no respect for Metria."

"His attitude does seem odd," Marrow agreed. "It was almost as if he thought she wouldn't like being married."

"He said that she was going to get what was coming to her," Gloha said, remembering. "And when I said that we weren't exactly Metria's friends, Magpie said it was all the better."

Trent shook his head. "Strange. I think we have not yet grasped the full import of this occasion."

They sat in silence for a while and a half, not getting up the gumption to retire after their arduous day.

Metria appeared, wearing a gauzy nightdress which showed the pink halter and panty beneath. "Oh, are you folk still up?" she asked, surprised.

"By inertia," Trent said. "Why are you here?"

"I made Veleno so deliriously happy that he pooped out. It will take him several moments to recover for the next bout. So I sneaked down to fetch a nice pie."

"But you don't need to eat, Metria," Gloha said.

"Not for me. For him. He'll be hungry, after all that effort."

Even Marrow seemed to be taken aback by this. "You are trying to do something nice for him that isn't what is strictly prescribed by the deal?"

"Well—yes," the demoness said defensively. "Can't a wife do something for her husband if she wants to?"

"It's almost as if you care," Graeboe remarked.

Metria looked nonplussed. "That must be an illusion."

Trent squinted at her, evidently thinking of something. "Say something mean about him," he suggested mildly.

Metria opened her mouth. "I—don't care to."

"If I didn't know better, I'd suspect you of having part of a soul," Trent said.

"That's nonsense! I'm just trying to make him diliriously happy for a few hours. It's a matter of professional pride."

"Since when do you have that kind of pride?" Gloha asked.

"Since—I got married," the demoness replied, surprised.

"That ceremony—it must have done more than marry you," Gloha said. "When I took the oath of nonhostility I felt invisible bonds close on me, binding me to what I swore. Did you feel that?"

"Why, yes," Metria said, similarly surprised. "I was so concerned with doing it exactly right that I didn't pay much attention. It did make me start relating to the castle, so I could pretend to summon the stork with him."

"Pretend?" Graeboe asked.

"We demons never summon storks unless we want to," Metria explained. "We just go through the motions, deluding mortals, but it isn't real. Who in her right mind would want to mess with a baby?"

"I would," Gloha said. "If I had the right—the right family."

Trent pursed his lips in the very mildest of expressions. "And you don't have the right family, Metria?"

"I didn't say that! Veleno's not a bad man, just isolated. There's nothing wrong with him that a good loving woman can't fix."

"And are you that woman?"

"Of course not!" Then she looked pained. "But—there's something. I don't know."

"Is it wonderful yet painful, leaving you so confused you hardly know what you feel?" Graeboe asked.

"That's it exactly!" the demoness agreed. "How did you know?"

"I think you are experiencing the first confused pangs of love," he said.

"I am? But—but that's what I was looking for!"

"And it isn't what you expected?" Gloha asked, interested.

"No. I don't know what I expected, but not this. It—I don't know if I like it."

"Love doesn't necessarily care whether you like it," Trent said sadly. "It can bring you enormous grief. But you would never trade it for any other experience. Metria, I believe that your wedding ceremony brought you half of Veleno's soul. Now you are able to experience the full range of human emotions and commitments."

"Not half of them?" Gloha asked.

"Half a soul is still a soul," he said. "It normally regenerates, becoming complete. You have a considerable experience ahead of you."

"But I didn't want a soul," Metria protested. "I just wanted to see what love is like."

"I think Professor Grossclout knew that," Graeboe said. "He knew you would be getting more than you wanted. He came to make sure it happened."

"Grossclout!" Metria exclaimed. "That infernal spook! He wanted to get back at me for never taking his classes seriously."

"I'd say he found a way," Trent said.

"What am I going to do with a soul?" she expostulated.

"You whatted?" Gloha asked.

"Shouted, yelled, howled, bellowed, proclaimed, argued earnestly—"

"Exclaimed?"

"Whatever," she agreed crossly. "Say, wait—I didn't say the word!"

"I still didn't understand it," Gloha said.

"Well, anyway," the demoness said tragically. "Where will I go, what will I do?"

"Frankly, my dear," Trent started, with three-fifths of a smile, "I don't—"

"Suffer," Graeboe said instead. "You'll suffer, Metria."

"Well, I'll have none of it. I'm going to—" She paused, distracted.

"You're going to what?" Marrow asked.

She sighed. "I'm going to get that pie for him." She puffed out.

Trent shook his head. "I think I wouldn't care to cross Professor Grossclout," he remarked.

"If that is his penalty for being crossed, I would gladly do it," Marrow said. "I want half a soul."

Gloha saw Graeboe look thoughtful, but he didn't comment. "Well, we had better sleep if we're going to," she said, standing.

Graeboe tried to stand, but didn't make it. "Perhaps I will remain here," he said.

He was trying to be gracious about his weakness, and not bother anyone else with it. Gloha didn't want to embarrass him by offering to carry him again. "Maybe I'll stay here too," she said.

"I should think it would be more comfortable in your private cell," Marrow said.

"Well, it might, but—" she started.

"So I shall be glad to carry Graeboe there," the skeleton finished. "He carried me before."

"That is kind of you," Graeboe agreed. The skeleton picked him up and walked away.

"I'll fetch pillows," Gloha said quickly.

But when she had several pillows, she realized that they were too big for her to carry. She would have to make the long trip to the highest cell with one pillow at a time. That promised to be tedious. It would also use up more of the time she had hoped to have for sleeping.

Metria reappeared. "Got a problem?" she inquired.

"None you need to concern yourself about," Gloha said shortly.

"Yes I do. You are a nice person who never did anyone any harm, and you deserve assistance. I'll carry those up."

Gloha was taken aback. Then she remembered the soul. The demoness had become a caring person. "Thank you, Metria."

"It's weird, having to be concerned how others feel," Metria remarked as she carried the pillows. "But this business of love—I'm so afraid I'll do something wrong, or that he'll do something wrong, though I know these concerns are foolish. Sometimes I'm happy and sometimes I'm terrified. I'm just so mixed up. I wish—"

After a moment Gloha realized that the demoness wanted to be asked. This was definitely not the old Metria. "What do you wish?"

"I wish I had a—someone to—to listen—to understand—to advise—I don't know what. This is all so new."

"You wish you had a friend," Gloha said in a burst of realization that brightened the passage.

"That must be it. But there isn't—demons don't have friends."

"Maybe they do if they want them," Gloha said.

"Who would ever want to be friends with a demon?" Metria asked plaintively.

Gloha saw that the demoness' problem was her problem too. She had gotten Metria into this, and it had saved Gloha from a horrible fate. Maybe the demoness had done it for her own selfish reason, without knowing the full consequence, but Gloha owed her a considerable favor. "I would, maybe," she said.

Metria paused on an upper landing. "Would what?" she asked cautiously.

"I would be your friend."

The demoness froze. "Oh, I couldn't ask," she said. "I—oh, thank you. I feel so much better now." She was smiling, but tears were flowing from her eyes.

"I haven't experienced love myself, exactly," Gloha said, touched. "But I think your feelings are normal."

"I hope they get untangled soon."

They reached the high chamber. Marrow and Graeboe were there, talking, but they stopped as the others arrived.

Metria set down the pillows. "I have to get back," she said. "But—"

"Pop in, anytime," Gloha said.

The demoness nodded, and faded out.

"I will depart now," Marrow said, and did so.

Gloha arranged the pillows to make Graeboe comfortable.

He seemed thoughtful as well as weak, but she decided not to ask what he and Marrow had been talking about. In a moment he was asleep, and in another, so was she.

Something was strange. The floor seemed to be sagging. That was impossible, of course, but Gloha couldn't just dismiss it. She sat up, looking around.

Dawn was brightening. Beyond the barred window a pink cloud was losing its color. The window looked slightly skew. She got up, knowing that it was merely an effect of the magic of perspective, but unable to restrain her curiosity. She touched a bar—and it felt not quite hard. Not soft, certainly, but not metallic. More like wood.

She looked up—and saw a dip in the ceiling. Imagination? She spread her wings and flew up to touch it. And it was slightly soft. And it gave a bit where her finger poked it. It *was* sagging!

Something was definitely amiss. She dropped to the floor. "Graeboe—I think we'd better get out of here."

He woke. "I think not."

"Not?"

"I don't think I can get up. I think my time is coming."

Something seemed to tear inside her. "No, Graeboe!" she cried. "Not yet. You haven't found your—your answer."

"I found enough. You must pry open the bars and fly out."

"Pry open the—! I can't do that!"

"The castle is dissolving. It means that Veleno has found someone who remembers her wedding the following morning. The enchantment is dissipating. You must escape before you are caught in the collapse.

Gloha realized that he had correctly understood the situation. That explained the sagging of the castle. The bars would no longer be strong enough to hold her, and that was the fastest exit. She went to them and wedged them apart as if they were strands of rubber. Looking out the window and down, she saw the entire castle leaning lopsidedly as its foundations lost their solidity.

She hurried back to Graeboe. "I'll take you too," she said.

"Gloha, it isn't worth your effort. I will be gone before the morning is done anyway. This is as good a way as any. But if you would—" He paused, somewhat as Metria had.

"What do you wish?" she asked, her heart hurting.

"If you would kiss me before you go—"

"I'm not going!" she cried. "Not without you." She got down, about to pick him up. But as she did so, she realized that the flight down, carrying him, would be perilous; she wasn't that strong a flyer. So she didn't gamble. She put her face down and kissed him on his little mouth.

Something went through her, like a gentle shock. Then the floor tilted, and she had to act. She hauled Graeboe up in her arms, scrambled to the window, and jammed through. It was slanting crazily, and the bars stretched readily. She lunged out, fell, spread her wings, and flew as hard as she could.

But it wasn't enough. Graeboe's weight bore her down, and she was falling too fast to land safely. She struggled to fly harder, but was able only to slow her descent. They were going to crash.

"Drop me!" Graeboe cried.

"No!" she cried back, hanging on to him more tightly.

The ground rushed up. Gloha closed her eyes.

She struck something soft and springy. She bounced.

She opened her eyes. She had landed on a big resilient cushion. It had enabled her to light harmlessly. But how had it come there?

The cushion opened a mouth as Gloha landed the second time. "Don't look so surprised," it said. "What are friends for, anyway?"

"Metria!" she cried gladly.

The cushion faded, leaving them on the ground. "Must see about Magician Trent," the lingering words came.

"Why did she save us?" Graeboe asked as she set him down on a nearby hummock.

"We're friends. We agreed to be, on the way up to the room last night. She needs a friend." Gloha looked up at the melting castle. "And it seems I needed one too."

"Ah. Because she is new to conscience and love. It must be difficult for her."

"It is. She has to sort it out all at once. But she must be succeeding, because the enchantment is ending. I'll help her all I can. After all, she saved me from something I very much didn't want." She glanced at the ground. "Twice."

"Which perhaps leads into my second question. Why didn't you drop me and save yourself, when it was apparent that you couldn't save us both?"

"I just couldn't!"

He did not pursue the matter. They watched the castle fold in on itself as its substance lost cohesion. Meanwhile the front door opened and nymphs ran out across the drawbridge, their hair streaming behind them. They had been freed, and were going home, where they would surely be welcomed. But where were Trent and Marrow?

Then those two emerged as well. They were the ones who had gotten the nymphs out.

"What about Veleno?" Gloha asked.

Metria appeared. "Are you kidding? I got him out first, of course. He's waiting over there."

They looked where she gestured. Veleno was lying on the ground, which accounted for why Gloha had overlooked him before. He had a dreamy smile on his face.

Gloha walked across to him. "Are you all right?"

"Never better," he replied. "I had to ask her to let me be for a while; there's only so much delirious happiness a man can stand all at once, when he's not used to it."

"I guess you did meet the demons' requirement," Gloha said. "You found a woman to love you."

"Metria's no mere woman. She's something else." He closed his eyes, and the dreamy smile returned. Evidently he was satisfied.

The castle continued to settle, as if on a very hot surface.

Smoke rose from it, fuzzing into the sky. It collapsed into a mound, and the mound shrank into a pile, and the pile bubbled into a molehill. Finally the last of it steamed away, leaving only a bare island in a dirty pool.

"Well, that's it, dear," Metria said to Veleno. "I was going to bug out after this point, but somehow I no longer want to. Let's go home to your village."

"Weren't you helping these folk to fulfill their own quests?" he asked.

"In my fashion. But now they're free, so they can go on about their business."

"That's true," Gloha said. "Metria has done her part, and helped us a great deal. We can handle things on our own now."

"All right," Veleno said. "We might as well go."

But now Metria demurred. "Maybe I should see them through to the completion of their quests. We can wait, after all; that village doesn't even know we're coming."

"Or care," Veleno agreed. "Maybe we should go somewhere else. I really don't care, as long as you're there."

"You must be ready for some more delirious delight," the demoness said, advancing on him.

"Well—"

"Perhaps we should find some food, and resume our journey," Trent said briskly.

"But Graeboe can't travel," Gloha said.

"We can surely help," Metria said.

"But why should you take the trouble?" Gloha asked her.

Metria approached her. "Please," she said quietly. "I have a husband, but I'm new at all this, and I have only one friend. I'm not ready to face it all alone."

"Oh," Gloha agreed quickly. "Of course."

"We may have another concern," Marrow said, his skull facing the sky.

There were large creatures flying rapidly toward them.

12
LOVE

Gloha recognized them. "The flying centaurs!" she
cried happily.

In a moment four centaurs landed. Two were
adult, and two were juvenile. Gloha flew up to make introductions. "Hello, Cheiron and Chex and Che and Cynthia,"
she said. "And Gwenny Goblin—why did you come here?"

"Metria said you needed help," the goblin girl chief said,
jumping down from Cheiron's back to give Gloha a hug.
"So we arranged for a contingent of goblins to come here
to rescue you. Naturally I had to come myself to make sure
they behave."

"And naturally I had to come with her, as her Companion," Che said.

"And naturally we wouldn't let them go into an unknown
and possibly dangerous situation alone," Chex said.

"But the situation has been resolved," Gloha said.
"Metria married my captor, and got half a soul, and the cas-

tle dissolved down to nothing. So we don't need rescue any more."

"That's too bad," Gwenny said.

"Too bad?" Gloha asked, surprised.

"Because the goblin forces will be arriving at any moment, and they'll be in a fighting mood."

"Oh." Gloha appreciated the problem. Goblin girls were always lovely, sweet, and nice, but goblin men were not like that. If there wasn't some enemy for them to fight, they were all too apt to find something else to fight, such as their friends.

"I wonder how the harpies will react," Metria remarked.

"They're coming too?" Gloha asked, alarmed.

"I tried to notify interested parties," the demoness said.

"It's a good thing the giants didn't hear of this," Graeboe said with a weak laugh.

"Of course they heard," Metria said. "You were in trouble too, weren't you? They said they'd gather a big force and tramp right over here."

Gloha was aghast. "Who else did you tell?"

"Nobody except the skeletons of the gourd."

Gloha was relieved. "At least they can't come out here. They're locked in the dream realm."

"Not if Trojan deems the matter important enough to give them a pass to the waking realm," Marrow said.

Trojan was the horse of a different color, who ruled the dream realm. He was a no-nonsense creature. "No danger of that," Gloha said, relieved.

There was the sound of marching. It grew louder. Not only that; it seemed to be coming from several directions. What was going on?

Gloha and the winged centaurs flew up to investigate from a suitable height. "Oh, no!" Gloha breathed.

For there were four groups converging. From the north came a rabble of goblins armed with clubs, spears, and stones. From the south came a screech of harpies armed with dungballs and explosive eggs. From the east came a crunch of giants; they were invisible, but their footprints could be seen advancing by giant steps. From the west came "a skeleton stiff!" Metria said, smoking into view at the same altitude.

"A skeleton what?" Gloha asked.

"Remains, cadaver, stink, decompose, body—"

"Corpse?"

"Whatev—no, that's not quite it. Band, force, squad, unit, team, crew, troop—"

"Corps?"

"—ver," the demoness agreed crossly.

"And they're all going to meet by the dirty pond," Cynthia said. She was flying beside Che Centaur, and they did make a nice couple, though both were still children. Gloha was glad to see that aspect of her adventure working out well.

"We'll just have to explain," Gloha said.

"That will not be easy," Chex said. "The goblins will obey Gwenny, grudgingly, but the others won't. They will want to have a big battle."

"And they are more or less natural enemies," Gloha said. "It was difficult to stop the goblins and harpies from going to war when my parents got together. I almost wish our captivity had lasted a little longer."

"Maybe Trent will know how to handle it," Cynthia said. "He was king for a while, wasn't he?"

"Yes," Gloha agreed. "He must have faced difficult situations before."

They flew down to rejoin the ground party. "There are goblins, harpies, giants, and skeletons converging," Gloha reported to Trent. "We need to stop them from quarreling."

The Magician nodded. "A distraction would be good. Perhaps some temporary quest to take their attention."

"Yes! But what?"

He glanced over to Graeboe. "I fear you are about to expire. What is your last wish?"

A horrible chill shuddered through Gloha. "Expire? Now?"

"I would like to be taken to some isolated region and transformed to my natural form," Graeboe said. "And I would like Marrow Bones to have my soul."

"Oh, I would not take your soul!" the skeleton protested.

"I would not care to have it be wasted, when it expected a longer life," Graeboe said. "I can not think of a worthier creature to have it."

"But you can't die!" Gloha cried. "You were supposed to be saved!"

"That appears to have been a vain hope," Graeboe said sadly. "I want Marrow to have my soul."

"Perhaps half of it," Trent said.

The sound of tramping was loud. At any moment the converging forces would appear. "I do not wish to intrude on a sensitive moment," Marrow said, "but I think that dealing with the assorted contingents should have priority."

"This is my notion," Trent said. Then, inexplicably, he addressed Graeboe again. "Did the Good Magician say anything else, except that help would come if you waited in this vicinity?"

"No, not that I recall," Graeboe said. "Just that I might be transported."

"Transported?" Gloha asked.

"Shipped, hauled, delivered, moved, carried, conveyed—" Metria said helpfully.

"Surely to the place suitable to my expiration," Graeboe agreed. "I must have misunderstood the message."

"That's easy to do, with Humfrey's words," Marrow said. "I may have similarly misunderstood Professor Grossclout's admonition to tarry near the volcano."

"I am not sure of that, in either case," Trent said. "Humfrey's Answers are always relevant, when understood. So are Grossclout's. Your fates may be linked, along with Gloha's."

Now the giant steps were so close the ground was quaking, and the harpy flight was appearing on the horizon. Why wasn't Trent paying attention?"

"That word," Trend said. "Could it have been 'transplanted'?"

"Why, yes, I believe it was," Graeboe agreed, surprised. "I misremembered it. But that must be merely another way to suggest that I would be moved to another locale."

"And you, Marrow," Trent said. "Was there anything else, however seemingly irrelevant, that Grossclout told you?"

The skeleton tapped his skull. "Only that it would be a fair trade. Since I have nothing to trade for a soul, that does not seem to relate."

The goblin army appeared to the north, and the skeleton crew to the west. The timing seemed perfect: all four groups would arrive together.

Trent turned back to Graeboe. "If you were to trade half your soul for something, what would that be?"

"I am not seeking to trade my soul," Graeboe objected. "I seek only to give it to a worthy person."

"Speaking hypothetically: what would be worth it?"

Graeboe made a wan smile. "My life, of course. But—"

"What kind of a transplant would give you life?"

"New blood. Since that is not possible—"

"Where does your blood come from?"

Graeboe shook his head. "I don't understand."

"I do," Cheiron Centaur said. "The blood comes from the bones, at least in part. He would need a bone transplant."

The others laughed at the impossibility of that. Except for Trent. "Or perhaps a marrow transplant?"

"Well, yes, of course," Cheiron agreed. "The center part of the bone. I thought that was understood."

The skeleton's jawbone dropped. "You mean I could trade some of my marrow, to give him life? I would gladly do that, regardless of the soul."

"But Graeboe's a giant," Gloha said. "Marrow doesn't

have enough in his whole body to provide more than one finger's worth."

"Not when Graeboe is in his present form," Trent pointed out.

The others stared at him. "That's right!" Marrow said. "He is small at the moment."

"Oh, Graeboe, you can be saved!" Gloha said. "Once you get better, you can be as you once were, an invisible giant." Yet somehow her joy in that realization was tempered.

"Thus perhaps we see the nature of the trade," Trent concluded. "Marrow for half a soul, and both achieve their objects."

Now the contingents from the four directions arrived. They drew up and flew down to a stop, forming a perfect square bounded by goblins, giants, harpies, and skeletons. The giants were indicated only by their imprints, but those were huge.

"I shall be happy to make that trade," Marrow said.

"And so shall I," Graeboe agreed, amazed.

"There is just one problem," Trend said. "As I recall, a marrow exchange has to be facilitated by bloodroot and a trans-plant. Does anyone know where such a plant grows?"

There were blank looks all around. No one knew.

"I think we have a search to make," Trent said. "Fortunately, we have a competent search party assembled, capable of checking land, air, and underground. In one of those regions there should be a plant." He looked around. "But we need to locate it before the day is out, because I think Graeboe will not survive until tomorrow."

"What does the plant look like?" Gloha asked.

"It is fairly small, with vinelike branches," Cheiron said. "Its leaves are green, and it has coiled projections terminating in spikes." He took a stick and made a sketch in the dirt. "Approximately this configuration." Then he drew an enlarged flower. "You can most readily identify it by its distinctive blossom."

"Let's see which contingent can find such a flower first," Trent said.

The word went out to the four groups. Immediately they scattered, seeking the trans-plant. The possible strife had been averted.

Cynthia looked thoughtful. "I dimly remember something about such a plant," she said. "Of course that was when I was a child, seventy years—" She caught herself. "Seven years ago. It may be gone now."

"Where did you hear it was?" Che inquired.

She turned a surprisingly competent little-girl smile on him. Che of course knew her origin and original age, but seemed to like her very well regardless. That was perhaps not surprising, for not only was she the only other winged centaur child in Xanth, who was most eager to get along well, she had more than a suggestion of her former and later prettiness. "I'd rather not say. Because if I'm wrong it will make me look even duller than I am. I think I'll just go look."

"Not alone," Chex said severely. "Not at your age, in this region."

"Oh," Cynthia said, momentarily discommoded. "Yes, of course. It's probably not there anyway."

"I will go with you," Chex said. "And you don't look dull." She was of course speaking literally. Cynthia's mind might be dull compared to that of a normal centaur, but her appearance was bright.

"Oh," Cynthia repeated, more cheerfully. "Yes." The two of them took off.

Gloha realized that Che wasn't going, because he was staying with Gwenny, whose companion he was. He never separated from her. It was clear that the two were as close as any two could be, but that this was friendship and not romance. It was a significant distinction. Cheiron stayed also, to give Gwenny a ride, because she couldn't fly. Thus Gwenny was directing the goblins from the back of a winged centaur, and no one seemed to find that remarkable.

Soon the only ones remaining by the pond were Gloha, Graeboe, Marrow, Trent, Metria, and Veleno—and the last two disappeared into the forest, theoretically to search, but probably to have privacy for another dose of delirious happiness. Gloha remained amazed how that had worked out, and a bit jealous. The demoness and the nymphomaniac had turned out to be right for each other, while Gloha had found nothing right for her. If only it had been someone like Magician Trent who had captured her in the castle, but younger and single—but her foolish little fancy was going offtrack again.

"Perhaps we should eat and rest now," Trent said. "Because when that plant is located, we shall likely have some traveling to do."

"Could it be brought here?" Gloha asked. "It would be better if Graeboe didn't have to travel."

"The bloodroot, yes. We need only a sprig of that. But I believe that the trans-plant itself can't be transplanted," he said. "Just as I can't transform myself. Some magic relates to oneself, and some to others. So we shall have to find a way to move Graeboe comfortably. Perhaps I can transform a volunteer into a form suitable for such service."

"Transform me!" Gloha said immediately.

"Please, no," Graeboe said. "I would not have you trouble yourself further on my behalf."

"But I want to help you. I can't stand the thought of you—" She couldn't finish.

"I have been already too much of a burden," he said. "You have been more than kind to me already."

"Perhaps we should accomplish the exchange," Marrow said. "Then there need be no further concern about burdens, for Graeboe will be healthy and able to be transformed to any form he wishes."

"Exactly," Gloha said. "He can be an invisible giant again. And I can help that happen by being transformed to a suitable carrying form."

"I think it will be better to get some other volunteer," Trent said.

"Why? When I want to help?"

"It's just an opinion," he said mildly.

Gloha decided not to argue further. She and Marrow went foraging for nuts and fruits and a blanket for Graeboe, because he seemed to be getting cold. Trent transformed a weed into a flame vine that provided heat. They ate a belated breakfast and rested. Gloha discovered that she was tired; the events of the morning had taken mental as well as physical toll. So she settled down on a cushion beside Graeboe and tried to relax. She knew she wouldn't really be able to rest until there was news of the trans-plant.

She woke some time later, somewhat refreshed. It seemed to be near noon. Graeboe was asleep beside her, wrapped in his blanket, still looking cold. Others were talking some distance away.

Metria popped in before her. "Mixed reports," she said. "The goblins are scouring the ground and underground. The harpies are checking the mountains and treetops. The giants and skeletons are checking far crannies together. They've found plenty of bloodroot. In fact, here's a sprig." She showed a blood-red root. "But there seems to be no trans-plant growing anywhere to be found."

Gloha didn't want to hear that, so she inquired about a detail. "The giants and skeletons are working together?"

"Yes. The giants can travel far, but aren't much for detail work like peeking into beerbarrel tree knotholes. So they are carrying handfuls of skeletons, and the skeletons do the peeking." The demoness smiled. "Some ordinary folk have freaked out when they peeked into houses."

Gloha could appreciate why. "I hope somebody finds it. It would be really mean of the Good Magician to tell him he'd find help, if it can't be."

"Yes, Humfrey always amused me before. Now I would be sorry to learn of such a deception."

"Well, you have a soul now." Gloha sat up. "I guess I haven't been much of a friend to you. I've been distracted."

"It's a funny thing," Metria said. "Once you said you would be my friend, I got much more confidence, and it was easier to adjust. I didn't need your advice."

"That's the way friendship works sometimes." She looked at Graeboe. "If only I could be more of a friend to him."

"You've done all you could, haven't you?"

"I haven't saved his life. I try to find ways to help, but I can't do what really counts."

The demoness looked unusually thoughtful, as if her recent experience had given her some insight. "I'm sure you'll find a way."

Then two centaurs appeared in the sky. Chex and Cynthia. "It was there!" Cynthia exclaimed, her pigtails bobbing. "Right where I'd heard it might be."

Gloha leaped up. "You found the trans-plant? Oh, wonderful!"

"Don't be overjoyed just yet," Chex said. "It is by no means easy to reach."

"We'll reach it anyway," Gloha said. "We have to. Where is it?"

"In a crevice on Mount Pin-A-Tuba. That's not a nice mountain."

Sudden dread surged through Gloha. "I know. Oh, this is awful. How will we ever get to it without being buried in burning ashes?"

Magician Trent strode up to join them. He accepted Metria's sprig of bloodroot and tucked it into a pocket. "I think the creatures who came to help us will have some real action after all. We shall have to lay siege to the mountain."

"But that won't get us safely into its crevice!" Gloha protested.

"It will if the distraction is sufficient."

Gloha saw the logic. The evil mountain wouldn't be able to keep track of every single goblin and harpy. If they were careful, and escaped its notice long enough, the ploy might work.

The retreat sounded, and the various parties began returning to the rendezvous. As they did, they got briefed. There were hollers and screeches as the goblins and harpies learned that violent action would be required, but abrupt silence when they found out the nature of the enemy. This was more of a challenge than they really cared for. But neither group could back down in the presence of the other. The skeletons were not as concerned, being less vulnerable to hot rocks. The giants were neutral; they could normally get away from something like that in two or three giant steps, but they knew that they could be hurt by flying boulders, and the closer they got to the mountain the worse it would be.

"Now we shall have to get moving," Trent said.

"But the siege hasn't even started," Gloha said.

"Precisely. We must seek a devious route that will take longer, so that the mountain never suspects the real object. The siege will be in place by the time Pin-A-Tuba might realize that an insignificant party is approaching—and then it may assume that this is merely a distraction from the real object. This is chancy, I agree, but seems to be the best course."

"What is the real object?" Gloha asked. "I mean, the one that we hope the mountain will think is the real object?"

"The harpies discovered a marvelous lake on the other side of the volcano from the trans-plant. They call it Miracle Lake. The apparent object will be to capture and exploit that lake."

"Why would anybody want a lake beside a mean-spirited volcano?"

"There are boats on that lake, floating at anchor. Barnacles grow on the bottoms of those boats. The surfaces of those barnacles are so highly glossy as to be reflective. They can be harvested and assembled into full-sized mirrors. Thus they are mirror-barnacles, or miracles for short."

"But mirrors can be made from glass or polished stone," she said. "Why go to the trouble of fashioning them from shiny barnacles?"

"They are magic barnacles. They make magic mirrors."

"Oh!" Gloha exclaimed, suddenly understanding. "I never knew where magic mirrors came from."

"There may be other origins," Trent said. "But I suspect that we have stumbled upon one of Magician Humfrey's secret sources. Certainly the mountain will zealously guard its treasure. So I think this is as good a diversion as any."

"I should think so," she agreed, impressed. "I wouldn't mind having one of those mirrors myself."

He smiled. "You have other business, I think."

"Oh, of course! I wasn't suggesting—" Then she realized that he was teasing her. His ways were sometimes so subtle that she had trouble interpreting them. That was part of what she liked about him. He was just so—so manly.

He turned to other business. "Metria and Veleno are now scouting out a possible route to the trans-plant. They seem to work well together."

"But Veleno can't go near that mountain."

"He can in his present form."

"His—?"

"I transformed him. He is a parrot legal, one of the few creatures the volcano tolerates near its cone. Perhaps because they are very good at arguing their cases."

"Arguing cases?" she asked blankly.

"Parrots are talkative birds, and these ones like to perform legal tasks, though they are neither secretary-birds nor lawyer-birds. They are merely paralegals. They argue Pin-A-Tuba's case that he has a right to sound off in as great a volume as he chooses, though he blows phenomenal amounts of gas and ash into the sky. So he doesn't object to their presence. Veleno is flying through the region, while Metria makes spot detail checks on the terrain. I think they'll get the job done."

"But why should Veleno help us? He was holding us captive, and he almost wanted to—to make me be his—"

"He was doing what he thought he had to, to achieve freedom from his enchantment," Trend said. "You caused Metria to marry him. He is grateful, and perhaps suffering some tinge of guilt. He believes that the guilt will not entirely dissipate until he has helped you achieve your quest, just as you helped him achieve his."

Gloha shook her head. "I suppose it does make sense. But why couldn't Metria explore the whole region herself?"

"Because she's a demoness, and the volcano doesn't much like demons. It seems that they used to play pranks on him, such as dropping stink bombs into his mouth. So whenever a demon materializes close by, Pin-A-Tuba lets fly with vigor and blasts it out of there. Metria can remain close only so long as she never materializes."

"But then she can't communicate with anyone, can she?"

"She can communicate with Veleno, because she has half his soul. So Veleno is indeed proving to be useful to our cause."

Gloha shook her head again. It was amazing how things could turn out.

Metria appeared. "We have a route," she reported. "I didn't have time to investigate every nuance, but I think it's good. It won't be fun, but it should get you there."

"Where's Veleno?"

"He paused to argue a case with another parrot legal who didn't recognize him. He'll be along soon."

Indeed, in only four moments the parrot winged in. He had bright purple plumage with orange stripes. Metria held out her hand, and he landed on it. She brought him in and kissed him on the beak. "I have been beakissed," he exclaimed, fluttering his wings. "There is no precedent."

"Are you ready for your next form?" Trent inquired.

"Proceed with your case, counselor," the parrot said.

The Magician put his hand close, and the parrot became a glob of goo. "Eeek!" Metria screamed in almost nymphly fashion, trying to hold the goo in her hands. But it slipped through her fingers and landed with a splat on the ground.

Metria turned to face Trent. "What did you do to my love?" she demanded. "He's all icky!"

"No he isn't," Trend said mildly. "He's merely not yet quite firm. He will shape up in a moment."

Sure enough, in exactly one moment the blob shaped itself into what appeared to be a reclining chair. Metria touched the surface. "Oh, he's like centaur hide," she said appreciatively.

"Precisely. He is ready to carry Graeboe to the transplant."

"But what kind of creature is he?" Gloha asked.

"A slowmud. A smaller cousin of Swiftmud. Large enough to carry one elf. He can hear and understand us, but can respond only with bubbles: white for yes, black for no, and shades of gray for other responses."

"Carry an elf?" Gloha asked. "You mean—?"

"Graeboe lacks the strength to make this trip," Trent reminded her. "We are fortunate that he was able to rest and recuperate enough to survive beyond noon."

That was certainly true. Graeboe remained asleep, or—

Gloha hastily checked him. His eyes were open, but his forehead was cool. "Oh, Graeboe, you're fading!" she said.

He gave her a reassuring smile, but it was a weak one.

"We need to reach that plant before the day is out," Trent said quietly. "Does your route permit that, Metria?"

"Yes, if you move right along," the demoness said. "I'll lead the way. I won't be able to solidify near the mountain, but Veleno will receive my communications."

"You had better lead invisibly from the start," Trent said. "So that we can work out the miscues before we get within range of the mountain."

"Gotcha," She smoked out.

He turned to Gloha. "I think it will be best if you move Graeboe to the chair."

Gloha agreed. She got down and slid her arms under the

elf form and the blanket. She heaved him up, wincing as she saw him wince. She set him carefully in the chair, which adjusted to accommodate the body. The surface of the slowmud was plush and did seem to be about as comfortable as it could be. Trent had chosen the transformation well.

"Lead on, Metria," Trent said.

The demoness did not appear. But Veleno started to move. He just slid smoothly along the ground, in the manner the larger Swiftmud had, evidently responding to Metria's hidden touch or silent word. Shared souls were wonderful.

"But we can't get there from here," Gloha said, hurrying after the slowmud, which was getting to respectable velocity. "It's beyond the Faun & Nymph Retreat, Lake Ogre-Chobee, and the Region of Madness. It took us days to come this far. How can we do it in hours?"

"Maybe we can go into ogre-drive," Trent said, unconcerned as they moved onto a slight hill. "Or take giant steps."

"But we're not—"

The hill rose into the air. "Eek!" Gloha cried, exactly like a nymph. She kicked her feet, flung her hair about, spread her wings, and flew up, alarmed.

Trent and Marrow sat down beside the chair. "On the other hand, let's just relax," Trent said. The group rising up beyond the tops of the trees.

Chex and Cynthia flew over to join Gloha. "I see you are on your way to the nasty mountain," the elder centaur said. "We can't go there, so we'll return home now. But please stop by when your quest is done."

"Yes, please do," Cynthia said. "I really enjoyed traveling with you and Magician Trent." There was just the suggestion of a flush as she mentioned the name, as if she had some unchildish memory. "I would hate to lose touch."

"I, uh, of course," Gloha said, somewhat discombobulated if not actually disconcerted, because she understood

Cynthia's memory all too well. Also, she was confused by the mysterious flying hill.

"I'm so glad I was able to help," Cynthia said.

"Yes. Thank you."

The centaurs flew away, looking somewhat like dam and filly, or more properly dam and future filly-in-law.

Then Gloha saw a giant footprint form in a field. Oh—an invisible giant was carrying them! One whose breath didn't smell. Now she realized that the hill the others rode on was in the general shape of a hand with a tarpaulin spread across it. Somehow she hadn't gotten the word about this detail.

She flew to the hand and landed. There was no sense wearing herself out with a long flight.

Then she remembered Trent's pun: take giant steps. On the other hand. Figures of speech to be taken literally. Darn the man!

In a surprisingly short time their flying island sank down to the land. In the distance was the peak of a smoking mountain. She saw other islands floating in, and realized that the armies of goblins, skeletons, and harpies were being similarly transported. "The giants can't approach the volcano for the same reason the demons can't," Trent remarked. "It seems that once an absentminded giant trod on one of Pin-A-Tuba's ash gardens, and now none of them are welcome. A boulder of hot rock can make an uncomfortable burn. But the giants are contributing to the effort in this manner before going home." He patted the tarp. "And we certainly appreciate the transportation." The flesh beneath gave a twitch of appreciation. Gloha knew why the giant did not speak; it would give away the operation if the mountain overheard.

They dismounted from the hand, and the tarp slid off and became limp. The hand had departed.

They were at the edge of a dry plain spread with what looked like dishes. Veleno, answering an invisible directive, slid briskly into it. Trent and Marrow paced it on either side. Gloha was left perplexed again.

Unable to subdue her curiosity, she went to inspect the closest of the dishes. It turned out to contain what looked like vanilla ice cream. What was that doing way out here in nowhere? She checked another. It contained several brownies, smelling very chocolaty. A third dish contained butterscotch pudding. Others had pie, cake, tarts, sweets, fruits, sugared nuts, and assorted other desserts.

Suddenly it registered. This wasn't a desert plain—it was a dessert plain! Filled with plain desserts. In fact it must be the region of Just Desserts she had heard about but never expected to visit.

Well, there was no sense in letting all this wonderful food go to waste. She picked up a dish with a mouth-watering slice of meringue pie. She was about to eat it when Marrow's skull turned to face her. "That may not be wise," the skeleton said. "Fumes from the volcano may have tainted these desserts."

Good point. She threw the pie away. But it looped around and came back to her hand. "Boo!" it said.

Astonished, she threw it away again, harder. It skated just above the ground in a big loop, and came right back to her. "Boo!" Couldn't she get rid of it?

"Boo-meringue pie, I believe," Marrow observed.

Oh. The kind that always came back to a person. So she held on to it for now; she'd find a way to get rid of it soon, she was sure.

She flew ahead to see what other wonders might be along this route. Beyond the desserts was a low valley. In it were hoods. Just assorted pointed or rounded headdresses, sitting there for anyone to take. She picked one up that was about right for her and put it on her head.

Immediately it closed on her forehead and ears with such force it was painful. She tried to take it off, but it clung, curling around her mouth, trying to suffocate her. Choking, she fell to the ground.

Then the hood climbed off her face. She gasped in a breath, not moving for the moment. The hood crawled to her hand and wrapped itself around the dish of pie. Then it rolled away with the pie.

Gloha sat up, staring after it. That was a robbing hood! A criminal type. And she, unsuspecting, had let it waylay her. What a fool she had been to trust a hood.

She got up, dusted herself off, and set forth again. She hoped the others had not seen her stupidity with the hood.

Beyond the hooded valley was a field with a single tree. The tree had branches with spinning needlelike spikes, leaves that radiated X rays, and tendrils that squirted jets of water or made horrible sucking sounds. The very sight of it made Gloha shiver with horror. That was a dentis tree! The most feared of all trees. Her teeth ached with the mere thought of getting within range of that monster.

The party caught up as she hovered, not daring to proceed. "No need to be concerned about that," Trent said reassuringly. "That's a dentis tree."

"I kn-know," she agreed, her teeth chattering.

"Such a tree can be very useful, when there's a toothache, I understand," Marrow said. "It doesn't bother folk with healthy teeth."

Veleno proceeded right past the tree. Gloha nerved herself and followed. She was relieved when the tree did not grab her.

Now the route descended into a broad, deep cleft. This was good, because it concealed them from the view of the mountain. But there was something odd about it. "I don't like it," she said.

"Like it it," a voice replied with an annoying inflection.

"Who said that?" she asked, not quite pleased.

"Said that that," the voice said with a sneer.

"Are you making fun of me?" she demanded.

"Fun of me me," it agreed ironically.

"Pay it no mind," Trent advised. "It's obviously a sar-chasm."

"Sar chasm chasm," the voice agreed tauntingly.

Gloha nodded, not trusting herself to speak again, because the chasm had a way of reversing and demeaning the import of whatever she said.

There was a remote clamor. It sounded like goblins and harpies hurling insults at each other. That was good news; it meant that the siege was starting. That should distract Mount Pin-A-Tuba from the real mission.

But soon there was another sound: that of distant thunder. Trent cocked his head. "Uh-oh," he said mildly.

"Could that be Fracto?" Marrow inquired.

"It surely could," Gloha said. "He always shows up at the worst times."

"Malign beings do seem to congregate," Trent agreed. "The evil cloud may have a pact with the evil mountain. Our siege alerted it."

"Well, as long as Fracto doesn't realize what we're up to."

The cloud moved in with dismaying speed. The sky darkened. Thunder crashed, and lightning jags taunted the land. The rain started.

"I think this chasm won't be suitable much longer," Trent said.

"Maybe if we hurry, we'll get out of it soon," Marrow said.

They hurried. Veleno fairly whizzed along. The rain came down more thickly, and the runoff from higher slopes poured into the chasm in assorted waterfalls. The base began to fill with water.

"Maybe we had better get out of this chasm," Gloha suggested. "I mean by getting straight out now, not trying to get out the far end of it."

"Metria is showing the route," Trent said. "She should know whether it is safe to leave the chasm now." He glanced at Veleno.

A black bubble came from a nozzle at the slowmud's front. That meant No. It wasn't safe to leave.

So they continued, as rapidly as they could. But the rainfall increased. Water sluiced into the chasm, and the runoff poured more thickly into it. Evidently this was one of the mountain's natural drainage clefts, excellent for travel during dry weather, but a disaster in a storm. Metria could not have known that Fracto would get into the act. The level not only rose in the chasm, it developed a turbulent flow. They had either to get out of the chasm, or fight that flow. It was getting more difficult.

"Still not safe to leave this depression?" Trent inquired mildly.

Another black bubble.

"I'll see for myself," Gloha said impatiently. She spread her wings and hauled herself into the air despite the buffeting of the winds. She got her head up above the level of the brink and peered out.

It was a hellish scene. The chasm was winding through a landscape of jagged rocks surrounded by ash. Steam rose from hot spots, and sinister smoke issued from meanlooking vents. There seemed to be no clear path through it except the chasm. Metria had signaled truly.

"Not safe," Gloha said shortly as she dropped back to the bottom. "We have to continue here."

"We shall have to float," Trent decided. "Slowmud can do it, and Marrow can form a boat for me, as he did before. But each can support only one person. We have one extra."

"Me," Gloha said. "I will have to go back, so that the rest of you can make it."

"No," Trent said firmly. "You must be along. It is your quest."

"But Graeboe has to be along, and so does Marrow. You don't mean that you will go back?"

"I fear for your safety if I am not with you. I may need to transform you if there is an emergency."

"Then transform me now, into a form that can handle this."

"I don't think that's wise."

"But we have to do *something*!" she cried despairingly.

"See if you can hang on to the slowmud," he said. "You can float without putting your weight on it."

She hadn't thought of that. Maybe it would work.

Trent kicked Marrow in the hipbone, and the skeleton flew apart and formed into the small boat. There was even a line of small bones extending across so that the slowmud could grab on. That way they wouldn't get separated in the rapids.

Trent found a long piece of driftwood he was able to beat into a crude paddle-pole. He got in the boat and jammed the pole down through the surging water as an anchor. Gloha saw now that the bone boat had flipper-bones below that served to propel the craft.

Meanwhile Veleno stopped trying to glide through the shallows and set out to float on the deeps. It did seem to work better, except that the swirling current tended to turn him around. Gloha grabbed on behind, and the current hauled her back, so that she served as a stabilizer. Then the slowmud was able to forge forward.

They moved slowly on up the river. Gloha hoped it would end soon, so that they could get back on land, but it seemed interminable. The rain kept pouring down, preventing the river from drying up. Fracto probably didn't realize that they were there, or he would have made it much worse. This was just the fringe of his effort to wash out the goblins and harpies elsewhere.

A dark ugly shape flapped over the chasm. Gloha saw its silhouette against the bleary sky. It looked like a vulture, only worse. It peered down with its beady eyes. It plopped a smelly poop into the water. That enabled Gloha to recognize it: the thing was a vulgar. Probably one of the mountain's mean-spirited creatures. What would happen if it spied them, and told Pin-A-Tuba?

Then two smaller ugly shapes appeared. "There's one!" the first screeched.

Harpies! Part of the siege force. Gloha had seldom been happier to see her winged relatives.

"Well, let's tear it to quivering bits!" the second harpy screeched enthusiastically.

The two dived for the vulgar. All three shapes disappeared beyond the chasm brink. There was a medley of screeching, and a grimy feather drifted down. The harpies had saved the little party from discovery.

They followed the chasm river around a turn, and came to a filling pool. Here it was slightly quieter, though the storm was still pounding overhead. They pulled over to the side, where it was shallow enough for them to get some temporary footing and rest briefly.

Trent looked back. "Trouble," he said mildly.

Gloha looked around, expecting some new threat. But there didn't seem to be anything. "What is it?" She noticed that the sar-chasm effect was gone; there was no longer a mean-spirited echo.

"Graeboe is leaving us."

"What?" But she knew what he meant. She pulled herself around to the side and looked at the elf-giant.

His pallor was worse. He was conscious, but looked as if he expected not to be so at any moment. The violence of the river travel had depleted his scant remaining strength.

Gloha was stricken. What good was this trip if the rigors of travel wiped Graeboe out before the trans-plant could heal him? "What can we do?" she asked plaintively.

"We can do nothing," he said gravely. "You can do much."

"I don't understand!"

"Tell him the truth."

"I haven't lied to him, or to anyone."

"Except to yourself, perhaps."

The Magician could be so irritating at times! What was he talking about? "What haven't I been truthful about?" she demanded. "How is it hurting Graeboe?"

"Your feeling."

"My feeling? I want him to be cured, so he can live and be a giant."

"Then tell him that."

Gloha shook her head, unkindly bemused. Graeboe was dying, and she was supposed to wish him a happy giant-hood? Yet she had to say something.

"I can't tell him the truth," she said with difficulty. "It would only hurt him, and diminish me. And you."

"I doubt it," he said with that infuriating mildness.

"Then *you* hear it first!" she snapped. "I am—am fascinated by you, and if I had my choice I would become a human woman and do everything with you that you had in mind for Cynthia." There: it was out, for whatever mischief it was worth.

He seemed unfazed. "I think not."

"Because you're not interested," she agreed dully.

"Oh, but I am."

"So you can just go on being amused by—" She paused. "What?"

"You are lovely, innocent, caring, faithful, and sincere. You are the kind of woman any man could love. You are a rare prize. And I could readily transform you to a fully human woman."

She stared at him. "You—you return my interest?"

"I do. I am as fascinated with you as you are with me, and for similar reason. You are to your gender what you see me to be in mine. We could have a wonderful time together."

Gloha shook her heady little head. "Forgive me, Magician, but I am having trouble believing this."

"Believe it. But understand the whole of it: it would not endure. Because my perspectives are not yours, my friends are not yours, and I am a Magician while you are not. I exist in a different realm, and that would surely alienate us from each other after the first flush of fulfillment faded. You will never be able to match me in magic, and if you join me you will sacrifice the heritage you have. You would come to resent your inability to fly, and you would be ashamed that you gave up the quality that made you unique: the unification in your person of the goblins and the harpies. And so it would be a mistaken affair without a future—even if I were not old and already married. This is not your true desire, or mine."

She reeled under his harsh and appallingly adult logic. Suddenly she saw her dream for what it was: an utterly foolish fancy. She had known it, but never quite accepted it. Now she could no longer deny it. She could not give up her heritage for any temporary tryst, no matter how handsome, intelligent, or magical the man. And he could not give up his, though he had gone so far as to confess being attracted to both Cynthia and Gloha herself. He was, physically, a young, healthy man; he noticed and responded to pretty women. The difference between them was that he had experience enough to appreciate the truth, and the discipline to be governed by his head rather than his passion.

"Thank you, Magician," she said at last. "You have marvelously clarified my mind." She wiped away her tears, but more replaced them immediately.

"Now you must do the same for Graeboe, before he dies."

"I should set him straight, the way you set me straight? I don't think I could be so cruel."

"The truth is seldom cruel. I think you owe it to him."

"Because he—he thinks he feels about me the way I thought I felt about you?"

"Yes. But there is a difference."

"Yes. He's dying. I'm not."

"So there is very little time."

He was relentless! But what else could she do? She did owe a dying man the truth. She returned to Graeboe.

She reached out of the water and took his hand under the blanket. It was as cold as hers, but his wasn't wet. The blanket seemed to have a water-repellent quality, so was protecting him from a soaking. "Graeboe, I wish you could hang on just enough longer so that you can be cured, and live your life as an invisible giant."

"Thank you," he breathed. "I wish you fulfillment in your quest." He closed his eyes. "If you will, ask Marrow Bones to come near."

She saw that he was about to die. Something burst inside her. "Oh, it's not true!" she cried. "I don't want you to be a giant!"

Slowly his eyes opened. He was faintly startled.

"I don't want you to be any other creature," she said, amazed at herself. "I just want you to be mine. I love you, Graeboe, and I wish I could m-marry you, and to h-hell with my quest!" She fetched his hand in to her face and kissed it. "Oh, Graeboe, it's impossible, and I'm so selfish, and you're such a good man, and I have no right, but please, please don't die. Even if it can't be anything between us, because I know I could never endure as a giantess any more than as a straight human woman, I want you to be healthy and happy."

"But I am not handsome or really smart, and I have no magic talent. A wonderful creature like you can do so much better."

"You're just a really decent guy, who needs me, as Trent does not," she agreed. "And that's all I ever wanted. My heart knew. Except—"

His hand warmed. "I'd rather be a winged goblin with you, than a giant without you," he said. "I love you too, Gloha, but did not want to impose."

"A winged goblin!" she exclaimed. That had never occurred to her. "Of course that's possible. You can be anything, when Trent transforms you. Oh, Graeboe, *you* are the one I want. I knew you liked me, but I never thought you'd be willing to give up your natural form, so I diverted myself with another notion. Just hang on, and *be* the fulfillment of my quest."

He smiled. "I think perhaps I can do that now."

She leaned over him and kissed his little face. "You must, Graeboe. I would be desolate without you."

"I did not want to live, without you."

And so he had been fading, having no reason to fight to survive. Magician Trent had known. Now the rest of the truth was out. She had been unblinded.

Graeboe closed his eyes again, but this time he seemed to be headed for a restorative sleep instead of a final fade-out. He should be able to survive until they reached the transplant.

They resumed their float up the river. The rain was still coming down, and total gloom covered the landscape, but now things seemed brighter.

Finally the chasm narrowed and gave out. They emerged on a slanting plain of hardened volcanic rock; the covering of ash had been washed off. What had been the chasm was now a mere indentation. Trent kicked Marrow back to his normal configuration, and they followed the indent around a curving surface until a new and jagged terrain appeared. There were ridges and spikes interspersed with a cracked-glaze pattern of crevices.

A hulking knuckle-walking brute came around a pile of stones. "Huh?" it exclaimed, spying them. Then it lifted its snout and sounded a howl. "Awooooo!"

The mountain took note. The rock shuddered. Steam issued from the little crevices. Boiling red lava appeared, flowing in pursuit of the steam.

"We may have a problem," Trent said mildly.

"Pin-A-Tuba knows we're here," Gloha agreed. "It's focusing on us. We'll never get through."

"Metria," Trent said. "Materialize."

The Demoness appeared. "You realize this means more mischief," she said.

"If you are willing to act as a decoy, we may be able to proceed."

She pursed her lips. "Follow the path up to that crack in the cone," she said, pointing. "I'll do what I can."

Then Metria fogged into smoke, and re-formed as a monstrous toad. "Come and get me, you numbskull!" the toad croaked. Gloha hoped that the mountain was not smart enough to realize that it had to be a fake; frogs, not toads, croaked. But maybe it didn't matter; the mountain would know she was a demoness, and go after her regardless.

The toad hopped, landing with a plop. "Can't catch me, firesnoot!" she called.

The lava fairly boiled out of the cracks, hissing as the rain struck it. It formed pools, then began to flow after the toad. Scattered bits of wood and brush burst into fire as the lava touched them in passing. The several runnels formed into one big one, gaining speed. They seemed to have forgotten about the main party, but there was so much lava that it spread out across much of the surface as it flowed.

Trent led the way quickly to the nearest ridge, so that they could avoid the burning rock flow. It surrounded their elevation like a shallow lake. There was nothing to do except follow the ridge on up.

The crest became higher and sharper. The lava still prevented them from returning to more level terrain, so they had to stay high. The ridge turned pointed, until the two sides met in a knifelike cut.

Veleno had no trouble. The slowmud simply slid across one side of the ridge, sticking to it like a snail. Graeboe rode along, firmly fastened in place. Gloha was able to fly just above the ridge, though the rain and gusts of wind made this nervous business. Marrow straddled the crest, having no flesh to be cut. That left Trent.

But Marrow solved that problem. With a kick he assumed the configuration of a platform across the top, braced by arm and leg bones on either side. Trent sat on this platform, and the skeleton skidded smartly along, carrying him. Gloha was even able to join them, so that she didn't have to fight the foggy winds.

Then another vulgar flapped by. "Awk!" it exclaimed, spying them. Then it headed directly for the mountain's cone.

"We had better hurry," Trent said mildly.

They hurried. The skeleton platform clattered along the ridge, and the slowmud kept the pace. The ridge seemed to lead toward the crack in the cone that Metria had pointed out, but it turned away at the last moment. They were stuck at the end of a long island, with molten rock flowing between them and the cone. There was a crevice that might be used as a path up the side of the cone, but they couldn't reach it.

Mount Pin-A-Tuba got the word. The cone rumbled. Then a torrent of ash spewed out the top. It was trying to catch them with its ash, but they were too close. The worst of the ash and hot stones were flying too far out.

Gloha could fly across, though she feared for her wings in the moderate rain of hot ash. But none of the others could. "Transform me into a roc bird. I'll carry you across."

"No. The volcano could orient on a target of that size, and drop fireballs on your wings. We need to stay small."

"I can help," Marrow's head said from the platform. "Kick me into a ladder. Then cross on me."

"Good notion. But how will I stand on this ridge without your support?"

The slowmud blew a white bubble. Then it slid up until its muddy snout crossed the razor edge. The mud caked up on either side of the ridge, dulling the edge.

"Thank you," Trent said. He got off the platform carefully and sat astride the ridge, his midsection protected by the hard rounded mud. Gloha hovered nervously near.

Then Trent hauled the bone platform up, held it over his right foot, and gave it a good kick. It flew apart, and formed into a double line of bones, connected by crossbones. In fact it was a rope ladder without rope.

There was a skeletal hand at each end. Trent lifted the bundled ladder and put it on the end of the ridge. The fingers felt around the rock until they found good fingerholds, and the hand clenched tightly. Then Trent held the other end up for Gloha. She took the bone-hand and flew across to the base of the cone. The bone rope strung out behind her. It was heavy, but for this short hop she could handle it. She landed on the crevice and bent down to set the hand there. The fingers got a good grip, and the bone ladder drew itself tight.

The slowmud slid up onto the ladder and started across. Progress was slow because there wasn't much surface for the mud to cling to, but it was getting there, and bringing Graeboe along.

Mount Pin-A-Tuba realized what was happening. He sounded an enraged honk. "Oompah!" So much ash shot out of the cone, so fast and high, that it didn't come down; it stayed up in the high air and cooled Xanth a degree. But he couldn't stop the crossing.

Veleno and Graeboe made it across. Then Trent started. He went on hands and knees, gripping the rungs of the ladder as if he were climbing.

But now Cumulo Fracto Nimbus, the evil storm cloud, came to the volcano's rescue. He huffed and puffed, trying to blow the man down. When that didn't work, he formed a terrible funnel. The funnel seemed to be sucking up everything it touched, and it had a lot of power. Trouble indeed!

Trent saw it. "Metria!" he called.

The demoness appeared. "You realize that my appearance here will just draw Pin-A-Tuba's attention to—" She saw the funnel. "Point taken. I'll handle this." She changed into the biggest stink horn Gloha had ever seen; It fairly festered with contained stench.

The funnel swept in, casting somewhat blindly about for the man on the ladder. The screaming sound of the winds around it drowned out almost all else. The stink horn moved to intercept the mouth of the funnel. In a quarter of a moment the horn was sucked in and up.

There was a pause. Then the funnel exploded with the foul-smelling noise typical of stink horns. BBBRRR-RRRUMMPPPOOPOOH!" The noise dissipated into a miasmic fog that saturated the region. It was all Gloha could do to keep from choking as the stench reached them. The demoness had certainly found the way to get rid of the evil cloud's mouth!

Not only that. Fracto himself had been so disrupted by the taste of the fetor weed that he was unable to continue raining. His fragments drifted away, and a beam of sunshine ventured down, though it wrinkled its rays at the lingering reek. Even the molten lava below was revolted; it blistered and solidified. Nobody could stand a stink horn.

The volcano continued to erupt impotently. Trent completed his crossing, then hauled in the ladder after him. They were all on the crevice-path now, and not far from their destination. To keep them safe, Gloha flew up with Marrow's ladder end and helped him catch hold higher on the path. Then the others used the ladder as a guardrail so they weren't in danger of falling off the steep slope.

But now the mountain used its last weapon. High above them black goo issued from a fissure. It slid slowly down the cone toward them.

Gloha, alarmed, flew up to investigate. But Marrow's skull, which was in the middle of the bone ladder, called out a warning. "That may be poison!"

She halted just outside its range. She caught the barest whiff: the same stuff they had encountered at the Magic Dust Village. This was the worst menace yet!

She flew back down. "We can't handle that. We must flee before it reaches us."

"I think not," Trent said.

"But it will kill us all except Marrow and Metria, and they aren't even a couple."

"It won't kill the trans-plant, because that's one of the mountain's precious possessions. If we join the plant, we should be safe."

Could it be? Gloha wasn't sure just how logical the volcano might be. It might wipe out the plant to be sure of getting the intruders. But she realized the Graeboe would die if they retreated now. So they had to gamble on the plant, perhaps in more than one respect.

"Let's hurry," she said.

Again they hurried, working their way up as the poison blob worked its way down. The first nauseating whiffs of gas drifted down, making them cough. Gloha worried about Graeboe; any little thing could wipe him out, and this wasn't little.

But as they got closer to the opening in the cone that the crevice was leading to, the terrible odor faded. Gloha looked up. The deadly glob was detouring, sliding away from the cave. Trent was right: the mountain wouldn't destroy its treasure.

They came into the open grotto. There in the recess grew the trans-plant, exactly as it had been described. It hardly looked unusual, but her excitement made it almost seem to glow.

"Now let's get this operation done," Trent said briskly, "before the mountain thinks of some other device to balk us."

Veleno carried Graeboe to one side of the plant. Marrow Bones resumed his regular form and went to the other side. Trent set the bloodroot sprig down between them.

Gloha thought that there would be some procedure or invocation, but the plant simply wrapped tendrils around Marrow's left leg bone, and others around Graeboe's right arm, while still others picked up the bloodroot. Then it lifted needle stickers, drilled one into the bone, and the other into one of the elf's veins. Gloha winced, watching, but knew better than to protest.

It took longer to get into the skeleton's hard bone than into the elf's soft arm. But the plant did another thing. It brought a large yellow flower around until it was leaning over Graeboe's body. It looked like a sunflower, but of course couldn't be, because this wasn't the right type of plant.

There was a glow from the flower. It bathed Graeboe. He writhed, but did not seem to be in actual pain. His flesh did not change, but Gloha was sure that something significant was happening.

"My understanding is limited," Trent said. "But I think that the patient's defective marrow has to be killed, so that the new marrow can takes its place. That must be the radiation that accomplishes that. Graeboe will die very soon if the transplant is not accomplished. The marrow of the donor is liquefied and mixed with the blood of the bloodroot, and that mix is put into the body of the recipient, and finds its own way into the bone. Something like that. We simply have to trust that the process is effective."

"Oh, I hope it is!" Gloha breathed. She couldn't bear to watch any more, so she turned her gaze outward. And froze.

A squadron of vulgars was flying toward the cave. They would be able to come right in and attack the party.

Trent followed her gaze. "We shall have to defend ourselves," he said mildly. "I think I shall this time have to transform you, Gloha."

She realized that he had declined to do so on the way in because she hadn't yet done the thing required to give Graeboe the will to live: declaring her love for him. She had had to remain in her natural form until then, so that he would be assured it was her. But now she was free to defend the group. "Yes, transform me," she agreed.

"Be careful to look at none of us," he said. "Never turn your gaze into the cave."

"Why not?"

But even as he spoke, he was transforming her. She found herself in a lizard body. A lizard? What good would this do? She almost turned to direct a questioning glance at him, but caught herself. So instead she gazed out at the swiftly approaching dirty birds.

The first bird met her gaze—and abruptly plummeted from the sky. What had happened?

The second looked at her—and dropped out too.

Then she realized what it was. Trent had transformed her into a basilisk! Her very gaze could kill.

She glared around, and vulgars dropped like burning stones. Soon none were left. She was more deadly than a fire-breathing dragon.

Suddenly she was herself again. "A little of that goes a long way," Trent remarked.

Now it was safe to look at the others. Nervous in retrospect about the damage she could have done, she was relieved.

More time must have passed than she had realized. The trans-plant was withdrawing its needles. She went to Graeboe. "How do you feel?" she asked anxiously.

He looked surprised. "Better. I feel the new marrow taking hold, revitalizing my blood. I think it will be a while before I am completely restored, but surely it is happening." He paused, glancing at the skeleton. "There is something I must do now. Help me up."

She put her arm around his shoulders and helped him stand. He did seem stronger, though still weak. Some magic was not instantaneous, but that did not lessen its value. He walked unsteadily across to Marrow. "You have given me life. Take half my soul." He extended his hand.

The skeleton reached down to clasp the flesh-hand in his bone-hand. "Now I will accept it," he said.

The hands touched. There was a glow. Gloha, in contact with Graeboe, felt an eerie thinning or separation, not painful, just uneasy. It was his soul fissioning.

Then their hands separated. Graeboe tottered, weakened again, and Gloha quickly supported him. Marrow fell back against the wall. "Oh!" he said in wonder.

Metria appeared. "Now you know what I feel like."

"I believe I do," Marrow said. "It is wonderful yet frightening."

"Exactly," the demoness agreed. She stepped in to kiss him on the fleshless mouth. "But you do get used to it, gradually. Especially if you have a friend."

"He has friends," Gloha said. Graeboe nodded agreement. Trent turned to the slowmud. "You have been most helpful," he said. "I think that any inconvenience you may have caused us has been ameliorated." Then Veleno was standing in his natural form.

"Yes!" Gloha agreed. "You risked your life to bring Graeboe here. I shall always be grateful." And she emulated Metria, flying up to plant a kiss on his surprised face.

"Now I think we had better get out of here before Pin-A-Tuba fields another ploy to dispatch us," Trent said. He went to the edge of the grotto and looked down. "I think we can't depart the way we came; the poison goo is all around."

"You could change me to a roc bird," Gloha said. "So I can carry the rest of you out."

"No, the volcano is alert for that. He's putting out hot rocks to set fire to feathers."

Gloha looked out. Pin-A-Tuba was sending a barrage of burning ashes into the air, furious that the party had won its way to the trans-plant. Lava and poison were strewn all across the ground. Their prospects for escape did look bleak.

Graeboe joined her. "I think I could make it out," he said. "In my natural form, invisible. I could step on the clean ridges, and be away before the volcano knows what is happening."

"Then by all means go," Gloha said. "The rest of us will follow when we are able."

"No. If I am able to do it, then we all are; I will carry you. You should be invisible too, if I curl my fingers around you."

"But you aren't invisible any more," Marrow reminded him. "And you are weakened by losing half your soul. I should not have taken it yet."

"I should be invisible when healthy. I am weak now, but healthy. And if I carry you, my soul will be reunited for that time. It might be a harrowing ride for you, but I believe I could do it. My natural body is familiar to me, and I should be able to keep my balance and step well."

Gloha looked at Trent. "Do you think—?"

The Magician nodded. "If he believes he can do it, he probably can. But it would be better to wait for him to recover more of his strength."

"I think not," Marrow said. "I believe I hear the scritching of nickelpedes."

"Nickelpedes!" Gloha cried in horror. "We can't stay here if they're coming. There'll be too many for Trent to transform, and they'll gouge out nickel-sized chunks of our flesh."

"Yes. I shall try to toss out as many as I can, but I fear a swarm."

Indeed, now they all could hear the scritching coming from deep inside the cave. As the mountain's creatures, the nickelpedes would not bother the trans-plant, but they would soon strip the flesh from any fleshly creatures they could get at. Gloha could become a basilisk again, but wouldn't be very effective against the antennae of creatures who were more interested in chomping than in looking. Pin-A-Tuba had found something they could not readily nullify.

Graeboe stood at the brink of the cave and extended his right hand toward Gloha. "All of you take hold of my fingers," he said. "Then transform me, Magician. I will try to hold you gently."

The offer would have been laughable if they had not understood what was about to happen, because the elf had the smallest hands of any of them. Gloha extended her hand to touch his tiny little finger; Marrow touched his next finger, Veleno his middle finger, Metria his forefinger, and Trent his thumb.

Suddenly Graeboe was gone. But the hand was there, incomparably larger—and invisible. Only their touches on the massive fingers gave them assurance.

Immediately they were scrambling up. Gloha had no trouble; she spread her wings and half flew to the top of the finger she was on. Marrow wrapped his skeletal arms around his finger. But Veleno and Trent were having problems. The nickelpedes were bursting into view, a swarming tide of them, pincers leading.

Metria fogged out. She reappeared behind Veleno in the form of an ogress. "Get up there, my love," she said, boosting him head over heels into the hand. Gloha saw him roll across the invisible surface and come to rest, bemused. "And you, Magician," she added, heaving Trent up similarly. Then she puffed into smoke just as the first nickelpede snapped at her feet.

The hand closed, carefully. They all tumbled together in the palm, held by loosely clenching fingers.

The hand lifted. Gloha righted herself and peered out between or through the invisible fingers. They were swinging way up through the air and the burning ashes, but they were protected by the giant's flesh.

Now the giant was tramping away from the mountain. Gloha saw a ridge squish flat, and a cleft fill in as if pressed by a phenomenal weight. Their speed was remarkable, for Graeboe was taking giant steps and not dawdling.

There was a sound behind: "OOMPAH!" Mount Pin-A-Tuba was venting his absolute rage at their escape. Such a torrent of material shot out of his cone that it was likely to cool Xanth another degree before it settled out. There were fiery boulders too, arcing down to fall all around them. But they were already getting safely out of range. They had made it!

The pace slowed. The giant stopped at a nice glade and brought his hand down so they could dismount. Then Trent faced the region where Graeboe stood. "What form would you like to assume now?" he called.

"I—" the giant's voice came. "I'm falling!"

Trent leaped for the hand. Then a naked winged goblin man was there, falling forward. Trent caught him. Had he not made the transformation, the giant might have fallen on the rest of them.

"Graeboe!" Gloha cried. "What's the matter?"

Then she saw for herself. His body was covered with terrible burns. He had been shielding them from that barrage, taking the burns without complaint. But he had been weak from his recent malady, and this had added intolerably to his burden.

Gloha whipped out her handkerchief. It had a bit of healing elixir in it. She needed all of it now. She dabbed it on Graeboe's burns and blisters, and they healed. When she ran out of dabs of elixir, she kissed the spots instead, and this seemed to work almost as well. "Oh my darling," she breathed as she worked. "You never said! You were getting all burned, protecting us—"

Trent had been holding Graeboe up, but Gloha's ministrations were rapidly restoring him, so Trent moved clear. Suddenly she realized that the ex-giant was not wearing anything. She moved to shield him from embarrassment— and suddenly was in his arms. They kissed.

After her head stopped spinning, Gloha drew back. "Of course you can be a giant if you really prefer. I never sought to—"

"I am getting healthier by the moment," Graeboe said. "Either get me some clothing, or take off yours."

The others laughed. Metria appeared with some clothing she had scrounged from somewhere. Soon Graeboe was decent.

But Gloha's trace of guilt remained. "You never asked me to become a giantess for you. I don't think it's right to make you change for me. So if you have any second or third thoughts—"

"Hold the tableau," the demoness said, and vanished.

"What's she up to?" Trent asked.

"Something nice, I'm sure," Veleno said. "She's a wonderful woman."

Gloha decided not to debate that, so she changed the subject. "I think I know what Graeboe and I will be doing," she said. "Also Veleno and Metria. Marrow will go home with his half soul to his family and share it with them. So all our quests have been accomplished. But what of you, Magician Trent? Are you going to fade out now?"

Trent looked thoughtful. "I must say I had forgotten how exhilarating youthful adventure could be. I believe I'll keep my youth for a while longer, and tell my wife to try it too. I think it is not yet time to fade out."

"I'm glad to hear that," Gloha said. She was understating the case, but didn't think it appropriate to say more.

Then the demoness reappeared. She handed Graeboe a mirror.

"What's this for?" he asked.

"It's a magic mirror the goblins liberated from a storehouse by Miracle Lake," Metria explained with a hint of the old mischief. "They said you should have it as a wedding present, and I think it's ideal. It will tell you anything your beloved seeks to hide. She'll have no secrets from you. You won't even need to ask her; just ask the mirror. Any private feelings, any doubts, any misgivings will be mercilessly revealed."

Graeboe nodded, unconcerned. "It's for you, my love," he said, handing it to Gloha. "Have a harpy time."

AUTHOR'S NOTE

I don't do routine Author's Notes; nevertheless, this one
is routine, so those who aren't interested in lists of cred-
its might as well skip to the last page.

Gloha's quest for a husband, and the talent of Surprise,
were suggested by Jeremy Brinkman. Lock Ness was from
Michael Cowan. The Sin Tax was defined by Susan Bates.
The Sock Her plant was hit by Patrick Geary. Joseph Slezak
Washed Her, Dried Her, and Boxed Her. The Glyph's original home was with Sharon Stegemeyer. Susanna Alvarez
figured out that the Gorgon's face could be made invisible
with a face mask illusion. Chris Anthony (no known relation to me) provided the Light and Heavy Bulbs, Com Pewter's Mouse, and the Shooting Star. Swiftmud flowed from
the Southwest Florida Water Management District. Robert
Christensen got the Ant Honey. Whose Fault was it? Lee
Mendham's fault. Cynthia Carman daydreamed Cynthia
Centaur's history when she was sick; Mare Imbri really gets
around. The Stare-way was suggested years ago—and I

can't remember the originator's name. Also belated credit to another suggestor of contact lenses for Gwenny Goblin, whom I should have credited before: Deana Livingston. The Three Mermaids were drawn by Julie Brady on one of the most decorative envelopes I have received, with their fascinating fronts on the front and their beautiful backs on the back, so I named them and put them into the story. Braille, who transcribes documents, was made by Rich Cormier. Jana's love for the centaur was described by Dana Bates, who is no known relation to Dana Demoness; how could she be, since the demoness is really Dara? The Draw Well was by Michael Portney. Alyson Dewsnap walked the Steppes. Misty Malmstrom walked the Board Walk. Robert Smith named Graeboe. Missy DeAngelis was the Spring Chicken. The Ant puns were by Dan the Man Watson, except for the AccountAnt by Mark E. Stringer. Roger Brannon turned objects to other objects. Barbara Hay Hummel described Gloha's harpy past and Veleno's past; we remember her from the days of Rose of Roogna and Okra Ogress. Panther Ginnett had the Death puns. Cathy Hudson presented Richard C. White, who longed for Xanth and finally reached it. There's more of a story there than I care to tell.

Janet Hines was mentioned in the Note for *Demons Don't Dream*, when she had an iris named after her. She had been paralyzed and blinded by an unkind ailment, but still liked Xanth. She died while I was writing this novel. So I took her to Xanth, as I did with our dog Bubbles in the last novel, and gave her back her motion and her sight, so she could have a better life there among her irises. I don't undertake to do this for other readers, but it seemed appropriate in this case.

Amanda Dickason drew the Girlfon. Julia Lalor described the Nymphomaniac. Stephanie Erb, who gave Kim the talent of erasure in the last novel, this time came up with the Notar Republic and the Parrot Legal. The Not-Holes were from L. Charles Gattuso. Shirwyn Dalgliesh suggested the consequence when Metria married. Jeff Snavely donated Marrow's marrow. Bridget Colvin crafted the Miracle mirror-barnacles. Dakota Hain tasted the Dessert desert, and E. Jeremy Parish ate the Boo-Meringue Pie. Matthew Brennan was the Hood. Jeffrey Ku drilled the Dentis Tree, and Brad Bell uttered the Sar-chasm.

There was half a slew of puns and suggestions left over, some going back to prior novels they weren't used in. My apologies to those folk who have been waiting forever minus a moment; I'll try to catch up on them in the next novel, *Geis of the Gargoyle*. The story lines take their devious turns, and avoid some notions I expect to use. There are a lot of puns, but the welfare of the story always comes first. (That ugly creature who just exploded with laughter is a critic; he thinks this is the first funny statement in the book.)

Jenny Elf did not appear in this novel—she's entitled to some time off, you know—but her namesake in Mundania continues to improve. But there can be snags. For example, when she was at Cumbersome Horsepital (no, it's not really called that; I got the name from *Letters to Jenny*, which has more of our relationship) to sharpen her computer skills, she was outside when another patient had a seizure. Jenny's attendant hurried to help, forgetting that Jenny's wheelchair was on a slope. Jenny, strapped in, went rolling off the path and over a bank and cracked her head on the ground. Several stitches, but no internal damage. Her main complaint was when they hauled her off for treatment without her makeup. She was sweet sixteen at the time, and makeup is important. Who says life in a wheelchair is dull?

My only adventure in this period was when I attended MagiCon, the World Science Fiction Convention in Orlando, Florida. I wasn't going to go, but my wife said she was tired of the dull home routine, so we went. My daughters were there, of course; they've been Con freaks since I made the mistake of taking them to NecronomiCon in Tampa a decade before, and now have attended more Cons than I have. I've never been to a World Con before. My attendance was unannounced; I had given no commitments in advance, because I wanted to do what I wanted to do, instead of what I was programmed to do, for once. It was interesting, and I met a number of figures in the field, including one who said I'd called him a Nazi. What bothered me was that he seemed to believe his charge, and insisted on it in the presence of two publishers. I have been charged with many things over the years, and I don't mean just bad writing, but this was the first time anyone had the nerve to do it to my face with witnesses. So I am pursing it as a matter of slander, and we'll see. All my other contacts were positive. My autographing session Sunday morning took almost an hour and a half; the word had leaked out and my fans were appearing. Barbara Hambly called hello from the next autographing table, and I got to meet Hal Clement, whose *Needle* and *Mission of Gravity* were part of my formative years in the genre. I regret that I didn't get to meet the Guest of Honor, Jack Vance, whom I regard as the finest fantasy writer extant. But that's the way of big conventions: there are so many things happening all at once that the things you want to do are squeezed out by the incidentals. So it was fun, once, but I won't rush to do it again. We picked up literature on the 1995 WorldCon in Glasgow, Scotland; we might attend that. I was born in England some time ago, but have never been back; it's about time.

Thus my quiet life in the months of AwGhost, SapTimber, and OctOgre 1992. Remember, if you want my catalog of titles and such ilk, call 1-800 HI PIERS.

PIERS ANTHONY
THE GRANDE MASTER